KATE HEWITT

The GIRL *on the* BOAT

W0008918

bookouture

Published by Bookouture in 2024

An imprint of Storyfire Ltd.
Carmelite House
50 Victoria Embankment
London EC4Y 0DZ

www.bookouture.com

ISBN: 978-1-83790-291-0
eBook ISBN: 978-1-83790-290-3

Dedicated to Tom Safran,
who first alerted me to the tragedy of the SS St Louis,
and told me about his grandmother who traveled on it, and sadly
lost her life at Auschwitz.
Thank you for sharing her powerful story.

PROLOGUE

JUNE 1946—PARIS

The café is small and shabby, tucked into a row of other cafés and *tabac* shops, cast in the looming shadow of the Eiffel Tower. On this bright summer's afternoon, the tables on the sidewalk are bustling with couples having coffee, smoking cigarettes, or toasting the day—the whole season even—with fresh champagne. Paris seems to be bursting with new hope and *joie de vivre*, nearly two years after its liberation.

The woman stands on the sidewalk, dressed in a worn overcoat, the light breeze blowing her hair into tangles about her face. She reties her scarf at her throat as her narrowed gaze scans the row of cafés, looking for one in particular. *Henri's.*

When she sees the faded lettering on the sign—tarnished gold on a red background, the paint peeling and weathered—her breath catches in her chest. It's still here.

But will they be?

She takes a determined step toward the café, and then falters. If they aren't there, she doesn't think she can bear it—and yet why would they be, after all this time? They'd last been together seven long years ago, huddled on the deck of a ship, wide-eyed with the terrible realization that on the very cusp of a new horizon, all their hopes were about to fade to nothing.

She reaches into her pocket and clasps her shard of emerald, running her fingers along its sharp edge, taking a perverse sort of comfort from the prick of it into the soft pad of her thumb. The four of them all have a similar shard, split from the same perfect jewel. Have the others kept theirs? Have they held them in their hands and studied the deep green gleam, like a fire burning within, remembering all the promises they'd made to each other, all the while knowing how hard—even impossible—they might be to keep? That they would find each other again. They would meet—here, at this place, this time. They would be four friends again, forever.

She takes a deep breath, lets it out slowly as she curls her fingers tightly around the piece of emerald, its sharpness cutting into her skin. She walks forward.

The door opens with a tinkle of bells; only a few people sit in the shadowy space, drinking and smoking at rickety tables and chairs. She takes a step inside, her gaze slowly sweeping around the room before coming to rest on the last person she spied, seated in the corner, a grizzled old man in a dusty black frock coat, his rheumy gaze trained indifferently on her as he smokes a cigar.

They aren't there. Of course they aren't.

The disappointment she feels is crashing, immense and unbearable, even though she's been telling herself for seven years to expect it. There has been a *war*, after all. A most terrible war. How on earth would four women who had been flung to the far corners of the earth be able to meet here, at a shabby café in Paris, on a certain month, day, and even hour? It had been a ridiculous idea, an absurd suggestion, and they'd all acknowledged it at the time, as well as after.

And yet they'd still agreed. They'd *promised*. June seventeenth, the year after the war was over. Four o'clock, at Henri's, in Paris, by the Eiffel Tower.

And here she is. Alone.

The door's bells tinkle again, and she whirls around, one hand pressed to her heart as she sees a young woman in the doorway. She stands tall and straight, with narrow shoulders, dark eyes, her hair covered with a scarf.

Before either of them have so much as moved, another woman rushes in behind her, breathless, her blond hair crimped, her mouth outlined in crimson lipstick.

"Hello," the woman says softly to her two friends.

Pain and recognition flash through the others' eyes as they look at each other in a silent acknowledgment of everything they've endured, all they've overcome to make it to this moment.

"I can't believe we are all here," the woman continues softly. "After all this time."

"Not all of us," the other woman replies, her voice quietly sorrowful.

"But she's coming, isn't she? She must be coming." The woman can't imagine it any other way, not now, not when three of them are already here. They all made it this far.

The silence that falls then feels like an ending. *After all this time...*

Slowly, decisively, the woman in the doorway shakes her head.

"She's not coming," she states with quiet, final certainty. "It's only us."

"But—"

"She's dead," the woman clarifies, her gaze dropping to the floor. "I know, because I was there when it happened."

CHAPTER 1

MAY 1939—HAMBURG, GERMANY

Hamburg was bristling with Gestapo and SS officers, but then it seemed everywhere was these days, a country on the cusp of war, although no one dared say, or even whisper, as much. No one even wanted to think it. Still, it was in the air, like a metallic tang, the scent of a storm, or maybe blood. Everyone could smell it. Everyone could see it—soldiers everywhere, goosestepping and saluting and always looking around, hands on holsters, eyes narrowed in speculation.

Sophie Weiss peered out the window of the taxi as it pulled away from the city's central station, drawing back as she watched two gray-coated, black-booted men swagger along Hachmannplatz, so sure of themselves in this brave new world that had no place for her or her family. Her heart gave an uneven lurch of fear before she drew a quick breath to steady herself.

Her family had got this far, she reminded herself, one hand pressed to her chest before she clenched both in her lap, lacing her fingers together tightly to keep them from trembling. There was no good reason to think they wouldn't finish their journey—or, really, begin it—on the cruise liner SS *St Louis*, leaving tomorrow evening from Hamburg for Havana, Cuba, and a new life for them all. A wonderful new life she could hardly wait to begin.

"Heinrich, please!" she exclaimed in gentle protest as her five-year-old half-brother scrambled across her lap, his elbow digging deep into her middle, to get a look out the window at the two officers striding by. He was obsessed with soldiers, surely an unhealthy preoccupation for a Jewish boy in Hitler's Germany, but, of course, he didn't understand any of the politics—he only saw smart uniforms, shiny boots, peaked caps, and was desperately, enviously impressed by it all. Still, Sophie thought as she rested one restraining hand on her brother's back, now was not the time to attract any notice.

All four of them were squeezed into the back of the taxi—her papa, her stepmother, little Heinrich, and her. Her brother had his nose pressed right against the glass and Margarete, her stepmother, let out a little whimper of distress as she tried to pull her son back, her fox fur sliding off one bony shoulder.

"*Please*, Heinrich," she implored, "don't peer out like that. Not now, darling." She glanced at the taxi driver, who had no real reason to suspect they were Jews—he hadn't asked to see their papers—but the man's face was worryingly impassive.

Heinrich settled grumpily between Sophie and his mother, wriggling deep into the seat so Sophie had to shift over, and now *she* was practically pressed against the glass.

She turned her face away from the window, as Margarete patted her husband placatingly on his arm. "Josef, we are almost there. I am sure it is all going to be all right."

Sophie pretended not to notice as her father nodded back, a mechanical bobbing of his head, before he muttered something unintelligible, his gaze unfocused, his chin drooping toward his chest. He had barely spoken during the entire train journey from Berlin, which had thankfully passed without incident; they'd even got a taxi from the station with no trouble, thanks in part to the fact that none of them looked like the Nazis' leering caricature of a Jew.

Her father was tall and distinguished, with a thin face and kindly blue eyes, although his figure was now stooped and haggard, his gaze so often timid and darting. Margarete had always been considered an imposing woman, tall and angular, ash blond and elegant, dressed in silk and fur, while Sophie, blue-eyed, blond-haired and petite, took after her mother, who had died shortly after her birth. Heinrich, with his cherubic blond locks, had even received a kindly pat on the head by an SS officer at the Anhalter Bahnhof in Berlin. Sophie and her stepmother had both held their breath in terror as Josef had looked on, agog and trembling, while Heinrich had blinked up at the officer and exclaimed that he liked his boots. The man had chuckled and chucked Heinrich on his chin before going on his way; Sophie and Margarete had exchanged watery looks as they'd both exhaled silent sighs of relief.

Now Sophie couldn't help but acknowledge that her father looked far older than his fifty-four years—grizzled, gray, rheumy-eyed, fearful. For the last six months, since the awful events of Kristallnacht, when his law office had been ransacked and he'd been taken into "protective custody" for two endless weeks, Sophie and her stepmother had both been participating in the fiction that Josef Weiss was not an empty shell of the man he'd once been, diminishing more day by day. Her stepmother willfully refused to see—or at least to acknowledge—how timid Josef had become, how he shrank and trembled anytime their apartment doorbell rang in one of Berlin's best neighborhoods; it had caused so much distress in the end that Sophie had removed the bell herself, quietly, without any notice or fuss. By then, there had been little point having it, anyway, as so few people came to their house, especially as her father's office had already been forced to shut its doors after Kristallnacht.

In the months since he'd arranged their passage on the *St*

Louis, he'd become convinced that, somehow, they would be kept from going, their visas would be confiscated, their tickets, as well. He'd imagined the Gestapo would come in the night, as they had before, hammering down the door, tromping through the house, taking them away.

Sophie had tried to reassure her father that they would be safe; the government had approved their immigration as well as their passage, as no Jew could leave Germany otherwise, but her father had simply shaken his head and muttered under his breath: "*Nein, nein, nur die Harten kommen in den Garten.*"

"We are the strong ones, Papa," Sophie had argued against his quotation of the old proverb, that only the strong could enter the garden, or really, survive. "We will come into the garden, I promise, when we board the *St Louis*. The Nazis won't be able to hurt us then. They are not the strong ones in Cuba, or America. We're going to be all right. We *are*."

Her father had clutched her hand, his own bony and claw-like, his eyes filled with tears. "Do you think so, *Schatzi*?" he'd asked hoarsely, using the endearment—treasure—that he'd always called her. "Do you really think so?"

"Yes, Papa, I do," she'd murmured as she'd patted his hand. "I really do."

She had to, because what was the alternative? She refused to live in fear the way her father did now. She would fight for her family's future, even if he no longer could.

Now, as they neared their destination, Sophie told herself that her father would surely gain back some of his strength and confidence once they were on board the ship. Away from the threat of arrest and imprisonment, in a world where Jews weren't allowed in shops, in parks, at theaters or restaurants, where you always had to look over your shoulder, fear the worst... Away from all of that, her father would find himself, his strength of conviction and *humanity* again. They all would. And they would start their new lives, their real lives, in America, once their visas were approved at the embassy in Havana. They would live in New York, as her father had said, where he had some contacts. He would practice law again; they would *live* again.

The driver of the taxi turned onto a side street off the main thoroughfare in the Neustadt neighborhood of the city, near to the port. After a few minutes of driving, he pulled up in front of the stoop of a modest hotel, a single, weathered door with a drooping awning. Her father had not wanted them to draw attention to themselves, and so had refused to entertain the notion of staying at a proper hotel, the Fairmont Hotel Vier Jahreszeiten or the Alster Hof, as they once might have, before all the laws that restricted Jews' lives had come into force, even though it perhaps would have been a better cover. Guests at such vaunted establishments, especially ones wearing jewels and furs, would not often be asked to show their papers, revealing passports stamped with a J and labeled either Israel or Sarah, no matter what their names were.

"We'll spend a quiet evening by ourselves," he'd insisted when he'd made the arrangements. His hands had shaken before he'd pressed his fingertips together, tried to steady his voice. "It's best if no one even knows we're there."

"Of course, Josef," Margarete had murmured. "Whatever you think is best."

Now, with a shaking hand, her father took out several bills to pay the driver while Margarete exited the taxi, Sophie following behind, holding Heinrich's hand, who was wriggling like a fish on a hook.

"Enough, Heinrich," she scolded, her voice sharpening a little as she yanked him back from the street, and her half-brother gave her a mutinous glare. He wasn't used to her being so stern; she, along with Margarete, had a propensity to indulge him. Today, however, Sophie felt too on edge to show the patience she normally would have. Despite her determination not to be afraid, she knew she was; her stomach felt hollow, an empty, cramping pit. What if something happened? What if it all went wrong?

She scanned the street for any dangers, but it was empty of pedestrians, nothing but wind blowing down it, chilly and damp from the harbor. Sophie, in her sprigged cotton spring dress, tried not to shiver.

Her stepmother drew her fox fur more closely about her shoulders as she glanced up at the hotel's modest front with a look of both apprehension and distaste. "Who knows what the food is like," she murmured, and Sophie gave her a small, sympathetic smile.

The only daughter of a wealthy banker, Margarete had grown up privileged and pampered; the restrictions against Jews had offended her as much as they'd shocked her, and six years on, she still chafed against them, albeit uselessly.

Sophie had tried to adopt a far more pragmatic and accepting attitude over the years, not wanting to become bitter, although it had been hard, as one comfort after another had been taken away—opportunity, education, and, most wrenchingly of all, friendship.

She was looking forward to being on the *St Louis*, an actual cruise liner, where they would be treated as regular, fare-paying customers rather than undesirables, despicable and degenerate.

Over the last few years, she'd done her best to accept how her bosom friends had dropped her when having a Jewish acquaintance had no longer been acceptable; she had, with determination, chosen not to resent the housemaid who had spat at her in the street even though she'd known Sophie since she was a small girl. Sophie had happily given the young woman her cast-off dresses, and Margarete had insisted she take a plate of supper home every night for her ailing mother. Now, however, they were beneath her notice; she'd looked at Sophie with hate in her eyes.

When the teacher who had treated Sophie as a doting pet, giving her the highest marks in the class, had forced her to sit at the back of the room and tell everyone that she had connived her way into her affections, after the laws on schooling had changed in 1936, Sophie had accepted it with the same stoicism her father had.

"People are weak," her father had said when she'd come to him once, with her grievances, her hurt. "And they are afraid. You must not take it personally, Sophie. It is so much bigger than you are." He'd smiled sadly. "And yet so much smaller."

"People should be stronger, then," Sophie had replied, and he'd patted her shoulder gently.

"Then you must lead by example."

And so she had, doing her best to shrug off all the petty slights, the deeper hurts, the lack of opportunities, and, worst of all, the loneliness. For the last three years, since she'd finished her education, she'd spent most of her time caring for Heinrich and daydreaming of when her life might truly begin.

And now, finally, it almost was.

Starting tomorrow, she would no longer have to face '*Juden verboten*' signs in every establishment's window, forbidding entry, or the glares or sneers on the street from those who knew she was Jewish; she would not have to tremble inwardly every time she passed a hard-faced man in uniform, wondering if he would stop her, assault her even, simply because he could. She would no longer have to live in fear, in loneliness, feeling cut off from everyone and everything she'd once known.

Starting tomorrow, she told herself as she mounted the steps of the hotel, her new life, one of possibility and *hope*, would finally begin.

CHAPTER 2

The quay in front of the SS *St Louis* was heaving with humanity—sailors and stevedores, SS officers and gawking passersby, curious about the nearly thousand Jews who were leaving the country with all their worldly belongings, yet no more than the equivalent of a handful of dollars in their pockets, thanks to stringent and grossly unfair immigration laws that had been imposed on them.

Fortunately, the Weisses' passage on the ship included all food, drink, and even entertainment, and Sophie's father had arranged to transfer as much of their savings as he could to a bank in New York some months ago, although, in order to do so, he'd had to relinquish fifty percent of all his assets to the German government. Still, he'd assured Sophie and her stepmother, it would be enough... if they could just get out of the country.

Upon arrival at the harbor, passengers had been directed to the cavernous Shed 76, where their papers would be processed, visas and passports checked, before they were at last allowed to board the ship. It was the last checkpoint in what had been a long, slow trudge of bureaucracy and injustice as they attempted to leave a country that no longer wanted them, but refused to let them go without paying a harsh penalty.

Once upon the cruise liner, they would finally be away from that; they would be safe. Or at least Sophie hoped they would; when they'd arrived at the harbor, she'd noticed, with a plunging sensation in her stomach, the black swastika painted on the ship's helm, reminding its passengers that it might be taking Jews to Cuba, but it was still a German ship, a *Nazi* ship, controlled by Hitler's forces.

She hoped her father hadn't spotted the darkly ominous sign. Margarete had been doing her best to distract him with her frivolous chatter, fussing about the clothes she'd sent ahead, and whether enough care would be taken with their trunks. Every so often, she gave Sophie a frightened, darting glance, reminding her of a sparrow desperately pecking for crumbs. Neither of them wanted Josef to fall into one of his dark moods of despair, or, worse, a mania of paranoia where he suspected everyone of being an informer. Not now, when they were so close.

As they moved through the long line in the shed, Sophie's heart skipped a nervous beat, and she smoothed down the bronze silk of her tea dress with hands that shook just a little. Margarete had insisted they dress appropriately for the occasion: their final farewell to a country that had come to despise them.

"I will not leave my homeland in rags," she'd stated that morning as she'd rolled her hair into an elegant chignon, her lips pursed in concentration as she'd stared hard at her reflection. "And, in any case, even SS officers respect a well-heeled personage."

Do they? Sophie had wondered, but she hadn't questioned her imposing stepmother.

Margarete had married her father seven years ago, just before the first race laws had come into force, and her father had still been a man of stature and reputation. Margarete had been kindly enough to Sophie, but, at twelve years old, she'd been suspicious of the sudden insertion of a stranger into their lives; her mother had died when she was a baby, and so for as long as Sophie could remember, it had simply been her and her father, a tender team of two.

To her credit, Margarete had done her best to woo her new stepdaughter with shopping trips and outings to the cinema, *Sachertorte* at Café Kranzler, and an embossed book of fairy tales that had been too young for her at the time, but beautiful all the same. Still, Sophie had not trusted this elegant woman with her brittle smile and bright eyes.

When Heinrich had been born, Sophie had felt as if her role in the family had been firmly displaced; why would her father concern himself with a querulous and spotty fourteen-year-old girl when he had a blond baby boy, dimpled and smiling, to dote on? And yet she'd doted on Heinrich, too, even though she hadn't meant to, at least not at first. She'd intended to ignore her baby brother, but it had proved impossible to resist his gummy smile, the way his chubby hands so often reached for her, winding about her neck as he pressed his round cheek to hers.

Now Sophie held tightly to Heinrich's hand as he tried to wriggle free, eager to explore, and they moved at a snail's pace in a long line of weary, worried passengers that snaked through the shed, the air turning hot and stuffy in the spring sunshine.

People had been boarding the ship since last night, with the Orthodox Jews going first, to avoid having to embark on the Sabbath. Since her own family observed only the high holy days, and sometimes not even those, such a consideration had not even occurred to Sophie.

She glanced around in both curiosity and sympathy at her fellow travelers and Jews—it was a motley group, many of them shabbily dressed, clutching battered, cardboard suitcases, while others were well-dressed and elegant, heading toward the first-class boarding gate. What they all shared, Sophie realized, were the anxious, careworn expressions—darting eyes, hunched shoulders, startling at any sudden noise. No amount of money, jewels or furs, it seemed, could change *that*.

"When are we going to get on the ship?" Heinrich demanded, tugging her hand hard enough to make Sophie wince. "I want to get on the ship!"

"Patience, little man," she replied gently. "We will get there soon, but we have to show them our tickets first. We are going on a big trip, you know!" Playfully, she tweaked his ear. "You can't go on a big trip without a ticket, can you? It's very important that you have one."

She glanced discreetly at the guards at the checkpoint ahead of them; their expressions were stony, mouths twisted in derision in a way Sophie recognized all too well. Even here, they hated the Jews, it seemed. Was there anyone, anywhere, who didn't?

Her father suddenly clutched at her arm. "Sophie," he hissed. "Those men... are they Gestapo?" He nodded anxiously toward the guards at the front of the line who were checking papers. "They look like Gestapo to me." His voice rose to a breathless squeak as he continued to clutch at her arm. "Gestapo—*here*—"

"No, no, Papa," Sophie said quickly, patting his hand, "they're just—" She stopped suddenly as she watched one of the guards shove a passenger hard in the shoulder, so he stumbled nearly to his knees, and, with a bored expression, the other emptied the man's case onto the floor, kicking at the flurry of clothes with his dirty boot. Her stomach hollowed out at the sight, and she had to swallow hard. They *were* Gestapo, or as good as. They were clearly no friend of Jews, at any rate—but then who was, these days?

Why, she wondered in an uncharacteristic burst of savagery, had the Hamburg-American—or Hapag—Line accepted Jewish passengers—and their hard-earned money—if they were going to treat them this way? As soon as she had the thought, she knew its answer; they had no choice. No one did. The Nazis inserted themselves into every institution—school, hospital, department store, even a pleasure-seeking cruise liner. They would not be safe, she thought, until they were sailing away from Germany... and maybe not even then.

"Don't worry, Papa," she told her father gently, patting his hand again as she made sure he kept his gaze on her, and not the passenger at the front of the line who was now on his hands and knees, head bowed as he scrabbled pathetically for his clothes, while the guards looked on, smirking.

She met her stepmother's eye, who had also witnessed the unpleasant scene, and they shared a brief look of understanding. They could not let Josef see what had happened.

"They are just guards," Sophie soothed. "Checking people's papers, and, as you know, everything is in order for us. You got the visas yourself!" A hundred and fifty dollars apiece, hardly an insignificant sum, from an official in the Cuban government. "Everything is going to be fine," she told her father firmly, determined to believe it herself. "Soon, we will be on the ship, and we will be safe. We will be having fun! Did you know there is a cinema on board? And a ballroom."

She'd read the brochure for the St Louis avidly over the last few months, studying the photographs of elegant state rooms and the many social and leisure areas the cruise liner had to offer. With room for a thousand passengers in first and tourist classes, as well as the crew, it wasn't the largest ship cruising the seas, but it had been furnished and decorated to a high standard, with many modern amenities. She had hardly believed they would be able to experience all its pleasures and wonders.

Her father continued to clutch her arm as he nodded slowly. "I pray you are right," he told her in a hoarse voice.

He'd never been a praying man, but since Kristallnacht, her

father had discovered his faith—or, perhaps, just the lack of it. After he'd returned from his weeks of protective custody, he'd begun intoning the night prayer over her and Heinrich before they went to bed: *Adonai, may it be your will that I lie down in peace and rise up in peace. Let not my thoughts, my dreams, or my daydreams disturb me. Watch over my family and those I love...*

As the line inched forward, Sophie's apprehension only grew. The guards were treating many passengers in a coarse and cruel way—upending their belongings, shoving them roughly as they glanced at their papers. While she had become used to seeing such treatment over the last few years, she worried about its effect on her father, especially at this crucial juncture. If he had some sort of breakdown right there at the gangplank, with Gestapo and crew members looking on, would they even let him on the ship—or would they drag him away, as he feared they would? And if they did, what then? They could hardly leave her father here in Germany. It would be the end of all their hopes.

Sophie glanced at Margarete and saw how she was chewing her nails—something she *never* did—and knew her stepmother was having the same anxious thoughts.

They simply could not come so close to salvation, Sophie thought, biting her lips in her worry, only to be turned away at the very last moment. She *wouldn't* let it happen... And yet she knew well enough just how powerless she was. She could not keep the guards from acting as they did; she could only attempt to distract her father.

"What do you think you'd like to do first on the ship?" she asked brightly. "The gymnasium, or the cinema? Or the social hall? I read in the brochure there was even a swimming pool. They'll fill it up with sea water when we're a day out. And it said they had tea dances and all sorts of things. There's a library, as well, with lots of books." She kept her wide smile in place, even though it made her cheeks ache, and, from the corner of her eye, she could still see the guards slouching about. "What do you think, Papa?" she asked again, but her father just stared at her blankly.

"I want to go in the swimming pool," Heinrich told her, tugging at her skirt. "Please, can we go in the swimming pool? Now?"

"Not yet, Heinie," Sophie told him, managing a laugh. "We're not on the ship, and in any case, it hasn't been filled yet! We can't go swim in an empty pool, can we?"

The sudden bright flash of a camera had her blinking in surprise, and Heinrich once more began straining at her hand.

"What was that... Are they taking photographs?" he asked eagerly. "Will we get our photograph taken, Sophie? Can we? Please? Please? I want a photograph!" He stood up straight, puffing his chest out in a way that made her smile. Despite her worry, her little brother's excitement was infectious.

"I shouldn't think so, Heinie," Sophie murmured, only to once again fall silent as they moved forward in the line and she saw that indeed there was a photographer, ostentatiously taking pictures of passengers as they passed by him.

She glanced at Margarete, who gave a little shrug of incomprehension. Why would they be taking photographs of Jewish emigrants, when for so long they had only seemed to want them gone?

A couple ahead of them paused in front of the photographer; they were even better dressed than Margarete at her most elegant; the woman in a mink stole and full-length evening gown of emerald satin, a diamond bracelet sliding down one slender wrist. Her dark hair was elegantly coiffed, her head tilted coquettishly as she swiveled this way and that, as if searching for the perfect angle.

Her husband was just as impressively attired, tall and broad-shouldered in a well-cut suit, his dark hair brilliantined to a gleaming slickness, his smile wide and white, master of his immediate domain. They posed for the photographer with the confident assurance of film stars well-used to the red carpet and the flash of cameras, while behind them, a dark-haired, sallow-faced young woman, tall and slender and around the same age as Sophie, and much more dourly dressed in a simple belted frock and plain overcoat, stood watching, a wry twist to her lips as she observed their obvious posturing.

She caught Sophie's inquisitive gaze and, after a second where they just stared at each other, she, very deliberately, rolled her eyes. Sophie found herself letting out a sudden, little laugh in return. The woman smiled then, and it transformed her face, lighting her eyes and brightening her complexion, making her seem almost beautiful. Sophie smiled back; she felt as if they had shared a joke, or even become friends. Perhaps she would try to make the young woman's acquaintance once on board the ship; she was in line for the first-class boarding gate, just as Sophie and her family were, so it was not outside the realm of possibility.

The photographer, however, had lowered his camera without snapping a single photo; the man in particular looked put out that he was not being photographed, his lips pursed in exasperation.

Sophie was now close enough to hear the photographer state flatly, "You are not the kind of subject the Reich wishes to highlight."

"Aren't we?" the man replied, puffing out his chest, clearly affronted.

The young woman exchanged another glance with Sophie, giving a little shrug of her narrow shoulders as if she was answering a question.

What, Sophie wondered, was going on? Who was the photographer, and who were these self-important people? Were they famous, or were they just acting as if they were?

Just then, a short, stocky man with the bearing of someone in the military, wearing the uniform of the Hamburg-American Line, stalked toward the photographer. Passengers waiting in line drew back, instantly apprehensive, tension crackling in the stuffy air of the shed as everyone watched on to see what would happen.

"How dare you take photographs of my passengers!" the short man declared in a voice taut with anger. "How dare you insinuate yourself in here, with your vicious and inappropriate propaganda!" He slapped the man hard on the shoulder, sending him staggering. "Out! Out of this shed—out, *out*!"

"I am here on orders of the Reich—" the man declared, cringing back from the man's continued short, stinging slaps as he clutched his camera to his chest. "You cannot keep me from following my—"

"This embarkation shed is the property of the Hamburg-American Line," the other man replied. "And here, I, as Captain of the SS *St Louis*, am in charge. If you do not leave at once, you will find yourself forcibly removed, and your equipment confiscated. *Out!*"

Sophie watched, both fascinated and horrified, as the photographer, in high dudgeon, gathered his belongings and then, with a dark look for the captain of their ship, scurried out of the shed. Her gaze caught the young woman's once more, and the other woman raised her dark eyebrows, another wry smile curving her lips. Sophie found herself grinning back. She most certainly would seek that young woman out once they were on board, she decided. After the bleak loneliness of the last few years, she could use a friend.

Fortunately, her father, while searching for his handkerchief, had managed to miss the entire altercation, and fifteen minutes later, they passed through the checkpoint without any incident. The guards, having viewed the captain's thunderous denunciation of the photographer, had ceased their intimidation tactics, and satisfied themselves with surly looks and growling tones, both of which Sophie—and even her father—were able to take in their stride.

As they walked through the first-class boarding gate, she exchanged a silent, grateful look with her stepmother and breathed a sigh of relief. They were finally on board; surely everything would be all right now.

Sophie glanced around in curiosity as they followed the flow of passengers down a corridor and up a flight of stairs to the deck of first-class berths, Heinrich pulling at her hand like a dog on a leash. She had a glimpse of elegant-looking receptions rooms positioned in the center of the ship, off an impressive main hall, before she followed her stepmother and father towards the sleeping accommodation.

"We'll get there, Heinie, don't worry," she laughed, wishing she could walk more slowly, to take in all the exquisite furnishings and fixtures of the ship. There would be time later, she supposed, during the two week journey, to explore all the interesting rooms.

Outside a hall that advertised itself as the Tanzplatz nightclub, rousing piano music could be heard. For a second, Sophie didn't recognize the lively tune, or maybe she simply didn't want to, but it only took a few seconds for her to realize what it was—the Horst Wessel song—the Nazi Party's unofficial anthem. Several men were singing along to it in loud, cheerful voices. *"The flag is high, our ranks are closed, the S.A. march with silent, solid steps..."*

"Liebe, what is it that they are playing?" Her father's voice was faint, his face pale as he clutched Margarete's arm.

"Never mind, Papa," Sophie replied quickly. "It doesn't matter. Let's get to our cabin. I'm sure we want to refresh ourselves before the ship leaves port."

"That song..." He shook his head, tears starting in his eyes.

"I knew it! I knew this ship was damned! Did you see the swastika on its helm? The Gestapo—"

"Every German ship must have a swastika, Josef," Margarete interrupted him, trying to sound breezy, Sophie thought, and not quite managing it. "It means nothing. There are no Gestapo here, certainly, and in a few hours, we will have left Germany behind forever."

Her father was shaking now, gazing around the ship's narrow corridor as if looking for enemies, as the rousing song continued to be banged out on a piano. "This ship... this ship is *damned*!"

"Papa, please, don't say such a thing," Sophie begged. Other passengers who had boarded were starting to stare; a few were casting them dark looks, shaking their heads, and whispering as they moved past them, to their own berths. No one wanted such a distressing portent of doom at the start of their journey. "Please—"

"May I help you?" A dark-haired man in the Hapag Line uniform stepped forward smoothly. "I am First Officer Ostermeyer. Do you need directions to your cabin?" He nodded toward the hatbox Margarete had looped over one arm; she hadn't wanted to trust it to the porters. "May I take that for you, madam?"

Margarete stared at the man dumbly, made speechless by his meticulous politeness. Much as her stepmother railed against the injustice and cruelty of the Nazis, when confronted with the opposite, she had no idea how to respond.

Neither did Sophie. Did this man mean it? Was it some kind of trick?

From the nightclub, the Horst Wessel song continued to play, accompanied by a handful of thunderous male voices.

"Please ignore that music," the first officer continued in a voice that was low and pleasant. "I apologize for any distress it might cause you."

Slowly, Margarete shook her head, still looking dumbfounded.

Sophie stepped forward, her heart beating hard. "Thank you, sir," she said quietly. "As you can see, my father is distressed. Our cabin is A-108. Could you kindly direct us?"

The smile the man gave her was quick and sure. "But of course, please follow me."

Still holding Heinrich's hand, Sophie followed the man down the corridor, her stepmother trailing behind, holding her father's arm as she murmured soothing words to him.

A few minutes later, they'd reach the door of their cabin. First Officer Ostermeyer opened it with a smiling flourish, asking if they needed anything else before departing.

Sophie stepped into the cabin, a shuddery breath escaping her in a rush. It was a lovely and well-appointed room, with two beds and matching dressers, a desk and chair, and an adjoining bathroom, complete with tub, toilet, and sink. She and Heinrich would share a connecting adjoining cabin, similarly styled.

Looking around, Sophie felt herself start to relax. They really had made it, they were safe, at last... And yet, with the piano music echoing in her ears, the memory of the surly guards, the photographer... it didn't quite feel that way.

"Look, Sophie, look!" Heinrich was clambering toward the porthole, pressing his nose against the glass, just as he had yesterday, with the taxi's window. "I can see the sea!"

"Well, I should hope so," Sophie replied as she managed a laugh. She joined him at the porthole, caressing his blond curls as she gazed out at the churning water of the harbor and tried to steady her nerves.

They'd made it, she told herself, willing herself to believe it, to trust in it. What could the Nazis do to them now?

She glanced back at her father and stepmother. Her father was sitting slumped on one of the beds, his hat in his hands, his head bowed. With a lurch of alarm, Sophie saw that tears were silently trickling down his wrinkled cheeks.

Margarete had closed the door of their cabin, exhaling shakily, before turning to her husband with a determinedly wide smile. "Shall we celebrate with champagne?" she asked, her voice high and bright as she did her best to ignore her husband's silent tears. "I could summon the steward to bring us a bottle. We should toast our journey!"

As much as Sophie wanted to celebrate, she could not imagine her father toasting their voyage—or anything—just now. He looked like a man in the depths of despair, not the pinnacle of celebration.

Slowly, he shook his head, a monotonous back and forth, as he stared at his wife, helpless in his grief. Sophie kept her hand on Heinrich's shoulder, anchoring him in place. Absorbed with the bustling view outside the porthole, her little brother thankfully did not notice the sorrowful drama playing out on their own personal stage, but she did, and it tore at her heart. She wanted her father to regain some of his energy and enthusiasm, the zest for life that had once been so much a part of him. She just didn't know how to help him find it again.

"Josef..." Margarete took a step toward him, one hand flung out toward him in supplication, her determined smile wavering at its edges. "We're safe now."

"Are we?" her father replied softly. He cocked his head to listen, and Sophie imagined she could almost hear the strains of the Horst Wessel song from the nightclub, filtering all the way down the corridor to their cabin.

It was impossible, of course, but she felt it all the same—the rousing tune, the hard voices. *Millions are looking to the swastika for hope... the day of freedom and of bread dawns!* Utter lies that had permeated and poisoned everything she'd once known and held dear. Would the same happen here?

"Pfft?" Margarete registered Josef's look with a dismissive

cluck of her tongue. "That song? It was only a few uppity crew. What of it? They've been taken in hand, I'm sure of it."

"They are never taken in hand, Margarete," he replied, running a weary hand through his hair. "They never will be."

"It doesn't matter," she insisted, "now that we're on this ship! There are no Nazis in Cuba."

"That remains to be seen." Her father drew a shaky breath as he squared his shoulders. "But you are right." The smile he gave both Sophie and her stepmother was watery and weak, but at least it was there. "We are on the ship," he said as he released a long, low sigh. Again, he managed a small smile. "That is something, I suppose."

"And, in just two weeks, we'll be in Havana," Margarete added, her voice hard and bright. "And then on to New York! We'll drink champagne at the Plaza Hotel, Josef. I've always wanted to see the Palm Court." Her eyes were glittering, her smile fierce. "You must stop your worrying, Josef. I tell you, nothing can stop us now."

CHAPTER 3

Sophie stood on the deck of the ship, her hands curled over the railing, as a short, piercing blast sounded.

"What's happening, Sophie?" Heinrich demanded as he stood on his tiptoes to try to see past the railing, his nose barely brushing the wooden banister. He'd been jumping up and down almost constantly since they'd got on the ship several hours ago. "Are we going? Are we finally going?"

"I think we are, Heinie." Sophie's smile trembled on her lips and her heart swelled with hope and joy as she watched the gangplanks hauled clear and the ropes slipped. She could hardly believe it was finally happening; they were actually leaving Germany, and all its painful memories, behind.

Bellowed commands passed from ship to shore as the crowd at the railing grew silent with both apprehension and awe. As Sophie glanced around at the solemn faces, she wondered how many of them had feared not being able to leave at all. The ship would be recalled; they would be forced to disembark, sent back to their homes, or worse, somewhere else.

It was what her father had feared. While Sophie and Margarete had taken Heinrich to a children's tea in the first-class dining room, Josef had stayed behind in the cabin, slumped on his bed, muttering prayers Sophie hadn't thought he believed in.

At least he'd roused himself to come to the railing now, to see the *St Louis* depart.

As the ship slowly and lumberingly began to move off from its moorings, not a single person on deck spoke a word. It felt as if everyone was holding their breath, waiting for disaster or deliverance—they didn't know which. The water churned up white foam and the cries from the shore of the stevedores became fainter and fainter as the ship made its way out of the harbor.

"The space between the ship and the land," someone called in a voice of hushed excitement. "It's growing!" He sounded amazed, incredulous.

Sophie watched, her hand tightly gripping her brother's, Margarete standing next to her, her arm slipped through her husband's, as if to keep him upright.

"Bang on eight o'clock," a woman nearby remarked, glancing at her watch in satisfaction. "Right on time."

"The Germans are never late," the man next to her replied sardonically. "Especially when it comes to Jews."

The ship was now chugging steadily away from the shore, and suddenly feeling rather shaky and emotional, Sophie turned away from the railing. She felt a need to stretch her legs, empty her mind. She knew she should ask Margarete if she would like her to put Heinrich to bed, or help her father back to the cabin, but for just a few moments, she wanted to feel young and free and unencumbered, this adventure rolling out in front of her like a red carpet.

"I'm going to take a stroll around the deck," she told her stepmother, a pronouncement as much as a question. "Just for a few minutes. Then I'll come back and read Heinrich a story before bed." She glanced at her father, who was staring out at the sea, a look of weary confusion on his face. "All right, Papa?"

"Hmm?" He turned back to her, blinking her into focus. "*Schatzi*...?"

Sophie reached over to squeeze his hand. "We're really going," she told him quietly, and his eyes crinkled in a faint smile as he nodded.

"Yes, we really are."

Sophie glanced back at her stepmother for permission she still felt she needed. For a second, Margarete looked as if she wanted to refuse Sophie's request; her face was pale and strained and Sophie knew her stepmother had come to rely heavily on her help with Heinrich, and even with Josef. But then Margarete's expression softened, and she gave a brief nod.

"Go on, then," she said. "But only a few minutes, mind."

"I promise."

As Sophie started down the deck, maneuvering around various knots of people, she felt her heart lighten, her soul start to soar. Freedom, if only for a few minutes! Away from the Nazis' oppression, from the cares and demands of her own family...

She felt a flash of guilt for thinking that way, but resolutely she pushed it aside. She had only a few minutes to enjoy this heady sense of possibility, and she did not want to squander them on pointless regrets or feelings of guilt.

As she came to the prow of the ship, the deck began to clear; most people were still on the shoreside, or else had gone back inside. Sophie breathed in the clean, cold, salt-smelling air, let the wind whip her hair from its usual neat French roll. Sea spray touched her cheeks and for a few seconds she closed her eyes, breathed in the scent of freedom. *At last...*

She could let all the cares that had weighed her down these last months and years fall away, leaving her feeling light and easy. In Havana, and then America, her father would regain his health and confidence. She'd make friends, maybe even go to university. She'd once had a dream of studying languages, before the government had banned Jews from all public schools and universities last year. But in America? All things were possible. She might even meet someone, a law student perhaps, or a doctor...

Sophie smiled wryly. Margarete would want her to meet someone with such social connections, but she didn't care so much about that. She wouldn't mind falling in love with a poet or a musician, or just an ordinary man with a nice smile and kind eyes. She'd never been in love, never known what it was like to have a man look at her with admiration in his eyes, speak to her with tenderness in his voice...

No matter what happened in Cuba and then America, Sophie just wanted life to *begin* the way it was meant to—love and adventure, learning and fun, laughter and hope, all waiting for her in America...

"You're not going to jump, are you?"

Startled, Sophie's eyes flew open, and she blinked the speaker into focus—it was the tall, dark-haired young woman who had been standing behind the glamorous couple and who had smiled at her like she'd made a friend. Sophie had looked for her at dinner, but since she and Margarete had gone to the children's tea with the other few dozen small children on board, as well as their carers, she hadn't really expected to see her, and she hadn't.

"Jump?" she repeated with a surprised laugh. "No, certainly not."

The woman nodded towards Sophie's hands, curled around the railing, almost, she realized, as if she'd been about to launch herself over. "Well, you looked as if you might have, but I'm glad to hear it's not a possibility. It would be a shame, having finally got *on* this ship, to get off it again so soon."

"It certainly would." Sophie took a step back from the railing as she eyed the young woman with unabashed curiosity.

Tall and slender, her shoulders thrown back and her gaze direct, she had a frank, unsentimental air about her that both intimidated and intrigued Sophie; this was a woman who was comfortable in herself in a way Sophie knew she wasn't. Not yet, anyway. Perhaps when she had more life experience, more confidence, she'd be like this young woman, eyeing the world in such a practical yet disinterested manner, confident and assured. She wasn't particularly beautiful, but Sophie decided she was striking, which was far better, with her dark hair pulled back into a simple bun and clear gray eyes. She wore the same drab dress from earlier, and it hung straight from her shoulders to her hips, belted loosely but revealing very little of what looked to be a boyish figure.

"Finished your inspection?" the woman asked, amused, and Sophie blushed, realizing belatedly how she'd been staring.

"Sorry. I was just... curious. I recognize you, from before."

"Yes, I know. I recognized you, as well. You came with your parents?"

"My father and stepmother. And my half-brother. He's only five."

"Ah." The woman nodded knowingly; the single syllable seemed to hold a wealth of meaning, and Sophie had the uncanny feeling that this woman understood her entire family situation without her having had to say a word about it.

"And you?" she asked. "Are you traveling alone?" Over half the passengers on the ship, Sophie knew, were women and children, traveling either to meet husbands and fathers, or sadly having to leave them behind, with hopes and promises that they would follow when they could.

The woman let out a short laugh of genuine amusement. "No, didn't you notice my parents making the usual display of themselves for that Nazi photographer?" She shook her head, smiling faintly, still amused. "I'm with them."

"They're your *parents*?" Sophie exclaimed in surprise. She'd assumed they were strangers, traveling separately. "But—"

"I know, I know," she cut her off with a slightly hard laugh, "they're nothing like me. Or, really, I'm nothing like them, thank goodness. But yes, they are my parents. Not that you'd know it. I suppose you thought I was their personal secretary or something?" She raised her eyebrows in query, while Sophie stared at her helplessly. She hadn't thought this woman had been associated with that glamorous couple at all. "Sometimes I do feel like that." She let out a little sigh, staring out into the darkness of the sea, before she gave a subtle shake of her head and turned back to Sophie. "Anyway. I'm Rosa Herzelfeld." She stuck out a hand for Sophie to shake.

"Sophie Weiss." She took Rosa's hand, who shook hers with a firm, almost manly grip. "Pleased to meet you."

"Likewise. I was hoping I'd see you on board. I haven't always been very good at making friends, but you seemed something of a kindred spirit."

"Do you really think so?" Sophie didn't even try to keep the surprised pleasure from her voice. She liked Rosa instinctively; her clear-eyed honesty made her trust her, or at least *want* to trust her. And after the loneliness and isolation of the last few years, she desperately wanted to make a friend, a good friend. A kindred spirit, like Rosa had said.

"Well, you laughed at my parents' ridiculousness, after all," Rosa replied dryly. "So that's something. Will you be staying in Havana, or will your family try to obtain visas for America?"

"America," Sophie replied. "New York. At least, I hope so. My father is—well, *was*, really—a lawyer and he has some connections in New York and Washington."

Once, Josef Weiss had been one of Berlin's most renowned lawyers, making a name for himself as an attorney in many prominent cases in the 1920s, fighting against the social clubs that had belonged to a seedy underworld of blackmail and prostitution. Back then, his opinion had been respected, feted; he'd lectured in Berlin's universities, and people from the public would often sit in on his trials to hear his opening and closing statements, with his trademark mixture of sophistication and subtle wit. Many such speeches had been reprinted in the *Berliner Tageblatt*, and once upon a time, various *bon mots* would be discussed and dissected at many of Berlin's intelligentsia's dinner tables.

That had all changed in 1933, when Hitler had come to power and Jews had been as good as expelled from the legal system, along with most other professions. Her father had only been allowed to continue to practice because of his age—as an '*Altanwalt*', or senior lawyer, who had come to the profession before 1914, he had been allowed to continue to work, although it had been in a depressingly diminished capacity. But of course, that had all changed after Kristallnacht.

"Always good to have connections," Rosa replied in that same dry voice.

"I imagine your father must have some, as well?" Sophie ventured. She thought of the man's gleaming hair and smile. He seemed like the sort who would know the right people.

"He collects connections the way other men collect stamps," Rosa offered with a sharp, little laugh. "So, yes. But whether they are the right ones..." She shrugged, pursing her lips, her gaze sliding away. "Who knows."

"Will you stay in Havana, then?" Sophie asked.

"We'll stay where my father can be most successful," Rosa replied. "He's a doctor."

Something about her tone made Sophie feel uncertain. There was a hardness in her new friend's face that she didn't know how to deal with, and so she decided to change the subject.

"Well, I'm looking forward to ten days on this ship," Sophie told her in a bright voice. "Food and dancing and entertainment —I heard there is a cinema on board, and there is even going to be a costume ball on the second to last night."

Rosa smiled faintly, and suddenly Sophie felt childish. Why should she be excited about such things, when they were fleeing for their very lives? When there were so many more important things to be thinking about?

"Yes, I heard the same," Rosa said after a moment. "It sounds like good fun. What are you going to dress up as? My mother's brought a Cleopatra costume, of all things, a wig included! She'll probably look a complete fright."

"I haven't thought that far ahead," Sophie admitted. They'd brought nothing for costumes; it had, she acknowledged, been just about the farthest thing from their minds. "But it's nice just to think of being able to do such things again," she said, "not that I ever really did them before." She'd only been thirteen when the first race laws had been enacted, and Heinrich had been born, and in so many ways her life had become so small— without adventure or romance, or even the possibility of either.

"Yes, I know what you mean." Rosa suddenly flung her arms wide as she tilted her face to the night sky. "We finally get a chance to live! *Really* live. I can't wait."

Sophie gazed at her, wishing she had the reckless confidence to throw her arms wide as well, turn her face to the heavens, but she knew she didn't; she feared she'd look ridiculous. "What do you want to do in Havana?" she asked. "Or America, if it comes to that?"

Rosa lowered her face as she dropped her arms, turning to face Sophie with a ferocity as well as a bleakness in her eyes. "*Anything*," she said, her voice coming out both determined and heartfelt.

Before Sophie could respond—not that she'd even known what to say—they heard heavy footsteps behind them. Rosa tensed as Sophie turned around at the sound of a man's sneering voice.

"Ah, two little Jewesses enjoying the night air. Better be careful you don't fall over—or get a push."

As he came closer, Sophie could see his face—pockmarked and leering. He wore the uniform of the Hapag crew, the brim of his cap pulled low, his fleshy lips twisted in a sneer. She took a step away from the railing, her mouth dry, her heart beating hard. Never mind the music or the photographer earlier, she hadn't expected the outright hostility of the man's attitude right here on the ship, completely undisguised. Before Sophie could think how to reply, Rosa spoke.

"I'd say the same of you," she remarked coolly. "Your little piano concert wasn't very popular this afternoon, as I recall, with the captain."

The man's face contorted with malevolence as he took a threatening step toward Rosa. "Shut up, you dirty little Jew," he told her in a low, menacing voice. "Or you really will need to be careful."

Rosa didn't move a muscle, even though the man was now looming over her, angry and ugly, and, Sophie thought, completely terrifying. How on earth was her new friend able to keep her nerve? Yet there she was, standing tall and straight, gray eyes flashing, chin tilted at a haughty angle as she faced the man down.

"Shall I tell Captain Schroeder about this little conversation?" Rosa asked pleasantly. "I'm sure he'd be interested to hear how his crew are treating the passengers, especially as First Officer Ostermeyer was so keen to make a good impression. The reputation of the Hapag Line is at stake, after all." She kept the man's gaze, even as he raised one meaty fist as if to strike her.

Sophie caught her breath, completely frozen in fear, as Rosa steadily eyed the man, without so much as a flinch or a wince.

Finally, after what felt like an absolute age, he slowly lowered his fist.

"I'll be watching you," he warned her in a growl, and then he pushed past her, hitting her hard in the shoulder, as he moved down the deck.

As his footsteps faded into the darkness, Sophie hurried to her new friend's side. "Are you all right?" she asked anxiously, as Rosa massaged her shoulder. "I can't believe your courage!"

In response, Rosa smiled wryly, and then promptly leaned over the ship's railing and threw up.

CHAPTER 4

By the next morning, which dawned sunny and bright, Sophie had managed to cast off the sense of anxiety and fear that had dogged her since the previous night's altercation.

Rosa, having wryly wiped her mouth with her handkerchief after being sick, had robustly declared, "I refuse to be cowed by some toady little stool pigeon like that. Even if the prospect of standing up to him was enough to make me lose my supper." She'd glanced down at her stained and crumpled handkerchief with a grimace. "I do apologize for such a display. I didn't think I'd actually be *sick!*" She had let out a slightly shaky laugh as she'd dabbed at her mouth.

"Never mind that," Sophie had told her. "I thought you were amazingly brave. I never could have spoken out the way you did."

She'd been, quite literally, quaking in her shoes. She wished she possessed Rosa's audacity as well as conviction, but she knew she didn't. Ever since Kristallnacht, she'd just wanted to be safe—and safety meant not speaking out, not rocking the boat or risking anything, in any way. It was a price Sophie knew, somewhat to her own shame, that she was more than willing to pay. For herself, and for her family.

"If courage is feeling terrified and doing it anyway, then maybe," Rosa had replied as she had folded her handkerchief and slipped it into her pocket. "Although it might just have been sheer foolishness. I'm just so *tired* of people like that—thinking they're better than I am, and for what? An accident of birth? A J stamped in my passport?" She had shaken her head, her mouth firming. "Anyway, never mind that lout. Captain Schroeder is on our side, at least, as far as I can tell."

Sophie had been intrigued by her seemingly inside knowledge. "Is he?" she had asked.

Rosa had raised her eyebrows. "Didn't you see him shout down that photographer, back in the shed?"

"Yes, but..." Sophie had paused, feeling her own inexperience compared to Rosa's seeming worldliness. She hadn't really understood the situation with the photographer at all, although she had felt as if she should have. What had been the captain's objection? "Why was he there in the first place, do you know?"

"To take photographs of Jews cringing and scraping and looking dirty and poor," Rosa had stated matter-of-factly. "That's why he didn't want to photograph my parents. They were far too glamorous for the Reich's newsreels that show good Germans how Jews are little better than rats—a nasty, germ-ridden infestation they'd best get rid of." Her lips had twisted. "No, he didn't want a snap of my parents, that much is certain. My father has made a career out of looking like the right sort of person."

"And yet he couldn't escape being Jewish, I suppose," Sophie had pointed out. She was curious about Rosa's relationship to her parents; she seemed to hold them in something close to contempt. And yet, no matter how glamorous her father looked, like so many others, he'd still been forced to leave the country.

"Well, he gave it a good try," Rosa had replied shortly. "But never mind that. I should get back, not that my parents will miss me. But why don't we meet up in the morning, have a wander around the ship? I want to have a good explore of everything."

Sophie was delighted by such an offer, even as she couldn't help but give a slight grimace of apology. "I'm afraid I'll most likely have my little brother with me—"

Rosa had shrugged her easy acceptance. "I don't mind if you don't."

"He'll probably be very excitable," Sophie had felt compelled to warn her new friend. Heinrich, no doubt, would be jumping up and down and pulling her everywhere the entire time. "But, yes, if you don't mind, then I certainly don't! And I'm desperate to explore the ship. What I've seen so far has looked amazing." She'd smiled, and Rosa had smiled back, their friendship firmly forged.

"Then it's a date."

Now, as the sun streamed through the porthole of their cabin, Sophie stood in front of the mirror, fussing with her appearance. She already knew Rosa wouldn't care what she wore, but Sophie felt a feminine – and, she supposed, a rather vain – desire to look her best as she went about the ship, and maybe met some of her fellow passengers. This was the first time she'd done anything like this—encountered new people, had any *fun*. She wanted to look the part.

She'd put her hair in pin curls last night, and now she combed her fingers through the carefully waved blond locks as they fell to her shoulders. She never wore makeup, although Margarete often did. Somehow, whenever Sophie dared to put on a slick of crimson lipstick or a touch of rouge, she felt like a little girl playing with a paintbox. She decided to forego makeup that morning—not that she even had any of her own—

and settle for a pair of pearl earrings her father had given her for her eighteenth birthday. They'd been her mother's, along with an emerald parure set—necklace, brooch, earrings, and bracelet —all of which she had meticulously sewn into the lining of her winter coat, at her stepmother's urging.

"There are some things you must make sure the Nazis don't get," Margarete had stated grimly. "Especially when they've taken so much already." She had sewn her own jewels into the lining of one of her coats, as well—a plain woolen one the Nazis would take no notice of. "Just in case," she'd told Sophie, her lips pursed as she'd bitten off a thread.

In case of what, Sophie wasn't entirely sure. But now their belongings were on the ship, she supposed they could unpick the linings of their coats and wear the jewels to dinner, or the costume party on the last evening, but she suspected Margarete would not be willing to do so until they reached Havana, or maybe even America. Then, and only then, would they truly be safe, no matter what assurances Margarete or Sophie had given to Josef.

But Sophie didn't want to think about any of that this morning. She didn't want to remember the Nazi photographer, or the Horst Wessel song being banged out on the piano, or the ugly, sneering face of the crew member calling Rosa a dirty little Jew. If there was a crew member or two who had something against Jews, well, what of it? Like Rosa had said, the captain was on their side. That was what mattered. Besides, the sun was shining, and her new friend was waiting, and she had the whole ship to explore. Today, Sophie decided, was a day for pleasure and possibility—for all the things that had been so woefully absent from her life for far too many years already.

"Come along, Heinrich," she told her little brother with brisk cheerfulness. He'd been kicking around the cabin since breakfast, restless and bored, jumping up and down on the bed, burrowing under the covers, and generally wearing his mother's nerves to a fray. "We're going to explore the ship. But you must be on your best behavior, or you won't get any dessert tonight." She wagged a playful finger at him while her brother's face lit up.

"Explore the ship? Can I see the engine room? And the bridge?"

Sophie let out a laugh as she rumpled his hair. "I'm not sure about that, but how about the cinema and the swimming pool? The gymnasium and the social hall?"

"I'd rather see the engine room," Heinrich replied, but he was hopping up and down with excitement. He wanted to escape the confines of their cabin just as much as Sophie did, if not more; her father was still looking dejected and Margarete was fussing around him, like a butterfly fluttering around a wilting flower. If Sophie entertained Heinrich for a few hours, she hoped that, with her stepmother's help, her father might regain some of his old equilibrium.

"I'll see you at lunchtime, Papa." She bent to kiss her father's withered cheek and gave her stepmother a fleeting smile before she took Heinrich's hand and stepped out into the corridor.

Up on the A deck, the sun was shining brightly, glinting off the sea which stretched endlessly in every direction. Until she looked out at all that ocean, Sophie hadn't realized how *freeing* it would feel to know Germany, with its goose-stepping Wehrmacht and gun-toting soldiers, the *verboten* signs on every doorway, was far away. With a ripple of unease, she once more recalled the sneering face of the man from last night. *I'll be watching you.* But he was just one man; he couldn't really do anything other than make empty threats, surely.

"Sophie, come on!" Heinrich tugged at her hand. "I want to see *everything*!"

"All right, little man, all right." Laughing, Sophie let herself be pulled along. "We're meeting my friend Rosa in the social hall, so let's start there."

The social hall was an enormous room, filled with tables and chairs and a double staircase that led to a balcony that ran the whole length of the chamber. At a little past nine o'clock in the morning, it held only a few dozen people scattered about, some reading or writing letters, others playing cards. The mood seemed cautiously muted, and Sophie wondered if the other passengers, like her father, had trouble truly believing they were finally free. Sitting comfortably in a well-appointed room with no restrictions or rules, no one to come along and knock the book out of your hands or shove you to the ground or shout for you to be on your way... such liberty seemed a simple thing, one she once would have taken for granted, but now it felt almost sacred.

"There you are!"

Sophie felt someone tap her on her shoulder, and she turned around to see Rosa smiling at her. She was wearing a shapeless dress, similar to the one she had on the day before, in a plain blue serge, and her dark hair was pulled back in a no-nonsense bun. She would have looked as stern as a schoolmarm, save for her ready smile and the sparkling warmth in her gray eyes. "And this must be your little brother."

"I'm Heinrich," he said, puffing out his chest importantly. "Who are you?"

"I'm Rosa," she replied with a laugh. "But don't you know it's rude to ask a lady her name in such a way? Although, I must admit, your forthrightness is refreshing."

Heinrich's forehead creased with confusion. "How am I supposed to ask?"

"You say, '*I am delighted to make your acquaintance,*'" Rosa told him in a voice of exaggerated graciousness, laughter still lurking in her eyes. "And then, '*May I have the pleasure of introducing myself?*'"

Sophie let out a gurgle of laughter. "I can't see Heinrich saying any of that!"

Her brother gave her a withering look. "I can," he insisted in a voice stiff with affront, and Rosa and Sophie exchanged smiling glances.

"Well, try it, then," Rosa told him, and the little boy drew himself up, as dignified as a count attending a ball.

"I am delighted to make your acquaintance, Rosa," he said in as serious a voice as Sophie had ever heard. "May I have the pleasure of introducing myself?"

Rosa gave a deep, sweeping curtsey in return. "You may, sir," she replied, and Heinrich held out his hand.

"My name is Heinrich Eduard Weiss," he intoned, and she took his hand. "Very pleased to meet you."

"And I, you," Rosa replied graciously, before she and Sophie lapsed into giggles.

Heinrich turned to Sophie, his expression caught between anxiety and affront. "I did it right, didn't I?"

"Oh, you did, Heinie, you did," Sophie assured him. "It was very well done! You are a proper little gentleman." As they started to walk along, she turned to Rosa and confessed in a low voice, "You've taught him more manners in a minute than my stepmother or I have in a year! I am impressed and ashamed all at once. I'm afraid we have both tended to spoil him."

"I don't think it's done him any harm," Rosa responded, "and considering the state of the world today, a Jewish child surely deserves a little spoiling. There's a tea dance this afternoon in the *Tanzplatz*. I think we should go and let Heinrich have all the cake he wants!"

"I think it might give him a stomachache," Sophie replied, "but I'm sure he won't mind."

"Cake?" Heinrich asked eagerly, catching the one crucial word from the conversation. "Can we have cake?"

. . .

They spent the next hour happily wandering around the ship, from the deserted gymnasium on A deck, to the sports deck, where a few dozen young people were trying their hand at shuffleboard. Heinrich had a go, pushing the disc along, his face screwed up with effort.

They toured the *Tanzplatz*, where they were setting up for the tea dance, thankfully with no Nazi songs being played on the piano. They peeked into the cinema, which was playing a film that evening, and the dining halls, which were being set for lunch, with tables of sparkling crystal and snowy white linen. As they explored the ship, Sophie felt her heart get lighter; people were starting to enjoy themselves, and the shadowed, anxious looks from the day before were already relaxing into shy, cautious pleasure—something she felt herself.

She and Rosa ended up in a couple of lounge chairs on the sun deck, while Heinrich played with a few other children, and they shared a pot of coffee.

"I've seen quite a number of children on their own," Sophie remarked as she glanced around at the young ones playing on the deck, some of them with no parents in sight. "Are some of them really traveling on the ship without any chaperones?"

"So, it would seem." Rosa nodded toward two girls, about five and seven years old, who were playing quietly together. "I met those two last night, Renata and Evelynne Aber. They're here completely by themselves, can you imagine? They're so little! Their father is already in Havana."

"And their mother?" Sophie asked.

Rosa shrugged. "They didn't mention her." She leaned over to put her coffee cup down just as the ball some of the children had been playing with suddenly bounced right up into her lap before smacking her in the face. "Oh...!" She fell back into her chair in surprise, one hand pressed to her cheek, coffee splashed on her skirt.

"I'm so very sorry." A young woman about their age came

hurrying toward them, her face tense with anxiety. "My sister threw the ball, and I was so clumsy, I wasn't able to catch it! Are you hurt?" She reached a hand out to Rosa before dropping it to her side.

"No, it just surprised me, that's all." Rosa rubbed her cheek and then smiled. "I suppose I should throw it back," she remarked teasingly, and, taking the ball from her lap, she tossed it gently to a young girl about ten years old, with blond braids and a fearful expression. She caught it with a shy smile, clutching the ball to her chest, and the older woman's face broke into a smile of relief, her shoulders sagging a little. She looked, Sophie thought, like someone who had carried a great burden for too long already.

"Thank you," she said quietly, her tone heartfelt. "You are very kind."

"You're traveling together?" Rosa asked, glancing curiously between the two.

The woman was small and slender with light brown hair pulled back into a loose bun. She had a small, pointed chin and bright hazel eyes, and Sophie thought she would be quite beautiful, if she didn't look so tense and unhappy.

"Yes... this is my sister, Lotte, and my name is Hannah. We're going to meet our father in Havana." Hannah put her hands on her sister's shoulders, as if anchoring her in place. She took a steadying breath and let it out slowly before straightening and then offering them both a quiet smile; it seemed as if it cost her something.

"It's nice you have someone to greet you," Rosa replied, her speculative glance moving between Hannah and her sister. There was, Sophie thought, an air of sadness about the sisters, like a dark fog surrounding them. "I don't know a soul in Havana."

"Nor do I," Sophie chimed in, smiling. She nodded toward

Heinrich, who was eyeing the ball in Lotte's hands with longing. "This is my brother, Heinrich. He's nearly six."

"I'm... t-t-t... ten," Lotte said quietly. She had a slight stammer, and after she spoke, she blushed and looked down at her feet, one skinny leg twisted around the other.

"Are you on your own?" Rosa asked. "We were just saying how many women are traveling by themselves, without husbands or fathers."

"Well, I certainly don't have a husband," Hannah replied, with something approaching humor, her hazel eyes briefly lightening to a golden-green. "But, yes, it is just the two of us." She tilted her chin at a determined angle, as if daring them to question it.

"Mutti... stayed... behind," Lotte offered, the words coming out painfully. She pressed her head against Hannah's shoulders and closed her eyes, while her sister cradled her protectively.

A silence fell as Sophie struggled to think what to say, and Rosa looked at them in quiet pity.

After a second, Hannah cleared her throat. "Thank you," she said, with quiet dignity, and with her arm still around Lotte, she began to turn.

"Wait!" Sophie called, not wanting to end their brief meeting in such a way. "We were thinking of going to the cinema tonight—they're showing a romantic story. Would you like to come with us?"

Hannah turned back to her slowly, her eyes wide. "To the cinema?" she asked, as if she couldn't quite believe—or trust—such an invitation.

"Well, yes." Sophie let out an uncertain little laugh. "We're allowed to go, aren't we, and I thought it might be fun. I've missed going." Jews had been barred from all cinemas, theaters, and sports grounds after Kristallnacht. Sophie had used to go with her father, before he'd married Margarete, and she'd taken

Heinrich to see *The Seven Ravens* last year, his first film, based on the Grimm fairy tales.

"Yes, do with come us," Rosa chimed in. "And Lotte, as well. I imagine it will be suitable."

"I..." Hannah glanced down at her sister, clearly torn. Like so many others, Sophie wondered, was she struggling to trust any kindness, no matter how small?

Lotte peered hopefully up at Hannah. "Can we?" she whispered, and Sophie's heart gave a little pang at the look of fierce tenderness that suffused Hannah's face as she looked down at her little sister. She seemed intensely protective of the young girl.

"Yes, of course we can, *Schatzi*," she murmured, stroking Lotte's hair. It was the same endearment Sophie's father used for her. "If you want to." She turned back to Sophie and Rosa, her expression now one of dignified politeness, her arm still around her sister. "Thank you very much for the invitation. I am delighted to accept."

"I am *delighted* to make your acquaintance!" Heinrich suddenly piped up, sounding positively triumphant, and Hannah looked startled as Rosa and Sophie erupted into giggles.

"I taught him that," Rosa explained, and as Sophie looked between her and Hannah, her heart swelled with pleasure. She'd made *two* friends, she thought, more than she'd had for so many years. It made her begin to believe that all the things she'd wanted—friendship and fun and maybe even romance—were no longer out of her reach. They were right here, for the taking.

CHAPTER 5

The mood in the cinema that evening was one of convivial expectation; the earlier fears and worries as people had boarded the ship seemed to have melted away in the bright sun and fresh air, and as Sophie headed into the theater with Rosa and Hannah, she felt positively buoyant.

It had been a lovely day, one of the loveliest she could remember. After meeting Hannah and Lotte, she and Rosa had agreed to meet Hannah not only at the cinema, but also at the tea dance that afternoon in the *Tanzplatz*. Sophie had rushed Heinrich through lunch, much to his disgruntlement, before bringing him back to the cabin for a rest so she could get ready.

She'd been pleased to see her father seeming somewhat revived; he and Margarete had strolled the deck, taking the air, and when Sophie had mentioned the cinema, he had agreed, at his wife's determinedly cheerful insistence, that they could all attend.

For the dance, Sophie had put on the dress of bronze silk she'd worn yesterday, and, impulsively, she'd even dabbed a bit of Margarete's rouge on her cheeks. It had all been for naught, as she hadn't even been asked to dance; the occasion had been attended mainly by older married couples quietly swaying together, and a few children darting around, stealing cakes from the silver trays on the buffet. Sophie hadn't minded because she, Hannah, and Rosa had all got to know each other over coffee and cake, while Heinrich and Lotte had played together, Lotte seeming to provide a surprisingly calming influence on her brother.

It had been so very lovely, to chat and laugh about silly things, the cares and fears of the last few years falling away almost—*almost*—as if they had never happened at all. At least, Sophie could pretend to herself, for a few moments, that they hadn't.

She could pretend that her best friend Ilse hadn't claimed not to know her when she'd run into her at Wertheim department store in Leipziger Platz—a store owned by Jews that was now run by Nazis, the family having, like Sophie's, to flee for their lives. The friend who had collapsed laughing on Sophie's bed, who had thrown her arms around her, who had promised—*promised*—that they would be bosom friends forever, had looked angry when Sophie had greeted her over the glove counter, and stormed away without saying a word.

She could pretend that she hadn't overheard a neighbor loudly calling her family "those dirty Jews" even though they'd had her and her family over for supper on more than one occasion, evenings filled with both laughter and flowing with wine.

She could pretend that she hadn't felt her insides turn liquid with fear when she'd seen two SS marching down the street, scowling at her, while she'd stood frozen, as scared as a rabbit.

She could pretend that she hadn't witnessed her father, the man she'd looked up to most in the world, crying like a child, while her stepmother had looked terrified, the world as they'd known it collapsing around them.

Yes, she wanted to pretend none of that had happened—

even if she knew she couldn't, not really. She could never forget. She could only maybe remember a little bit less... especially when she was drinking coffee and eating a delicious slice of *Sachertorte*, and learning about her new friends' lives.

Not, as it happened, that either Rosa or Hannah were very forthcoming about those lives, at least not at first. Sophie felt too shy to ask many questions, and besides a few barbed comments about her parents, Rosa seemed almost dismissive about her past life, although Sophie had managed to glean that she'd lived in Berlin as well, albeit in a much grander neighborhood—one of the large houses in Wannsee, most of which, Sophie knew, had been taken by Nazis.

Hannah had told them she was from Dusseldorf; her father was already in Havana, working for a bank, and her mother had remained in Germany.

"Will she join you in Cuba, when she is able?" Sophie had asked with sympathy; she could only imagine how difficult it must be, for a mother to send her two daughters, aged only ten and seventeen, off across the ocean, and in such turbulent times as these.

"No." Hannah's voice was firm, her expression flat. "She won't. She's divorced my father and taken up with an SS officer, as it happens. They'll get married one day, I should think. That's what she's hoping for, anyway." At Sophie's startled look, she had explained, "She's not Jewish, you see. We're *Mischlinge*." She had used the derogatory term the Nazis had coined for those who only had one Jewish parent, her face and voice both devoid of emotion.

Sophie wasn't able to keep from gaping for a few stunned seconds. "But... you mean... your mother's *left* you?" she had finally asked.

"I suppose, in truth, *we've* left *her*," Hannah had replied with an attempt at levity that sounded a bit too brittle. "Not that we had much choice in the matter." She had drawn herself up, taking a sip of coffee, with her hands clenched around the fragile porcelain, her slim knuckles turning white. "She has a new life. And so will we."

Sophie had no idea what to say to that. She couldn't imagine Margarete being willing to leave Heinrich. *She* couldn't imagine leaving Heinrich, and she was only his half-sister.

"Parents don't always love their children," Rosa had stated matter-of-factly. She had stabbed her fork into her slice of *Sachertorte*. "They should, but they don't."

"And your parents?" Hannah had asked as Rosa ate her bite of cake, one eyebrow arched in query. "You sound as if you speak from experience."

"Well." Rosa had given a little shrug as she swallowed. "I suppose they love me in their own way. But they love each other far more—or, really, my mother loves my father, utterly adores him, as it happens, and my father... well, he loves himself." She had let out a little sigh as she tossed her fork onto her plate with a clatter. "But maybe I'm being unfair. Maybe things will be different in Cuba, when there are no Nazis for him to impress. Although maybe there will be. They seem to be everywhere."

"How does a Jew impress a Nazi?" Sophie couldn't keep the surprise from her voice.

Rosa's mouth had twisted. "You'd be surprised."

A silence had fallen over the table and Sophie had half-wished she hadn't asked so many questions. They were trying to escape all that, weren't they? That was why they were on the *St Louis* in the first place. Determined to lift their mood, she had straightened, giving a little clap of her hands. "I don't know about you, but I came here to dance. Who's up for a waltz?"

Rosa had glanced at her, amused. "Are you asking me to dance?"

"I don't see a suitable gentleman anywhere, so..." Sophie had spread her hands, smiling, feeling both bold and silly. She wanted to have some *fun*. And while she would have been thrilled to have a man ask her to dance, there weren't any available. It didn't mean she had to stay a wallflower.

After a second's pause, Rosa had laughed and stood up. "I don't see any, either! Very well, then, let's shock everyone here and have a waltz." She had glanced back at Hannah. "You'll have to cut in halfway through, so you get a turn. That will shock some of these old biddies even more!"

Hannah had looked startled by the suggestion, but then she had offered a small smile. "I wouldn't dream of it. I'll dance with Lotte."

Laughing, they had made two unlikely couples on the dance floor—Rosa and Sophie together, and Lotte carefully following Hannah's steps, her head only coming up a little past her elbow.

"I want to dance, too," Heinrich had complained, tugging on Sophie's sleeve, and so she had let him stand on her feet—wincing a bit at the pain, even as she and Rosa had collapsed in giggles—and dance with them, an unlikely trio hobbling along. An elderly couple dancing with stiff dignity had given them a frosty look as they'd whirled past, but Sophie didn't mind. She couldn't remember when she'd last laughed so much. She was, she thought happily, finally having some fun.

Now, several hours later, Sophie, Rosa and Hannah walked arm in arm into the theater. Lotte and Heinrich, tired out by the day's activities, were both tucked up in their beds, and Margarete and her father had come in after them, slipping into one of the back rows.

Sophie had always loved the buzz of the cinema—the murmur of voices, the air of expectancy as the lights dimmed and the screen crackled to life. She loved being swept up in a story—any story—and feeling as if it carried her away for a few blissful hours. It had been a long time since she'd been able to experience that.

"Do you know what film it is?" Hannah whispered, and Sophie shook her head.

"Only that it's meant to be a romantic story. I'm afraid I haven't kept up with films at all."

"Well, why would you, when you weren't allowed to see any?" Rosa replied dryly. A certain hardness flashed across her face before she gave one of her more habitual wry smiles. "I don't even care what it is. I just want to watch something."

"Yes, exactly," Sophie agreed.

Just then, the lights dimmed, and the three women settled into their seats, sharing a few expectant, covert smiles as they waited for the screen to come to life. Sophie's stomach flared with anticipation. Once, she might have considered going to the cinema an everyday affair, but since Kristallnacht, it felt like an unthinkable luxury, a wonderful treat.

An image flashed onto the screen, and a collective gasp of shocked horror ran through the crowd as they saw a close-up of Adolf Hitler's face—his eyes narrowed to angry slits, his mouth screwed up, spittle flying as he spoke in his usual robust fashion.

"Worldwide Jewish influences are clamoring for an inter-ventionist war against Germany!" he declared, his hand slicing through the air. "The Jews are a parasite living on the Germany body... we must once and for all get rid of the idea that the Jewish race was created by God..."

Sophie sat frozen in her seat as the newsreel continued—shots of Germany's army mobilizing for war; crowds of cringing Jews, faceless under wide-brimmed hats, scuttling along an alleyway, almost as if they were rats, as Rosa had said, all with Hitler's usual decisive oratory as he spoke of the sword, and fire, and blood, and destruction. The destruction of the Jews, their "final day of reckoning."

As the newsreel went on, the initial gasps of surprise turned to murmurs of upset and discontent. Sophie's stomach roiled and her head felt light. Having been banned from cinemas for the last seven months, she hadn't seen nor heard such pernicious propaganda in a long time; Margarete had forbidden anyone to listen to the radio after her father had come back from Kristallnacht. And Sophie's life had shrunk to her family, her home, and the occasional brief outing to shops. She'd resented the restrictions, the utter smallness of her life under the Nazis, and yet now she realized just how much she'd been protected from.

"I will not tolerate this!" A man in the front row, with slicked-back hair, wearing a dinner jacket, stood up, bristling with affront, his elegant wife alongside him. With a jolt of surprise, Sophie realized she recognized them—they were Rosa's parents. "This is an outrage!" he declared as he strode from the theater, his wife following in his wake, her hands fluttering at her sides.

The murmurs of dismay and confusion grew, a wave of worry and grief. Just when everyone had been starting to believe they were safe, Sophie thought, *this* happened. It was like that altercation with the member of crew all over again. Why was it being allowed? Who had approved this newsreel?

"The film's started now," Rosa stated quietly. "Do either of you want to watch it?"

Sophie didn't know what she wanted anymore. Like just about everyone else in the theater, she felt too jumbled up and upset to watch something light and frothy, or even anything at all. "I—" she began, only to stop suddenly when a ragged cry burst out at the back of the room, and then a man ran, stumbling and sobbing, from the theater.

"Josef!" Margarete called and chased after her husband.

"Isn't that...?" Rosa began, and Sophie nodded.

"My father." Her stomach cramped with anxiety. "I should go help him."

Fumbling a bit, she rose from her seat and walked quickly out of the cinema. As the doors closed behind her, she heard a burst of violin music, a trill of laughter. The romantic story, whatever it was, had started.

The lobby outside the theater was empty, save for Rosa's parents, huddled together by the doors. Her father was still fuming, his wife clearly trying to placate him, her face tilted up to her husband in appeal, one hand fluttering toward his arm like a butterfly afraid to land.

"I'm sure it was an oversight, Fritz," she implored. "They could not have meant it to be shown, surely."

"Even as an oversight, it is *inexcusable!*" Rosa's father drew himself up, chest puffed out. "I will *not* allow it!"

"*Fritz—*"

He turned away from his wife in an abrupt movement that to Sophie seemed dismissive and even unkind. "I am going to insist on speaking to the purser," he stated and began to stalk away.

As he left the lobby, his wife's shoulders slumped as she watched him go.

Sophie approached her. "Excuse me," she asked quietly, "but did you see the man who ran from the theater, after you and your husband came out? He was quite upset. Do you know where he went?"

The woman looked at her with blank eyes; her face was pale and heavily powdered, her lips blood-red, although she had the same coloring and slender build as her daughter. "A man..." she asked dazedly, as if she did not understand the word.

"He was upset," Sophie repeated, insistent now. "He was accompanied by his wife. They must have gone somewhere—" Sophie's voice caught. She couldn't bear the thought that the newsreel might have sent her father spiraling downward yet again.

The woman simply shook her head, turning away from her as if she were of no concern. No wonder Rosa disdained her parents, Sophie thought with a sudden spurt of bitterness. They didn't seem inclined to consider anyone but themselves. She pushed the feeling away, determined to find her father. Perhaps he'd gone back to the cabin.

As she hurried along the darkened corridor, her stomach continued to churn with anxiety. She already knew that her father's public display would be upsetting to both him and Margarete; even in his diminished state, he hated being seen as a spectacle or an object of pity, and after tonight, Sophie suspected he would be seen as both. His distress would then lead to Margarete's, which would increase his own—an endless, dispiriting cycle. Already, Sophie knew she would struggle to be able to stop it, and yet she had to try.

When she got back to their cabin, however, she saw all was dark and quiet. Heinrich was tucked up in bed, fast asleep. She slipped out again, glancing up and down the corridor, wondering where to go. Where would her father go? He'd eschew crowds, she knew that, so there was no point looking in the social hall or any of the other public areas.

Would he go out on deck? Now that night had fallen, the wind off the sea had to be bitter.

Sophie headed down the corridor and then slipped outside, drawing her light cardigan more closely around her as the chilly wind buffeted her. Above her, the wide night sky was inked with stars, a scattering of pinpricks of lights that seemed tiny and irrelevant in the endless expanse of night. She shivered, both from the cold and that unending darkness, and then she started down the deck, empty at this time of night, as she'd known it would be. *Where* was her father?

"Josef—" Her stepmother's cry sounded as if it had been torn from her lips, flung to the sky.

Sophie started running.

As she rounded the corner, she saw her father bent over the ship's railing, almost as if he intended to fling himself right into the sea.

"Papa!" Sophie hardly recognized her own terrified scream as she lurched toward him. "Papa, please! *Don't!*"

Her father was sobbing, his shoulders shaking, his body bent over the railing. "I *told* you!" he half-wept, half-raged. "I *told* you this ship was doomed, damned! *Damned!* It is not safe. The Gestapo will come for us, they will come and, by God, I won't let them. Not this time! I'll die first!"

To Sophie's horror, he hitched one leg over the railing, his eyes wild and unfocused, caught in the terror of his own desperate nightmares.

Margarete let out a shriek of fear as he balanced on the railing, one foot barely touching the deck, the sea churning darkly far below. "*Josef!* No, please! Don't!"

Sophie threw herself at her father, wrapping her arms around him as he fought and clawed at her, until they both fell back, landing hard onto the deck, so the wind was knocked out of her and for a second, as her father sobbed next to her, she found she couldn't breathe. Her mouth opened and closed as she tried to catch her breath, her senses swimming.

"Josef, Josef..." Margarete was weeping quietly as she knelt next to her husband.

Sophie blinked up at the sky as a gasp finally rattled through her and she sucked in the much-needed air. Then, to her surprise, a slender hand stretched down toward her.

"Let me help you up," a quiet voice said, and Sophie turned to see a young woman she didn't recognize standing next to her. She had glossy chestnut hair pulled back into a neat roll, and there was a stillness to her slender form that suggested a steadiness at her center, even a peace. She gazed calmly at Sophie with dark blue eyes, waiting for her reply.

Wordlessly, Sophie took her hand, and the woman helped her to her feet.

"The best thing is a bit of brandy," she said in a low voice, nodding to Sophie's father, who was still weeping openly, shaking his head as tears trickled down his cheeks. "But only a drop or two. Do you know your way back to your cabin?"

"Yes, but my little brother is sleeping there—"

The woman nodded in immediate understanding. "The library is empty at this time of night. You can take him there."

"I don't know where the library is," Sophie whispered. She suddenly felt near tears, overwhelmed by everything that had happened. In the seven months since Kristallnacht, her father had never come so close to disaster, to death. The thought made her feel lightheaded, and for a second, she swayed.

Immediately, the woman stepped forward and slid her arm through Sophie's. "You've had a shock," she murmured. "All of you. Let me show you to the library."

The next few moments passed in a surreal blur as the woman guided the three of them to a quiet corner of the library, Josef dazed and unresisting. While Sophie stood there numbly, her stepmother sitting next to her father, holding his hand, the woman arranged for a steward to bring a snifter of brandy.

Her father drank it in two quick gulps, wiping his mouth with his sleeve. "I'm sorry," he told Sophie, his expression one of pleading pathos as he choked back the last of his tears. "I'm so sorry."

Sophie nodded jerkily. "You don't need to be sorry, Papa. But you're safe here. We're all safe."

Her father shook his head, a constant back and forth that had Sophie worrying he might start again with the tears, the portents of doom and despair.

She turned to the woman who was standing quietly by the door. "Thank you," she told her in a low voice. "You have been so very kind and helpful, and I don't even know your name."

"Rachel Blau," the woman replied with a small, sympathetic smile. "And it is no trouble." She paused before she nodded toward Sophie's father. "Give him time." She let the words fall into the stillness. "We are all hoping for a new life in Havana. If you ever need anything..." She reached out to gently touch Sophie's arm. "God bless you," she murmured.

She smiled fleetingly once more and, as she slipped through the doors of the library, Sophie wondered if she had, in the most unexpected circumstances, made another friend.

CHAPTER 6

"There is no Rachel Blau in first-class."

The steward's voice was kind but firm as Sophie stared at him in dismay, embarrassed by her obvious assumption. She'd been trying to find Rachel Blau, to thank her for her help with her father, but she'd only been looking in the first-class lounges and other areas. Of course, there were plenty of passengers in tourist class, but they were kept more or less separate from those in first, with their own public rooms and dining halls.

"I see, thank you," she told him, ducking her head. "I'll look for Miss Blau elsewhere." She gave the steward a brief smile of farewell as she walked slowly down the corridor.

The SS *St Louis* had docked in Cherbourg on Monday, to some passengers' apprehension; it was, they feared, an opportunity for more Nazi involvement in the ship, but the only things that had come on board in France had been crates of fresh fruit and vegetables, along with more passengers.

"But why no fresh water?" Sophie had heard a woman ask fretfully as she'd peered at the launches bobbing across the water, toward the ship. "Do they want to kill us with thirst?"

"Maybe we have enough already," her husband had replied placatingly, and the woman had shaken her head.

"Or maybe the French have *poisoned* the water," she had said darkly. "They hate Jews, as well…"

There had been many rumors flying around about the cruise liner since it had left Hamburg four days ago, and some of them, Sophie feared, were warranted. Rosa had told her about the 'Gestapo firemen' who were on board, it was stated, for safety reasons, but the reality was that there *were* Gestapo on the ship, just as her father had feared. Sophie hoped he didn't discover the truth; since rushing out of the cinema, he'd barely left their cabin, or even his bed. Margarete was distraught, and Sophie had taken complete charge of Heinrich. He'd become good friends with Lotte, while Sophie, Rosa, and Hannah had spent much of their days together, exploring.

"Any luck?" Rosa asked as Sophie rejoined her friends at a table in a quiet corner of the bustling social hall.

Sophie shook her head. "She must be in tourist class, which I should have considered. I feel foolish, that I didn't."

"Hardly your fault," Rosa replied with a bracing smile. "Why not take a look in some of the tourist-class areas?" She raised her eyebrows teasingly. "You can slum it for a bit!"

Sophie smiled back weakly; the tourist-class areas were, as far as she knew, respectable and well turned out, but they were still distinctly separate from their more luxurious first-class accommodation.

"I suppose I could try," she replied hesitantly. "I only wanted to thank her. She was so very kind."

"How is your father?" Hannah asked, and Sophie glanced at Heinrich, involved in a card game with Lotte, before she answered in a low voice.

"He's still not well. The worst I've seen, really. He'll barely get out of bed, and he keeps muttering things…" She stopped, her throat thickening with tears as she pictured her father as she'd seen him that morning, lying there, looking so wretched and afraid, while Margarete had sat next to him, bathing his forehead with a cold cloth, her own face drawn and anxious.

Sophie had so hoped her father would improve on this journey, but right now that seemed to be only desperate, wishful thinking.

"Give it time," Hannah advised gently. "We've only been at sea a few days. It has taken that long for many of us to be accustomed to feeling safe, and with what your father has experienced, it will take longer for him."

"Yes..." Sophie had told her friends about her father being taken into protective custody after Kristallnacht; they had been sympathetic, of course, but their own experiences had seemed very different. Rosa's family—for a reason Sophie couldn't yet discern—had seemed to escape most of the Nazis' persecutions, as had Hannah's, since her father had been in Havana for more than a year and her mother wasn't Jewish. Still, Sophie had been able to tell from their sometimes somber expressions, as well as the things they chose *not* to say, that they'd had their own trials.

Now, she glanced at Rosa, who had been silent for the last few minutes, a faint frown turning down the corners of her wide mouth.

"What is it?" Sophie asked, apprehension already digging its familiar claws into the pit of her stomach. She felt as if she were always bracing for the next bad thing—the photographer, the Horst Wessel song, the newsreel... What next?

"I don't know." Rosa sighed as she shrugged restively, smoothing down the skirt of her plain gray dress, her gaze roving over the various groups of people in the social hall without settling on anyone. "It could be nothing. It probably is..."

Apprehension was fast turning into alarm. If she wasn't careful, Sophie thought, she'd become as paranoid as her father —except, what if he *wasn't* paranoid? So many little things had happened on this trip already to cause panic. "Rosa, what is it?" she asked, her voice catching. "You sound as if you know something—"

"Yes, what is it?" Hannah chimed in, leaning forward, her fingers knotted tightly in her lap. Sophie knew she was anxious about the journey, especially for her sister's sake. "Has something happened?"

"I don't think so," Rosa replied as she turned back to look at Sophie and Hannah, her expression still clouded. "But Captain Schroeder was talking to my father. I heard them this morning, just outside our cabin. The captain was inviting him to inspect the bridge... my father is like that," she explained, as if one of them had asked a question, although Sophie and Hannah had both remained silent, wide-eyed as they listened to Rosa, wondering what she was going to say next. "He gets to know all the right people, and they defer to him—yes, even as a Jew. They always have. Anyway, according to the captain, it seems there might be some kind of trouble in Havana. He was concerned about the possibility, at least."

"*Trouble?*" Hannah's voice was sharp as she glanced worriedly at Lotte, who was bent over the cards with Heinrich, both absorbed in their game. "What kind of trouble?"

Rosa shook her head as she spread her hands wide. "I don't know. The captain didn't want to say, at least not then. But I suspect it has something to do with the government there, and whether they want a thousand Jews landing on their shores."

"But we have visas!" Sophie protested. Bought at a hundred and fifty dollars apiece, from an official in the Cuban government. How could they be denied entry?

"And my father's already there!" Hannah added, her face pale, her voice loud enough that both Heinrich and Lotte looked up from their game, foreheads furrowed.

"Hannah, wh-why are you sh-shouting?" Lotte asked, her stammer pronounced in her anxiety.

"I'm not shouting, *Schatzi*," Hannah replied quickly with a forced smile. "I was just excited." She bit her lip as she glanced between Sophie and Rosa. "I don't believe it," she stated in a low voice. "It can't be true."

"What can't be true?" Heinrich asked, and Sophie shushed him.

"Not for your ears, little man," she chided, smiling to soften the scolding, although her stomach was churning at Rosa's words. "Now, it's almost teatime. Shall we see if we can find some cake?" There seemed to be a never-ending parade of meals on the ship—breakfast, morning coffee and *Kuchen*, lunch, afternoon tea, supper, and then snacks before bed. Sophie couldn't remember the last time she had eaten so much, or so well, although her appetite had vanished now. "Lotte, would you like to come?" she asked.

"Lotte can go with me," Hannah interjected, scrambling up from her seat. She took her sister's hand, shooting Sophie a semi-apologetic smile. Sophie knew her friend was fiercely protective of her sister, and she could hardly blame her for it. With her shyness and her stammer, as well as a mother who had as good as abandoned her, Lotte seemed in need of protecting.

"We'll all go!" Rosa decided as she rose from her seat. "I could certainly do with some cake. When could I not?" She smiled, her eyes full of humor, although Sophie thought she still looked strained.

Yet it was easy—almost—to banish any thoughts about possible trouble in Havana once they were sitting at a table decked out with sparkling crystal and freshly starched linen, being served thick slices of delicious *Schwarzwälder Kirschtorte*, or Black Forest cake, by a white-gloved steward, while a three-piece string trio played quietly in the corner of the dining room, accompanied by the low murmur of voices, the tinkle of laughter.

They were full fee-paying passengers, Sophie told herself,

and every single one of them had a visa that had been approved by the Cuban government; they wouldn't have been able to board the ship otherwise. The Cuban government had to know already that the ship had left Hamburg, and surely it had to have approved the SS St Louis's travel plan. They couldn't have got this far otherwise. They couldn't have even left port.

"Heinrich, you have chocolate all over your face," Sophie admonished, and she wiped her little brother's mouth with the heavy damask napkin that she'd spread across his lap.

Somehow, this ordinary little action steadied her, gave her a sense of perspective that she knew she needed. The captain might be worried, she told herself, but that was all it was. A worry, not a reality, and one Rosa might have misunderstood. The ship was continuing its journey across the Atlantic; they must be a thousand miles or more from Germany already.

There was no way they would ever have to go back.

The next morning, with Heinrich playing with Lotte, watched by Hannah and Rosa, Sophie decided to make a concerted effort to find Rachel Blau. She knew there wasn't any real reason to track her down; Rachel had helped, and Sophie had already thanked her. And yet something about the other woman, her gentleness, the way she'd looked at Sophie with such sympathy and understanding... well, it made her want to find her. And it gave her something to do that wasn't worrying about her father.

That morning, he'd refused to go to breakfast, and when Margarete had tried to talk to him, he'd pulled the covers over his head, whimpering and moaning as he curled into a fetal ball beneath them.

"He's getting worse," her stepmother had confessed in a low voice as she and Sophie stood in the corridor outside the cabin after Josef had fallen into a restless doze. "He keeps saying the

Gestapo are going to come for him... he gets so agitated, Sophie." Margarete had pressed her fingers to her lips as she shook her head. "I don't know what to do."

Looking at Margarete, Sophie had realized, with a jolt, how tired and old her stepmother had become, and in just a few days. The lines in her face were carved deeper, and she hadn't bothered to do her hair or makeup the way she normally would. Her dress was wrinkled, a sweater thrown carelessly over her thin shoulders. She looked haggard and careworn, and when they were supposed to finally feel free and lighthearted.

"Do you want me to sit with him?" Sophie had suggested. "You could go out, take the air for a little while..."

Margarete had shaken her head. "My place is with him," she'd stated firmly. "And he gets so upset if I'm not nearby. I should go back." She'd turned to the door, and Sophie had watched her go with sorrow.

They'd both insisted on believing that things would be better in Havana, but what if that simply wasn't true? And what if they never even *got* to Havana? She didn't want to give Rosa's vague warnings much credence, but she wondered if she should. And yet what could she do about any of it? She was as powerless on the *St Louis* as she had been in Berlin.

Still, Sophie did her best to thrust the worries from her mind as she went in search of Rachel Blau in the tourist-class lounges. It took her over an hour to move through the various rooms—like first class, the tourist class had its own library, a social hall, a reading and writing room, a dining hall. As Sophie walked slowly through each one, she started to feel conspicuous, then ridiculous. What exactly was she hoping to achieve by coming here? What would she even say to Rachel if she found her? And yet, for a reason Sophie couldn't quite fathom, she kept going.

A few people glanced at her in apprehension or suspicion, clearly wondering why she was moving so slowly through the rooms, peering at faces as subtly as she could, but obviously not discreetly enough. A few passengers stared at her pointedly, until Sophie looked away, blushing in embarrassment. As she came to the end of the reading and writing room, having not seen any sign of Rachel at all in any of the tourist-class areas, she mentally shook her head at her own folly.

With regret, she turned around, retracing her steps through the room, only to stop in surprise when she saw Rachel herself coming through the doors.

"Oh, it's you!" Sophie blurted the words before she could think of better ones.

Rachel looked at her in surprise, and then back quickly at the man following her into the room. He was dressed in a shabby dark suit and was walking with hesitant steps, his head lowered. His hair was thin and sandy, his body slender and seeming defeated, somehow. The way his shoulders were hunched, his chin tucked low... he reminded her, Sophie realized, of her father; old before his time, seemingly broken.

Rachel tucked her arm through the man's as she turned back to Sophie. "Hello. I didn't expect to see you here," she told her with a small, questioning smile.

"I was looking for you, actually," Sophie admitted, blushing.

Rachel's forehead crinkled in concern. "You were?"

"I just... wanted to thank you for your kindness, that night on the deck. I don't know what I would have done without you—"

"You would have managed." Rachel's tone was gentle, her eyes kind. "If you had to."

"I'm not sure about that," Sophie replied.

"How's your father?" Rachel asked.

"He's—well, he's as best as he can be, I suppose," Sophie answered shakily. To her embarrassment, her voice wavered and then cracked. Trying to smile, she brushed at her eyes. "I'm so sorry—"

"Wait a moment." Rachel turned back to the man whose arm was still tucked in hers. His expression seemed both troubled and vacant; he seemed unable to meet anyone's eye, looking around the room with a distracted yet indifferent air. "Franz, let me get you a seat somewhere comfortable."

Sophie stood there uncertainly as Rachel walked the man to a quiet corner and gently settled him into a chair, murmuring to him all the while. Then she motioned to Sophie and took a seat a few tables away from the man, gesturing for her to join her.

"Franz will be all right for a bit," she told her. "And I think you could use a cup of coffee, or maybe something stronger?" The smile she gave her was whimsical, her dark blue eyes lightening to the color of the sky.

"Coffee would be wonderful," Sophie replied. "But..." She glanced uncertainly at Franz, who was sitting by himself, his hands in his lap as he simply stared into space. Had he suffered like her father? And who was he to Rachel? He seemed too young to be her father, too old to be anything else.

"He'll be all right," Rachel repeated quietly. "He likes being alone, these days. He prefers the quiet."

"Oh, I see..." Sophie said uncertainly, although she didn't, not really.

As if sensing her unspoken question, Rachel stated quietly, "Franz is my husband." Sophie tried not to look surprised; the man sitting quietly by himself, staring at his hands, seemed far older than Rachel, who looked only to be a few years older than Sophie herself. Sophie had assumed he was in his thirties or forties even, judging by his thinning hair, sagging skin, the stoop of his shoulders.

"He was in Dachau until two weeks ago," Rachel explained. Her voice was calm and matter-of-fact, with only a trace of sorrow. "The government told him he had to leave the country within the month, or he would be re-arrested. We were very fortunate to get passage on this ship."

"I'm so sorry," Sophie said, appalled. She had heard about the camp, first for political prisoners, and then for dissidents and Jews, and its rumors of beatings, hard labor, and torture.

Rachel's eyebrows lifted. "I assumed, from the other night, your father had experienced something similar."

"He was in protective custody," Sophie allowed. "I don't know where." Rachel's eyebrows lifted further, and a sickening idea dawned. "You don't think he was actually somewhere like Dachau?" She hadn't let herself think about the possibility of that, although she realized she should have.

"My husband was said to be in protective custody," Rachel replied, "for seven months."

"Since Kristallnacht?"

Rachel nodded and Sophie found she had to swallow hard.

Why, she wondered, was she finding this such a shock? She'd assumed her father had remained in Berlin, at the prison where he'd first been taken, although none of the police had been willing to give any information when she'd gone to ask. Why that was easier to stomach than the dreaded Dachau, she didn't know, but somehow it had been, even though she'd seen the bruises on his face, had been unable to deny how fearful and diminished he'd become since his arrest and subsequent release.

"What does your husband say about his time in Dachau?" Sophie asked in a low voice.

Rachel shook her head. "He does not speak of it."

"Nor does my father."

"Perhaps it is better that way." Rachel gestured to a steward, who came forward, and she asked him to bring coffee.

"What will you do in Havana?" Sophie asked once they were settled with their drinks.

Rachel had first poured a cup, made it milky and sweet, and brought it over to Franz, who had smiled at her gratefully as he took it in both hands, and Rachel had gently stroked his hair, her face softening with what looked like both love and grief. He was like a child, Sophie thought, and Rachel was acting as his mother, treating him so tenderly, smoothing his hair away from his creased brow. The sight of them together was both beautiful and terribly sad.

"Find a way to make a living, as best as we can," Rachel answered Sophie's question as she took a sip of her coffee. Her gaze flitted to her husband, who sat with his cup in his hands, as if he'd forgotten it was there. Her mouth drooped a little before she straightened as she turned her gaze back to Sophie. "I used to be a history teacher, before the laws changed. I don't know if I will be able to teach in Cuba. I have a book on the Spanish language, but I must admit, it is slow going. I am not a natural when it comes to languages." She smiled faintly, and Sophie couldn't help but admire her courage as well as her quietly cheerful pragmatism. It had been hard enough having her father imprisoned for two weeks—but a husband, for seven *months*?

"I don't know much Spanish," Sophie replied, "but I do have something of a knack for languages. Well, a bit." She ducked her head shyly, worried it had sounded as if she were boasting. "I was hoping to study languages at university, but it never came to pass. But if you'd like some tuition, or to study together...?" She trailed off, unsure if her suggestion was too forward or not. She wanted to repay Rachel for her kindness in some way, and yet more than that, she wanted to be the other woman's friend. Like Sophie, she seemed as if she could use one.

"Would you?" Rachel's expression brightened, her eyes lighting, her mouth curving. "That would be marvelous."

"We only have a few days left, but we could make a start." Sophie found herself brightening as the idea took hold. "My friends, Hannah and Rosa, might enjoy it, as well. They don't know any Spanish. We could form a little class!"

"Hannah and Rosa?" Rachel's expression clouded for a moment. "Are they in first class, as well?"

"Yes, but we could have the classes on the sports deck," Sophie replied quickly. "That's available to everyone, and it would give Heinrich—my little brother—and Lotte—Hannah's sister—a chance to play." Inadvertently, she glanced at Franz.

"Franz would enjoy the sunshine," Rachel commented. "Especially now that it is starting to get warmer." Impulsively, she reached over to touch Sophie's hand. "Thank you for your kindness. I realize I don't even know your name!"

Sophie let out an embarrassed little laugh. "Sophie. Sophie Weiss."

"Thank you, Sophie," Rachel said quietly. "I didn't realize until you came to find me how much I could use a friend."

CHAPTER 7

WEDNESDAY, MAY 24, 1939

The air was balmy and the sun warm on the sports deck as Hannah, Rosa, Rachel, and Sophie made their little group, sitting on deckchairs, Rachel's Spanish book open on Sophie's lap. Nearby, Heinrich and Lotte were playing with Renata and Evelynne Aber, the two young girls who were traveling by themselves. They had taken them under their wing, and the girls were often found nearby. Franz was lounging in a deckchair, his book forgotten in his lap.

Sophie could hardly believe over a week had already passed, the days sliding into one another as the ship moved inexorably west, toward freedom. As the weather had warmed, and as they'd traveled farther and farther from Germany, her father's mood had begun to lift, if only a little. He'd gone to the dining hall for his meals, and on Saturday he had even attended worship in the *Tanzplatz*; there had been over a hundred men present, ten times the required amount to hold a service. Sophie had noticed a few crew members looking down from the gallery, their expression a mixture of curiosity and scorn as they'd whispered among themselves.

With a ripple of trepidation, she'd spotted the leering, pockmarked face of the man who had accosted her and Rosa that first night—she hadn't seen him since—and the sight of his sneer was enough to cause a shiver of apprehension to run through her, although she had quickly suppressed it. He was one man, she'd reminded herself, and, like Rosa had said, Captain Schroeder was on their side.

Her father hadn't noticed the crew members, at least, and they'd been able to hold the service, which certainly spoke to the captain's support. Yet there had been other events on the ship that some whispered might be harbingers of doom—a man in first class had died, and had to be buried at sea, his body slipped into the water at eleven o'clock at night, with no fanfare or fuss. There had been dark mutterings that it had been foul play, even outright murder; one of the Gestapo firemen, perhaps, had roughed him up. The prospect struck terror in Sophie's heart, but Rosa had assured her, rather grimly, that the man had died of natural causes, admittedly brought on by anxiety. She knew because her father had been selected to be on a small committee of select passengers who communicated with the captain.

Still, the whole episode had made everyone on board uneasy.

"So, the captain is still expecting trouble?" Sophie had asked when Rosa had told her about the committee, and her friend had shrugged.

"Who knows? He doesn't seem to want to say much, but at least we're still heading in the right direction. We're only a few days off Havana, now."

Tomorrow night was the costume ball, the traditional end-of-voyage party, two days before the *St Louis* came into port. God willing, they would all disembark by Saturday afternoon. Sophie held tightly to that thought, chose to consider it a promise, as she continued to help her friends learn Spanish.

"All right, Hannah," Sophie said with an encouraging smile. "How do you say, 'I'd like to buy a loaf of bread'?"

Hannah sighed, her gaze cast to the sky, as she tried to remember the words. The tension and unhappiness that had shown in her face at the start of the voyage had started to ease; she was blossoming into a beautiful woman, with her wide mouth and hazel eyes. When she looked at Lotte, it was more with love than anxiety.

"Let me see..." she began, pausing before she stated carefully, saying each word with precision, "*Quis... quisiera comprar... una barra... de pan?*"

She looked hopefully at Sophie, who gave a little clap of approbation.

"Very good! Rosa? How do you say, 'I'd like to buy a cup of coffee?'"

Rosa's dark, straight eyebrows drew together as she gazed off into the distance in thought. "*Me gustaria...*" she began, only to shake her head, her sigh turning impatient. "Oh, what does it matter? I can point to it if I really want to buy a cup of coffee, and in any case, we'll be going to America as soon as we can. I don't intend to stay in Havana for very long."

"Yes, but—" Sophie stopped as Rosa abruptly rose from her chair and headed toward the railing, leaning her elbows on it as she lifted her face to the salty sea breeze.

"Perhaps we have finished our lesson for today?" Rachel suggested with a small, understanding smile, her blue eyes crinkling at the corners. "Coffee and bread, what more do we need, after all?"

"I have, I think," Hannah replied. "I promised Lotte we'd go swimming today, now that it's warm enough." In the last day or two, the weather had become hotter, the sunshine like a benediction, reminding them of just how far they'd traveled. "I could take Heinrich too, if you like?"

"And I might bring Franz along," Rachel suggested. "He

likes to dip his toes in the water, at least." Although her husband often still looked tired and anxious, he'd become a bit more animated, and Sophie was glad to see him starting to take an interest in his surroundings.

"All right, thank you," she told Hannah. As she closed the book in her lap, Sophie glanced again at Rosa. "Perhaps I'll join you in a bit."

When the others left with the children and Franz, Sophie joined Rosa at the railing. Her friend's eyes were closed, her face lifted to the sunlight.

"I'm sorry," she said, without opening her eyes. "I don't mean to cause a fuss."

"You didn't." Sophie paused, thinking about what to say next. Rosa seemed to have been in good spirits these last few days; they all had. It had become easier to banish any worries the farther they traveled from Germany, and the change in weather had only increased their optimism. "What's wrong?" she finally asked her friend quietly. "I don't think you're just frustrated with learning Spanish."

"No." Rosa opened her eyes as she lowered her head to gaze down at the sea churning below; deep blue, flecked with white foam. The ocean stretched, shimmering under the sunlight, in every direction, an endless world of water. "A crew member threw himself overboard last night," she confessed quietly. "My father heard it in one of these passenger committee meetings of his. He was a Russian émigré, a Jew."

Sophie stared at her, appalled. "On... on purpose?"

"He wasn't killed, if that's what you mean. Although, with the way things have been, I'm not surprised you might think it! A few people saw him do it. One tried to stop him, but..." She shook her head hopelessly.

"Was... was his body recovered?"

"No." Rosa shook her head. "They conducted a search, but

at the rate we're traveling, it was near impossible. They didn't find him."

"He killed himself?" Sophie stated dazedly. "But why?"

"He was afraid. Despairing, the way so many are trying not to be." Rosa gazed at the water, her lips pressed together. "I have a bad feeling, Sophie," she said in a low voice. "Not just about the crew member, but... everything." She hesitated before continuing, "My father seems so strained. He said he was given a tour of the engine room yesterday, and he saw copies of that wretched newspaper—*Der Stürmer*—about, and Nazi slogans all over the crew's noticeboard. And as he passed, some of the crew members whispered '*Juden raus*' at him."

Juden raus. Jews, out. Sophie swallowed hard. She wasn't all that surprised, and yet it still took her aback. The ship stewards and other crew members who served them above had all been so kind, so meticulously polite. And yet it stood to reason that there were others who, like so many, hated the Jews.

"So, it wasn't just that one man," she remarked, with an attempt at a dismissive shrug. "Well, what of it? We'll be in Havana in just a little more than two days, and we'll never have to see them again."

Rosa did not reply for a moment. "Why," she finally asked, "did the Nazis let us go?"

"From Germany?" Sophie was startled. "They want rid of us, Rosa. You know that."

"Yes," Rosa agreed, her lips pursed. "They want rid of us. But do they want us to lead happy, full lives in Havana? Do they want to show the world how we can manage, how we can succeed, away from Germany?"

Sophie shook her head slowly. "What are you saying?"

"I don't know." Rosa knuckled her eyes, her expression turning almost pained. "I don't know. I'm just so afraid. And so is my father. And that scares me as much as anything else, because he wasn't afraid the whole time we lived in Berlin, under Hitler. It's only now..."

"Why did he emigrate, if he wasn't afraid?"

"Pragmatism. He saw the way the wind was blowing, and it was against us. He knew his good fortune wouldn't last forever."

Sophie still wasn't sure how Rosa's father had managed to emerge from six years of Nazi rule seemingly so unscathed, but her friend never went into particulars and so she didn't feel she could ask. "And what exactly is he afraid of now?" she asked instead.

"Something going terribly wrong, I suppose. The Cuban government refusing us entry... or worse."

"But we have our visas—" Sophie protested, as she had before.

Rosa turned to give her a direct look, the ghost of her old, wry smile flitting about her lips. "What is a visa," she replied, "but a piece of paper?"

Sophie was silent for a long moment. "Then, if they refuse us," she said finally, "another country will accept us. The United States, even, since so many of us are planning to go there, anyway. This is just bureaucratic red tape, nothing more, surely?"

"Maybe..." Rosa allowed, and then she roused herself, straightening and smiling at Sophie with her usual, determined cheerfulness. "In any case, there is no point worrying about it. The sun is too bright and the sky too blue to spend another moment in the doldrums, thinking through all the what ifs. Shall we join the others at the pool? And then we need to sort out our costumes for tomorrow night! I'm planning on going as a pirate."

"A pirate!" Sophie was impressed.

"And what about you?" Rosa asked. "An Egyptian pharaoh queen or a geisha girl? You can do marvels with bedsheets, you know."

"Neither," Sophie replied with a laugh. "I wouldn't dare. Maybe as a... a ghost, or something. Covered up, certainly!" She had not given her costume much thought; she'd been excited simply to go to a party.

"Well, we'll see about that," Rosa remarked, linking her arm through Sophie's as they headed toward the pool. "I think we all should have lots of fun, anyway. Who knows when we'll next go to a big party like this?"

The social hall was bedecked with balloons and streamers for the costume party the next evening, and a band was playing lively Glenn Miller tunes as Sophie headed in with her friends.

She felt almost giddy with excitement; never mind when they might next go to such a party, Sophie couldn't remember when she last had, if ever. With Hitler coming to power when she'd been thirteen, and then the further race laws being enacted two years later, Sophie had missed so much of the usual entertainments and indiscretions of youth. Not that she intended to do anything indiscreet tonight, of course, but she was looking forward to dancing and drinking champagne... maybe even catching a young man's eye. She smiled at the fanciful notion.

While they'd been getting ready, Rosa had told her about the couples she'd stumbled upon when she'd taken the air the other night, pressed close together in niches and tucked under the companionways.

"They were like rabbits in a cornfield," she'd chortled, only to laugh harder at Sophie's beet-red face at such a thought. "Sophie Weiss!" Rosa had exclaimed. "Why, you look more prudish than my maiden auntie, not that I have one. Are you so embarrassed?"

"No," Sophie had lied. But how could she not be embarrassed? She'd never even gone on a date. She'd not even been kissed, never mind anything more than that.

"Perhaps you'll have a kiss during the costume party," Rosa had suggested. "With some handsome young man. Would it be your first?"

"Leave her alone, Rosa," Hannah had interjected good-naturedly. "First or not, there's hardly enough men here for us all to dance with, let alone share kisses with." The way she spoke made Sophie suspect she'd had her fair share of kisses, as had Rosa, and certainly Rachel, as a married woman. Somehow, she was the only innocent one, and it made her feel like a child.

Maybe she would have a first kiss tonight, she thought rebelliously, even if she couldn't actually envision it happening. She would like it to, one day. She had dreams of romance along with adventure, once they made it to America.

"There may not be enough male passengers," Rosa had said to Hannah, "but some of the women were with members of the crew."

Sophie had drawn back, shocked. "But I thought you said the crew were all Nazis...!"

"Not *all* of them. And even a Nazi, it seems, is sometimes willing to kiss a Jew, especially if she's pretty enough."

There had seemed to be nothing to say to that.

Now, Sophie twitched the veil—made from one of Hannah's lace-edged slips—that was part of her costume as a princess—"Or harem girl," Rosa had teased, with a knowing cackle while Sophie had tried not to blush.

Rosa was dressed in jodhpurs and riding boots, purloined from her mother's extensive wardrobe, complete with riding crop which she flicked expertly. Hannah and Lotte were dressed as pirates, with eyepatches and nightshirts, again taken from Rosa's parents' wardrobe. Rachel had eschewed a costume for a more sedate outfit and was wearing a plain evening gown in dark blue, brightened by a garland of flowers. Franz, in an evening suit, looked better than Sophie had seen him all voyage, his hair neatly combed, his expression almost alert, although he remained very quiet.

Sophie's father and Margarete had joined the festivities, much to her stepmother's delight, as she'd always enjoyed a party. They had chosen not to wear costumes; Margarete was in black satin with pearls and evening gloves, her father in a tuxedo.

"Papa, you look very handsome," Sophie told him, kissing his cheek, and her father smiled and squeezed her hand, the small gesture seeming to convey an ocean of sentiment—gratitude as well as grief, hope as well as apology. Sophie was just grateful that he seemed so much more himself than he had in a long while, and hoped he would be even more so once they'd reached Havana.

"Now, who are you going to dance with?" Rosa mused as the four friends stood to one side of the social hall, perusing all the couples flying about the floor.

There was an air of almost wild gaiety among the passengers, a sense of freedom tinged, Sophie thought, with desperation. No one knew quite what awaited them in Havana, what trials or triumphs, but here at least, they could have fun—forget for a time, whatever they needed to, while still hoping, and even yearning, for the future. Heinrich and Lotte had been allowed to come to the beginning of the party, full of excitement, completely unaware of any possible tensions, before they'd been ushered to bed.

"I could dance with you again?" Sophie teased. "I didn't mind it the first time!" Already the tea dance, a little over week ago, felt like an age away. They'd just been getting to know each other, and now they were all firm friends. As she watched her friends laughing, Sophie hoped they would stay in touch once they reached Cuba.

"True," Rosa acknowledged with a wry smile, "but I think a

gentleman would be far preferable." Her narrowed gaze swept the room, while Sophie laughed and shook her head.

"How about a toast?" Hannah suggested. "With champagne?" The "ship money" they were allowed to use on board, as part of their passage, would be worthless once the voyage was over, and so everyone was eager to spend it.

"Ooh, champagne, yes please!" Rosa replied with a laugh. "What do you say, Rachel? Sophie?"

"Oh yes!" Sophie exclaimed, a thrill of excitement running through her. Wasn't this what she'd wanted? Champagne and dancing and friends all around? Her heart swelled with both happiness and hope.

Rachel smiled shyly. "That would be lovely, Hannah."

A few minutes later, a steward had provided them with a dewy bottle and four flutes, pouring them each a drink with gracious alacrity.

"What shall we toast to?" Hannah asked as she took a flute and held it aloft.

"To the future?" Sophie suggested. She glanced down at the bubbles zinging through her glass. She'd only had champagne a handful of times in her life, and even then only a few cautious sips. There had never been much reason to celebrate.

"To Havana?" Rachel added, smiling as she hefted her glass.

"To the future, to Havana, and to us," Rosa declared firmly. "Four friends forever!"

"Forever!" they all agreed and, as one, they raised their glasses, clinking merrily as the band played on and couples whirled by.

They drank, eyes dancing over the rims of their flutes, and Sophie nearly had a coughing fit as the bubbles raced up her nose, the champagne tart on her tongue, making her lips pucker.

"Oh Sophie," Rosa exclaimed, patting her on the back, "you need some more practice!"

"I suppose I do," Sophie agreed with a laugh, and wiped her

streaming eyes. She wasn't even embarrassed; her inexperience didn't bother her now, because she was finally doing what she'd always wanted to do, feeling what she'd longed to feel. Hope and happiness. A sense of the future stretching out in front of her, forever, not something looming dark and dangerous, but rather one that was shining and bright. What a lovely feeling it was!

"We must all stay in touch once we reach Havana," she proclaimed in earnest, and Rosa smiled.

"Of course we will," she replied cheerfully. "Shall we meet for cocktails at Hotel Inglaterra? I saw a brochure and they have a rooftop terrace that looks out over the whole city."

"Not just once for cocktails, though," Sophie persisted, a sudden anxiety clutching at her that this would all slip away as they went their separate ways. "For... for *life!*" She looked around at her three friends, hoping they felt as she did. This wasn't just the friendship version of a shipboard romance, but something real and lasting. Wasn't it?

"For life," Hannah agreed with a quiet smile. "I think I'll be staying in Havana, but I suppose I could visit New York. I've always wanted to see the Statue of Liberty."

"I'll be in Havana too, I think," Rachel chimed in. "But we could all meet in New York, couldn't we? What fun that would be!"

"Smile, girls!" a man called, and they turned to see the ship's photographer—not the Nazi one from boarding—holding his camera aloft.

The four women moved together, their glasses held aloft, dazzling smiles in place.

To the future, Sophie thought as she lifted her chin, *to Havana, and to us.*

CHAPTER 8

SATURDAY, MAY 27, 1939—HAVANA

The stately baroque bell towers of Havana Cathedral and the towering walls of the ancient harbor fortress El Morro gleamed under the golden morning sunlight as Sophie stood on deck, gazing at Cuba's shoreline, although still a long way off. The balmy, tropical breeze blew over her, cooling her heated cheeks, as a few boats bobbed in distance, in the blue-green water of the city's harbor. Everything about the scene was unfamiliar, entrancing—the buildings in the distance, the vivid hue of the harbor, the little fishing boats and their swarthy occupants. They'd arrived at last, and it was entirely different from Germany.

Very early that morning, the SS *St Louis* had dropped anchor, the steady chug of her engines finally coming to a labored stop, so it felt as if the whole world had been plunged into silence. Sophie had woken up, blinking in the darkness, letting the stillness settle through her, and, with it, peace.

Finally, *finally*, they had arrived in Cuba, and yet when she'd ventured up onto the deck before breakfast, holding Heinrich's hand as he pranced on his tiptoes in excitement, it had seemed, to her bemusement and concern, that they hadn't arrived—not quite, anyway. Instead of being moored in the harbor, next to several other passenger ships, the *St Louis* was some distance off, having either chosen not to enter the sanctuary of the city's port, or, more worryingly, having been forbidden to do so.

As passengers breakfasted on coffee and rolls, rumors had swept through the tables of the dining hall that morning, as to why the ship had not yet entered the city's harbor. A steward had suggested the harbor was not deep enough for a ship the size of the *St Louis*; a passenger had remarked that he'd seen a yellow quarantine flag hoisted earlier, and so the ship would not be allowed any closer until all the passengers had passed their medical inspections. Someone else had said that they'd heard that the ship's papers might not be in order; then yet another soul had claimed that it was actually the passengers' papers that weren't in order.

Whatever the cause, they were very close to Havana, Sophie told herself, trying to ignore the sense of dread that was starting to swirl in her stomach as she recalled Rosa's words... *Why did the Nazis let us go?* It didn't matter, she insisted in the disquiet of her own mind, because they *had*, and they were here. Almost. She could even *see* the city, shining under the bright Caribbean sun.

In any case, there had been more than enough to occupy herself with that morning; from dawn, she and Margarete had been flying about the cabin, trying to finish the last of their packing, while Heinrich had spun like a top around the cramped room, too excited to stay still, and Sophie's father had sat on his bed, his hat in his hands, his shoulders slumped and his head hanging low, looking tired and troubled once again.

Sophie had given him a fleeting smile of encouragement as she'd dodged out of Heinrich's way. "You're so excited, little man!" she'd exclaimed, doing her best to hold onto her patience as she nearly tripped over him in her hurry to finish packing one of their cases. "It won't be long now, but please do try to stay out of the way." Her stepmother, Sophie had thought, was looking as if she'd used up all her patience over an hour ago.

In the end, Sophie, along with Rosa and Hannah, had decided to go up to the deck after breakfast, with Heinrich and Lotte in tow, so Margarete and her father could have a little peace. Sophie was as eager to catch another glimpse of Havana as her brother was; after nearly two weeks of nothing but endless ocean, the sight of land—shimmering so promisingly in the distance—had felt like a miracle, and a much-needed one at that. Sophie couldn't wait to inspect and explore, even if it had to be from a distance.

Although the *St Louis* wasn't in the harbor itself, there was still plenty of bustling activity going on in the waters all around them. A boat containing a white-suited Cuban official chugged from the harbor and then came alongside the ship; Sophie heard someone say he was the Port Authority doctor. She watched him climb aboard with trepidation as well as curiosity.

"Apparently, we'll all have to be inspected, to make sure we're not carrying some dreadful disease," Rosa remarked, joining her at the railing, her elbows propped on the burnished wood as she squinted in the bright sunlight. "Even though Captain Schroeder gave a sworn statement that we weren't, it seems they still need to make sure." She frowned, her eyes narrowed as her gaze swept the distant shoreline, with its gleaming white buildings and scattering of palm trees.

"It's just contagious diseases they're concerned about, isn't it?" Hannah asked as she clutched her sister's hand. Sophie knew she was worried on Lotte's behalf; a simple stammer was enough to make a Nazi doctor cast a questioning eye over the girl's health.

"It will be fine, I'm sure," Rosa replied, patting Hannah's arm. "It's just a formality."

Sophie glanced at her friend, who seemed, with some determination, to have adopted an air of breezy confidence. After her wobble a few days ago, when she'd told Sophie her fears about some kind of trouble once they reached their destination, she now seemed completely dismissive of anything but total success, a change which should have heartened Sophie, but somehow didn't.

"We'll be toasting our new lives in the Inglaterra Hotel by sunset," Rosa pronounced as they gazed at the aquamarine waters of the city's harbor glinting under the sunlight as if they'd been strewn with diamonds, and Sophie hoped desperately that it was true.

Along with the ship's doctor, several small fishing boats had made their way toward the St Louis, bobbing alongside as the occupants called up in Spanish or broken English, offering fresh fruit for sale—baskets of bananas and coconuts, armfuls of oranges and mangoes, all of it looking exotic and extremely delicious to Sophie.

"I've never seen so much fruit!" Rosa exclaimed, and she tossed a few coins to one of the fishermen in exchange for a bunch of bright yellow bananas that he hoisted up on a rope. "We must each have one," she insisted, handing the fruit around.

Heinrich happily munched his, but Sophie found her stomach was now churning with too many nerves to manage more than a bite.

She was excited, yes, and she was hopeful—so hopeful—and she kept telling herself that if she just believed enough, they really would be at the elegant Inglaterra Hotel by sundown that night, toasting each other with cocktails—not that she'd ever even had a cocktail. And yet she could imagine it... the four of them around a table on the roof terrace, hoisting glasses filled with some interesting and exotic drink, the warm, tropical breeze blowing over them, the ocean glimmering under the setting sun, the first pale glimpse of moon...

She so wanted it to be true... and yet, she still couldn't keep from wondering and worrying. *Why* hadn't the ship gone into the harbor? Why did no one know on board seem to know the reason, not even Rosa's father, who usually acted as if he knew everything? Sophie hadn't spoken to him much over the course of the voyage, but when she had, she'd found him portentous and a bit condescending. He was clearly pleased to be in the captain's confidence—except he wasn't, at least not on this particular point.

Still, Sophie didn't have too much time to dwell on it, for the rest of the morning was taken up with the medical inspections, a long line of passengers snaking through the social hall, the air humid and hot, children running around, or else wilting against their parents' legs, a sense of anxiety once more tautening the mood on the ship like a thrum in the air as people slowly inched forward to be looked over by the medical inspectors; fortunately, all the passengers passed without comment or notice.

"Thank God," Margarete whispered fervently as she shepherded Josef past the bored-looking inspector. Both she and Sophie had been concerned that the doctors might notice his vacant look, the murmuring under his breath, his mental fragility. Although his mood had improved over the last week, having the ship moored so far out of the harbor had caused him anxiety.

"They must have some plan," he muttered plaintively to Sophie as they left the social hall, Sophie pulling Heinrich along behind her, Margarete with her arm still around Josef. "Some terrible plan..."

"I'm sure it will all be sorted out soon, Papa," Sophie soothed. "You know how slow bureaucracy can be. That's all it is." She kept her voice bright with a conviction she didn't entirely feel.

After settling her father with her stepmother in the reading room with a carafe of coffee and a few cakes, Sophie headed back up to the promenade deck with Heinrich to join her friends. Hannah and Rosa were already at the railing, looking out at the vibrant scenes playing out over the water, while Rachel had gone to settle Franz somewhere quiet.

Sophie enjoyed simply being in the warm air and sunshine; already her hair had started to lighten, and freckles had come out on her nose.

"You passed through all right?" she asked Hannah as Heinrich and Lotte went off to play.

"Yes, thankfully. The doctors didn't seem interested at all."

"I wonder why that was," Rosa remarked, her head cocked as her gaze scanned the horizon as if looking for enemies.

"What do you mean?" Hannah's voice sharpened with concern, her eyes narrowing. "I suppose it was nothing more than a formality, since Captain Schroeder had already stated that all the passengers were in good health. Isn't that what you said yourself?"

"A formality," Rosa replied softly, "or a charade?"

"Oh, not that again!" Hannah sounded almost angry as she turned to glare at Rosa. "Don't be the voice of doom, Rosa. We are in Havana, we can *see* it right there!" She flung one hand out to the harbor and its crowd of buildings, the blank, brick walls of the imposing El Murro. "Why shouldn't we be allowed into the country?" Her voice trembled. "My *father* is there. He is waiting for us. He has an apartment all ready for us."

"I'm sorry," Rosa replied, sounding genuinely apologetic, yet still firm. "I wish as much as you do, Hannah, that I am being gloomy and nothing more." She cast her troubled gaze to the horizon once more. "I'm just... afraid."

"I thought that was past," Sophie protested, in the tone of someone trying to jolly another along, determined not to give into her own anxieties. "You've seemed so cheerful these last few days. What about the cocktails at the Inglaterra Hotel? I'm quite looking forward to them, you know. Frau Spanier told me that I must try a piña colada." Sophie heard how bright and brittle she sounded, and she fell, rather abruptly, silent.

"I've tried to be cheerful, it's true," Rosa admitted quietly. "God knows, I've wanted to be." She pressed her lips together as she stared out at the ocean. "But there are too many things..."

"*What* things?" Hannah burst out, looking angry again, her fists clenched as if she were ready to do battle.

Rosa, however, remained unfazed by her friend's seeming aggression. "The ship not being allowed in the harbor," Rosa stated calmly. "The doctors barely looking at us, as if it didn't matter whether we were ill or not. The immigration officers came on board at six o'clock this morning, and not one has even lifted a finger! They're eating sausages and drinking beer in the dining hall, and not bothering with any of us."

"My father wrote that they do things differently in Cuba," Hannah countered, sounding both defensive and insistent. "They say 'later' and they mean days or weeks, or even months. They tell you something is impossible and what they really mean is, it is difficult, and they need more money." She shrugged, smiling defiantly, her chin held high. "At least that's what he said. Why can't this be the same, simply the way the Cubans do things?"

Rosa stared at her for a moment, her lips pursed, her gray eyes drooping at the corners. She looked torn between exasperation and pity, but then, to Sophie's—and Hannah's—surprise, she pulled the other woman into a quick, hard hug. "*Sehr wahr, Hase*," she murmured, the friendly endearment *bunny* seeming to spring naturally to her lips. "*Sehr wahr*, very true. Forgive me, for being so gloomy. I don't mean it."

For a second, Hannah had looked startled that Rosa had embraced her. Although they'd all become good friends over the last two weeks, their relationships had not included much physical affection. But then, as Sophie looked on, Hannah returned the hug, her arms wrapped around Rosa as she clung to the other woman as if drawing both strength and succor from her. Rosa closed her eyes for a moment, a look of something like pain on her face, and Sophie knew, with a chilling certainty, that whatever reassurances she'd given to Hannah just then, she hadn't meant them. She was still afraid... and maybe she had good reason to be.

"Renata! *Bist du da, Mausi*? Evelynne!"

The sound of someone calling out in German from one of the little boats bobbing by the side of the ship had all three women rushing to the railing. A man in a light linen suit was waving his straw boater in the air, half-crouched in a small boat rowed by a Cuban, his expression one of both hope and anxiety as he called out again. "Renata! Evelynne!"

"It must be their father, Herr Aber!" Hannah exclaimed. "He's come to find them!" She turned to look for the two little girls who had spent much of the voyage with Heinrich and Lotte. "Renata, Evelynne! Girls, girls! Your father is here!"

Both girls ran to the railing, jumping up and down in their excitement as they caught sight of their father; Hannah lifted one up, and Rosa the other, so they could see him better. As excited as they obviously were, Sophie saw a hint of confusion in their eyes, and with a rush of pity, she realized it had been so long since the girls had seen their dear father that they didn't entirely recognize him. Thankfully, this did not seem to dim their enthusiasm in the least.

"Papa!" Renate cried. "Papa, you're here!"

"We had ice cream!" Evelynne told him. "Every day! And we've been swimming!"

Herr Aber let out a laugh that was a half sob, wiping his eyes as he smiled. "I am so, so glad to see you, little ones," he called up, before his expression turned anxious. "Girls, my dear girls, do you have visas?" He turned to Hannah, who was still hoisting up Renata. "*Fräulein*, do you know if their mother arranged their visas?"

"Yes, they're all arranged," Hannah called back. "With the Cuban government. There is no need to worry." She put Renata back down before wiping her own forehead, and Rosa set Evelynne back on her feet. "Goodness, it's hot out here," Hannah told Sophie. "I suppose we'll all have to get used to this weather."

"Ah, that's good, about the visas," Herr Aber called back. "I hope it won't be too long before they are able to come off the ship... Be good, girls! Be good for your papa!"

Rosa leaned over, her elbows braced on the railing. "Do you know what is taking so long for us to disembark?" she called to Herr Aber.

He looked up at her, shaking his head. "It is the way of this country, I am afraid. Slowly, slowly! You must have patience. Maybe a siesta!" He let out a laugh while Rosa smiled thinly and thanked him.

"You see," Hannah told her. "I said it was the Cuban way. We really don't need to worry, Rosa."

"No," Rosa murmured back, "I don't suppose we do."

The rest of that sultry Saturday passed slowly, every hour seeming to limp by as they waited for news. After lunch, Sophie put Heinrich down for a nap in the cool of the cabin; he'd been up with the rest of them since the crack of dawn. She felt hot and tired and tetchy herself, and yet too highly strung to rest. Rosa's warnings kept echoing in her ears, along with her assurances. She didn't know which to believe.

At half past three, with Heinrich still asleep, Sophie went back onto the promenade deck to see if there had been any news. Her friends were lounging about, looking limp in the heat, but Hannah's voice rang with excitement as she told her that four Cuban passengers, as well as a woman and her two children, had been allowed to disembark just a short while ago.

"What!" Sophie stared at her in surprise. "A German woman?"

"Yes, Frau Bonné, do you recall her? Her little girl Beatrice had a birthday party yesterday. She turned five."

"Yes, of course." It had been arranged by a steward, and both Heinrich and Lotte, as well as many of the other children on the voyage, had been invited. Sophie pressed her wrist to her forehead, desperate for a cooling breeze. In the stillness of the afternoon, the heat felt as if it had settled like a heavy shroud on the ship; the humidity made it hard to move, even to breathe. She had never encountered anything like it before. "Why was she allowed," she asked Hannah, "and nobody else?"

"The immigration official asked for them especially," Rachel replied. She'd come out to the deck, now that, like Heinrich, Franz was sleeping, and was perched on the edge of a deckchair, her hands folded in her lap. "I saw him. He wasn't even interested in seeing their landing permits. He just said they could leave the ship, and they did, almost that very moment."

Sophie glanced at Rosa to see her reaction, but her friend's face was impassive, her arms folded. What could any of it mean?

"I asked one of the police on board when the rest of us might disembark," Rachel continued. "He said '*despues de Pentecostes*', which means after Pentecost. It's a Christian holiday that takes place tomorrow."

"After," Sophie repeated, a mixture of relief and anxiety rolling through her. Could it really be that simple? "Why did no one tell us that before? Do we just have to wait until Monday?" It seemed both ages away, and yet no time at all, if it meant they really would finally get off this ship...

"No cocktails at the Inglaterra tonight, then," Hannah said

with a high, sure laugh. "But Monday evening, most certainly! Piña coladas all around!" She tilted her chin, her hazel eyes flashing, as if daring anyone to contradict her. The ferocity she so often exhibited defending her sister, Sophie thought, had been transferred to defending the sure and certain hope that they would be able to disembark.

Slowly, Rosa turned to smile at them all. She looked tired, and older than her twenty-one years. "Monday evening," she agreed, and the corners of her mouth tilted up in a smile that to Sophie seemed forced; there was something sad about the curve of her lips, even defeated. "And then," she continued, her smile creeping up at its edges, "we'll toast our new lives in Havana."

CHAPTER 9

WEDNESDAY, MAY 31, 1939

The decks of the SS *St Louis* shimmered in the intense heat, underneath a hazy blue sky. With the temperature registering over a hundred degrees outside, it was too hot and humid to remain on deck for very long, although it was also the only place to get some fresh air. Sophie had taken to coming up to the sports deck with Heinrich for a quarter of an hour every so often, before retreating to the cooler, shadowy rooms below.

After Sunday—*despues de Pentecostes*—the mood on the ship had sunk into an almost lethargic despair. The *St Louis* continued to remain outside the harbor, and the only people who had left the ship since it had arrived in Cuba were a handful of members of the crew, who had, with the captain's reluctance, been given shore leave. Rosa and Sophie had watched them go with a sense of bitterness; they'd been rowdy and jovial, out for a night's pleasure in the town, while nearly a thousand passengers looked on, aggrieved and despairing.

Over the last few days, the passengers of the *St Louis* had begun to feel more and more as if they were trapped in a floating prison. Since Monday, police boats had surrounded the ship, along with a motley array of fishing vessels that continued to offer fresh fruit. Occasionally, visitors would come from the shore, including Herr Aber, who was still working hard to get his girls off the ship. Hannah and Lotte's father had come, as well, on Sunday afternoon, waving and crying from a boat as they'd waved and wept back.

"He'll arrange something, I'm sure of it," Hannah had said fiercely, over and over again, as if daring anyone to contradict her. No one had had the heart to, or the conviction to offer their agreement.

Sophie knew from Rosa, and her father's part in the captain's passenger committee, that the situation was bad, and growing worse by the hour. On Monday night, when nothing had changed despite everyone eagerly waiting in a constant state of determined expectation, suitcases still packed, their pressed traveling clothes put on once more, she and Sophie had gone for a walk along the promenade deck, in the cool of the night.

"It's worse than I thought," Rosa had stated quietly as they'd walked side by side, the water nothing but blackness below, occasionally swept by the searchlights from the police boats. Apparently, they were there to make sure no one jumped off—whether to escape the ship or this life, Rosa had remarked dryly, was up for debate. "Much worse."

Sophie's stomach had clenched, and she'd had to take several deep, calming breaths before she was able to speak. "How bad?" she had asked, bracing herself for Rosa's response.

A long, weary sigh had escaped her friend, as if coming from the very depths of her being. "It seems the Cubans don't want us there at all. My father thinks the *Abwehr* have been stirring up hatred against Jews in Cuba for some time."

Sophie had frowned. "The *Abwehr*?"

"The Nazis' military intelligence—"

"Yes, I know," Sophie had replied, "but surely they're not in

Cuba?" She had been so sure—so *wanting* to be sure—that they had left such things back in Germany.

"They're everywhere, Sophie," Rosa had replied bleakly, turning to face her head on, her mouth set, her shoulders slumped. "Everywhere. My father thinks this voyage was nothing but another one of the Nazis' propaganda tricks, to show the world that *nobody* wants Jews—not Germany, not Cuba, not anyone, anywhere. The newspapers in America and England have been quite cool on the whole situation, apparently—not much in their news at all. No one really cares, or even *wants* to care about us."

"But..." Sophie had found she could only gape, horrified, as she struggled to absorb the full, awful meaning of what Rosa was telling her. "But we have *visas*..."

Rosa had shaken her head. "Not worth the paper they're printed on, apparently. Some government official was giving them out on his own as if they were candy! It was just a way for him to make money. They were never actually approved, so they don't amount to anything."

Sophie had flung one hand out to the railing to steady herself; she had felt as if the very deck had shifted beneath her feet, as if they were back out on the wild, heaving ocean rather than so close—*so close*—to the calm waters of Havana's safe harbor. All the certainties she'd been counting on—and, in truth, by this point, there hadn't been that many—had been swept away in light of these awful revelations.

"But why?" she had asked finally, her voice catching as she slowly shook her head. "The Nazis wanted rid of us—"

"They want to *destroy* us," Rosa had stated. "It's not the same thing."

Sophie had turned to gaze out at the harbor, the lights of the city twinkling in the distance, reflected as bright, blurred pinpoints that danced across the water. Under a half-moon, the walls of El Murro were nothing more than shadowy outlines, a sense of darkness in the midst of the usually busy harbor.

So close. If she was brave enough, she could swim it, Sophie had thought, although the police boats would surely stop her. In any case, she would never leave Heinrich or her father or stepmother behind. But how could they have crossed an entire ocean, and now be in full view of Havana itself, and not be allowed in?

It was monstrous. And the Nazis, she acknowledged bleakly, were monstrous.

Slowly, she had turned back to Rosa. "So, what do the Nazis want to happen?" she had asked. "For us to stay on this—this *death ship*—forever?" She had pictured them circling the globe, drifting on the sea, going nowhere. Her father had said the ship was damned, Sophie had recalled, and it seemed he might have been right.

Rosa had shrugged. "I don't know what they want. Maybe they haven't thought it through properly. They're achieving something, though, aren't they, by the simple fact that we're still here?" She had let out a huff of breath. "My father told me the Cuban president, Bru, is dithering and dallying because it is an election year, and he doesn't want to go against the will of the people."

"And the people don't like Jews, because the *Abwehr* has been stirring them up," Sophie had finished as she recalled what Rosa had said. "Are we really all to be sacrificed for the sake of an *election?*"

Rosa had spread her hands wide, grimly accepting. "It would appear so."

They had continued walking along the darkened deck in a morose silence; there seemed nothing more to say. There was nothing they could do.

"So, what will happen?" Sophie had asked eventually. She knew Rosa couldn't give her a definitive answer, but she'd come to trust her friend's wisdom, as well as her insider knowledge, gleaned from her father and his role on the passenger committee.

"My father said the committee has been sending cables to various politicians and newspapers," Rosa had told her. "In the hope that they will be able to garner support. The United States might take us if Cuba doesn't."

"Do you think so?" Sophie's voice had lifted in eager hope. "But that would be even better—"

Rosa had shaken her head. "I don't know, Sophie. I just don't know. It seems so complicated. My father doesn't think the captain is telling him everything—the Gestapo on board have been searching people's rooms, roughing them up even. They broke a man's nose, my father said, but the captain hasn't mentioned anything about that."

"They have?" Sophie's stomach had plunged unpleasantly. That was a worse thing than what she'd encountered so far—the Horst Wessel song, the crewman's sneer. What if they found her father? She didn't think he would recover from such rough treatment, not a second time.

Rosa had let out a despondent sigh. "I knew they were on board, of course, but they've become bolder. They're not afraid of showing their true colors, the way that crewman did the first night." She'd shivered, wrapping her arms around herself as if she were cold, despite the sultry air bathing them like warm silk. "I don't know what will happen now," she had finished quietly, and it sounded like a confession.

Now, on Wednesday morning, Sophie stood at the deck with Heinrich, Havana's shoreline shimmering in the heat haze. Heinrich tugged impatiently on her hand; he wanted to go swimming, but with the heat, the pool had become too crowded.

Yesterday, First Officer Ostermeyer had announced that

there would be no more divisions between the first and tourist classes; all passengers could use all areas of the ship. Sophie had been grateful, as she'd never been truly comfortable with the division, and it meant she could see more of Rachel, but it also meant that the nicer first-class lounges and leisure areas were often heaving with people.

Half of the passengers, Sophie had thought as she'd looked around, seemed intent on enjoying what, on the surface, could seem like a tropical paradise, nothing more than a lovely holiday —whiling away the hours lounging by the pool, eating meals in the dining hall. She'd seen several young women in swimming costumes, flirting with members of the crew, tossing their heads back and laughing as if they hadn't a care in the world.

The other half, like her, seemed on the brink of despair, or something even darker. Her father had plunged into depression once more, and worse, a growing paranoia. He kept insisting the Gestapo were coming for him, that they were on the ship, knocking on doors, looking for him. Sophie didn't know how to reply, because she knew now that they *were* on the ship, but she hoped, at least, they weren't looking for her father. The truth was, however, that she didn't feel as if she knew anything anymore. She'd never expected to still be here, waiting, worrying, nearly three weeks after they'd started their journey, with their prospects seeming bleaker now than ever.

"Sophie, please. I want to go to the pool." Heinrich yanked on her hand again, hard enough to hurt.

"Enough, Heinrich!" Sophie's voice came out far more sharply than it usually did as she turned to her little brother, her brows drawn together in a scowl.

Immediately, Heinrich's eyes filled with tears. "Sophie..." His voice wobbled and she took a steadying breath.

"I'm sorry, Heinie." She knelt to give him a quick hug, both of them sticky with heat. She was never cross with him, but the events of the last few days had left her feeling distinctly on edge, her nerves frayed to a thread. "I didn't mean to snap. It's only, darling, that the pool is so crowded. I wouldn't be able to see you, amidst all the people, and I wouldn't want you to get into any trouble."

"I can swim," Heinrich insisted stubbornly, and Sophie tried to smile. Her brother couldn't swim *that* well, she knew, although he certainly gave it his all, kicking and splashing with happy abandon.

"Even so, Heinie. I'm sorry, but we'll have to wait. I'm sure it will clear later. I'll take you today, I promise." She kissed his plump cheek, but he did not seem all that mollified.

"Sophie, you'll never guess what has happened!" Hannah hurried up to them, her whole face alight as she held Lotte's hand, who trotted behind a little bit. "The Aber girls have left the ship! They were in their swimsuits, dripping with water, would you believe, when their father came aboard. They've gone to Havana!"

"*They* were swimming," Heinrich declared grumpily, yanking at her hand again. Sophie ignored him.

"Renata and Evelynne are gone?" she asked Hannah, hardly able to believe it.

"Just a few moments ago." Hannah's face was flushed, her eyes shining. "Don't you see, Sophie, if they can leave the ship, then, surely, we can, as well? I know my father will be able to arrange it. Lotte and I might be in Havana by tomorrow!"

Her father could arrange it, Sophie thought, but what about her own family? Her father was currently curled up in bed, his face turned to the wall. He wasn't able to arrange anything.

"I'm so glad for them," Sophie said at last, despite the fear that lined her stomach like acid. "And I'm sure it will be your turn very soon, Hannah. This is such good news."

Hannah reached out to grasp her hand. "It will be *all* our turns," she insisted, her smile wide, her face practically radiant. Sophie wished she had her friend's certainty.

Leaving Hannah and Lotte on the deck, she dragged a reluctant Heinrich back to the cabin, where Margarete was sitting at the desk, her chin propped in her hand, looking incredibly weary. Sophie's father was asleep.

"My friend Hannah told me the little Aber girls have been taken off the ship," Sophie told Margarete in a low voice, after settling Heinrich with a book of fairy tales. He flipped through it disconsolately, gazing at the illustrated plates without much interest.

"Have they?" Margarete perked up, lifting her head from her hand. "That is surely good news for all of us."

"Hannah's father is trying to get her and her sister off the ship. He has connections, apparently, that he is able to use."

Margarete gave a short nod of understanding. "All the better for him, I suppose."

"What about our connections?" Sophie asked tentatively. "Papa mentioned having friends in New York and Washington. Could we contact them? Perhaps they could act on our behalf. Others have sent cables to various people. If we know anyone of influence..." Margarete stared at her, an arrested look on her face, as Sophie continued quickly, "I am speaking on everyone's behalf, not just ours. If people hear about what is happening here, they might bestir themselves. Maybe America will take all of us, then."

"Maybe," Margarete replied after a moment, sounding unconvinced, or perhaps just weary. She glanced at Josef, who was still sleeping. "I suppose I could send a few cables to the people your father mentioned. He will not be able to do it, at any rate." A shaky breath escaped her. "We must try everything."

Just then, her father suddenly startled awake, lurching upright with a gasp as if he'd been prodded. "The Gestapo!" His voice shook and his eyes were wide and dazed with terror, his hands stretched out in front of him. "The Gestapo—they're coming—"

"No, no, Papa," Sophie said quickly, hurrying over to pat his am. "There are no Gestapo here. You are safe—"

"No, no, no..." Her father shook her off as he started moaning, dropping his head into his hands as he rocked back and forth. "No, no, I'd rather die than go back to Germany! I will die first, I tell you!"

"Josef, *Liebe,* no one is going back to Germany," Margarete assured him, her voice trembling, although she tried to smile. "We are in beautiful Havana, in Cuba—"

"No!" The word came out in an unexpected roar, and both Sophie and her stepmother drew back, startled and dismayed by the unexpected, angry outburst. "I won't do it!" Josef declared as he staggered up from the bed. "I won't do it! I won't let them take me! They won't, they *won't!"*

"Papa, no one is going to take you—" Sophie exclaimed, reaching out to him.

"Josef—" Margarete stood up and reached for her husband's arm. "Josef, please—"

"I *won't!"* With both hands, he pushed his wife's shoulders hard, so Margarete fell back onto the floor with a little scream.

"Mama!" Heinrich called, sounding scared. He tossed his book aside as he ran to his mother.

"Papa—" Sophie began, only to have her father throw open the door and run from the cabin.

"Get him!" Margarete gasped out, waving Sophie away as she tried to help her up from the floor. "Get him, Sophie, please!"

It felt like a nightmarish repeat of that evening over two weeks ago, when her father had run from the cinema. Sophie hurried down the corridor, calling her father's name, heedless of the people who poked their heads out of their cabins, looking curious or concerned, or, in some cases, wearily disinterested.

"Papa!" Sophie burst out onto the deck, slipping and nearly falling in her haste as she ran down the length of the ship, looking for her father. A few people were standing at the railing or sitting in deckchairs, drawing back as she raced along. "*Papa!*" She looked around wildly, but she could see no sign of him.

"*Fräulein,* may I help you?" A member of the crew stepped forward, his tone polite, his eyebrows drawn together in concern. "What is the trouble?"

Sophie turned to him, gasping for breath. "My... my father... I'm afraid... I'm afraid he's going to..." She couldn't bear to put it into words.

Just then, someone screamed, and Sophie turned to see her father bursting out of the men's lavatory and racing down the deck. Blood streamed from both wrists as he launched himself toward the ship's railing.

"*Papa, no!*" The words were ripped from Sophie's throat as she lunged toward her father, only to be held back by the seaman.

"*Fräulein,* it is too dangerous—"

"My *father!*" Sophie screamed, only to watch in horror as her father clambered up to balance precariously on top of the railing, arms outflung and dripping blood, before he threw himself into the foaming waters far below.

CHAPTER 10

FRIDAY, JUNE 2, 1939

"Has there been any news of your father?"

Rachel's face was wreathed in kindly concern as she sat next to Sophie in the first-class reading room. Sophie had been sitting there, Rosa keeping vigil beside her, for most of the afternoon, while Hannah had kindly taken Heinrich and Lotte to the swimming pool, and Margarete attempted to sleep.

"No, not since yesterday," she replied dully.

Wordlessly, they all exchanged tense glances. Sophie felt both numb and exhausted, having moved in a dazed torpor through the days since her father had thrown himself into the sea. The seaman who had held her back had, with immense courage, jumped in after him, and attempted to save him, while her father had thrust himself away from the man, sobbing and screaming that he wanted only to die.

Sophie had watched from the deck above, stricken, as the seaman had, with the help of two policeman, rescued and subdued her father. In the bottom of the police launch, they'd bandaged his wrists and then he'd been taken, under guard, to a hospital in Havana, where he remained. Although he had lost a great deal of blood, they'd been told yesterday afternoon that he was likely to survive—and be returned to the ship when his condition was stable.

While this was certainly good news, her father's suicide attempt had darkened the mood of everyone on board. Captain Schroeder had instructed the first officer and purser to conduct a nightly suicide watch, patrolling the corridors and decks throughout the evening hours, in case anyone else was driven to the edge of despair. The jollity that some passengers had determinedly been affecting had vanished completely, and now everyone looked pale and taut with anxiety. The Gestapo firemen had continued to act dangerously emboldened, searching rooms and occasionally roughing up passengers. There was no longer any sense that they had truly fled Germany, that they were safe.

And now, today, with her father still in the hospital in Havana, they had received the news that the ship was going to have to heave anchor; that morning, President Bru had decreed that the St Louis could no longer stay in Cuban waters. They had to put out to sea and go who knew where.

"Does the captain have a plan, do you think?" Rachel asked, and Rosa and Sophie both shrugged. No one seemed to know anything.

"What happens," Sophie wondered aloud, "if my father is still in hospital when we leave?" It was a question her friends couldn't answer, and yet she still felt compelled to ask it, to voice that terrible fear. "I'd like to think he'd be safe," she'd continued quietly, "but I just don't know…"

Her father's mental state was even more fragile than his physical one, and Havana no longer seemed the safe haven Sophie had once assumed it was. Never mind drinking cocktails at the Inglaterra, she thought bitterly. The city appeared to be a hotbed of anti-Jewish feeling. Perhaps it was better they were leaving; some passengers were insisting that America would still accept them. As long as they waited until her father was back on board...

"Captain Schroeder has said they can't possibly leave tonight," Rosa told her bracingly. "He has to take on fresh food and water first. My father says we won't move at least until tomorrow afternoon."

"That's something, then," Rachel offered with a small smile. She'd been quiet and tense lately; like Sophie's father, her husband Franz was struggling under these new, uncertain conditions, falling completely silent or sometimes disappearing for hours at a time, wandering around the ship, Rachel didn't even know where. She'd found him in the kindergarten once, and another time in the gymnasium. Each time, she'd led him back to their cabin, as docile as a child, but she was clearly worried.

"But where will we go?" Sophie asked. For so long, she'd tried to hold onto her hope, her belief, that things would turn out for the better, but now she felt only a deep, weary despair. Why should things turn out for the better this time? They certainly hadn't before.

"Some are saying Miami," Rosa offered. "Maybe Washington. Not too far."

"Somewhere, anyway," Rachel added with a smile. "We have to go *somewhere*."

Did they? It seemed no one wanted this ship of the damned, or its passengers. Her father's suicide attempt had made the newspapers, and still no one seemed to be rousing themselves for the thousand souls aboard the SS *St Louis*. No one wanted to know, never mind care.

The sudden click of heels on the parquet floor of the reading room had all three women turning. Sophie was startled to see her stepmother walking toward her with fierce purpose. For the last few days, Margarete had barely left the cabin, so distraught was she about her husband's condition. Now, however, she wore a smart, belted dress of black taffeta, and her face was powdered, her lips slicked with crimson, her eyes burning darkly in her pale face.

"Margarete—" Sophie half-rose from her chair as she looked at her stepmother in alarmed query. "Has something happened? Have you had any news?"

"Of your father? No." Margarete's tone was tense. Her gaze flicked to Rachel and Rosa, and then back to Sophie again. "We must talk in private, Sophie."

"Of course." Rachel rose from her seat with quiet dignity. "We will leave you in peace."

"There's no need," Margarete replied briefly, without meeting the other woman's eye. "We'll go back to our cabin."

Sophie turned back to her friends. "Can you look after Heinrich for me, if I'm not here when Hannah brings him back—"

"Of course," Rachel said quickly. Lightly, she squeezed Sophie's hand. "We are always here to help."

"I know." Sophie found she had to blink back sudden tears. She had never had such good friends as these three women. They had chatted and laughed and danced and dreamed. And they had wept and held each other when life had seemed so terribly uncertain. She would miss them, whenever they went their separate ways, although that seemed a far-off prospect at the moment, as their fates remained altogether undecided. "What's going on?" Sophie asked Margarete once she'd closed the door. Curiosity gave way to alarm as her stepmother paced the confines of the cabin, chafing her hands together as if she were cold. "You said there's been no news about Papa—"

"No, no news about him." Margarete whirled around to face Sophie. "I have had a reply to one of my cables. A colleague of your father's—although I've never met the man or his wife myself. They live in Washington."

"They do?" Sophie stared at her stepmother, trying to decipher her mood. She seemed agitated, but also as if she had news of import. Surely, if she'd heard back from someone, it was positive... But why did Margarete look so anxious? "What did he say?"

"Their names are Stanley and Barbara Tyler," she continued, her voice high and fast. "Your father met Mr. Tyler at a conference in London, ten or so years ago, I think."

"And they are willing to help?"

"Yes." Margarete hesitated for a single second before continuing, "Another family, the Annenbergs, Jews from Philadelphia, have arranged transport from the ship. There is room for six passengers."

Sophie blinked, incredulous, hope like a fragile, fledgling thing inside her. "*Six—*"

"A police launch will take you to Havana tonight," Margarete continued hurriedly, as if she had to get the words out as fast as she could. "Your visa has already been stamped. And from there, a chartered airplane to Miami, and then onto Washington. The Tylers are ready to welcome you. They live in a grand house on Massachusetts Avenue. You can stay with them as long as you need to."

Sophie stared at her stepmother for a long moment, noting the hectic color in her cheeks, her fierce, determined stare. "*We,*" she said slowly. "The Tylers are ready to welcome *us.* We're *all* going." Her voice rose, high and thin, nearly hysterical. "Margarete, we're all going! You said there were six places—"

"The other places have already been taken," Margarete cut across her. "You can imagine how in demand they are. I don't know how they were chosen, but it doesn't matter. You know I cannot leave your father. And I will not be separated from Heinrich. He would not want to be separated from me." She pressed her lips together, her bony arms folded across her chest. "It must be you, Sophie. Only you."

"No." The refusal came with swift certainty as she shook her head, hard enough to make her ears ring. "I'm not going to go on my own! I won't abandon you or—"

"You must." Margarete took a step toward her, seeming almost angry as she loomed over Sophie, her hands now clenched into fists at her sides. "You must! Do you think it was easy, arranging this? Do you think there will be another chance like it? You'd be a fool not to take it. We'd all be fools. You'd make a fool of me, Sophie, of your father."

"I *can't.*" Sophie stared at her pleadingly, her arms outstretched, her heart beating hard. "Please, Margarete. I can't leave you all. Papa, Heinrich..." Her *friends.* How would they feel, to know she'd abandoned them, simply to save her own skin? "It wouldn't be right."

"Has anything been right about this godforsaken voyage?" Margarete demanded, her voice hoarse and raw. "Anything at all? You must take this chance and save yourself, Sophie. I insist upon it. Besides, if you are in America, it might help us to get there, as well. You know how they always prefer people to have family already in the country."

Sophie stared at her helplessly. "But what will happen to you?"

"Pfft." Margarete waved a hand in airy dismissal, although her face and voice were both tense. "It will only be a delay. We will be in America before the end of next week, most likely, reunited." Margarete's gaze flitted away from her as her chest rose and fell in frenzied breaths, her panicked breathing the only sound in the room.

"You're lying," Sophie stated after a tense moment. She shook her head slowly. "If it was going to be as easy as that, you wouldn't be demanding I leave tonight. You wouldn't say that me being there would help to get you all in."

"It doesn't matter," Margarete insisted. "Whenever we come. You must take this opportunity. I insist upon it!"

Sophie set her jaw. "I won't," she stated flatly. She had not defied her stepmother in any significant way since she'd been a truculent twelve-year-old, kicking against this new, unwelcome influence in her life. "I won't leave you, or Papa, or Heinrich. It wouldn't be right. It wouldn't be *fair*."

Margarete stepped forward and, in one deliberate movement, she slapped Sophie hard across the face, so her head whipped back, her cheek stinging, her eyes watering.

Stunned, Sophie pressed one hand to her throbbing cheek. "*Margarete—*"

"You're going," her stepmother stated, and now she sounded cold. "This is not the time for your absurd theatrics. You are not upon the stage."

Sophie blinked rapidly to keep her tears from falling. "I'm not trying to be dramatic," she whispered. "I don't want to leave you."

"Do not make our sacrifices worthless," Margarete replied harshly. "This is what your father would want. If he were here and well, he would be insisting upon it even more than I am." For a second, her voice caught, broke. "Sophie, if I could save my son, don't you think I would?"

Sophie blinked back more tears. "Send Heinrich then—"

"I cannot send a child on his own, and there is only room for one!" Margarete exclaimed, her voice rising to an impassioned shriek. "And your father would want this for you. I know it, and so do you. It might help us, in the end, as well. Sophie, you *must* go."

They stared at each other, both of them breathing heavily, Sophie's cheek still throbbing. She couldn't believe her stepmother had raised her hand to her; in all their years together, she never had before. And to leave for America... *tonight*...

She couldn't do it. She wouldn't. And yet, even so, she felt the inexorable shifting of her own will, her stepmother's, like the pull of the tide that she was not strong enough to resist. If this was what her father wanted for her, and Sophie knew, with bone-deep certainty that it was, she could not refuse him. If her going to America could help get her family there one day, as well... She could not stand on pointless principles when lives were at stake. When her own was.

"What will I say to my friends?" she whispered, and Margarete clucked in dismissal.

"Say goodbye and Godspeed," she replied tartly. "And do it quickly, because the launch leaves before sunset."

Sophie felt an increasing sense of unreality as she packed a single case, with only a few of her clothes. Margarete had told her there wasn't room for anything more, and she would get the rest of her things when they were all together again, "very soon." But she didn't meet her eye as she said it.

As Sophie laid her coat down on top of her clothes, she felt the sharp bulkiness of the jewels sewn into the lining. Her mother's emerald, a handful of diamonds. With sudden determination, she whirled back to Margarete, who had been watching her, beady-eyed, her arms folded.

"Papa brought jeweler's tools..." Sophie recalled. "Where are they?" Her father had packed them in case they needed to break the jewels up into smaller pieces for sale or barter.

Margarete tutted. "What on earth do you need such tools for?"

"I'm going to split one of my mother's emeralds into four pieces," Sophie stated. "As a token, for each of my friends."

"You'd waste a precious jewel on people you've only just met?" Margarete's elegant eyebrows rose in disdainful disbelief.

"They're the best friends I've ever had," Sophie stated with quiet feeling. "I want to remember them. I want them to remember me."

Margarete stared at her wordlessly for a long moment and

then she went and fetched the tools from her father's leather bag, chisel and hammer and cutting board, handing them to Sophie without a word.

Sophie made a small cut in the lining of her coat and eased out a few of the jewels, while Margarete watched, silent yet still scathing. She picked one of the larger emeralds, an oval pendant in a setting of gold filigree, and held it in the palm of her hand, feeling its weight, the cool smoothness of the stone. Her fingers closed around it, clasping it tightly.

"You are ridiculously sentimental," Margarete burst out, unable to keep from saying something any longer. "To waste that jewel on a few girls you'll never see again!"

"I *will* see them again," Sophie replied fervently. "I will."

Margarete just shook her head.

"When do I go?" Sophie asked, her voice cracking. She could hardly believe this was happening; life felt as if it was blurring by, even as she stood there, emerald in hand, completely still.

"As soon as possible. They are assembling on B deck. The purser, Mueller, told me you should be quick, if you can."

"They won't leave without me?"

Margarete's mouth tightened. "I pray not."

Sophie nodded resolutely. This was it, then. One last farewell for her friends, and then...

The utter unknown.

She swallowed hard and, setting the emerald on the slate cutting board, she positioned the chisel at the emerald's base and then brought the hammer down.

Back up on the sports deck, life had continued as before, as every day had on this damned ship—without news, without hope. Rachel and Rosa were lolling back in their deckchairs, sleepy in the sun, although anxiety was never far from their eyes.

"Sophie!" Rachel straightened in her chair. "What did your stepmother want?"

"Where is Hannah?" Sophie asked, her voice tight with tension. "And Heinrich?"

Rachel frowned. "They're still at the pool."

"I need to speak to you all," Sophie said. Her voice hitched and Rosa frowned.

"Sophie, what—"

"Please, wait. Let's get Heinrich and Lotte settled, and then..." She found she couldn't say anything more.

"What's happened?" Rosa asked, her voice turning sharp. "Something has happened!"

"Yes, but... please. I'll tell you. Just..." She shook her head.

It was only a matter of a few moments to fetch Heinrich from the pool, salty from the water and protesting having to return to the cabin.

"Just for a little while, Heinie," Sophie pleaded. She had the urge to catch him up in her arms, smother him with kisses, imprint him on her very soul. She deposited him with a tense and unhappy Margarete before she gathered her friends in a quiet corner of the first-class reading room.

"Sophie, what on earth is going on?" Rosa asked, her voice caught between concern and impatience. "All this mystery and drama!"

"No mystery, no drama." Sophie's voice trembled. She held the jagged shards of emerald in a small bag; it had not been easy to break, taking several hard strikes of the chisel before the precious jewel began to crack and split. "I just wanted to tell you what... what is happening."

"What *is* happening?" Hannah demanded, frowning. She looked caught between anger and alarm, as she so often was.

Rachel simply shook her head slightly, both concerned and confused.

Sophie gazed between them all, her three dear friends. They had only known each other three weeks—three *weeks*—and yet it felt like a lifetime. It *had* been a lifetime, one of hope and despair, of laughter and tears, of fear and determination. How could she leave them? How could she tell them she was leaving?

"My stepmother..." she began, and then had to stop again.

Rosa tutted, and Rachel smiled in gentle encouragement. Hannah still looked as if she wasn't sure what to feel.

"My father has connections in America," Sophie said in a rush. "A family in Washington. My stepmother sent a cable... she has arranged for me to leave the ship... to go to America..." She trailed off at the look of blatant shock on all three of her friends' faces.

"You're... *leaving*?" Rosa finally said.

Sophie could only nod. Her heart felt like a bird beating in her chest, wings flapping wildly.

"When?" Rachel asked, still looking stunned.

"Tonight. Very soon, in fact. I came to... to say goodbye." Her voice caught as she glanced at Hannah, who hadn't spoken. She'd folded her arms and her lips were pursed, her eyes narrowed nearly to slits. "I'm so sorry..." Sophie choked.

"How can you be leaving?" Hannah spat suddenly, "when Lotte and I are not able to? My father is in Havana! He's *right there!*" She flung one hand out, a shudder going through her whole body as she struggled not to cry.

"I'm so sorry," Sophie said again, wretchedly. She wrung her hands, hating how abandoned Hannah clearly felt. "I didn't want to go, but my stepmother—Margarete—she insisted." She touched one hand to her still-stinging cheek, remembering that shocking slap. "She said it would be wrong for me *not* to go, after the sacrifices my family has made. It's what my father would have wanted—"

"It's what we all want," Hannah burst out bitterly. "Lucky you, though."

"Hannah." Rachel sounded quietly reproving. "Sophie must take this chance. You would take it, if you'd been offered it. You know you would."

Hannah merely shrugged in reply, her shoulders hunched, her back half-turned from Sophie. She hated the thought that she might part from her friends in such a way.

"I don't want this to be farewell forever," she insisted, her voice breaking. "You three have been my best friends. I haven't..." She paused, struggling to keep her voice even. "My best friend back in Berlin, Ilse, was a gentile. After the race laws, she turned her back on me completely. I... I never had another friend like her, not until I met you three." She tried for a smile, but it wobbled and slid off her face. "Please..."

"Oh, Sophie," Rosa said with quiet sorrow. "I hope and pray we'll see each other again, as well." But she did not sound convinced, and why should she?

"Listen," Sophie said. "I have a jewel, an emerald, from my mother." She held up the bag. "I split it into four shards, so we can each have a piece to remember one another by. And one day—*one day*—we'll meet again. We will."

Rosa still looked skeptical. "You should keep any jewels," she said, nodding to the bag. "You might need them."

"No." Sophie shook her head, vehement. "I want us each to have a piece. A talisman of sorts. And when we're together again —and we will be—we'll fit the pieces back together. We'll be whole again." She gazed at each of them in turn, her face filled with hope, with hunger. She so wanted this to mean something.

"Oh, very well," Hannah replied restively. "It's a bit dramatic, but if you insist."

It was, Sophie knew, as good as an apology for her earlier bitterness.

Carefully, she withdrew the shards of emerald, jagged and green, and handed them solemnly to each woman. Rosa studied hers with academic interest before her fingers closed tightly around it. Hannah took hers and slipped it quickly into her pocket. Rachel smiled gently at Sophie as she took her own piece, letting it rest in the palm of her hand.

"How on earth did you manage to split it?" she asked. "Emeralds are almost as hard as diamonds."

"It wasn't easy," Sophie admitted with a wobbly laugh. "But my father had brought jeweler's tools."

"Still, you must have had to give it a good whack," Rachel remarked.

"And now what?" Rosa asked, gazing down at the splinter of emerald in the palm of her hand. "How on earth will we ever find each other again? We don't even know where we're going."

"I'll send a cable when I arrive, so you know my address. And you can write to me, with your own addresses, when you know them. Please write," she implored. "Let me know when you're settled, so I can write you back. We must keep in touch. We *must*."

"And one day," Rachel said softly, "we'll meet again. Where?"

"In New York?" Rosa suggested wryly. "Somewhere in America, where we'll all be living."

A brief silence rested on the little group, the looks on everyone's faces making Sophie think they all knew what wishful thinking that was, even if they didn't want to say as much.

"In America," she agreed, "or maybe somewhere in Europe —Paris? Somewhere wonderful. We can decide later, because we're all going to stay in touch." She gazed at each of them in both challenge and plea. "Aren't we?"

"Yes, we are," Hannah said quietly. She raised her shard of

emerald. "We're the Emerald Sisters," she quipped, smiling faintly. "And the next time we see each other, it will be somewhere elegant in Paris or New York or who knows where, drinking champagne!"

"Or piña coladas," Rachel added, with a small smile.

"I think Paris," Rosa said decisively. "There's a little café by the Eiffel Tower I've been to. Henri's. We'll meet there on the same day as today, the second of June, at..." She glanced at her watch. "Four o'clock!"

"What year?" Hannah asked, sounding skeptical, and Rosa shrugged.

"As soon as it's safe."

They all fell silent, not needing to acknowledge that none of them had any idea when that would be.

Then, in turn Rosa, Rachel and Sophie each raised their shard of emerald as Hannah had done, the light catching the green shattered jewels, and making them glint.

"To the Emerald Sisters," they repeated solemnly, a sacred vow, and in the wide darkness of their eyes, Sophie saw and felt her friends' fear, as well as her own. They had made promises to each other, yes, but it was beyond each and every one of them whether they were ones that could be kept.

CHAPTER 11

All around her, the sea stretched, endlessly dark, save for the pinpoints of lights from the various police launches surrounding the St Louis. Sophie sat on a bench, shoved up next to a stout woman with a face like stone who had not spoken a word since the six passengers from the St Louis had boarded the police launch. No one had said anything, save for the two Cuban policemen who were escorting them to shore, who laughed and chatted easily, as if this were an amusing jaunt, rather than a flight for their lives.

Sophie's suitcase banged against her knees as the little boat bobbed up and down in the dark waters. She clenched her jaw against the tears that threatened when she thought of her father, of Margarete, of Heinrich. She'd barely said goodbye to him; Margarete hadn't wanted him to become upset. When Sophie had kissed Heinrich, he'd squirmed away, impatient, restless, while she'd longed to hold onto him, burrow her face into his chubby shoulder and breathe in his little boy smell of sunshine and sweat. When, she'd wondered, would she see him again? How big would he be?

As for her friends... they'd hugged her each in turn, the

farewell terribly solemn, almost as if it was a ritual, a ceremony. A funeral of sorts. Rosa had grasped her hard, like a warning, or maybe a promise, and then she'd stepped back quickly, brushing at her eyes as she'd looked away. Hannah had clung to her, mumbling into her shoulder, "I'm sorry..." Sophie had hugged her back with all the warmth she felt. And Rachel, dear, gentle Rachel, had kissed her cheek. "God be with you, Sophie," she'd whispered.

"And with you..."

Sophie had choked out more promises to write, to see each other again, but this time her friends had not parroted them back. Did any of them really believe they'd meet again? And yet... they'd promised.

In a few days, the *St Louis* might be docked in Miami. Her friends might be in America. They might meet again in a week, or even less! Like with so many other things about this doomed voyage, Sophie was desperate to believe it.

"When we get to the shore," one of the policemen stated in broken, heavily accented English, "there will be a plane. You must stay together. No one go—anyplace else." He raised one thick finger in warning. Sophie and the five other passengers—an assortment of people from first class she barely recognized—all nodded silently.

Ten minutes later, they were at the harborside. As Sophie stepped off the launch, she could hardly believe she was actually in Cuba. After weeks of gazing at it from afar, here she was, her feet on firm earth. How far away was her father? she wondered. She had not, of course, been able to say goodbye to him, and she had no idea when she might see him again... if ever. He'd already attempted to end his life once. What if he tried again?

"Come, come!" one of the policemen urged them on impatiently, and the other nudged Sophie in her back.

Grabbing her suitcase tightly, she started walking, her steps unsteady. A small plane was waiting on an airfield only a short distance away. With a growing sense of unreality, Sophie clambered aboard. She had never been in an airplane before, and as for what came after... it felt utterly unfathomable.

Still, no one had spoken. When she met a man's eye by accident, he looked away, a guilty flush staining his cheeks. Did they all feel like she did, Sophie wondered, like rats abandoning a sinking ship? Like traitors. She swallowed hard and hugged her suitcase to her, telling herself she would see her family soon.

Just a few minutes later, they were in the air. Sophie could hardly believe it had been so easy. No one had looked at her passport, or her visa that had been stamped with approval in her absence. After weeks of feeling as though getting to Havana was virtually impossible, she'd already been and gone. The next stop was Miami.

Her stomach plunged unpleasantly as the little plane rose and then banked. She already had no desire ever to go in one again. Judging by the looks on her fellow passengers' faces, none of them were enjoying this flight through the stars.

The rest of the night passed in a dazed and silent blur. The flight to Florida took two hours, and then they all waited in an empty hangar before they were taken onto their next destinations. None of the passengers seemed to know anything; Sophie had the sense that they were afraid to ask questions, in case any of them were sent back, although wildly, she thought she wouldn't even mind. She wanted to see her family again, her friends...

Eventually, a uniformed official—Sophie had no idea who— gestured to them to leave. Three of them would be going onto Washington; the others were going to New York. Numbly, Sophie wondered whether anyone would even be waiting for her in Washington. What would she do if there wasn't?

Three hours later, in the gray light of pre-dawn, they touched down at Bolling Air Force Base, just outside Washington DC. On stiff and shaky legs, Sophie emerged from the plane, blinking in the dim light. After passing through a cursory customs inspection, she stood on the edge of the airfield, swaying with exhaustion, wondering what on earth she was meant to do now.

"Miss Weiss?"

Sophie blinked to see a tall, broad-shouldered man in a gray uniform and cap walking toward her. White teeth gleamed in his dark face, his skin the color of one of her father's cigars. Sophie blinked again, startled; she'd only seen a handful of black people in her whole life before.

"*Ja*—yes," Sophie stammered, switching from German to English. She'd had lessons since she was a child, but she was not fluent. "I am... I am Sophie Weiss..."

"I'm Herman, the Tylers' driver. I'm to take you home to their place."

Home? She had no idea what that word meant anymore, but the mere thought of it made her throat tighten with unshed tears and she slipped her hand into her pocket, her fingers curling around the shard of emerald.

Herman took her suitcase easily, carrying it as if it weighed nothing, and, still smiling, started walking toward a gleaming silver car. He put her case in the trunk and then opened the door for her. Sophie slid inside, the leather interior soft and inviting. She felt as if she'd woken up in a dream.

"You must be tired, Miss," Herman said as he started the car. "It's not too long of a trip back to the Tylers, but you ought to rest."

"Yes," Sophie said, her eyes already fluttering closed. Too much had happened in too short a space of time, and she needed some respite from the strangeness, if only for a few minutes.

She startled awake sometime later, she didn't know how long, to find it was a bright, sunlit morning, and the car had pulled up a sweeping drive to park in front of a large brick house, three rows of windows glinting in the morning light. It was one of the most impressive houses Sophie had ever seen, practically a mansion, all in its own expanse of verdant green lawn.

"The Tylers said you could go right to bed," Herman told her. "They won't expect you for breakfast."

"Thank you," Sophie said, wishing her English was better. She thought she could understand what the chauffeur was saying, but she felt too tired to make any kind of lengthy reply.

Herman ushered her to the front door, while he, to her surprise, went around the back. As she stepped into a large, elegant foyer with a floor of black and white checkered marble, a chandelier suspended above sparkling in the morning sunlight, a woman in the gray uniform and frilly apron of a housekeeper or maid bustled toward her.

"We've been waiting for you. Miss Barbara said to take you right up to bed, where you can get some sleep. Wake up when you need to, and I'll have breakfast ready for you right away. I'm Esther, Herman's wife."

Sophie stared at the woman, her face full of kindness, still too tired and disorientated to find any more words than yet another murmured "thank you."

"That's all right, Miss Sophie," the housekeeper assured her. "You look fit to drop. Let me show you to your room."

Dazedly, Sophie followed her up a sweeping, circular staircase to a plushly carpeted corridor, with several doors leading off to various bedrooms. It all looked incredibly elegant and expensive, vast rooms hinted at beyond doors left ajar. The whole house was silent, and she wondered where the Tylers were, and when she would meet them, these strangers who had been kind enough to take her in.

"Here's your room, honey," Esther said, standing aside so Sophie could enter the biggest bedroom she'd ever seen, twice the size of her old room back in Berlin. A four-poster stood on its own dais, and what looked like an acre of carpet stretched out in front of it, with a matching bureau, wardrobe, writing desk, and divan. Two long, sashed windows overlooked the garden, a verdant oasis of green right in the middle of the city.

"This is... good," Sophie managed, wishing she could be a bit more eloquent. She knew more English than this, but she was too tired to remember it now.

Esther looked a little startled by her response, and Sophie wondered if she'd misspoken. Or was it simply her German accent, which she knew sounded thick?

The other woman quickly masked her surprise, though, with another wide smile. "If you need anything, let me know," she said, and then stepped out of the room, closing the door behind her.

Sophie looked around again in wonder; she'd never seen anything so elegant before, and she'd always thought her own house had been a place of some luxury and refinement. Still, it had been nothing like this.

Too exhausted to explore or do anything more than take a few steps into the room, she kicked off her shoes, peeled the dress from her body, and then fell into bed, and a deep sleep, almost immediately.

When Sophie woke, the room was flooded with sunlight and stiflingly hot. Lying on top of her covers in only her slip, she was soaked in sweat. Slowly, she rolled up to a seated position, still feeling dazed by everything that had occurred in the last twenty-four hours. Had it been only yesterday that she'd been sitting with her friends on the St Louis, wondering what would happen, where they would all end up? And now she was here. Alone.

Still feeling sleepy, Sophie rose from the bed and walked to the window. Outside, the grass was a bright green, as soft and deep as velvet, the lawn fringed with luxuriant oaks and pines. It looked wonderfully inviting, despite the heat. After three weeks on board a ship, Sophie longed to feel the grass under her feet, hear the wind whispering through the trees.

She turned from the window, deciding she should wash and dress and then ready herself to meet her hosts. Her luxurious bedroom included an adjoining bathroom, complete with a sink, toilet, and deep, claw-footed tub. Feeling absurdly extravagant, Sophie ran a lukewarm bath, grateful to wash off the sweat and dust of travel.

She dressed quickly in the bronze taffeta tea dress she'd worn to board the ship, wanting to make a good impression. The Tylers were obviously wealthy and well-connected people, and already Sophie felt as if she had a standard to live up to.

As she came down the sweeping staircase, the emptiness of the house seemed to reverberate all around her. Then Esther hurried in from the back of the house, through a swinging door.

"Ah, Miss Sophie! You're up. I hope you had a good rest and are ready for some breakfast."

Belatedly, Sophie realized just how empty her stomach was. She hadn't eaten anything since yesterday lunchtime. "Yes... please, Esther." She spoke carefully, wanting to be understood, and the housekeeper beamed.

"All right, then. You set yourself down in the dining room and I'll bring it all in a jiffy."

As Esther went back toward the kitchen, Sophie walked slowly to the dining room. It was a long, elegant room with a table of burnished mahogany that seated sixteen. Matching mahogany cupboards flanked a fireplace against the far wall, filled with pieces of gold-edged porcelain. Heavy gold drapes hung at the windows, framing the view of the front drive, Massachusetts Avenue beyond. Margarete had told her last night, while she'd been packing, that the Tylers lived in one of the most elegant neighborhoods in the city. She hadn't really been able to consider such things then but now, looking out at the stately homes lining the broad avenue, Sophie could believe it.

"Ah, here we are."

She turned to see Esther bringing a tray that was positively brimming with food, much of which Sophie didn't recognize.

"Got to fill you up," the housekeeper told her cheerfully. "You're a scrawny little thing."

Sophie didn't know what scrawny meant, but she could guess.

"Thank you," she said meekly, and sat down as Esther unloaded all the dishes. There was a pot of coffee as well as ones containing cream and sugar, a bowl of scrambled eggs and a rack of toast. There were also two fluffy biscuits, a tureen of gravy, and something that looked like porridge, but Sophie suspected wasn't.

"That's grits," Esther explained, following her gaze. "You can't have a breakfast without grits."

"Grits?" The word was unfamiliar to her.

"Boiled cornmeal," Esther explained. "You put a little honey on it, and it will slip right down. Now, can I get you anything else?"

Overwhelmed, Sophie shook her head. "Thank you," she said again, and with a nod and a bob that was almost like a curtsey, Esther turned from the room.

Sophie poured herself some coffee, a wave of homesickness sweeping over her. As friendly as the housekeeper was, and as welcome the food, everything felt incredibly foreign and strange. And where were the Tylers? She would have thought they would have greeted her by now, and the fact that they hadn't made her feel the same sort of unease that she'd had on the St Louis... something wasn't right.

Despite her hunger, Sophie found she could only pick at her breakfast, because her stomach was churning so much. She wanted to meet the Tylers, and she also wanted to discover some news about the *St Louis*. A whole day had passed; maybe the United States had already agreed to give the refugees entry. And what about her father? Was he back on the ship? Perhaps she could arrange to send a cable to the St Louis.

She'd just finished her coffee when she heard the front door open and close, followed by the click of heels on the marble floor of the foyer.

"Good afternoon, Miss Barbara," Esther said, coming into the hall.

Sophie was jolted. Was it already afternoon?

"Hello, Esther. Is our little refugee awake yet?" The voice of the woman was clipped, with a sardonic edge that had Sophie instinctively stiffening.

"She sure is, Miss Barbara. Just eating her breakfast right now."

"I see."

Barbara Tyler walked into the doorway of the dining room, standing there for a moment as if posing for a painting. She wore a belted jacket and wide skirt, both in deep pink taffeta, and she was easing off a white glove from one hand, finger by finger. Her head was cocked, her dark hair pulled back in an elegant knot as she eyed Sophie speculatively. She had a bony face, dark eyes, and a beaky nose. She wasn't smiling.

Sophie rose from the table quickly, bumping the dishes in her haste. "*Gut*... good morning," she said, and Barbara let out a sharp crack of laughter.

"Oh my goodness, don't you sound *German*?" she exclaimed, sounding both appalled and fascinated. "Of course," she added quickly, "we've nothing against the Germans. Stanley admires quite a few of Hitler's economic policies. He's certainly got the country up and running again, hasn't he?"

Sophie stared at her uncertainly. Had her hostess just

defended Hitler, or had she, in her imperfect grasp of English, misunderstood? Either way, she didn't know how to reply.

"Well, I suppose you could take lessons," Barbara remarked carelessly as she came and sat down opposite Sophie, dropping her gloves onto the table. "Elocution and all that. Esther? Coffee?"

"Of course, Miss Barbara." Esther hurried out of the room.

Barbara propped her chin in her hand as she gave Sophie a thorough look, her lashes half-lowered. "You're a very pretty girl," she remarked, but it didn't quite sound like a compliment. "I thought Jews all had dark hair."

Sophie stiffened before she carefully lowered herself back into her chair. *And all Jews have big noses, as well*, she thought sourly. Barbara Tyler sounded as if she'd gleaned her information from Nazi propaganda newsreels. "Not all," she said, making sure to enunciate. She certainly didn't want to be accused of sounding too *German*, even if she was.

Esther came back in with another pot of coffee and a cup and saucer, which she placed in front of Barbara before stepping back to wait behind her chair, her head slightly bowed. Barbara ignored her completely.

"I wonder," Sophie asked hesitantly. "May I see a newspaper?"

Barbara raised her thin, penciled eyebrows. "A newspaper? Whatever for?"

"For news about the ship. And... my family."

Barbara glanced wordlessly at Esther, who left quickly, returning with copies of both the *New York Times* and the *Washington Post*, which she laid next to Sophie's plate.

Sophie's family had had a maid as well as a cook back in Berlin, before the race laws anyway, but they'd never treated their servants the way Barbara treated hers, as if they were completely beneath notice.

"Thank you," she said to Barbara, and then, a bit pointedly, she turned to Esther. "Thank you."

Under Barbara's beady, speculative gaze, Sophie scanned the headlines of both papers. *Hitler Reported Ousting Generals Opposing Him. Manton Testifies to Big Cash Loans from Litigants. Loss of 85 Feared in Submarine as Tide Engulfs It.* There was nothing, not one headline or article, about the *St Louis*, or the predicament of the refugees.

Sophie's stomach cramped at the realization. She'd thought, from what Rosa had said, that the papers were full of news about the plight of the ship, especially after her father's suicide attempt. Rosa had mentioned a headline citing 'The Ship of the Damned'—her father's prophetic words in print. But here she could see nothing, not even a criticism of the whole venture. It was as if the ship didn't exist—truly a ghost ship packed with a thousand souls, cruising the empty waters, just as Rosa had said, going nowhere.

She glanced up to see Barbara watching her with a faint, knowing look on her face, not quite a smile, but almost. "I thought there would be something," she stated carefully. "Some news."

Barbara shrugged. "I'm not sure people are too concerned about a German ship in Cuba," she remarked. She tapped a cigarette from a long, slim case and lit it, blowing out a plume of smoke as she gazed at Sophie through narrowed eyes. "But at least you're safe, aren't you? Your mother assured Stanley your family would be here by the end of the week. A happy reunion." Her lips curved.

"She's not my mother," Sophie replied, before she realized she did not know the word in English for what Margarete was to her. "But yes. I hope they will."

"We all hope so," Barbara replied, and Sophie had the uncomfortable sense that she wasn't repeating the sentiment out of concern for Sophie or her family, but because she wanted her gone.

Why, Sophie wondered, had the Tylers agreed to take her in, in the first place? At that moment, as she looked down at the papers again simply to escape her hostess' assessing stare, she wanted to be gone, as well. She wished she'd stood her ground with Margarete and had refused to come. She'd rather be on that doomed ship with her friends and family, than here with this woman who reminded her of a crow, looking at her with sharp eyes, beak and talons at the ready.

Right then, Sophie hoped more than ever that her stepmother's assurances were true... that they'd all be reunited in just a few days.

CHAPTER 12

The heat of Washington DC was an oppressive blanket that Sophie felt was smothering her. She'd thought she'd become at least *somewhat* used to the soaring temperatures while on board the *St Louis*, but away from the cooling sea breezes, she found the sticky humidity almost unbearable.

She spent the hottest part of each day in her bedroom, lying in just her slip and waiting for news. Sometimes, she took out her sliver of emerald and held it to the light, gazing into the gleam of its greenness as if it were an oracle that could give her the answers she so longed for. Thinking about her family, her friends, having no idea how they fared—or where they might go —was even more unbearable than the heat.

For the rest of the time, she tried to take an active interest in her hosts and their lives, but it had become uncomfortably clear that Barbara Tyler had no interest in including her in any of her daily activities. She was often gone straight after breakfast, to shopping or a bridge party or coffee with friends, and Sophie was never invited. She obviously had no interest in getting to know her guest.

Stanley Tyler was another, even more uncomfortable

matter. He'd arrived home on Sophie's first full day at the house, full of booming bonhomie and sweeping gestures. A tall, broad man with a florid complexion and sporting a natty checkered suit, he'd embraced Sophie with all the warmth his wife had not shown her—and then some. Kissing her on both cheeks, holding her hands several seconds more than she'd like... it had left Sophie feeling flustered in an entirely different, but just as unpleasant, way.

"Your father was such a *good* man," he'd reminisced as he'd splashed cognac into a snifter from a crystal decanter on the extensive drinks table in their living room. "He kept hold of such *principles*." He spoke as if he'd discarded such inconvenient things himself some time ago.

"We hope he will be released from hospital soon," Sophie had replied, and Stanley's thick eyebrows had risen in surprise.

"*Released...* my dear, I thought he'd died."

"Died?" She'd stared at him in shock, flushing under his surprised, sympathetic stare. "No... no..." Unless her stepmother had kept such a dreadful thing from her? But surely not. Surely not!

"That must have been my misunderstanding," he'd murmured, tossing back his cognac. "I apologize for causing you any distress."

Sophie had merely shaken her head, her heart hammering with the very idea that her father might have died. But, no, surely he couldn't have. She would have known. Margarete would have told her. She would have to send a cable to her stepmother, to find out what news she could, as soon as possible, as well as one to her friends, to let them know her address.

"Doesn't she sound *German?*" Barbara had interjected, sounding amused, and Stanley had given his wife a rather irritated look.

"Well, she is German." He'd turned back to Sophie. "It's a bad business, with this ship. I'm afraid the government is in something of a quandary over it. Roosevelt doesn't want to know about it, you see. He won't say a word to anyone. It's as if the blasted thing doesn't exist."

Having blushed just a few minutes before, Sophie had then felt herself go pale and lightheaded. A ghost ship, indeed, then. "But..." She had swallowed hard. "Why?"

Stanley had shrugged. "Rumor is, he's thinking of running for a third term. It's not done here, you know, generally speaking. Washington refused to do it, and Grant and Theodore Roosevelt tried, but failed. But if the Sphinx himself decides to do it... well, I'm afraid what's happening over in Germany isn't of much interest to most people here. They don't want to get the US involved in all that drama in Europe... well, you can understand it, can't you?"

"I..." Sophie had found she did not have the English to reply, or even understand all Stanley had been saying. The Sphinx? Was that the president? And did her host really mean that people didn't care about the plight of the Jews, herself included? He had been looking at her with a kind of academic disinterest, as if they were talking about the weather, and Barbara had been studying her nails, yet this was her *life* they were talking about. Her family's lives, her friends' lives. She thought of Rosa, Hannah, Rachel, the last time they'd seen each other, saying goodbye, each of them holding their shards of emerald.

"So, Roosevelt doesn't want to rock the boat, as it were..." He'd finished, grimacing good-naturedly. "Sorry, that's a terrible pun. But Morgenthau—he's the Secretary of the Treasury—well, he's on your side, of course. He's a Jew, as well, you see."

Sophie had shaken her head. "Are you saying the United States will not accept the refugees," she'd finally asked in careful, hesitant English, "because... because of an election?" Just like with President Bru of Cuba. The self-interest of these important men made her want to spit or scream or both.

"That's about the size of it," Stanley had agreed as he'd finished his cognac with relish. "But, like I said, Morgenthau's hoping to do something, and his family has a lot of influence, a lot of money. Millionaires in New York, don't you know. He's thought about maybe having the refugees taken to the Virgin Islands... now, that's not a bad life, hey?" He had let out a laugh as he jangled the change in his trouser pocket.

Sophie had had to swallow hard. "Please," she'd asked. "May I send a cable to my family?"

Stanley had taken her to the Western Union office the next morning, to send a cable to the *St Louis*. He'd insisted on driving himself, dismissing Herman, and patted the seat next to him as he slid behind the wheel.

"This is a brand-new Lincoln Continental," he told her as he stroked the leather. "Not for sale yet to the general public, but I got it hot off the assembly line. It helps to have connections."

Sophie had the urge to snap something about using such connections for good, and not just to get a fancy car, but the language defeated her, and in any case, she knew she should not be rude to her host. In the little more than twenty-four hours since she'd been at the Tylers', she'd come to dislike them both for different reasons, and yet she knew she still should be grateful to them for taking her in it at all... even if she didn't entirely understand why they had.

At the Western Union office, amidst the clacking machines, the telegraph operators with their visors and ink-stained fingers working away, she painstakingly composed a cable, assuring Margarete of her safe arrival and asking for news of her father and the fate of the ship. She also sent one to Rosa, asking her to give her address to her friends, and cable her when there was any news.

On the way home, Stanley slung his arm over the back of her seat, his fingers brushing uncomfortably against Sophie's shoulder. "I wouldn't worry too much, if I were you," he told her breezily. "They'll wash up somewhere, no doubt. I've heard talk that Cuba might still take them for the right price, or even Honduras, or the Dominican Republic. Four hundred and fifty grand they want, though, and that's not chicken feed."

Sophie didn't understand everything he'd said, but she got the gist. The *St Louis* had nowhere to go, and she could only pray that it found a friendly port soon. Because if it didn't... well, she simply couldn't bear to think about that. Some country simply *had* to take in the *St Louis*.

Margarete replied to her cable the next day; a messenger boy delivered it to the house and Sophie had to ask for it from Barbara, who, after giving her the slip of paper, insisted she read it in her presence.

"Your father on board," Sophie read in a trembling voice. "Ship heading to Miami." She'd looked up with tears in her eyes. "Miami! They'll be here soon, then."

"What a relief," Barbara replied, sounding disinterested.

Sophie turned away, unable to hide her tears.

That evening, however, Stanley had different news. "The US Coast Guard turned them away from American waters outside Miami," he told Sophie at dinner, with an apologetic grimace. "It was a political decision."

She stared at him, stricken. "What... what does that mean for the ship?"

He shrugged. "I don't know. Maybe a deal can be worked out. Otherwise... they'll have to go back to Germany."

"*Germany!*" Sophie rose from the table with a screech of her chair, her whole body trembling at the utterly terrible thought. If her father went back to Germany in his state... he'd collapse, and that was if he wasn't arrested first. And what about Rachel's Franz, who would surely be arrested the moment he stepped on shore? Perhaps they'd arrest everyone on board, simply because they could. And even if they didn't... what good could possibly await her family, her friends, back in Germany? "No, no," she whispered frantically, biting her lips. "That cannot be, that cannot be..."

"It may not happen," Stanley said quickly. He looked as if he regretted telling her what he'd learned. "Morgenthau is still working on something. And the Joint."

"The Joint?"

"The American Jewish Joint Distribution Committee. They're trying to raise money for the passengers."

Sophie was desperate to hold onto whatever hope she could, no matter how slender the thread. "So, the ship might still be able to dock?"

Stanley shrugged uncomfortably. "Maybe."

By Friday, when Sophie had been at the Tylers for almost a week, she finally learned the fate of the *St Louis*. They had been turned away a final time from America and were heading back across the ocean. Margarete had sent another cable, this one insisting that they were likely to be let into England; Stanley admitted that the rest of the world was not looking too kindly on the US's refusal to take in the refugees. Too late, their plight had captured the public's imagination. The ship was already a thousand miles into the Atlantic.

Sophie tortured herself, imagining how her father must have taken this news. He would be distraught, if not completely despairing... he might even try to kill himself again. She knew Margarete would keep such news from her, and her ignorance both infuriated and shamed her. She needed to know the truth, no matter how much it hurt.

And what about her friends? Hannah would be worried about Lotte, and Rachel about Franz. And what of Rosa? Her father might have had some sort of understanding with the Nazis, but Sophie doubted Rosa thought it would last very long. If any of them were forced back to Germany, their lives would be in danger... just as those of her family would be.

And meanwhile, what on earth was she to do, alone in Washington? She could not live with the Tylers indefinitely; Barbara's unfriendliness had made that clear, and in any case, Sophie knew she didn't want to. Stanley's jocular familiarity made her as uncomfortable as his wife's iciness. Staying at the beautiful mansion on Massachusetts Avenue for any length of time would, she feared, be untenable.

Yet what else could she do? She had no friends in the city, and no money; as a single woman, she had no way to access the funds her father had sent on to New York. Her grasp of English was little more than passable. She had spent her leisure hours practicing speaking, as well as listening to the radio or reading books, in an effort to improve her English, and a week on, she felt she had a better understanding of the language, but she still sounded, as Barbara had acidly remarked, German.

Yet why, Sophie wondered bitterly, should Americans resent her sounding German as much as being Jewish? Or was it simply that they didn't like anyone who appeared foreign or different? And she knew she was both.

If her family ended up in England, she told herself, perhaps she could join them there. She knew it wasn't necessarily as simple as that; getting a visa could be difficult, as well as time consuming and expensive. Even if she did manage it, it would be weeks, or even months, before it could be arranged, if not longer... And they might not get to England, at all. They might be forced back to Germany...

In the meantime, she knew, she needed to think of a plan.

.   .   .

Ten days after she'd arrived in Washington, and a full month after the *St Louis* had set sail from Hamburg, Sophie received another cable from her stepmother, this one the best news she could have hoped for, considering the circumstances.

We are saved. England, Belgium, Netherlands, and France taking all passengers between them. Will write when we are settled.

"No one is going back to Germany," she told Barbara and Stanley, brushing the tears from her eyes as a choked laugh of pure relief escaped her. "Isn't it wonderful?"

"I told you it would all work out," Stanley replied with a booming laugh. They were all in the living room before dinner, having drinks, as was the Tylers' custom. Barbara always had a cocktail, usually a sidecar; Stanley a whisky. Sophie tried to demur, but Stanley often insisted she have a cherry brandy, at the very least. "Didn't I?" he continued as he poured more whiskey into his glass. "Nothing to worry about at all." He made it sound as if everyone's lives had been tied up neatly with a bow, and all thanks to him.

"What will you do, my dear?" Barbara asked after a pause, her tone all too pointed. She took a sip of her cocktail, her eyes narrowed over the rim of her glass. "Will you join them in one of those countries, do you think?"

Sophie had known such a question would be coming, and she was prepared. "I will look into making arrangements to do so as soon as possible," she told her hosts. Her voice was sure, her words carefully enunciated. "When Margarete writes to tell me where they have arrived, I will travel to meet them as soon as I can."

There was a prickly, uncomfortable silence; Sophie noted that neither Barbara nor Stanley looked particularly pleased by her words. Barbara looked oddly annoyed, and Stanley seemed ill at ease, tugging at his short collar.

"Well, now," he said at last, "there's no need to get into all of that just now. It will be a while yet, before you hear any news." He turned to his wife. "Won't it, Barb?" he asked, his tone meaningful.

"Yes," Barbara replied without looking at him, "I suppose it will."

"In any case, we should celebrate," Stanley continued, his tone turning jolly. "There's a party tomorrow night at the Mcleans'—why don't we bring Sophie with us, Barbara? Show her the 'heart of the nation' in style!"

Barbara eyed her husband coolly from where she was artfully draped over a velvet chair. "I'm sure she doesn't have anything to wear," she replied.

Sophie flushed in both mortification and anger; her hostess could not have sounded less enthused by the prospect, although she didn't particularly relish the idea of going to a party, either.

"You can lend her something, can't you?" Stanley eyed Sophie up and down in a way that felt far too familiar. "You're about the same size, although she's a bit shorter. Still, neither of you have too much meat on your bones, do you? Good thing I like my girls skinny." He winked at Sophie, who quickly looked away, affecting not to notice, as her stomach roiled.

"I'm sure I can," Barbara replied after a pause.

The next afternoon, Sophie found herself sitting on a powder puff stool in Barbara's bedroom—she and Stanley, Sophie realized, did not share a room—while her hostess threw an armful of dresses across the bed, in a rainbow of colorful silks and satins. After her seeming reluctance to give Sophie an outfit for the party, Barbara had now, rather unsettlingly, entered into the spirit of the thing, taking it as her personal mission to dress Sophie appropriately.

"You've a lovely, trim little figure, haven't you?" she remarked as she riffled through the dresses on the bed. "Something nipped in at the waist should suit you nicely, and in a jewel tone, I think, with your pale skin and green eyes... cat's eyes!" She spoke in a high, fast voice that Sophie suspected was meant to pass for enthusiasm. She wasn't quite sure what to make of it all.

"I don't mind what I wear, Mrs. Tyler," she told her. "Really, I don't. I can wear my bronze taffeta—"

"Nonsense, you've worn that thing to death already, and I'm sorry to say, my dear, but it is a *trifle* dated." Barbara stood up, her hands planted on her bony hips, dark eyes narrowed. "Now, let's see. How about the emerald satin? No, too grownup. You're only nineteen, and when you have the bloom of youth, you should make the most of it." She let out a brief sigh, and for a second, her expression seemed resigned, even sad. Sophie didn't know how old her hostess was, but she guessed around the same age as Margarete, around forty.

"How long have you and Mr. Tyler been married?" she asked hesitantly, thinking it would be nice to get to know her hosts a bit more, yet still bracing herself for Barbara's acid tongue.

"Twenty years," she replied on another small sigh. "I was only twenty-one—not much more than your age—when we met. He turned my head immediately." She did not sound particularly pleased by the fact. "Here we are." Barbara shook out a dress in peach satin. "The peach will warm up your skin and complement your eyes. Try it on."

She handed the gown to Sophie, who took it with some uncertainty. Was she meant to strip down right here, in front of Barbara's all too assessing gaze?

"Oh, come now, we're both women," Barbara exclaimed on a brittle laugh. "You could be my daughter."

Sophie had never felt so far from being this woman's daughter, but she unbuttoned her plain blouse and slipped off her skirt, so she was standing in just her brassiere and slip. Quickly, she put on the dress, wriggling it over her hips and slipping her arms through the wide, ruched straps.

"I'll do up the buttons in the back," Barbara told her, and Sophie turned around, trying not to tense as the older woman's cold fingers brushed her bare spine. "I would have had a daughter the same age as you, you know," Barbara said after a moment. She was close enough that Sophie could feel her breath on the nape of her neck. "She would have been nineteen in December. That's when she was due, you see."

"What..." Sophie swallowed. "What happened?"

"She came too early. I was only about six months gone. She was a lovely little thing, though, just so tiny. Little fists curled up by her face." For a second, Barbara's fingers stilled on the buttons.

"I'm so sorry," Sophie whispered.

"Well." Barbara finished doing up the buttons and then placed her hands on Sophie's shoulders, turning her around. When Sophie dared to glance up at her, she thought her face looked as hard as ever. "That will do, I think. I've got heels to match, and I think we're about the same size. Do you have any silk stockings?"

"Yes—"

"And some jewels, of course. Do you have any?"

Sophie thought of the shard of emerald she carried with her everywhere. Even now, it was in her skirt pocket. "Yes," she replied, "from my mother."

For a second, Barbara's expression softened. "Your mother died, didn't she, when you were young?"

"Yes, of the Spanish flu. I was only a baby."

"Well." Barbara's expression tightened once more. "Pearls would go nicely with it, or diamonds, if they're not too showy." She reached for her cigarette case on her vanity table. "You'll do, I suppose," she said, like a dismissal, as she tapped a cigarette out from the case. No matter what warmth they might have just shared, Sophie knew she had been dismissed.

CHAPTER 13

The party was at Friendship House, the magnificent residence of the wealthy and well-connected McLean family, out on Wisconsin Avenue. In the car on the way over, Stanley told Sophie something about their hosts—Evalyn McLean was a socialite and heiress whose family made their money from Colorado gold. Her husband, Ned, had once owned the *Washington Post*, but had been declared insane and committed to a psychiatric hospital in Maryland six years ago.

"Oh, how sad," Sophie exclaimed, appalled, and Stanley, puffing on his cigar, smiled comfortably.

"Well, it suited Evie well enough. She'd been trying to divorce him for two years."

"Still, it was a scandal," Barbara put in. "I'd rather have an ex-husband than an insane one." She gave her husband a pointed look.

"Beggars can't be choosers, my dear," Stanley replied with a saccharine smile and Barbara's eyebrows lifted.

"I don't believe I was the beggar in our particular union," she replied with asperity, and Stanley's expression darkened. He puffed even more furiously on his cigar and said nothing. "In any case," Barbara told Sophie, turning to her, "the remarkable thing about Evalyn McLean is that she *owns* the Hope Diamond. She bought it from Cartier about thirty years ago. It's always a matter of gossip whether she chooses to wear it or not. We'll see tonight."

Sophie had never heard of the Hope Diamond, but she nodded as if she had, touching the small diamond pendant around her neck that had belonged to her mother.

The sun was just starting to set over the endless, verdant lawns as Herman turned the Lincoln Continental up Friendship House's sweeping drive. Sophie had never seen so much excess—greenhouses, gazebos, a golf course and stables were all visible as they drove toward the huge mansion of white stucco that reminded Sophie of the White House, only even more splendid.

Herman drove under a porte-cochere and a liveried footman stepped forward to open the passenger door.

"Welcome to Friendship House," he greeted them.

Stanley, getting out first, merely grunted in reply.

Sophie smiled warmly at the man as she stepped out; she'd become used to almost all servants and those in other jobs perceived as menial being black, but she resisted the way her hosts—and so many others—ignored the people who made their lives so much easier. It reminded her a bit too much of the way the Nazis treated Jews—as beneath their notice, somehow subhuman. She vowed she would never treat another human being with the same lack of dignity with which she herself had been treated.

She followed Stanley and Barbara up the marble steps to a wide veranda that was filled with guests looking to escape the stifling heat of the ballroom inside. Potted palms and masses of fresh flowers filled the space, and waiters circulated with trays of champagne. Everywhere Sophie looked, there were people—

elegant and well-dressed, the men giving brash laughs and the women looking languid.

Stanley fetched three flutes of champagne and handed one each to Barbara and Sophie before tossing his own back in a single swallow.

"Right, I'm off," he announced, and startled, Sophie watched him stride away.

"Where is he going?" she asked Barbara.

"To hobnob and toady," Barbara replied as she sipped her own champagne. "It's the only reason he comes to these things. To get ahead."

Sophie had never heard of either hobnobbing or toadying, but she thought she understood what Barbara meant. In any case, she was relieved to be rid of Stanley's company for a little while. When she'd come down the stairs this evening, he'd whistled at her before spanning her waist with his hands and lifting her right in the air.

"Don't you look *bee-yoo-to-ful*," he'd exclaimed, planting a smacking kiss on her cheek. Sophie had been mortified. Barbara, she'd seen, had watched the whole thing, eyes narrowed, lips pursed, saying nothing.

Now, Barbara gave a sigh and nodded toward the circulating crowds. "I suppose I should introduce you to people," she said, sounding less than enthused about the prospect.

"There's no need," Sophie told her quickly. She didn't think she could manage small talk in English with strangers who might remark how *German* she sounded, just as Barbara had. "I don't mind going around by myself." She intended to find a corner to hide herself away in.

Barbara cocked her head, her gaze sweeping slowly over her. "All right, then," she replied, lifting one thin shoulder in a shrug. "Suit yourself." She turned away, moving across the veranda to mingle with a group of women around her age.

Sophie breathed a sigh of relief. She didn't mind being

alone; in fact, she preferred being away from Barbara's narrowed stare, Stanley's overfamiliarity. She would explore the ballroom and enjoy being in such grandiose surroundings. She'd write to Margarete about it, she thought, once she had her family's address. She imagined her stepmother would enjoy the descriptions of the house and party, in all their excesses.

Slipping through the chatting crowds, Sophie went through one set of the five French doors that opened out onto the veranda. She found herself in a drawing room, with a door connecting to the other rooms the French doors on the veranda opened into—a card room, a music room, a billiards room, and a dining room. In each room, people were chatting, laughing, smoking, drinking, and circulating—and no one paid any attention to her.

She wandered through each room, until she came to the magnificent Georgian ballroom adjacent, with a seventeen-piece orchestra set up at one end, although no one was dancing yet.

"Were you thinking of having a whirl?"

Sophie turned around in surprise at the voice, which had been young and friendly. A man in a dinner jacket and dark trousers stood there, smiling easily. His brown hair was swept away from a high forehead and his eyes crinkled at the corners. Sophie judged him to be around thirty, maybe a bit older.

"I was... just looking," she replied, horrified to hear how thick her accent sounded. In her nervousness at being addressed, she hadn't been able to speak as clearly as she normally would have.

The man's eyes narrowed, although not in an unfriendly way. "May I ask, where are you from?" he inquired, and she blushed.

"I have recently arrived from Germany."

"Germany!" He whistled low under his breath. "Are you one of the lucky ones who made the quota, then?"

Sophie knew of the quota—the number of German refugees the United States gave visas to in any given year. For the last few years, it had been around twenty-seven thousand, although only a fraction of those had actually been issued, and some not even to Jews.

"I do not consider myself lucky," she replied rather stiffly, and the man's face collapsed briefly into apology.

"I'm sorry, that was clumsy of me. Of course you don't. When did you arrive?"

"Two weeks ago." Had it really been only two weeks since she'd been with her family, her friends? She thought of the costume ball, the four of them lifting their flutes of champagne, feeling so hopeful. What were Rosa, Hannah, and Rachel feeling now, halfway over the Atlantic, heading back to Europe on the verge of war?

"Two weeks!" the man exclaimed. "You're fresh off the boat, then."

A bitter laugh escaped Sophie; he could have no idea about the boat she was so fresh from.

The man frowned. "Sorry, did I say something...?"

"I was on the *St Louis*," she told him, doing her best to speak as clearly as she could. "Do you know it?"

"The *St Louis*... you mean the ship that was hanging around Cuba?" he exclaimed in surprise. "It's been sent back to Europe now, hasn't it?"

Her throat thickening with tears, Sophie nodded.

"How did you manage to get off it, then?" He spoke with curiosity rather than judgment, and swallowing her tears, Sophie managed to answer.

"My father had connections. I do not know exactly how it happened, but I was issued a visa."

"And your family?" he asked, his voice softening with sympathy. "Where are they?"

"They are still on the ship." For a second, Sophie pictured

Heinrich—his blond curls, his bright blue eyes, the way he'd wind his arms around her neck. *Please, Sophie, please can we...*

Swiftly, she brushed a tear from the corner of her eye.

"Oh shucks, I'm sorry, that must be rough," the man said, his voice filled with sympathy. "Look, let me get you another drink."

Sophie was too concerned with not breaking down in public to reply, but just a few moments later, the man returned with two drinks, an olive floating in each one's amber liquid. He handed one to Sophie with a smile.

"I hope you like martinis."

She took a sip and promptly choked. "Oh...!" she spluttered. So this was a cocktail.

"Sorry, they're pretty strong. Maybe this is a good time to introduce myself. I'm John Howard, naval attaché. And you are...?"

"Sophie Weiss." She paused and then added, "Jewish refugee."

"Nice to meet you, Miss Weiss. If you're not too fond of that martini, how about we get something to eat instead?"

Gratefully, Sophie nodded, and John Howard took the glass from her before leading her to the massive buffet in the dining room. There was beef and shrimp, a dozen cold salads, sandwiches and olives, different kinds of cheese and crackers, as well as petit fours and dainty little cakes. There hadn't been such a spread even in the first-class dining room of the *St Louis*.

After they'd filled their plates, John drew her to a couple of upholstered chairs in a corner of the room. Briefly, Sophie wondered at the propriety of eating alone with a man she didn't know, but as the room was full of guests, she decided it wouldn't raise too many eyebrows, and John Howard seemed kind.

"So, how are you finding America?" he asked as he forked a piece of beef and popped it in his mouth. "Or really, Washington? This town can be a pit of vipers, let me tell you."

Sophie didn't know what a pit of vipers meant, but from his tone, she suspected it was not complimentary. "I have not been here long enough to know," she replied honestly. She'd seen very little of the city besides the Tylers' house and the Western Union telegraph office.

"Where are you staying? Did the Jewish Community Center fix you up some place?"

Sophie frowned. "The Jewish...?"

"The Jewish Community Center, on 16th Street. It's where most refugees go for help. They can get you housing, a job, that sort of thing. And they have plenty of social occasions, as well. I've got a neighbor who goes there quite a bit. He's not a refugee, but he's Jewish."

"I... didn't know," Sophie replied, her mind whirling. Could she find a way to get to this Center? Perhaps they could help her find some sort of future in this city, away from the Tylers, at least until she was able to be reunited with her family. The possibility filled her with hope. Maybe she wasn't as alone as she felt she was.

"So where are you staying, if you don't mind me asking?" John asked. "Do you have friends here? You must, if you've found yourself at this 'do.'"

"I'm staying with Stanley and Barbara Tyler," Sophie told him. "My father knew Mr. Tyler from a long time ago."

Something flashed across his face—irritation, perhaps, or even disgust?

Impulsively, Sophie laid a hand on his arm for a brief second, before taking it away again. "Please," she said. "If you know something, tell me."

"About the Tylers?" He shrugged. "Stanley Tyler is a lawyer and a lobbyist, with a finger stuck in every pie he can find. Some people think he's aiming for political office one day." He paused and then added frankly, "If he's a friend of your father's, well and good, but I wouldn't call him a friend of mine."

"Nor mine," Sophie replied quickly, and John frowned.

"He hasn't... bothered you?"

She blushed and shook her head, knowing what he meant and yet too embarrassed to make any actual reply.

"Well..." He took a card out of the inside pocket of his dinner jacket. "This is my card. If you need any help... or anything like that... you can reach me on that number." He nodded to the card.

"Thank you," Sophie murmured, touched by his thoughtfulness. "That's very kind."

"Well, you've had a tough time of it. Do you know where your family will end up?"

"Not yet, but at least not Germany."

"No." He was thoughtful for a moment, gazing down at his plate of half-eaten food. "You know, there will be a war," he said finally, his tone almost gentle. "Hitler has already taken Austria and Czechoslovakia... we can't let him have much more."

Sophie looked up at him sharply. "*We?*" she repeated.

John grimaced wryly. "That's the crux of it, isn't it? Americans don't want a war. They don't want to trouble themselves over anything in Europe, but Great Britain has a different opinion on that."

Sophie thought of Barbara's comments on a similar theme. "So, America will allow Hitler to continue?" she surmised. "And do what he wants?"

John sighed. "I don't know. We can't have jackboots marching all over Europe either, not that many would agree with me right now. The US is a big enough country that they don't need to worry about the rest of the world. At least, they don't *think* they do."

"It must be very nice for them, then," Sophie replied, unable to keep the bitterness from her voice.

"And for you, too," John reminded her. "You're one of us now, aren't you?"

Except she didn't feel remotely American, Sophie thought. She might be allowed to stay in this strange and bewildering country, but her heart was somewhere over the Atlantic—with her father and stepmother and Heinrich, and with Rosa, Rachel, and Hannah.

It was after midnight before Barbara found Sophie, who had retired to a corner of the library, to tell her they were leaving. After her conversation with John Howard, Sophie had wandered through the gardens and then ended up passing the hours by reading in the library, while the guests had become progressively more raucous—and drunk.

She'd wanted to go to parties like this for years, she'd thought wryly. She'd wanted to sip champagne and dance and laugh and *live* life, and yet now that she actually could, the whole prospect soured her stomach. She didn't want any of it, not like this, anyway.

"Have you been sitting in the corner this whole time?" Barbara exclaimed. She looked tired and older than her years; her face powder had settled into the creases between her nose and mouth, and her lipstick had faded to a dull red. "What a waste of a night. And of my dress."

"I did talk to some people," Sophie replied, mentally amending that to one person. No one else had shown any interest in her, and she'd been glad of the fact. "I didn't mind. It was interesting to see all the guests."

"Your English is getting better," Barbara remarked, and turned away.

Sophie followed her out to the car, where Stanley was lounging against the fender. Even before he'd spoken, she could tell he was very drunk. His face was florid and there was a mean look in his eyes that made her tense.

"Well, weren't you the little *flirt*," he told her sourly, and Sophie jerked back in shock.

"Pardon?"

"Get in the car, Stanley," Barbara said tiredly. "Before you make even more of a fool of yourself."

Swearing under his breath, he got into the passenger seat while Barbara and Sophie slid into the back.

Sophie glanced at Herman, whose expression was completely, carefully bland as he started the car.

"I saw her," Stanley grumbled as they started down the drive. "Flirting with some no-name guy in Naval Intelligence."

"Were you?" Barbara asked, more out of curiosity than anything else, as she turned to Sophie.

"I... I spoke to a man, yes," Sophie stammered. "He asked about the *St Louis*. He was very kind."

"Drinking martinis and looking *very* pally," Stanley continued, and Sophie flushed.

"Were you... spying on me?" she asked, and Barbara let out a hoot of jaded laughter.

"She's told you now, Stan!" she remarked with weary humor, and no one said anything further until they were back at the house on Massachusetts Avenue.

All Sophie wanted to do was escape up to her bedroom. This evening had made her realize, more than ever, that she needed to leave the Tylers' house. Tomorrow, she vowed, she would go to this Jewish Community Center and ask for their help. She would find a way out of here, no matter what it took.

"Thank you for this evening," she told Barbara stiffly. Stanley had gone to the drinks table in the living room, but Sophie could feel him watching her. "I will return the gown in the morning."

Barbara waved her away. "Keep it. The color doesn't suit me, anyway."

Sophie nodded her thanks and then hurried up the stairs, away from Stanley's accusing gaze. She heard the ice rattle in his glass as she made it to the landing.

Alone in her room, she breathed a sigh of relief and then, with trembling hands, began to undo the buttons down her back. It wasn't easy, and she only managed half before she wriggled out of the dress and hung it over a chair, glad to be out of it, and finished with the whole evening.

She was just about to take off her slip and slip into her nightgown when a heavy thud of a knock sounded at the door. Sophie stiffened, holding her nightgown to her chest.

"Barbara?" she called hesitantly. "I am going to bed. I'll return the dress in the morning if you want it—"

"It's not Barbara," Stanley slurred, and then pushed open the door.

CHAPTER 14

Sophie stood completely still, frozen in shock, as Stanley lumbered into her room, reminding her of a shambling—and dangerous—bear. He held his cognac glass aloft and a few amber drops spilled onto the pristine cream carpet, his eyes narrowed to dark slits.

"Well, aren't you looking as pretty as a peach," he remarked as he kicked the door shut behind him. More cognac sloshed from his glass.

Sophie stared at him, her mind a terrified blank, as he started walking toward her. She felt more frightened now than she had when the crewman on the *St Louis* had called Rosa a dirty little Jew. More frightened, even, than when she'd seen her father catapult himself off the deck of the ship.

She opened her mouth, yet no words came out, and Stanley was coming closer.

"Please..." she finally managed. "*Bitte...*"

"Oh, you're going to beg me?" Stanley replied with a laugh as he carelessly tossed his glass onto a dresser. "I like that. And in German, too. I didn't realize you knew how to talk dirty."

"*Nein...* no," Sophie tried again. "Please, Mr. Tyler, leave me alone."

"Why should I?" he asked, his tone turning almost lazy. "You've been driving me crazy for two weeks now, tossing your pretty little head, giving me those pretty-please, wide-eyed looks, and all the while butter wouldn't melt in your mouth? I don't think so." He reached out one thick arm and wrapped it around her waist, pulling her to him.

Sophie's chest collided with his before her brain kicked into gear and she tried her hardest to pull away, squirming against him, kicking his shins.

"Ooh, feisty," he slurred, and she thought she might be sick.

"*Nein... nein,*" she half-sobbed as he landed a slobbery kiss on her cheek. She twisted away from him, but he took her jaw in his hand and wrenched her head back, so she was forced to face him, his heavy body pressed against hers.

"Now, we don't need to make this difficult," he growled, the cognac-fueled fumes of his hot breath making her dizzy. "I can be nice to you, Sophie. Real nice, if you let me."

"No," she wept, too pinned by his arms to struggle more than a little. "No, *please.* I don't want this. Please. *Bitte...*"

"Come on, now..." He ground his body into hers as his mouth found hers, forcing her lips apart.

Futilely, Sophie tried to kick against him, wriggling in his tight embrace, unable to move much more than a little.

Then, suddenly and with no warning, his arms slackened and with a choking gasp, Sophie stumbled away, falling to her knees. She wrapped her arms around herself, blinking up to see Stanley sitting slumped on the carpet, one hand to his head.

Barbara was standing over him, the empty glass of cognac in her hand.

"Aw, Barbara, we were just having a little fun," he complained, rubbing his head.

She must have hit him with the glass, Sophie realized. Had

she heard her screaming? Had she suspected something like this might happen? Barbara didn't look horrified or even surprised; if anything, she seemed wearily annoyed.

"It didn't look like fun to me," she remarked coolly. "The last thing you need right now, Stanley, is a rape charge."

"You think the police would believe some German-speaking little Jew who's fresh off the boat?" Stanley sneered.

Sophie recoiled, horrified by his careless words almost as much as the attack on her person. This man was meant to be a friend of her father's. How could he speak about her in such a way?

Barbara stared dispassionately at her husband for a moment. "Go to bed," she said finally, her voice flat, and, to Sophie's surprise, Stanley lumbered up from the floor, casting her a malevolent look, before he slouched out of the room, slamming the door behind him.

A shudder escaped Sophie as she hugged her arms around herself. The night was as sultry as any other recently, but she felt icy cold inside.

"Put some clothes on," Barbara said in the same tone she'd told her husband to go to bed.

Gulping, Sophie slipped on her nightgown and then reached for her dressing gown from the hook on the door.

"Th-thank you," she managed as she knotted the sash tightly. "For saving me."

"I was saving him as much as you," Barbara returned. "I meant what I said. The last thing he needs right now is a rape charge. He wants to hold office one day."

Sophie simply stared, having no idea what to say to that.

Barbara sighed. "I'm sorry for you, because I know you weren't asking for it. But you'll have to leave. In the morning."

Sophie nodded, even though the prospect filled her with dread. She wanted to leave, yes, but to be tossed out with nowhere to go was another matter entirely. Still, she knew

Barbara was right. She could not, and would not, stay under this roof another night. "Yes," she told her. "I will."

"The only reason we took you in was because you were young and pretty," Barbara told her wearily. "Oh, I know Stanley liked to say how he was doing his bit, all for your father, blah, blah, *blah,* but it wasn't any of that. He'd seen a photograph of you when you were small, that your father had shown him. *'Head full of blond curls, face like a china doll'* was what he said when he got that cable. And he knew you had to be no more than twenty. *That's* why, in case you were wondering, which I suspect you were."

Sophie stared at her speechlessly, too shaken by the night's events to formulate a reply.

Barbara turned to the door. "Be gone by breakfast," she said, and then she opened the door and slipped out into the corridor.

Alone again, Sophie sank onto her bed, pressing her hands to her face. She felt too shocked and horrified for tears, and more alone than she'd ever felt before. She knew not one soul in this entire country who could help her; as kindly as John Howard had been, she could hardly ask him to bail her out after a single evening's acquaintance! Her only hope, she realized dully, was the Jewish Community Center... and all she knew was that it was on 16th Street, and she didn't even know where that was. Somehow, she told herself, she'd figure it out. She'd find a way. Because, really, what other choice did she have?

The next morning, Sophie was up just a little after dawn, the day already sticky and hot. She'd barely slept last night, even with the door locked and a chair put under the handle, just in case. Every creak or sigh of wind had her startling awake, her heart racing, straining to hear. When she finally lay down again, trying to sleep, her mind would race with fears of all that lay ahead, so utterly unknown.

Now, however, in the early-morning light, she felt more resolved. She washed and dressed before packing her single suitcase; she left the peach silk evening gown hanging in the wardrobe. She never wanted to wear or even see it again. She glanced once around the opulent room and then, taking a deep breath, unlocked the door and tiptoed downstairs as quietly as she could.

The house was quiet; Sophie doubted even Esther or Herman were stirring yet. It was barely past six o'clock. She reached for the handle of the front door only to be stopped by a woman's voice.

"Now, honey, there's no need to creep out of here like a burglar. I got you some breakfast in the kitchen. You come fill your belly before you leave." Esther stood in the foyer, her arms folded over her ample bosom, her smile kindly.

"I..." Sophie swallowed. "Thank you," she whispered, and she followed Esther into the kitchen.

Unlike the rest of the house, in all its opulence, the kitchen was a homely room that was clearly Esther's domain. She set a bowl of porridge swimming with honey and a cup of coffee down on the table and nodded to Sophie to take a seat.

"You get that in you."

"Thank you," Sophie murmured. She wrapped her hands around the mug of coffee before she looked up at Esther. "Do you... do you know what happened?"

"Honey, I know everything that happens in this place," Esther said her, tone turning grim. "I'm sorry to say it, but Lord knows it was only a matter of time before he went for you." She shook her head, her mouth tightening.

Sophie gulped and nodded. "I don't know what to do."

"You got a place to go?"

"No, but I hope the Jewish Community Center might help me. Do you know where 16th Street is?"

Esther nodded. "It's not that far from here. Maybe half a mile."

Sophie took a steadying sip of her coffee. She could manage that.

"If they ain't got something for you," Esther continued, "then you come back here, all right? My cousin Lorna's got a little boarding house on I Street. She might have some space for you, if I ask her."

"Thank you," Sophie replied, her voice catching. The older woman's kindness meant so much to her, especially now. "Thank you, Esther."

"It's nothing, honey. The least I can do."

A sudden thought occurred to Sophie, and she let out a little gasp. "My family... they will try to write to me here, with their new address—"

"I can hold any letters for you," Esther assured her. "I'll pass them on, wherever you end up. Don't you worry your head about that."

Sophie sat back with a sigh of relief. "Thank you," she said again, and Esther smiled.

"You eat up that porridge, now. You need a good meal on your bones."

An hour later, with her belly full and the sun already starting to blaze down, Sophie followed Esther's directions down Massachusetts Avenue to the massive and magnificent Dupont Circle, already starting to fill with traffic, even though it wasn't yet past eight in the morning.

Her suitcase banged against her knees as she walked round the circle, trying to find a place to cross northwest to P Street. Cars honked and buses rumbled as she looked futilely for a break in the traffic. Finally, she darted across, jumping in fright when a driver blared his horn and shouted at her to get out of the way. Safe on the opposite sidewalk, she started down P Street. Her dress was sticking to her back and her heart was thundering in her chest.

It was the first time she'd actually been out in the city by herself; the only other times she'd left the Tylers' house had been in Stanley's Lincoln Continental. Now, Sophie was conscious of the jostle of humanity as people headed to work, the blaze of the sun, the occasional dark look she received for being a young woman alone, carrying a suitcase. They couldn't possibly suspect she was German and Jewish... could they?

Twenty minutes later, she finally came to 16th Street and Q, the address of the Jewish Community Center, according to Esther. The building was stately and impressive, as so many buildings in this city seemed to be, with a wide set of steps leading up to a set of three wooden doors, set apart by Corinthian pillars. Above, the words 'Jewish Community Center' were engraved into the stone. Sophie was both heartened and intimidated by all the grandeur—the Center clearly had the means to support Jewish refugees... but would they help her?

There was only one way to find out.

She headed up the steps and opened the door to the Center, which led into a large foyer of black and white checkered marble and long, high windows.

A woman with dark hair and eyes and a brisk, friendly manner at a desk looked up with a smile. "You're looking a little lost," she remarked, cheerfully enough. "May I help you?"

"I..." Sophie found she was too overcome to speak. Her English had abandoned her; *everything* had abandoned her. She simply blinked at the woman, speechless and staring.

To her grateful surprise, the woman did not seem fazed by her response. "Why don't you sit down?" she suggested in a gentler tone. "Would you like a glass of water? It's going to be a scorcher today."

Wordlessly, Sophie nodded. She found herself guided to a chair, and the woman took the suitcase from her limp fingers and set it to one side. She returned a moment later with a glass of water, which Sophie drank thirstily.

"Thank you," she murmured, embarrassed by her earlier display. "I am very grateful."

"Now, how can we help you?" the woman asked. She looked to be in her thirties, with a trim figure and a practical, pragmatic attitude.

"I have arrived in this country recently," Sophie explained haltingly. "My family was on the St Louis... the ship that went to Cuba. My father arranged for me to come here, but it is no longer... I can't..." She paused, swallowing, and started again. "I have nowhere to go. And I need work."

The woman nodded slowly, seeming unsurprised by such news. "We can help with housing and employment," she said, "but I'm afraid there is a shortage of the first at the moment. You'd have to go on a waiting list for housing for at least a few weeks—do you have anywhere to stay in the meantime?"

Sophie thought of Esther's offer. "Maybe..."

"All right, then. We'll put you on the list, and as for work... your English is decent, which is good. Can you type?"

Sophie bit her lip. "I can learn."

The woman raised her eyebrows, nodding her acceptance. "Dictation, stenography, anything like that?"

Misery filled Sophie as she shook her head. She'd finished her education at sixteen and had no real practical skills. "I can learn," she said again, a bit desperately.

The woman nodded slowly. "All right, then, it's a start. Plenty come here without any skills at all, so don't you worry."

"You're very kind," Sophie whispered.

"You've had a tough time, haven't you?" the woman observed in sympathy. "So many have. We'll do our best to help you, I promise." She paused before adding in apology, "Not everyone wants to hire German Jews, I'm afraid. They don't always like foreigners, although plenty of the highfalutin type don't mind rubbing shoulders with Nazis!" She grimaced. "But never mind that. I'm sure we'll be able to find you something."

"I was going to study languages at university," Sophie ventured. "I can speak French and a bit of Spanish, as well as English, and German, of course."

"Can you?" The woman brightened. "That's something, then. I'll make sure to put it on your form. Let me take down your details and then we'll see what we can find."

Several hours later, having filled out a dozen different forms and had a lunch of soup and bread in the Center's café, Sophie was walking under the hot sun back to Massachusetts Avenue. The woman who had helped her, Sadie Danvers, had been kind and welcoming, and Sophie had felt almost as if she'd made a friend. Like her, Sadie was Jewish, but she'd lived her whole life in the United States; she'd never even been to Europe.

"My great-grandparents came from Poland about eighty years ago," she'd told Sophie with a smile. "But we're all Americans now."

Sophie could only smile politely at that. She didn't feel at all American, and she doubted she ever would... especially if she found a way to reunite with her family.

Sadie had told her to check in with the Center every morning for work. She hoped to have something for Sophie within a week or two, which was encouraging but also felt like an eternity. How, Sophie wondered, was she going to live? Eat? She had no money, and she didn't even know how to sell the jewels still hidden in the lining of her coat.

Instinctively, Sophie reached into her pocket for the shard of emerald, her fingers closing around it, drawing comfort from its shape. Where was the *St Louis*, she wondered. When would it reach Europe? Another week, at least, and then it would be several weeks before she received any letters, any news of her family and friends' whereabouts, and she could potentially arrange her own voyage. It felt like a long time—a very long time indeed.

Back at the Tylers' house, Sophie crept around to the back door, trying to be as unobtrusive as possible. She rapped once, softly, breathing a sigh of relief when Esther opened it almost immediately.

"Ah, honey. How did you find it?"

Briefly, Sophie told her what she'd discovered. "Would I be able to stay with your cousin, Esther?" she asked hesitantly. "I'm sorry to have to ask. Perhaps I could do some work there... cleaning or cooking? I don't want to be any trouble."

"You won't be any trouble," Esther assured her. "I can't take you over until this evening, though, because I've got to work. You all right to sit and wait in this kitchen? I know it's hot."

"Of course," Sophie replied. Barbara and Stanley were both out, and in any case, she didn't think she'd run into either of them in the kitchen. "But please let me help you."

Esther looked scandalized. "Honey, that's not how it's done here," she told her, shaking her head, and Sophie stared at her, confused.

"What do you mean?"

"You're a white woman, and I'm not," Esther stated bluntly. "I can't have you helping me in the kitchen or anywhere else."

"But no one will be looking," Sophie pointed out. "Please... I want to be busy."

Esther frowned, but then, after a long moment, she gave a reluctant nod. "All right, then. But Lord help us if someone sees."

. . .

Sophie spent the next few hours happily occupied in the kitchen, peeling potatoes, washing dishes, and generally making herself useful. She hadn't spent all that much time in a kitchen before, since they'd had a maid until last year, but she didn't mind getting her hands dirty, or elbow-deep in soap suds. It felt good to keep her body occupied, because then her mind was somewhat distracted as well, and she didn't have to dwell on last night's attack or the utter uncertainty of her future, both of which had the power to freeze the breath in her lungs, and her stomach to cramp with anxiety.

Part of her longed to be back on the *St Louis* with her friends and family, even though she knew their future was even more uncertain than hers. Was she selfish, to think that way? To feel jealous, that they were at least together, while she was here, all alone? Except, of course, they weren't together. Everyone would be split apart, just as the emerald was. England, Belgium, the Netherlands, France. Where would they all end up? And if war came to Europe, as John Howard had said it surely would...

But no, she couldn't let herself think that way, because otherwise she would become paralyzed with fear, when there was nothing—absolutely nothing—she could do about any of it. The *St Louis* would reach Europe soon, Sophie told herself. And then her parents and friends would write, and she would be able to write them back.

Maybe then she wouldn't feel so alone.

CHAPTER 15

JULY 1939—WASHINGTON DC

Sophie had been at the boarding house on I Street for three weeks before the Jewish Community Center had a job for her, and she could finally make some of her own money. Although the mistress of the boarding house, Francine Bryson, had been welcoming enough, Sophie was all too aware that she was there on charity.

As she'd promised, Esther had taken her after she'd finished her day's work. They'd had to take the bus, since Herman wasn't allowed to use the car for personal reasons, and Sophie had been shocked when Esther had sat at the back, in the 'colored' section, while Sophie had taken a seat up front. She'd followed Esther to the back as a matter of habit, only to have the housekeeper turn around and hiss, "Not back here, child! You white folks sit up front."

It seemed entirely unfair and wrong for such a delineation to be made, and it had reminded Sophie painfully of being back in Berlin, when it was the Jews who were forbidden from entering certain shops or buildings; the Jews who had to sit on only certain park benches marked with a yellow stripe; the Jews who were treated as second-class citizens, or not even that—just as black people seemed to be here.

When they'd got off the bus, she'd asked Esther about it.

Esther had let out a huff of tired laughter. "Lord, child, that's just the way it is. One rule for white folks, another for colored. It's never going to change." She'd sounded both practical and resigned, shrugging the question aside as if it was of little importance.

"But it's not fair," Sophie had stated quietly.

Esther had given her a startled glance. "No, but what's it matter to you? You've got enough to be worrying about with your own folk, I should think."

"Yes..." Although surely one injustice begot another. How would the Americans ever bestir themselves to care about how the Jews all the way over in Germany were treated, when they were creating similarly unjust laws right here at home? It was a terribly dispiriting prospect. If a war did come, Sophie suspected America needed to be in it. But maybe, she told herself, it wouldn't come to that...

The boarding house on I Street was a narrow townhouse near George Washington University, three stories, with a porch out front and a scrappy yard of grass and a few pecan trees in the back. Sophie could smell the Potomac River on the humid breeze, a not altogether pleasant aroma. Esther had taken Sophie round to the back, where a comfortably round woman in her forties was stirring an enormous pot of beans at the stove.

"Lord, Esther, what are you doing coming round here with no warning?" she had exclaimed, sounding pleased to see her cousin, despite her scolding words. "And who's this little thing?"

Esther had introduced Sophie and explained the situation. "You got a place for her, Lorna? Just for a little while."

Lorna had clucked her tongue, hands planted on her ample hips as she shook her head back and forth. "What are these people like? Yes, I can find a place for her up with Mattie in the attic, especially if she does a bit of work round here to pay for her keep. I don't think Miss Bryson will say no, but I'll have to ask."

"All right, then." With a groan of satisfaction, Esther had lowered herself into a kitchen chair while Lorna went to check with the mistress of the house. A few minutes later, Sophie had been summoned to the front room—a small, rather drab room with an old sofa, a couple of armchairs, a record player and a large Silvertone radio. A tiny scrap of a woman, her white hair piled on top of her head, had been perched in one of the armchairs. She had reminded Sophie of a little, bright-eyed bird.

"Miss Bryson," she had said in greeting, and bobbed something of a curtsey. "I'm very pleased to meet you."

"What manners," Miss Bryson had replied, looking pleased. "And your English is surprisingly good. Did you really just come from Germany, child?"

Sophie had nodded. "Yes, Miss. A few weeks ago."

"Lord! You poor thing." She had shaken her head and clucked her tongue, just as Lorna had. "Well, I'm all for Christian charity, of course," she had stated after a moment. "You can have a room in the attic and three meals a day if you help Lorna in the kitchen and with the housework. For a few weeks," she had qualified. "I suppose you'll find better accommodation soon enough, with your own people?"

"Yes, Miss." Sophie had certainly hoped she would. As relieved as she was to be out of the Tylers' house, she knew she needed a situation that was more stable... or to find a way to join her parents back in Europe.

Her room in the attic was tiny and airless, shared with Lorna's daughter, Mattie, a pretty twenty-one-year-old with plenty of fire and sass—far more than Sophie had. Although she currently worked as a housemaid in one of the great houses on Massachusetts Avenue, just like the Tylers', she'd taken a secretarial course and had aspirations of obtaining an office job. Her attitude, Sophie found, was the opposite of Esther's.

"Things are going to change!" she had declared. "It's been almost eighty years since we got our freedom, and we have *rights*." Her dark eyes had sparked with fire. "There isn't a reason in the world why I can't work in an office downtown, save for the color of my skin."

When they'd spoken about how things were back in Germany, Mattie had been incredulous. "You mean, they don't let you in stores and places even though you're *white*?"

Sophie had let out a small, sad laugh. "In Germany, it isn't the color of your skin that matters," she had told Mattie. "It's what they think is the color of your blood. Jews' blood is tainted, or so they say."

Mattie had shaken her head, condemning yet still incredulous. "Lord," she'd exclaimed, "what's wrong with this world?"

Sophie had no good answer to that question.

Sophie soon settled into a routine of cleaning and cooking, scrubbing and sweeping, sleeping every night on the thin mattress in little more than her slip, for the Southern summer had arrived, good and proper, and it was, Lorna said, "as hot as Hades, and as wet as a river."

Sophie had never known anything like it—the stickiness made her want to wash every morning and night; she would fetch a basin of water from the pump in the yard and try to cool herself down with a damp cloth. And as the days and then the weeks passed, she waited for news from her family and friends, as well as the possibility of a job.

She'd learned in late June that all the refugees from the *St Louis* had safely arrived in Great Britain, Belgium, the Netherlands, or France, although where her loved ones had ended up, she still didn't know. It would take weeks for a letter to arrive, and there had been no further cables.

Sophie had taken the habit of visiting the Jewish Community Center every morning to see if anything had come up; even if nothing had, she enjoyed being in the dim, cool rooms, hearing German spoken occasionally, and being able to talk to like-minded people. Many of the Jews in Washington, and not just refugees, congregated there—there were dances on the roof terrace, ice cream socials, and even sporting events. Only that year, the Center had built a new wing with handball courts.

Sophie hadn't had the time or even the inclination to take advantage of much of it at all, but she'd met a few friendly people, which made her hopeful that she might meet more in time—if she stayed in America. Part of her still longed to return to her family, even as the news from Europe grew more dire every day. Violent rallies were being held in the Polish city of Danzig, demanding "liberation". The Nazis and Soviets were said to be considering a non-aggression pact. Germany was rearming at a terrifying rate, and even the American newspapers were declaring that "war in Europe was imminent." All of it filled Sophie with a deep and abiding terror, and yet she forced herself to listen to *Elmer Davis and the News* each evening, five minutes before eight o'clock, and the nightly talent show that all the tenants in the house gathered round for. You could even vote for the winner by telephone, although the boarding house didn't have one.

In mid-July, Sophie finally had some good news.

"Sophie!" Sadie rose from her desk with a smile when Sophie slipped through the front door with a sigh of relief; it was much cooler inside the Center. "I have good news for you today."

"You do?" Her heart lifted, although she remained cautious. Lorna's daughter, Mattie, had interviewed for three secretary jobs, only to be turned away when they'd discovered she wasn't white. Sophie worried the same thing might happen to her, for being Jewish. Sadie had practically warned her that might happen, especially when a potential employer heard her German accent.

"A position has come up, right here at the Center," Sadie told her with a smile. "As you can imagine, we're getting more and more refugees, and many of them speak little English. We need a German speaker to take down their information and help communicate what we can offer. Do you think you'd be interested?" She grimaced a little. "I have to tell you, the pay is fairly dire, but you'd get your lunch, and the company is the best!" She gave her a cheeky smile, which had Sophie laughing. She'd appreciated Sadie's cheerful good humor these last few weeks; even when there hadn't been a job available, she'd kept Sophie's spirits up with her briskly positive attitude. "Twenty dollars a week," Sadie continued, "with Saturdays off and every other Sunday. What do you think?"

"Yes, please," Sophie replied immediately. She wasn't really sure how far twenty dollars a week would go, but she was desperate to earn her own money. She hadn't yet had to resort to selling one of the jewels still tucked in the lining of her coat, and she wasn't sure she'd even know how to go about it, but she relished the idea of a regular paycheck.

"Wonderful," Sadie told her. "We'll get to work together! You'll have your own desk in the office—it's not much, but it does the job." She showed Sophie her own little workstation, complete with battered desk and a couple of chairs, tucked in the corner by some metal filing cabinets. Sophie was thrilled with it all.

She learned that evening, however, that her change in circumstances meant she could no longer share the attic with

Mattie. She wasn't a charitable cause any longer, but a proper tenant with a living wage. Miss Bryson told her she should move downstairs to a room not much bigger than the one she'd been sharing, and pay ten dollars a week for it, plus breakfast and dinner five days a week. Sophie thought she would have rather stayed in the attic with Mattie, but she moved down accordingly, even though her new room would take half of her wages.

As she put away her few clothes in the bureau, she tried to suppress the pang of loneliness she felt; such feelings would sweep over her suddenly, taking her by surprise with their force. As grateful as she was for the strides she'd made since coming to America, at certain times like this, when she saw how few belongings she had, and thought about how few people she knew, she realized how dreadfully alone she still felt. She'd made friends, yes—Sadie and Mattie, for a start—but the whole world she inhabited, that *they* did, still felt altogether unfamiliar and strange.

A tap on her door made her turn. Samantha Reeves, the other female tenant, stood on the threshold, polite but unsmiling, as ever. There were four other tenants at Miss Bryson's house, two men and two women, and they tended to keep to themselves, working all day in various jobs, and spending their evenings listening to the radio. Occasionally, someone might go out on the weekend, but all in all, Miss Bryson ran a quiet and respectable house. Still, perhaps now that she was truly one of them, Sophie thought, she'd get to know them a bit better.

"Miss Weiss?" Samantha said from the doorway, her tone no-nonsense. "You have a visitor."

A visitor? Sophie had no idea who it could be. "Thank you, Miss Reeves," she replied, and hurried downstairs.

No one was in the front room, where visitors usually waited, and so Sophie went back to the kitchen.

Esther sat at the table, drinking lemonade with Lorna, but she hefted herself up as soon as Sophie came in. "Miss Sophie! I thought I'd better come see you as soon I could, once I saw these." From the pocket of her dress, she withdrew two thin envelopes, in blue airmail paper.

"*Letters!*" Sophie exclaimed. "Oh, Esther, thank you." She took them, clutching them to her chest, filled with both hope and trepidation at the thought of what they might contain. As much as she longed to tear open the envelopes and read the letters right away, she knew it was only polite to chat with Esther for a little while, at least. The trip from Massachusetts Avenue to I Street was long and hot on the bus; Esther had been very kind to make it on her behalf. "How have you been?" she asked, only to have Esther let out a roar of laughter.

"Now aren't you all politeness! Never mind me, child, you go read those letters in private. I know you want to. Don't worry, I'll keep."

"Thank you," Sophie murmured, and she hurried back up to her room.

Sitting on the edge of her bed, the letters in her hand, she had a moment's tremor of true fear. She almost didn't want to open them, in case they contained bad news. What if her father had had a relapse, or worse? What if her family was in a dangerous situation? And what about the others—were they from Rosa or Rachel? Hannah? How were they and their families? Where had they all ended up? Were they safe? Were they well?

Sophie knew there was only one way to find out.

Carefully, she slit the first envelope and unfolded the tissue-thin paper, recognizing Margarete's elegant cursive right away.

Dear Sophie,

What a long and strange journey it has been, but here we are at last. We arrived in Antwerp nearly a week ago, with some relief, as the conditions on the St Louis had deteriorated, with a dearth of fresh food and water. By the end of our voyage, we were all eating soup and bread and not much more.

Unfortunately, things were not much better in Belgium. I had hoped in another country, away from Germany, we might be treated decently, but we were hustled out of Antwerp and put on a train with wooden seats and no food or water. The doors were locked, as well, as if we were prisoners, and perhaps we were, for there was a gang of Nazi youths handing out flyers to us printed with the words, "We want to help the Jews, too, we'll give them a rope and a nail." What a welcome!!

Thankfully, your father did not see any of it, and, to its credit, the government got rid of the thugs fairly quickly. Still, it was all quite unsettling, although I suppose nothing more than we Jews should expect these days.

We are now staying in a boarding house in Brussels, a shabby little place but adequate enough, although apparently it is only meant to be temporary. Where we will end up, I have no idea—it is clear that not all of Belgian society is in agreement about welcoming Jews to their small country...!

Our great hope is that we will join you in America. We wait for our quota number to come up, and pray it won't be too long, as the news from Germany grows worse every day. Your father is so glad you are safe in America, Sophie, as am I. Our sacrifice was well worth it. Heinrich misses you, as you can well imagine, and your father sends his love. You may write to us at this address, although I do not know how long we will be allowed to stay here.

All my love, Margarete

Sophie looked up from the letter, staring blindly out the window at a pecan tree, its green, leafy branches brushing her window. It all sounded so much worse than she'd hoped, or even feared, and she suspected Margarete was sparing her the worst of it. How was her father coping with such change, such *trauma*? Her stepmother had not said, and Sophie knew that had to be intentional, which meant he *wasn't* coping with it, maybe not at all.

And Heinrich... poor, dear Heinrich, so little and probably so confused, cooped up in some shabby boarding house in a strange city. He'd become used to being coddled, having his way, and while Sophie couldn't regret spoiling her baby brother, she wondered how he would manage under such difficult conditions, without her there to distract and cheer him up, chivvy him along.

Sighing, she brushed impatiently at her eyes, feeling she didn't have a right to her tears. *She* was safe, she reminded herself fiercely. She had nothing to complain about, not like the rest of her family and friends. It felt like the most treacherous betrayal of not just them, but of herself. Once again, and more bitterly than ever, she wondered how she could have gone in such a fashion. Fled like a criminal, left everyone she'd ever loved, and for what? This half-life she was living, in a foreign country, where she knew no one?

Swallowing the last of her tears, she slit the next envelope. This letter was from Rosa.

Dear Sophie,

Well, I told you I'd write once I received your address, although I'm not sure how much there is to say. The voyage back to Europe was pretty dire—none of the jolly mood going over! I saw that awful member of crew, and you'll never guess

*what he did when he saw me—drew his finger across his throat!
God help us all.*

*Everyone was terribly fearful—there were, I regret to say,
two more suicides. When we heard that we wouldn't be going
to Germany, everyone was so relieved, but then, of course, we
didn't know where we were going. A week ago, my family and
I arrived in England. Hannah and Lotte have gone to France,
Rachel and Franz to the Netherlands. Isn't it strange, how
we've all been cast to the four winds? It's made me more determined than ever that we meet again, once the world is safe.*

*Everyone in England seems to talk of war as if it is an
inevitability. I pray it isn't. My father seems to think his
connections will get us to America, but I'm not sure anyone
here is impressed by the people he knows. We're staying in a
hostel in London, a wretched little place, but at least we're
allowed in the shops, and no one asks for our papers.*

*I hope you've landed on your feet and are too busy dancing
the Lindy Hop with some handsome American to read this!
I've kept my emerald safe—I'm thinking of making it into a
necklace, so it never leaves me.*

As ever, Rosa

Sophie let out a shaky laugh as she reread the letter. It
sounded so much like Rosa, she could almost imagine her friend
was right here in the room with her, her lips twisting wryly, her
dark eyebrows lifting. If only she was! Sophie missed her, as
well as her family, with a desperation that felt like a physical
pain in her stomach, an emptiness and a hunger.

At least she could finally write Rosa and her family, she told
herself. And hopefully, Rachel and Hannah would write soon,
with their own news. But, Sophie acknowledged, it was
painfully clear that there was no way she would be able to travel
to Belgium to be with her family. She realized she'd known that

all along, even if she hadn't wanted to acknowledge it. It had been glaringly obvious, with all the reports in the news. She just hoped and prayed her father's quota number would come up, and her family would be able to join her here in Washington DC... or wherever they all ended up, when they were together again, at last.

CHAPTER 16

APRIL 1940—WASHINGTON DC

It had been nine months since Sophie had started working at the Jewish Community Center, and nearly eight since war had been declared in Europe.

That Sunday morning, they'd all sat around the Silvertone, somberly listening to the news. The ultimatum that Great Britain had given Germany to remove troops from Poland had been on everyone's lips for days, although many still shrugged it off as not America's concern. To many Americans, the events were too far away to care about, across an entire ocean, easy enough to dismiss, or even forget.

And yet they'd all been affected by hearing Neville Chamberlain's, the British prime minister's, grave voice crackling on the radio. Sophie had listened with a sense of unreality that crept over her like a numbing fog.

"This morning, the British ambassador in Berlin handed the German government a final note, stating that unless we heard from them by eleven o'clock that they were prepared at once to withdraw their troops from Poland, a state of war would exist between us. I have to tell you now that no such undertaking has been received, and that, consequently, this country is at war with Germany."

A stunned silence among their little group had followed this announcement; Sophie didn't think anyone had truly believed it had come to this, and yet it had. It *had*. What would it mean for her family? Her friends?

"War..." Miss Bryson had murmured faintly, her fingers pressed to her lips. "*Again...*"

Samantha had shaken her head slowly, her lips tightening, and Jack Wells had scowled, muttering something about it not being their business, while William Fawber had grimaced and struck up a cigarette even though he wasn't meant to smoke indoors. Sophie could barely listen to the rest of the speech. She had felt dizzy and numb, as well as strangely, unsettlingly relieved; at least now, at last, someone was fighting Hitler's evil. Someone was standing up and saying no more, *no more*. Surely that was a good thing, even if it was terribly frightening, as well? She had listened to the end of his speech with something almost like hope:

"Now, may God bless you all and may He defend the right. For it is evil things that we shall be fighting against—brute force, bad faith, injustice, oppression and persecution. And against them I am certain that the right will prevail."

The right will prevail. How she had longed to hold onto that hope! Perhaps it would mean she'd see her family sooner; surely the United States would allow more refugees into the country, now that Germany was at war with Great Britain and France, and the situation was clearly so very desperate? Maybe her father's number would finally come up.

Her work at the Jewish Community Center had certainly seemed busier over the last few months, as floods of Jewish refugees came through, looking for work and housing, and mostly hope, after so many dark and desperate years, trying simply to survive.

Even as their stories tore at her heart, Sophie loved being able to help the people who had struggled and feared just as she had, and still did. She held the hands of weeping mothers and fathers and let babies crawl on her lap and tug on her ears; she hugged children who looked shell-shocked and dazed, and she pressed cups of tea into the hands of the elderly, who seemed childlike in their confusion, their utter incredulity at what had happened to them, how they'd arrived at this point.

The refugees came from all over Europe, including Belgium, but when she'd had another letter from Margarete in October, there was still no word on when her family might be able to emigrate; the quota number remained elusive, ever beyond their reach. Still, Sophie held onto hope. Surely, *surely* it was only a matter of time... so many others had been able to make the journey. Why not her family?

Sometimes hope felt like the only thing she had, for while her life in Washington had certainly improved, with money in her pocket and a safe place to stay, she still felt, at times, unbearably lonely. She still felt she was perceived as a foreigner by most, even though her English had improved greatly, and she was now able to speak fluently, with only a trace of an accent.

She'd made a few friends at the Center, especially Sadie, who always invited her to the various social events held there, cheerfully jollying her along when Sophie, out of instinct, held back. She had gone to an ice cream social and a dance on the roof terrace, keeping to the edges of both, too shy to make conversation with strangers, and also feeling she didn't deserve to dig into a banana split or whirl about a dance floor, not when her father, Margarete and Heinrich had to share a small, squalid apartment with two other families, or Rosa wrote about the blackouts in England, and the food rationing that was sure to be introduced. For those she loved, the future loomed, terrifyingly uncertain.

Although, at times, during that fall and winter, oddly it had felt as if nothing was really happening; journalists in Great Britain had dubbed it "the phoney war," as the British Army took no land operations and the day-to-day activities of everyone remained unchanged.

At least, almost everyone.

In the spring, Rosa had written to her to explain how her family's circumstances were about to change quite drastically; as a recently arrived German, never mind that he was a Jew, her father was likely to be taken into protective custody and interned at a camp somewhere in the north of England. If it happened, Rosa had written, she and her mother would accompany him—her mother out of solidarity, and Rosa because she had nowhere else to go.

Sophie was furious on her friend's behalf—how could the British government actually think German *Jews* were a danger to their national security? When she'd written as much to Rosa, her friend had had a sanguine, and rather chilling, reply: *Well, Sophie, you don't know my father. It might be that he should be in such a place, after all.*

Sophie had no idea what to make of that. Rosa had hinted as much during the voyage, yet she could scarcely give it credence. What was Rosa saying? That her father was a *Nazi?* How could a Jew possibly be a Nazi? It made no sense to Sophie at all.

In December, she had finally heard from Rachel and Hannah; Rachel wrote that she was in a boarding house in Haarlem, and Franz seemed much better; he had found work and they were hopeful that the war would not reach their borders. Hannah was living on the outskirts of Paris, working as a secretary, and Lotte was in school. Hannah's letter was brief, almost terse, and Sophie feared their friendship had been irreparably damaged by her fleeing the *St Louis*. She knew it had been a bitter pill, indeed, for Hannah to swallow, when her own father had been waiting for her in Havana, with ready, open arms, only to have them remain empty.

As the months went on, Sophie couldn't keep from tormenting herself about how she'd acted back on the *St Louis*. She'd fled to save her own skin, that was the hard truth of it, the one she hated to face. Margarete might have slapped her—*once* —but Sophie could have defied her stepmother. Heaven knew, she'd done it before, as a sulky thirteen-year-old. Why had she acted so cowed, so *cowardly*, when it had mattered the absolute most?

Out of selfishness, Sophie had thought bitterly, angry only at herself. She couldn't stand the thought, the terrible truth of it, and yet it was one she had to live with, day after day after painful day. The only thing that helped was knowing the good she was doing now, helping the refugees who had had the great fortune of coming through the Jewish Community Center's doors.

Every time she scooped a frightened little child into her arms, she thought of Heinrich and the way he tugged on her hand, wound his arms around her neck. Every time she patted an elderly man's wrinkled hand, she remembered her father's silent tears. And every time she smiled in sympathy at a hard-eyed woman determined to protect her family, she remembered Margarete and didn't blame her for what she'd done. Margarete had been acting on her behalf and in her interest; Sophie knew she could never blame her stepmother for that. She could just blame herself for accepting the offer.

As spring came to the city, the news from Europe began to intensify. Rationing had been introduced in Great Britain; Germany had announced that all British merchant ships would be classed as enemy warships. As the city had burst into bloom with its hundreds of cherry blossom trees—a gift from Japan nearly thirty years earlier—the storm clouds had gathered over Europe, and German troops amassed on the borders of Denmark and Norway.

Nearly every night, the tenants of Miss Bryson's boarding

house gathered solemnly around the Silvertone to listen to William L. Shirer reporting to America from Berlin. Every time Sophie heard his signature opening, "This is Berlin. I'm William L. Shirer," her stomach cramped with tension and anxiety. What alarming news would he report next? What terrible thing might have happened, so close to the people she loved? At least his calm, steady voice was comforting, and the matter-of-fact way he reported Germany's actions helped, as well.

And yet the news grew worse—Germany's aggression, Great Britain's response, the Soviets fighting Finland, the whole of Europe holding its breath. Then, in April, Germany invaded Denmark and Norway. It was expected and yet, as with the start of the war back in September, completely shocking at the same time. Germany was trying to take control of a whole other country; why, Sophie thought, would anyone think Hitler would be satisfied with Czechoslovakia, Austria, and Poland? He would keep going, maybe until he owned the whole world, and Jews would not be allowed anywhere on the face of the earth.

"How can they just *do* that?" Samantha demanded, sounding so personally aggrieved that Sophie nearly smiled. She could almost imagine the no-nonsense schoolteacher taking Hitler by the ear and giving him a good scolding.

Jack made a scoffing noise, while William shook his head slowly. "Ladies and gentlemen," he intoned grimly, "the *phoney* war has just ended."

It still felt unreal as Sophie took the trolley to work the next morning, amidst a sea of pink cherry blossoms. The city was the most beautiful this time of year, the weather balmy without being sticky or hot, Washington's many impressive marble and granite monuments gleaming under the bright spring sunshine.

As Sophie entered the Jewish Community Center, Sadie gave her a sympathetic look and a quick pat of her hand. "I suppose you heard the news."

Sophie nodded back. "About Denmark and Norway? Yes."

"They might not get any farther, you know."

Sophie managed a tight nod. "They might not." She'd looked at a map of Europe in the big atlas Miss Bryson kept in the living room, and with her finger had traced the length from Norway to Belgium. It was far, she had consoled herself, while acknowledging that it was not *that* far. And what about the Netherlands, which was even closer to Denmark than Belgium? How must Rachel and Franz be feeling, knowing that Germany was invading a country so near to them?

She put her hand in her pocket and closed her fingers around the shard of emerald that she still carried with her everywhere, a talisman, a keepsake, letting the jagged edge of the jewel bite into her fingers, relishing that little sting of pain. *Please keep them safe*, she prayed, hoping that after so much strife and struggle, God might finally listen.

Now she pushed such thoughts away as she tucked her purse under her desk and pulled out her chair. She wanted to be distracted from her worries by her work; she had reams of paperwork to go through, as every refugee that came through the Center had to be documented and filed before they could be offered help. The more swiftly Sophie went through their papers, taking down their information and translating it, the faster they could find themselves in housing and jobs.

At lunchtime, Sophie walked to Logan Circle, a few blocks away, to eat her sandwich under the warm spring sunshine. She often met Mattie there, as it was a primarily black community, and they could sit on a park bench and eat together without anyone causing a fuss. Over the last ten months, Sophie had come to realize just how segregated Washington DC really was; the Jewish Community Center was on the edge of a predominantly black area of shops and homes, where white people never went.

"And the stuff you find in these shops isn't as good as the stuff you find in the white areas," Mattie had told her matter-of-factly. "Of course not."

"It was similar in Berlin," Sophie had replied. "Jews could go into the shops, but only at the end of the day, when almost everything had been taken. And some shopkeepers wouldn't serve you anyway, no matter whether you were allowed in or not."

Mattie had shaken her head in disgust, as she often did when Sophie told her such things. "So much wrong with the world." she'd lamented.

Today, however, Sophie wasn't thinking about that, but rather about the invasion of Denmark and Norway. It weighed heavily on her mind, not knowing if her parents were safe, if her friends were. She pictured Heinrich's tear-streaked face as he clung to Margarete, or Rachel and Franz huddled together in fear, and she felt a stabbing pain in her chest, as if her heart was literally being rent in two. How could she keep on living, day after mundane day, when such terrible things were happening?

Mattie immediately saw her emotions in her face as she approached the bench where they usually met. "The sun is out today, and the birds are singing," she remarked with raised eyebrows. "Why are you looking so long in the face?"

"I'm worried about the invasion," Sophie admitted quietly.

Mattie eyed her with sympathy. "Denmark isn't anywhere near Belgium."

"But it's close enough."

Her friend sighed and briefly touched her hand, something she'd never dare do back at the boarding house, in the presence of other white people. "You know there's nothing you can do about it, except pray."

"Yes, I know." Sophie nodded. She'd tried to pray, and

sometimes she got as far as *Dear God, please...* but not much farther. "It doesn't keep me from worrying, though."

"It sure doesn't." Mattie sighed again as she unwrapped her ham sandwich from its wax paper and took a bite.

"How's your work?" Sophie asked. Mattie had recently got a job as a secretary to a black lawyer, and had been enjoying it, although she was fuming that a black criminal lawyer only had black clients—something else that had been similar in Germany, with Jews.

"It's all right. Mr. George is a good man to work for, but he has a hard row to hoe. Most people think a black person's guilty just by looking at them, you know? The juries have already made up their minds, based on the color of someone's skin."

"Things are going to change, remember?" Sophie replied, parroting her friend's words back to her. "Something *has* to change."

"Yes, well," Mattie replied on a sigh, "it had better soon."

A male voice had them both stilling in surprise. "Miss... Weiss, isn't it? From Friendship House?"

Sophie turned to see a slender man with thinning brown hair standing in front of her, his hat in his hand. Although he looked familiar, it took a second for her to place him, until she remembered his warm smile as he'd handed her a martini— which she'd nearly spat out! He'd been kind to her at that party, over a year ago now. "Mr. Howard!" she exclaimed. "Yes, you have a very good memory."

"As do you," he replied, smiling. "I'm sorry to interrupt your conversation." He gave Mattie a little bow, which made her smile faintly. It wasn't often, Sophie knew, that a white man would treat her with such courtesy. "I simply wondered how you were. Have you settled into life here?"

"Yes, I think so. Actually, I have you to thank for recommending the Jewish Community Center to me. I have a job there now."

"Wonderful!" The smile that broke across his face was warm and genuine. "I am so very glad to hear that." He hesitated for a brief moment before asking, "Are you still residing with the Tylers?"

Sophie tensed a little at that, and the memory of what residing with the Tylers had led to—an awful night she wanted only to forget. She had not seen Stanley or Barbara since she'd moved to the boarding house, and she was glad of it. She still saw Esther sometimes, when she came to visit her cousin, and she was always pleased to see her. "No, I've found my own accommodation," she replied after a second's pause. "In a boarding house on I Street."

"I'm very glad to hear that, as well." He cocked his head, his gaze sweeping over her thoughtfully. "May I say your English is really quite impressive now. You sound completely fluent. Like a native."

"Well, it has been nine months," Sophie replied, smiling, and Mr. Howard nodded.

"Still... that is quite a short period of time, to become so accomplished. You clearly have a great gift with languages. Do you speak any others, besides German?"

Startled, Sophie replied, "French and a little Spanish."

"French?" His eyebrows rose. "Are you fluent in that, as well?"

She shrugged, nonplussed and a bit bemused by his line of questioning. "Mostly. I haven't practiced it in some time, however."

"I see." He nodded again, and then nodded at Mattie. "Lovely to see you both. I'm glad I now know where to find you, Miss Weiss, at the Jewish Community Center." He replaced his hat on his head, doffing it once before he walked smartly away.

Sophie stared at his retreating back, wondering what on earth that conversation had really been about. Had he just been making idle chitchat? It hadn't quite seemed like that, but what else could it have been?

"Where do you know him from?" Mattie asked, sounding as mystified as she felt.

"I met him at a party, back when I was living with the Tylers. He was kind to me. He works with the Navy." Naval Intelligence, she remembered Stanley saying. "We only spoke for a short while, though, and I haven't seen him since."

"Well, that was something of an odd conversation," Mattie remarked. "He almost sounded like he *intended* to see you again. I have to say, I think he's a bit old for you. He looks over thirty."

And she was only just turned twenty; she'd spent her birthday back in March at the boarding house, and Lorna had made her a special dinner. "I don't think he has any romantic inclinations," Sophie told her friend. She knew she didn't. She had not thought of romance once since coming to Washington; there had been too many other cares to occupy her mind. "I'm quite sure he was just being polite."

Mattie still looked skeptical. "But asking about your languages?"

Sophie shrugged as she finished her sandwich, scrunching the wax paper up into a ball. "I think he was just making conversation," she dismissed.

Still, the odd conversation with John Howard played at the fringes of her mind as she headed back to work. *Why* had he asked about her languages? Her thoughts jumped to intriguing possibilities; could he actually be thinking of recruiting her to work for the Navy? Would she want to? Or was she being ridiculous, thinking that was even a remote possibility? She was a twenty-year-old German refugee, with no formal education past age sixteen. Why on earth would the American government recruit her for anything?

She laughed softly, shaking her head. She was letting her

imagination run away with herself, simply because she so wanted to be *useful*. If she worked for the government, Sophie wondered, would she feel less guilty about those she'd left behind?

Unfortunately, she thought she wouldn't. Nothing could make up for fleeing the *St Louis* and abandoning all her family and friends.

Several weeks passed with Sophie hardly able to bear to listen to the news every night. Denmark had surrendered on the very first day of the attack, while Norway continued to hold out—but for how long? Allied troops had landed at Narvik and Namsos and were attempting to attack German troops in Trondheim from both the north and the south. Meanwhile, the reports on the news had suggested that Germany might bypass France's invulnerable Maginot Line and invade the country through the north... that was, the Netherlands and Belgium.

It hadn't happened yet, though, and Sophie was desperate to believe it never would. Hitler wouldn't be so audacious, so *arrogant*, as to take over even more of Europe? How much more did he *want*?

In early May, the news grew even more dire. The Germans had reached Andalsnes, and the Allies had to evacuate Namsos.

"Those bastards are *winning*," William had exclaimed as they'd listened on the radio, before excusing himself for speaking such language in front of ladies.

"Who cares?" Jack had replied grumpily, and Miss Bryson had given him a reproving look.

Sophie went to work with a heavier heart than ever the next day. Everyone expected Norway to surrender any day, and then what country would be next? The Netherlands? Belgium? What would happen to Rachel and Franz? To her father and Margarete and dear little Heinrich? She could hardly bear to imagine it—the sound of jackboots on the pavement, tanks rolling through the streets, Heinrich's tear-streaked face at the window... There had been so little news from them, since war had been declared.

She'd seen newsreels of what had happened in Norway when she and Sadie had gone to the cinema the other day; Sadie had reached over and held her hand tightly, a silent sign of solidarity. Although her friend didn't feel the danger and immediacy of the war in Europe the way Sophie did, she'd appreciated the sentiment.

All day at work, Sophie struggled to concentrate even on the most basic of tasks; she felt as if she were walking through a fog, barely aware of what was around her. All she could think about was what was happening in Europe. All she could imagine was her family, her friends, cowering in terror...

"Listen," Sadie said, stopping by her desk when they'd finished for the day. Sophie blinked up at her, startled back into the present—a beautiful spring evening in a lovely, peaceful city. "A bunch of us are going out tonight. I know you don't like to go out very much—don't bother to deny it!—but Jack Campbell is playing at the Mayfair Club, and you ought to come. Forget all these troubles, just for a little while."

Forget her troubles? As much as she wanted to, Sophie doubted it was likely, and yet she knew Sadie was right. She couldn't exist in this maelstrom of anxiety forever; for one thing, it was utterly exhausting.

"Come on," Sadie urged. "Let your hair down, just this once."

Sophie frowned in bemused confusion. "Let my hair down?" she asked, touching her neat French roll. It was an expression she hadn't heard before.

Sadie laughed. "*Relax*, I mean!" She touched Sophie's hand briefly. "Come with us, Sophie. You deserve a break, away from all this." She gestured to the cluttered desk in the Center's office, but Sophie knew she meant much more. *This*—the waves of worries and fears that battered her like a storm, relentless and never-ending, so often threatening to overwhelm her. A few hours enjoying herself felt like an unimaginable luxury, a treat she didn't deserve, no matter what Sadie said.

"I don't know..." she began, meaning it as a refusal, only to stop when Sadie leaned forward, over her desk.

"Look," Sadie said quietly, "a lot of the refugees who come through here feel terrible guilt, because they got away while others didn't. You're not alone in that, Sophie, but just because you feel it, doesn't mean you *should*."

Sophie stared at her friend, shocked that she'd seen and understood so much about her, when she'd never admitted as much to her, or to anyone. "You don't know that," she replied in a near-whisper, her voice choking a little. "I left everyone on that ship. *Everyone*..."

"I know, but you told me yourself your stepmother wanted you to go," Sadie replied staunchly. "Insisted upon it, even. What would staying have proved? Nothing. Absolutely nothing." She shook her head firmly. "Please, come out with us."

Sophie opened her mouth to say no—as she so often did—when she suddenly pictured Margarete's face, those dark, flashing eyes, that pursed red mouth. Her stepmother would want her to take advantage of every opportunity of her new life, she realized. She could imagine her remarking in her acerbic way, *I didn't send you to Washington to hide away from life, but to live it, Sophie! Otherwise what was our sacrifice for?*

A tiny smile twitched her mouth at the thought. Sadie was right; was there any point in hiding herself away as she had been? It wasn't as if her friends or family could even see her supposed penance. At heart, it was a selfish indulgence, only for her own sake.

"All right," she told Sadie, a heady sense of recklessness suddenly seizing her. "I'll come."

CHAPTER 17

The Mayfair Club was on 14th Street, in the city's theater district. Nicknamed the "Café of all Nations," its walls were adorned with murals of scenes and flags from every country imaginable, and its art deco interior was furnished with sleek tables of chrome and black, with white banquettes upholstered in turquoise. The waitresses were dressed in the native garb of different countries; the one representing the Netherlands even wore wooden clogs.

"I pity her," Sadie whispered as they watched the waitress carefully clomp her way between tables. "They look awfully uncomfortable."

Sophie giggled back, feeling nervous and excited all at once. The club had a far more sophisticated feel than the rather sedate dances on the Jewish Community Center's roof terrace. Here was a place where all of Washington was rubbing shoulders—government officials, military personnel, office workers, socialites. She was surprised to see the mix of black and white people among the crowded tables; in a supper club, at least, segregation did not seem so present.

Carefully, she smoothed down the front of her bronze

taffeta dress, the color now faded and the fabric worn, but still the only suitable garment she had to wear out of an evening. Over the last few months, she'd considered buying another dress, but her wages were so low, and every extra penny she saved, either for postage for letters, or simply to tuck away for a rainy day. If her family did make it to America, they would need all the money they could to survive. She wasn't about to waste any of her hard-earned dollars on mere fripperies.

"Let's find a table," Sadie said, as she wound her way through the crowded club. "And drinks! I'm parched."

Besides Sadie, there were three others there from the Center that Sophie knew, if not that well—Elizabeth, a single woman in her thirties, and two men, Jacob and Adam, who seemed to be acting as dates for Sadie and Elizabeth. Sophie didn't particularly mind feeling like a fifth wheel, but she was certainly conscious of it as they all sat down—Sadie and Jacob on one side of the table, Elizabeth and Adam on the other, and her alone at the end.

"What can I get you ladies for drinks?" Jacob asked as he stood up to go to the bar.

"Whiskey sour for me," Sadie replied blithely.

"Sidecar for me," Elizabeth said.

Sophie, still having no real experience of cocktails, stammered, "I'll... I'll have a lemonade."

"Lemonade!" Elizabeth exclaimed, rolling her eyes, while Sadie shot Sophie a quick, sympathetic look. "You can't come to the Mayfair Club and have *lemonade*."

"How about a splash of gin with it?" Sadie suggested kindly, and Sophie blushed, feeling like a child.

"Very well," she mumbled, looking down at her lap. In that moment, she wished she hadn't gone out at all.

This is the life you wished for, she silently mocked herself, *once upon time. Cocktails and dancing and handsome men—you wanted it all, Sophie, well, now you have it. But at what cost?*

"Sophie," Sadie said quietly, touching her hand, "you can have a lemonade if you really want to."

"It's fine." Sophie looked up, forcing a smile. "It's not often I go to a place like this, after all. I think I'll have what you're having." Her smile turned up even more at the corners, making her cheeks hurt.

Sadie looked dubious, but Jacob, wanting to get going, remarked jovially, "Two whiskey sours and a sidecar coming right up!"

Sophie clenched her hands in her lap, telling herself, rather futilely, to relax. This was what she'd wanted, wasn't it? What Margarete wanted for her? A fun-loving, freewheeling life, all the opportunities and pleasures. This was what she'd pined for, back on the St Louis. Cocktails, like they'd promised to have in Havana, at the Inglaterra Hotel. It seemed a lifetime ago.

As much as she was trying to enjoy the evening, all she could think about was her poor father, terrified and cooped up in some boarding house somewhere, as Germans troops drew ever closer. And of Heinrich, curled up on his own, wondering where his sister had gone. Or Rosa, interned in England and as good as a prisoner. Hannah, slaving away as a secretary in France, worried for Lotte, fearing for their safety. And Rachel and Franz, in the Netherlands, even closer to the German invasion than everyone else... They were all in danger. Every single one—except her.

"Here we are!" Jacob set a tray of cocktails down on the table with a flourish.

Sadie handed one to Sophie, who took a sip and then tried not to wince at the medicinal taste. Although the taste of the alcohol was muted by the addition of ginger and lemon, it still felt strong to her, a girl who had had little more than a few sips of champagne in her entire life.

"Do you like it?" Sadie asked, and once again, Sophie was

seized by a sense of recklessness—except right now it felt a little more like desperation.

"Yes," she stated firmly, taking another sip that went down a bit more smoothly. "I love it."

Jack Campbell had come onto the floor to play the piano, and as the first few lazy notes floated over the room, the conversation died down and Sophie was able to sip her drink as her gaze moved slowly over the motley crowd. Everyone looked sophisticated, she thought, and as if they belonged here. Everyone except her.

Well, what of it? She told herself sternly. She needed to stop feeling so stupidly sorry for herself. She was fortunate to be here at all, she *knew* that. She'd been invited. She could enjoy herself if she wanted to... the trouble was, she didn't know if she actually did. But, for Margarete's sake and maybe her own, she'd try.

"Sam!"

Startled, Sophie stopped perusing the crowd and found a sandy-haired man with friendly hazel eyes standing by their table. He had a muscular build and an open, freckled face. Jacob had stood up and was pumping his hand enthusiastically.

"It's so good to see you! How have you been keeping?"

"Well enough, I suppose, all things considered." The man had a twangy sort of American accent that was different from the drawl of the Southern accent, or the clipped tones of the metropolitan Washingtonian one, that Sophie had become used to. She didn't recognize it.

"Pull up a chair," Jacob entreated. "Join us, unless you're here with someone else?"

"Just a few guys from the Yard," Sam replied. "I'd be glad to join you."

After he'd fetched a chair, Jacob went around making introductions. "Miss Danvers, Miss Brown, Miss Weiss," he said. "And I think you know Adam already. We all work at the

Jewish Community Center. Everyone, this is Sam Jackson, who works at the Navy Yard."

Everyone murmured their hellos, while Sam smiled and nodded back. "Nice to meet you all," he said. His eyes crinkled at the corners as his gaze seemed to rest on Sophie for a beat longer than she'd expected, and she found herself fighting the urge to look away. Had he noticed her German surname, her accent? Was he wondering about who she was?

She took another sip of her drink, this time unable to keep from wincing slightly at its strong taste. Out of the corner of her eye, she caught Sam Jackson's twitch of a smile, and she realized he'd noticed her reaction. She pretended not to have seen it, taking another sip. This time she thankfully managed not to wince.

The conversation drifted around her in eddies and currents, as everyone talked about the Center, the Navy Yard, and of course the war in Europe.

"Denmark and Norway now," Sam remarked. "Netherlands and Belgium next, I shouldn't doubt, and sooner than anyone thinks, I'm afraid."

This time, Sophie couldn't keep from flinching, and it had nothing to do with her drink. Once again, Sam noticed.

"You disagree?" he asked, with a smile of frank curiosity, as if it were a mere matter of intellectual debate, which, for him, she supposed it was.

Carefully, Sophie set down her drink. "I would *like* to disagree with you," she replied. "My parents are in Belgium, waiting to emigrate."

"Sophie came from Germany almost a year ago now," Sadie put in.

"I'm so sorry," Sam said quietly and sincerely, his gaze trained on Sophie, a flush coming out on his cheeks. "I had no idea. I didn't mean to sound cavalier. I do apologize."

Sophie inclined her head in acceptance of his apology. It

was easy to sound cavalier—to *feel* cavalier—when you had no vested interest in the outcome. She knew that, she understood it, but sometimes it was hard not to feel bitter at how easy it seemed for everyone else.

After a second's awkward pause, the conversation moved on. Sophie looked away, letting her gaze move around the supper club and all its sophisticated clientele once more, trying to seem unaffected, but she could feel Sam's golden-green eyes on her, steady and thoughtful, and inwardly she squirmed. Had she been rude, speaking the way she had? He seemed like a kind man. She should have been more understanding.

After twenty minutes or so of desultory conversation, Jack Campbell invited a band to join him, and a tune was struck that had people jumping up from their seats and taking to the dance floor. The others paired off easily, leaving Sophie alone with Sam. So, she really had been a fifth wheel, she thought ruefully. She didn't mind; she wasn't dreaming of romance anymore the way she once had.

"Care to?"

She blinked up in surprise to see Sam Jackson standing in front of her, one hand outstretched in invitation.

"I..." She licked her lips. "I'm not a very good dancer."

His smile was crooked, endearing, "Neither am I."

Sophie felt she couldn't refuse without seeming terribly rude, especially as she'd already been somewhat curt in her reply earlier. Still, she felt nervous about the prospect of dancing with Sam Jackson, a man with kind eyes and a knowing smile. He hadn't even touched her and she already felt all jumbled up inside.

"Very well," she replied after a moment, fearing she sounded ungracious when she knew she was really only nervous.

She took his hand, his dry palm sliding across hers in a way that made her strangely aware of his touch. No tingle or sparks, not quite, but something close to it. A sense of heightened experience; suddenly, the room felt warmer, the music louder, and she could once more taste whiskey and lemon on her tongue.

"I really can't dance," she warned him with a shaky laugh as, around them, everyone whirled and gyrated in the energetic Lindy Hop. "I'm hopeless. My stepmother taught me to waltz, and that's all, but I wasn't even very good at that."

"A good box step should never be looked down upon," Sam replied with mock seriousness and an easy smile. His hand was warm, resting on her waist, the other clasped in hers as they moved sedately about the room, not even attempting the whirls and twirls of the couples around them.

After a few moments, Sophie felt herself start to relax.

"This isn't so bad, is it?" Sam remarked teasingly, his eyes crinkling down at her.

"I suppose not," Sophie replied, so grudgingly that Sam threw back his head and laughed, a sound of both humor and joy that made Sophie smile. It had been a long time since she'd heard someone laugh like that, with such genuine, good-hearted amusement.

"Most girls I know like dancing," he commented, sounding both curious and thoughtful.

Sophie risked a glance upwards. "I'm not like most girls," she replied quietly, and Sam's laughing expression dimmed.

"No," he agreed somberly. "I don't suppose you are."

Sophie swallowed, feeling like she'd clumsily ruined the mood... if there even had been a mood to begin with. She realized she rather hoped there had been. "I'm sorry," she blurted. "I'm not very good at any of this."

Sam cocked an eyebrow. "Any...?"

"Parties. Dancing. Flirting." She bit her lip as a flush of mortification swept over her face. *Flirting...!* Why on earth had she said such a thing? Sam Jackson wasn't *flirting* with her... and she certainly wasn't flirting with him.

Fortunately, he seemed remarkably unfazed. "You seem to be doing all right to me with all three," he told her, and Sophie blushed with both pleasure and embarrassment. She had no idea how to reply.

After another minute or two, the music ended, and Sophie stepped back, dropping Sam's hand as though it might have burned her. He stepped back as well, and she found, perversely, that she suddenly missed the warmth of his palm on her waist. She felt flustered, and then flustered for feeling flustered. She really was all jumbled up.

"It's getting late," she murmured, looking away from him.

"May I walk you back to your home?" Sam asked.

"That's not necessary..." Sophie protested, startled but also shyly pleased.

"No, but I want to." His eyes crinkled again. "If you'd let me?"

Sophie turned to look at him, trying to sort out the complicated tangle of her own feelings—excitement, that a kind, handsome man seemed interested in her; nervousness, because she'd never been in such a position before; and, as always, the ever-present and irritating guilt that she was enjoying such an opportunity when her family and friends could not.

"Well?" Sam asked gently.

She glanced at the others from their party, who were still dancing. Sophie suspected they would all stay out quite late, and she was already feeling weary.

"All right, thank you," she finally said. "I'll just tell Sadie that I'm going."

Sadie was thrilled when Sophie told her Sam was walking her home. "I thought he seemed a bit sweet on you," she said with a grin. "Enjoy yourself, Sophie."

Sophie managed a small smile. "I'll try," she replied.

Outside, the air still held the warmth of spring, even though it was nearing ten o'clock at night. Sophie slung her purse over her shoulder as she fell into step with Sam.

"Where do you live?" he asked, his hands in the pockets of his trousers.

"I Street and 16th Street, about a mile from here." She glanced at him in apology. "You don't have to walk me all that way..."

"I don't mind. I don't have to work tomorrow, anyway, and it's a nice evening." He tilted his head up to the starlit sky. "Spring in Washington is my favorite season, I think."

"Better than summer," Sophie agreed. "I arrived here in June, and I'd never felt such heat—and such stickiness!"

"Yes, and the stink from the Potomac, as well." He glanced at her, smiling, before he asked seriously, "How is it that you are here, and your family is in Belgium?"

Sophie's throat thickened and, haltingly, she explained about being on the *St Louis*.

"That was in the news," Sam recalled, shaking his head. "It must have been a truly dreadful time. I'm so sorry."

"Not so dreadful for me, though, really," Sophie replied, her throat still thick. "I escaped."

"And thank God you did." He paused mid-step to study her, his forehead furrowed. "I'm sure your family will be able to emigrate soon. The US is accepting so many more Germans now, what with the war on."

"Yes, one hopes." She swallowed hard and looked away, not wanting him to see how emotional she felt. "What about you?" she asked after they'd walked in silence for a few minutes. "Did I hear you say you worked at a yard?"

"The Navy Yard," Sam explained. "I'm a naval engineer. I help to repair and reinforce ships, that sort of thing. I've been in Washington for a year now, but I'm hoping to be posted soon."

"Posted?"

"To a naval base, I don't know where yet. I'm just waiting

for my orders." He paused before saying, "America is going to get involved in this war. Everyone in the military knows it. It's just a matter of time."

"Do you really think so?" Sophie heard both the hope and anxiety in her voice. "People here seem so against the idea, sometimes…" She thought of her fellow tenants' grumbling.

"Well, no one likes the idea of war, do they?" Sam replied with a sadly rueful smile. "The fighting, the danger and deprivation, the potential losses. But Hitler is on a murderous rampage. We can't stand by and watch him storm through Europe forever."

"No," Sophie agreed. Sam sounded so matter-of-fact, so practical, she thought, yet as part of the Navy, he would surely be caught up in it, maybe even on the front lines one day. Was he scared? She didn't know him well enough to ask, but she found his certainty reassuring. "This is my boarding house," she said after a few more moments of walking, when they'd reached Miss Bryson's house, the leaves of the pecan trees whispering in the spring breeze. "Thank you for walking me home."

"May I see you again?" Sam asked, stopping to turn and face her. "Next week, perhaps? I'm working through the weekend, but I'm free on a Thursday evening. We could go to dinner and a movie?" His eyebrows lifted. "If you wanted to?"

Did she? It sounded wonderful, and yet so strangely foreign, like something that only happened to other people, not her. For nearly a year, Sophie had kept her head down, working as many hours at the Jewish Community Center as she could, and spending her evenings huddled in front of the radio, waiting for news. She'd been in the United States coming up to a year, and yet, in some respects, she felt as if she hadn't started truly living yet.

Maybe she should… not in *spite* of the friends and family she'd left behind, but *because* of them. Why waste her life, the opportunities she'd been given, out of some misplaced sense of penance?

Instinctively, her hand slipped into the pocket of her coat and her fingers curled around the shard of emerald, hard enough to hurt. *Rosa, Hannah, Rachel*, she thought. *Do you still have yours? Are you well? Are you safe?*

The silence reverberated all around her, as Sam waited for her response. "All right, thank you," Sophie said, feeling a smile bloom in her heart and spread across her face. "That sounds lovely."

CHAPTER 18

When Sadie heard that Sophie had a date with Sam—although Sophie had protested that it wasn't *actually* a date, at least not much of one—she insisted that she buy a new dress.

"You've trotted out that bronze taffeta for nearly a year now," Sadie stated, wagging a warning finger, her eyes dancing playfully. "It's a lovely dress, it's true, but you can see for yourself the fabric's gone all shiny in places and it's also out of style by at least two years, I'm sorry to say."

"It's perfectly fine—" Sophie began to protest, more out of habit than conviction. She hadn't bought any new clothes since she'd arrived in Washington, and the ones she had were starting to look decidedly shabby.

"*Sophie.*" Sadie planted her hands on her hips as she gave her a stern look. "You can afford a dress. I know the JCC doesn't pay all that much, but you barely spend a penny as it is, on anything. We'll go to Woodies at lunch and find you something marvelous. I'll drag you there myself, if you refuse!"

Sophie felt she had no choice but to agree, and, in truth, she didn't actually mind. She did need a new dress, whether she wanted one or not... and the truth was, she *wanted* one. One that she chose and bought for herself, an independent woman making her own way. Besides, when had she last treated herself to anything? Her austere lifestyle, Sophie acknowledged, sometimes felt a little wearing. Guilt, she realized, feeling it all the same, only fired you for so long.

Woodward & Lothrop, known as Woodies, was the city's oldest department store, a behemoth of a building on 10th, 11th, F and G Streets. It was ten stories high and had everything anyone could imagine ever needing to buy—including dresses. Sophie had gone into the massive store to buy a few basic necessities, but she'd never felt the need to buy a dress.

Now she walked slowly through the women's wear section, hardly daring to finger the elegant dresses hanging from racks in every material and shade she could have wanted. Vases of chrysanthemums were interspersed throughout the department, and sophisticated-looking assistants hovered discreetly, waiting to be of assistance. It reminded Sophie a little of the old days in Berlin, when Margarete had taken her shopping at Wertheim or Jandorf—glass counters, marble floors, the scent of expensive perfume on the air. She felt as if she'd tumbled back in time, even as she kept looking determinedly toward the future.

"Now, it's likely to be warm out, so you'll want something to keep cool in," Sadie mused as she browsed the racks with a focused officiousness. "And a nice springy color, I think, but nothing too insipid. You're twenty, after all, not a child!"

"Insipid?" Although Sophie was pretty well fluent in English now, it was not a word she had come across before, although she thought she could guess the meaning.

"Boring," Sadie explained with a laugh. "Like some sort of infantile fainting lily. What stupid men think they want." For a second, her eyes flashed, and Sophie wondered if she had some personal experience of such men. She knew Sadie went out on quite a few dates, but had yet to find her own Mr. Right. "You need something with a bit more spark, I think," Sadie continued, "because I know you have it in you, even if you act as if you don't."

Sophie was already shaking her head, a matter of instinct. "Sadie, I'm not sure—"

"How about this one?" Sadie held out a dress in pale green chiffon, decorated with tiny daisies. It had flounced sleeves and a darted waist before flaring out in a frothy skirt, to just a few inches below the knee.

Sophie fingered the material, a sudden sense of longing welling up inside her. She hadn't realized just how much she'd missed having pretty clothes until that moment. And not just pretty clothes, but the life that went with them.

"I can tell by your face that you like it," Sadie declared as she gave a firm nod. "All right, let's have you try it on."

Half an hour later, Sophie was heading back to work with not just the dress, but a pair of ankle-strap heels and a set of silk-trimmed underwear, all wrapped in tissue paper and tucked into a paper bag decorated with the Woodies' label. She could hardly believe she'd let Sadie talk her into buying so much—and yet she had. She hadn't even had to try that hard, Sophie knew. It had been so much fun, to try on pretty clothes and feel young and silly and hopeful, if just for a little while.

An unsettling thought suddenly occurred to her. What, she wondered, had happened to all of Margarete's elegant clothes, her silks and satins, her furs and stoles? She'd packed most of them in trunks on the St Louis... but did she still have them in Belgium? If she did, Sophie doubted she had any occasion to wear them. She had no idea how dire her family's circumstances were, but she was almost certain they were worse than her stepmother let on to her in her letters, with her deliberately brief descriptions of where they lived and what they were doing —which seemed mainly to be waiting for their quota number to come up.

Yet here she was, jauntily traipsing through the spring-filled city, with new clothes and shoes and underwear in a bag. Guilt soured her stomach, her whole mood. Margarete might not want her to feel guilty about it, Sophie thought, but would Hannah? Rosa? Rachel? Would her friends be glad she was safe and free, while they were not? She realized she didn't know the answer.

By Saturday, the day of the dinner and movie—the *date*—Sophie had worked herself up into something of a seething bundle of nerves. She'd written to Rosa about the whole thing, even though she knew, of course, her friend would not receive the letter for weeks, if not longer. Still, it had helped to put it all down on paper, providing a little much-needed levity.

> *I don't know much about him except that he works as a naval engineer, and he has kind eyes that crinkle at the corners... do I sound besotted? Because I assure you, I am not! It is nice to have a bit of attention, though, I must admit. It's been such a long time... really, it's been forever! You guessed how inexperienced I was back on the St Louis, and the truth is, I've never had a man look at me the way Sam Jackson does... now I really do sound besotted! He says that America is going to get involved in the war... he sounded quite certain. It gave me hope, and I hope it does you, as well, because surely if a country as large as the United States comes against Hitler, he won't last for long! That is my hope, anyway, as well as my prayer. The war feels as if it has barely begun, and yet I already long for it to be over, as I'm sure you do...*

Today, however, thoughts of war seemed far from the minds of anyone in the city. It was a warm, breezy day, the cherry blossoms at the last peak of their pink, puffball blowsiness, just starting to go brown at their edges, the city aglow in spring sunshine.

Up in her tiny bedroom, Sophie stared at her reflection in the small square of mirror, a fluttering mix of apprehension and excitement warring inside her. She was wearing her new dress and shoes—and even her new underwear—and Mattie, getting into the spirit of the occasion, had helped to style her hair into sideswept pin curls. She'd even borrowed a bit of pink lipstick and rouge from Samantha, who had also seemed enthused about her so-called date, but Sophie had the urge now to wipe it off. Did she look ridiculous? She *felt* ridiculous, but she recognized that she also felt pretty, and it was a strange yet wonderful sensation.

For one evening, one precious, fleeting evening, she knew she wanted to feel like any other young, pretty girl out with a gentleman, without a care in the world... even if she felt burdened by far too many. She could let them slip off her shoulders for a few hours, surely? Just for a few hours...

"Miss Sophie!" Mattie's voice floated up the stairs, laced with excitement. "Your gentleman caller is here."

Her gentleman caller. Sophie took a deep breath, pressing one hand to her middle to calm the nerves jumping inside her like a jar of crickets. Another breath, and then she turned from her reflection and headed downstairs.

Sam whistled under his breath when he saw her, a smile splitting his face. "Don't you look swell," he said, and Sophie blushed in response. He'd scrubbed up nicely himself, she thought, wearing a white linen suit with a light blue shirt. A tremor went through her, of excitement and nervousness. Already, the evening felt as if it were brimming with possibility.

They walked out into the dusky evening, the sun just

starting to sink in an orange glow below the city's buildings, the air still holding the warmth of the day.

"I brought my car," Sam told her. "I figured it was a little far to walk, especially in those shoes." He nodded toward Sophie's heels, making her blush yet again.

"I'm not sure I could walk a few blocks in these," she admitted. "I'm not used to wearing them. I probably look as if I'm walking across broken glass!"

"Not at all," Sam replied gallantly. "Although I can't imagine walking in those things! But, like I said, I think you look swell. But if it helps..." He offered her his arm, which Sophie took after a second's pause. She rested her fingers on his forearm, feeling the warm muscles underneath the linen of his suit jacket. Her heart skipped a funny little beat.

Sam opened the door of his Ford coupe and Sophie slid inside, her skirt whispering against the leather seat. A few minutes later, they were driving towards the restaurant Sam had chosen, the Roma, an Italian restaurant in Cleveland Park that he promised her served "the best manicotti." Since Sophie didn't even know what manicotti was, she supposed she wouldn't be able to tell if it was the best or not, but she was excited to try it. She'd hardly ever tasted Italian food.

She kept her hands folded in her lap, feeling overcome with nerves, yet also terribly excited, too. Sam was easy at the wheel, chatting about the weather, the movie they were going to see, springtime in Washington. Sophie managed to make some desultory replies, even as her heart and mind both raced with anticipation and a tingling awareness of the man next to her.

The sky was livid with the reds and oranges of the sunset as they parked at Roma and Sam led her to the terrace in the rear, where they could enjoy the fading remnants of the spectacular sunset while they ate their supper.

Sophie glanced around the terrace, with its tinkling fountain, trellises trailing grapevines, and even an accordionist strolling among the diners, playing soulful music.

"Goodness," she said, impressed by it all, and Sam laughed.

"I know, you'd never find a place like this where I'm from," he told her. "It's all mom-and-pop diners and not much else."

"Where are you from?" Sophie asked as she took her seat, spreading her napkin in her lap.

"Wisconsin. You might never have heard of it. It's a boring old state, but it's home."

"I've heard of Wisconsin Avenue," Sophie replied with a smile. It wasn't far from her boarding house.

"Of course!" Sam nodded, smiling. "Well, the state is just above Chicago, on Lake Michigan." He held up his hand, fingers spread. "Michigan's shaped like a mitten, and my parents have a farm, here by the thumb, growing corn and cattle. That's where I grew up."

"On a farm?" Somehow, Sophie couldn't keep the surprise from her voice, and Sam laughed again.

"Yes, I'm a farm boy, I'm afraid. Still wet behind the ears by this city's standards, anyway. I grew up working on the farm all hours with my brother and two sisters. I love Mom and Pop to death, but the truth is, I couldn't wait to get away. I didn't want to husk corn for the rest of my life." He smiled wryly, ducking his head as if abashed. Sophie found she was charmed.

A waiter came to take their drink orders, and Sam raised his eyebrows in question. "The Chianti is pretty good here," he told her, "And it goes well with the manicotti."

Sophie didn't know enough about anything to make a comment, but she was willing to follow Sam's lead. "Sounds lovely."

They ordered—Chianti, garlic bread, and the renowned manicotti—and when the waiter had left, Sam gave her a thoughtful, serious look. "So, you grew up in Germany?" he asked, and Sophie nodded.

"Yes, in Berlin. My father was a lawyer, before Hitler's laws forbade him to practice. He was quite well known, in his day." She spoke with more sorrow than pride.

Sam shook his head, grimacing in both apology and sympathy. "I can't imagine what it was like."

"No." Sophie fell silent for a moment.

Trying to remember the days of her childhood, before Hitler came to power and everyone she'd ever known seemed to have decided they hated the Jews, hated *her*, felt like remembering a fairy tale, or an old film, blurred with age. None of it felt quite real. Had she once been young and silly, concerning herself with ballet lessons and birthday cake?

She remembered her father taking her to Café Kranzler on her tenth birthday; there had been balloons and delicious *Sachertorte*, and for her present, he'd given her a beautiful doll with a painted porcelain face. Where was that doll now? She had no idea what had happened to it, or to all the belongings they hadn't been able to take with them on the *St Louis*. She hadn't thought to miss any of them, until now.

"I'm sorry," Sam said, reaching over to briefly touch her hand, his fingers brushing hers. "I didn't mean to make you sad."

"You didn't," Sophie replied quickly, her gaze trained on his hand resting on hers. "It's only it seems such a long time ago. Everything has changed so much. It's hard to remember what life was like before it did. It feels like it all happened to someone else."

"Yes, it must." He shook his head slowly, before grimacing. "I don't think any of us can imagine what life must be like over there."

"Black people can," Sophie replied with just the slightest touch of asperity. She knew, of course, that Sam wasn't to blame for the city's segregation laws, but just about every American she'd met seemed to abide by them affably enough, a state of affairs which both frustrated and infuriated her. "My friend

Mattie can't ride on the bus with me or go into certain shops or theaters, or anything like that—just the way *I* couldn't, back in Berlin. I imagine she knows what it feels like, at least a little bit." She caught her breath, wondering if she'd said too much, sounded too passionate. But what of it? She felt it, all the same.

Sam looked surprised, and then thoughtful. "I never thought about it that way," he admitted, thankfully not sounding offended that Sophie had spoken so heatedly. "But I suppose she does, in a way. There aren't the same kind of segregation laws in Wisconsin as there are here in Washington, although there are certain... traditions, I suppose." He smiled apologetically, cocking his head. "It's unfortunate, I realize. But maybe it takes an outsider to point them out."

The waiter came with the bottle of wine, and poured them both glasses of rich, ruby-red liquid.

"Anyway," Sophie said as she took a sip, letting its velvety warmth seep through her. "I didn't mean to make such speeches. What movie are we going to see?"

"*Star Dust* is playing at the Sylvan. I thought that might be a nice one."

"All right." Sophie hadn't heard of it, but she liked the sound of it—surely something called *Star Dust* couldn't be too grim! She knew she didn't want to see anything war-related. The war occupied her thoughts enough as it was.

The rest of the evening passed by pleasantly indeed, without any talk of either the past or the future, which suited Sophie just fine. She was happy enough to listen to Sam talk about his job at the Navy Yard, and she told him about her work at the Jewish Community Center. They ate manicotti stuffed with prosciutto and ricotta until Sophie's stomach ached with how much she'd eaten; Sam had been right, the manicotti was wonderful, and she'd never eaten anything like it before. Sam had insisted they share a piece of tiramisu for dessert, and by the time she tottered out of the restaurant, Sophie was positively stuffed, as well as a little lightheaded from the wine.

She was also feeling flushed with pleasure from being under Sam's gentlemanly and admiring gaze for the last few hours. She didn't think she was imagining the warmth in his hazel eyes, the slow curling of his mouth as he smiled. He had such an open, friendly face, such a genuine kindness and warmth to him, that she felt herself unfurling like a flower in the sun.

When he'd put his hand on the small of her back as they'd left the restaurant, she'd suddenly turned fizzy inside, like sparks were going off in her stomach. Twenty years old, and she'd never felt this way before! She was glad to feel it now, to feel alive in a way she never had before. The terrors of war, the fear for her family and friends... right then, it all seemed far away, as Sam guided her back to the car, pressing his hand gently to the small of her back one last time before he reached over to open her door.

Star Dust, a frothy film about an up-and-coming movie star, was just the sort of light entertainment Sophie needed. She was tantalizingly conscious of Sam sitting next to her in the darkened theater, the sharp, pine scent of his cologne, his hand lying on the armrest so close to hers. He'd bought a nickel bag of popcorn to share, and every time she dipped her fingers into the bag, she felt a thrill, wondering if their hands would brush. They never did, but it was exciting, all the same.

By the time they'd finished the movie and headed back to his car, it was nearing midnight. As Sam pulled up in front of Miss Bryson's boarding house, Sophie felt both sleepy and very much wide awake, especially when she registered the rather intent look in Sam's eyes as he turned to her. Her heart did a little flip, and she found she had to catch her breath. Was he going to kiss her? Did she want him to? Yes, she realized, she very much did.

"I'm going to be shipping out in the next few months, as I said before," he told her in his steady way, "but I'd like to see you again before then, if I may." He smiled wryly. "If you want me to, that is. I had a really nice time tonight, and I'd like to do it again, if you would."

Sophie took in the warmth in his hazel eyes, the easy openness of his smile. Sam, she thought, was both kind and uncomplicated, an open book of a person, his life laid out like a map for anyone to see and observe. In comparison, she felt like something complex and crumpled up, a mess of uncertainty and confusion, guilt and fear that she could hardly bear to voice. And yet... tonight, she'd just been a girl in a pretty dress, out with a man who wanted to see her again.

And right then, that was all she wanted to be.

"Yes," she told him, knowing she meant it. "I would. That would be... very nice." She gave a small, self-conscious laugh. "Very nice indeed."

"I'm glad." His gaze lingered on hers for a second more, until Sophie felt herself start to blush.

He walked her to her door, and they stood in the shadow of the porch, Sam looking serious while Sophie smiled nervously, not quite sure how to say goodbye, wondering if he was going to kiss her and not at all sure how to show that she'd like him to. Then he stepped forward and brushed her lips in the gentlest of kisses, no more than a whisper of breath, of touch, like a butterfly had landed on her mouth and then flitted away again. It made her feel dizzy with pleasure, and yet already wanting more. Her first kiss, Sophie thought, her head spinning a little. It had been short and painfully sweet; something about its innocence made her ache.

"Goodnight, Sophie," Sam whispered, and he waited until she'd slipped inside before he left the porch and headed back to his car.

Sophie stood there for a moment, her back to the door, her

fingers pressed to her lips. A little giggle escaped her in a bubble of sound, and it was then she registered the sound of the radio, even at this late hour. She walked into the living room, starting in surprise at Miss Bryson, Samantha, William and Jack all gathered around the Silvertone.

"What..." she began, only to fall silent as Miss Bryson turned to her, her face full of sympathy.

"My dear," she said, holding out her hands to Sophie. "We've only just heard on the radio. Germany has invaded France and the Low Countries."

CHAPTER 19

AUGUST 1940

In retrospect, it all happened so fast. It took only weeks, but it felt as if it had taken mere days, or even hours, so quickly did Europe collapse under Hitler's relentless onslaught, a veritable house of cards under the relentless steel of Germany's Panzers.

By the middle of June, the Netherlands, Belgium, and France had all fallen to the Nazis. The Netherlands had surrendered after just five short days; Belgium after a little more than two weeks. France had managed to hold out a little longer, but when the British troops were forced to evacuate Dunkirk at the beginning of June, leaving no Allied forces on mainland Europe, all hope seemed lost.

It felt as if Hitler had as good as won the war, before it had barely been able to start. Three more countries now under his command, including those where her family and friends all lived! Sophie could hardly believe it. She couldn't *bear* to believe it—her father and Margarete, Heinrich, Hannah, Rachel... all under the Nazis' rule again. It felt like a nightmare from which there was no waking, and yet it was a shock every time she thought of it, the news jolting through her as if she'd heard it for the first time. *No, it couldn't be,* she kept thinking, while knowing that it was.

Sophie found herself walking around in a daze, a shadow of herself, and yet somehow, she made herself keep going, one foot in front of the other, day after day. She worked at the Jewish Community Center; she comforted Jewish refugees; she translated reports and typed up files; she ate and drank and chatted and sometimes she even smiled. She went out with Sam several more times, taking comfort in his easy presence, his ready sympathy. When she'd broken down in tears once, talking about her family, he'd put his arms around her and she'd rested her head against his solid chest, feeling safe, truly safe, for the first time in memory. *And yet her family wasn't...*

Still, she was grateful for Sam's presence in her life. Being with him felt simple, while so much else in her life was not, his company easy and undemanding and yet exciting, too. He kissed her at the end of every date, a chaste brush of her lips which set her heart to fluttering, but he never pushed for more, and even though part of her longed for it, she realized she was relieved. She felt too fractured inside to offer him anything else just then, as much as she liked him, and he seemed to understand that by intuition.

And yet, despite the pleasure of his company and the busyness of her days, in the middle of the night, she often woke up with her heart racing, eyes straining in the dark, gasping for breath as if she'd run a race, as if she was trying to escape a dark and malevolent formless force that was chasing her. She tried, at the same time, to imagine and not imagine, what was happening to her family and friends, everyone she'd ever known, so far away.

She'd learned through the news that a German military government had been set up in Belgium, run by General Alexander von Falkenhausen. He had authorized a tax on all Belgians to pay for "external occupation costs," which amounted to a staggering two-thirds of Belgium's national income. Food, fuel, and clothing were being strictly rationed, but so far, no laws against Jews had been enacted, and they were free to live as they had before.

As for Rachel in the Netherlands and Hannah in France, according to news reports, those countries, like Belgium, had enacted no specifically anti-Jewish legislation... yet. But would they? It was a question that haunted her. Although Sophie knew her family and friends would be facing deprivation, she hoped and prayed it would become no worse than that, and the Nazis wouldn't subject Jews in their newly conquered territories to the same harsh laws and practices they had back in Germany. It felt like so much wishful thinking, but she had no choice but to hope for the best, because she knew there was so very little she could do about any of it.

The flood of Jewish refugees that had come into the Center in 1939 slowed to a trickle as 1940 wore on, despite the hundreds of thousands still on the visa waiting list. With the war in Europe, travel across the Atlantic had become increasingly dangerous and prohibitive for anyone, never mind refugees with little money or other resources. Sophie's role at the JCC had turned into more general typing and filing than translating or helping refugees, and while she appreciated still being in work, she missed the old aspects of her job, comforting those in distress, giving hope to the weary and travelworn, and even using her German.

While the tenants of Miss Bryson gathered around the old Silvertone most evenings to hear William L. Shirer's nightly report from Berlin, Sophie started to sense a changing mood among her fellow boarders, or at least one in particular. Jack, an insurance clerk who generally kept to himself, had started making more vociferous comments after Shirer's report, about how Europe "needed to take care of itself" and America should stay "well out of it." Sophie held her tongue when he made

these remarks, even as he looked around the room with a chal-
lenging glint in his eye, as if spoiling for a fight. She wasn't
about to give him one, but it still made her feel uneasy and
afraid. How many people in this country thought like he did?
How many Americans resented the fact that Europe was domi-
nating the news, that refugees like herself were invading their
country?

In early August, they listened to General Pershing, the
former commander of the American Expeditionary Forces, give
a nationwide broadcast, demanding that aid be sent to Great
Britain. "Democracy and liberty have been overthrown on the
continent of Europe," he proclaimed over the crackling
airwaves. "Only the British are left to defend democracy and
liberty in Europe. By sending help to the British, we can still
hope with confidence to keep the war on the other side of the
Atlantic Ocean, where the enemies of liberty, if possible, should
be defeated."

"Amen," Samantha murmured, only for Jack to suddenly
jump up from his seat as if he'd been stung by a bee.

"Why should the United States bail out Britain?" he
demanded, startling everyone with his fury. "We're strong
enough that no foreign nation can invade us. Our shores are in
no danger. We can stand apart—alone—and so we should!"

"Mr. Wells," Miss Bryson reproved, drawing herself up in
affront. "I will not have any shouting in my living room."

"I'm sorry, Miss Bryson," he replied, not sounding terribly
contrite, "but we should all feel strongly about this. You
remember the last war, don't you?"

Miss Bryson drew herself up even further, her dark eyes
flashing like buttons in her small, wrinkled face. "I assure you I
do," she told him coldly. "My brother died in that war."

A startled, somber silence followed this pronouncement;
Sophie didn't think anyone had known that Miss Bryson had
even had a brother, never mind lost one in the Great War. She

tended to maintain something of a distance between herself and her tenants.

"I am sorry to hear that," Jack continued after a pause, sounding a bit more apologetic than he had before, "but if that's so, you should be fighting against us joining this war like I am. We don't want to be dragged down into Europe's mess, and lose good men—sons and brothers and husbands—again, do we, and for *what*? Something that's happening thousands of miles away that has nothing to do with us?"

"Or is it just you'd rather not fight yourself?" Samantha interjected sharply. Her expression was taut, her eyes snapping. "You sound like a coward, Mr. Wells, if you ask me."

Jack's face flushed a dull red. "I'm nothing of the sort," he replied with stiff dignity. "I'm just talking sense. Do you know there's nearly a million members of the America First Committee? We're writing to members of Congress—"

"Don't tell me you're part of that shameful group," Samantha returned, drawing back, her mouth twisted with distaste. "I don't know anyone who would admit to such a thing!"

"Oh, really? There's nothing shameful about it," Jack replied heatedly. "Charles Lindbergh is a member, and he's spoken in public about it! He's a national hero—"

"I don't care about Lindbergh," Samantha cut him off coldly. She turned to the other tenant, who had been silently smoking this whole time; Miss Bryson had relaxed the rules about smoking indoors, and she now allowed it in the front room only. "Mr. Fawber," Samantha asked in appeal, "don't you agree with me? We must support the British in their fight against Hitler."

William was silent for a long moment, while Sophie waited in growing apprehension. It had been bad enough having Jack mouthing off, but was William going to agree with him?

"I can't see the problem with giving aid," he said at last,

stubbing out his cigarette. "But sending men over—boots on the ground—is another matter entirely."

"Is it?" Samantha demanded. "Do you know what Hitler is doing over there? He's storming all over Europe! And what about how he's treating the Jews—"

Jack made a scoffing sound that had Sophie tensing all the more.

Samantha's eyes narrowed. "Do you not care about that, Mr. Wells?" she asked quietly.

Jack gave her a rather surly glance. "Like I've said, it's none of our business."

"Sophie is Jewish, you know," Samantha said, and Sophie felt herself flushing, hating being put under such sudden scrutiny by her fellow housemates. She and Samantha had become a bit closer over the last few months, sometimes sharing a pot of coffee and a chat in the evening, and Sophie had told her about her background. Now she almost wished she hadn't, especially when Jack gave her a none too friendly look. He must have known she was Jewish, even if it had never been discussed openly before.

"What of it?" he asked with a dismissive shrug.

"Her family—"

"Samantha, please," Sophie interjected quietly. "I think we've learned enough about Mr. Wells' opinions."

"I'll give you one more opinion, for free," Jack replied, his face twisting in malice as he glared at her. "I don't give a damn about what Hitler is doing to the Jews. It's his country to run, and he can do as he sees fit. And everyone knows how money-grubbing the Jews are, anyway. They control the banks, even over here! Why shouldn't they have a few regulations on their activity, teach them their place? They can't have everything their own way."

Sophie felt an icy wave of shock sweep through her as she stared at him, seeing the true malevolence in his face for the first time. She'd had no idea he'd thought that way about Jews, about *her*. They'd never spoken much, and she supposed she now knew why. Could he really think Jews deserved the treatment they were getting? The thought was an abomination.

"Mr. Wells," Miss Bryson stated in tremulous tones, "I will not allow such talk in my boarding house. If you are going to use such language, I have no choice but to ask you to leave." Sophie's landlady stared down her tenant, and everyone else held their breath.

"I don't want to stay in a Jew-lover's house, anyway," Jack spat, and he stormed from the room.

A terrible silence ensued; Sophie had no idea where to look. She felt both icy and hot at the same time, and deeply shocked, as well as humiliated. She'd never encountered such open, virulent antisemitism in America before, and it left her shaken, wondering how many others quietly—or not so quietly—held the same opinions.

"Sophie, I'm so sorry," Samantha said after a moment, her tone one of quiet contrition. "Perhaps I shouldn't have pushed him so."

"It doesn't matter," Sophie replied numbly. "You're not responsible for his opinions."

"I don't like such altercations in my house," Miss Bryson stated, drawing her cardigan about her shoulders. "If we cannot all get along, then we simply will not be able to listen to the radio anymore."

That hardly seemed like a reasonable solution, but Sophie wasn't about to say so. William, she noticed, had not said a word and was being careful not to meet her eye. She had a feeling he did not share Samantha's strong sentiments about the war or the treatment of Jews.

Doing her best to keep her expression even, Sophie started tidying up the tea things and then took them back to the kitchen.

"Are you all right?" Samantha asked as she followed her to the back of the house. "That was most unpleasant. I'm sorry, I had no idea he felt as strongly as that."

"As strongly?" Sophie put the tray by the sink before turning around to face her friend. "But you suspected?"

"Well, he's always grumbled a bit when we listen to the reports from Berlin, hasn't he? Under his breath."

Yes, he had, but Sophie hadn't really paid too much attention, because she'd been so concerned with catching every word of those reports. "I suppose," she replied.

"Please don't let it get to you," Samantha implored. "So many believe that America should involve itself in the war now. And look how Britain is controlling the skies! Some say they'll send the Luftwaffe packing soon."

The so-called Battle of Britain had been going on all summer. Sophie didn't think it would be over as quickly as that, however, despite her friend's optimism. Great Britain was holding its own, but only just, and meanwhile, Hitler controlled much of Europe.

"It doesn't bother me," she told Samantha, mostly honestly, because the truth was, she couldn't suppress a feeling of hurt, and even of shame, although she tried. "I'm afraid I have far more serious things to worry about."

Samantha's face creased in concern. "Have you heard from your family recently?"

Sophie shook her head. She'd had a letter from Hannah back in July; it must have been sent before the fall of France. She'd been heartened by her friend's warmth in the letter; Hannah had even mentioned the little café where they hoped to meet, after the war.

I've been to Henri's, where Rosa suggested we meet. It's a funny little place, right by the Eiffel Tower. I bought Lotte a hot chocolate and imagined the four of us there, drinking champagne and celebrating our new lives. Sometimes that is what keeps me getting out of bed every morning! I'm sorry I seemed angry with you, on the ship. I'm not anymore.

And yet, Sophie had thought as she'd folded up the letter, she was still angry with herself.

"I don't imagine many letters will get through now," she told Samantha. "Or at least not easily." She'd heard through the Jewish Community Center that letters from Europe could still be sent through the Red Cross, or through a private mail service through Lisbon, but it was slow, as well as expensive. In any case, she hadn't had any letters from anyone in well over a month, and she hated not knowing what was going on. She had no idea if her father or Margarete or Heinrich were safe and well; if they were warm, fed, *alive*. Somehow, she had to find a contentment, or at least an acceptance, in the not knowing, but it was hard.

"I really am sorry about Mr. Wells," Samantha persisted after a moment. "I don't know anyone who thinks the way he does—"

"It seems a million other people do, at least," Sophie replied, trying to sound wry. It was better than feeling hurt, and what did she really care if Jack Wells, who had barely said a word to her anyway, disliked Jews? Or if the million members of America First did? It wasn't as if he could actually do anything about it. At least she hoped he couldn't. And it looked as if he'd now be leaving the boarding house, anyway.

"I've heard talk that if Roosevelt wins a third term, we'll almost certainly enter the war," Samantha told her, clearly trying to bolster her spirits. "Whether people such as Mr. Wells want it or not."

Roosevelt had recently won his party's nomination at the convention last month; he'd claimed he would only run if he was "drafted"—his choice of word—but had then more or less rigged the convention to vote for him, setting it in Chicago, where he had a great deal of support, packing the galleries and even controlling the sound system to have everyone shout "The world wants Roosevelt!"

But, Sophie wondered despondently, did the world want war?

A week later, Sam took her out to the Potomac for a concert of the city's symphony orchestra, set on a barge in the middle of the river, as part of their "sunset symphony series." It was a sweltering day, the sky a pale blue and the leaves of the trees seeming to hang limply in the humidity. A year on, Sophie had almost got used to the heat; she wore a sleeveless cotton dress and kept her hair in a French roll to avoid it frizzing damply.

Hundreds, if not thousands, of Washingtonians were out on the lawn behind the Lincoln Memorial, sitting on the steps that led down to the Watergate, a natural amphitheater for the orchestra out on the river.

"Look at all the people," Sophie exclaimed, for besides the many people on the lawn and steps, there were dozens of canoes and other small boats surrounding the barge, trying to get a closer seat. She'd never seen anything like it.

"It's quite something, isn't it?" Sam returned. "I came last year for the first time and found it remarkable."

They found a comfortable spot and Sam spread out a blanket; Sophie had packed chicken sandwiches and cold bottles of Coca-Cola for their picnic. As she settled herself, she felt her spirits lift a little. It was hard not to be happy on such a beautiful evening, with the sky striated into streaks of red and orange, the sounds of the orchestra tuning up floating on the summer air, and a handsome man sitting next to her, all kindness and solicitude.

They listened to the first two pieces—Tchaikovsky's 1812

Overture and another piece by Strauss—before Sam turned to her, his easy, open face looking uncharacteristically shadowed and serious.

"Sophie," he said, and her stomach flipped, and not in a good way. He looked too somber for it to be good news.

"What is it?" she asked unsteadily.

"Remember I told you I'd be shipping out one day?"

Yes, back when they'd first met. They hadn't really talked about it since; as the months had slipped past, Sophie had let herself forget. "Yes..." she answered, the word trailing away as she waited for what he was going to say next, already knowing she did not want to hear it.

"Well, I finally got my orders. I'm going to Puget Sound, to help refit a battleship for the next few months. I leave next week."

Next week. Sophie stared at him in dismayed surprise. She hadn't realized he might be leaving as soon as that, and she knew just how much she'd miss their times together, his sweet kisses. "Oh..." she said, and then found she couldn't say anything else.

Sam took her hand in his, his long, lean fingers tightening on hers. "I know we haven't been stepping out all that long, but can I ask... that is, I want to ask you..." He paused, swallowing, his expression endearingly sincere and even a little anxious in a way that made Sophie smile despite the deep dismay she felt at his news. "Sophie," he asked, "will you be my girl?"

Sophie blinked at him in surprise and pleasure. She thought she knew what that meant, from hearing the phrase in movies and novels, but she wasn't entirely sure. At least, she wasn't sure what *Sam* meant by it. How could she be his girl, when he would be all the way across the country?

Sam seemed to understand her hesitation because he continued, smiling as he held her hand in his, "What I mean is, will you write to me, and I'll write to you? And you won't—well, you won't step out with any other fellows while I'm away? And when I come back... we'll see each other again. I should get leave in November, maybe, and I could come back then."

Sophie couldn't imagine "stepping out" with anyone else. The only man she wanted was Sam. But what was he really asking her?

"Are you asking me to wait for you?" she replied as she searched his face. Did Sam have serious intentions toward her? They'd never talked about the future, about things like marriage or children. Sophie hadn't even dared to think of them. But now, if Sam wanted her to wait... was that what he meant?

"Well..." He swallowed, smiling wryly. "Yes, I guess I am asking that." He let out an uncertain, little laugh. "Are you willing to wait for me, Sophie?"

She glanced down at their joined hands, fingers twined, his grip so solid and sure and safe. She thought she might be at least a little in love with Sam Jackson—not that she entirely knew what love felt like—and she thought one day she could be truly, deeply in love with him, if she let herself. And yet...

She took a quick breath and then forced herself to ask, "What about the fact that I'm Jewish?"

A silence ensued, one that made her feel uneasy. She made herself glance up from their joined hands.

Sam was staring at her, his forehead creased with what looked like confusion. "What about it?"

"Does it matter to you?"

He cocked his head. "Should it?"

"I don't know," Sophie admitted honestly. "It would matter in Germany, of course, and it seems to matter to a lot of people here, as well. More than I expected." She thought of Jack Wells' face, twisted in derision and dislike. He'd left the boarding house the day after that awful altercation, and while she couldn't help but be glad, his departure had ended up causing a certain frisson in the atmosphere at Miss Bryson's house. Sometimes, Sophie had caught the older woman gazing at her in a way that made her wonder if Miss Bryson regretted asking Jack Wells to leave, and if she thought Sophie was more trouble than she was worth. Miss Bryson hadn't yet been able to find another tenant to replace him.

Sam squeezed her hand. "It doesn't matter to me, Sophie. I promise you it doesn't. Does it matter that I'm *not* Jewish?"

"No," she admitted honestly. "My family was never very religious that way, although sometimes I felt we ought to be. If we're going to be singled out for being Jewish, well, perhaps we should act Jewish." She let out a short laugh and Sam smiled and squeezed her hand again.

"Then that's sorted," he said. "So, what do you think? Will you be my girl?"

It seemed like such an easy question to answer, and yet she still hesitated. Her being Jewish might not matter to him now, but what about when—if—they married? What if they had children? Would he want his children raised Protestant, the way she knew he had been? Would his parents? And what about her —would she want her children raised Jewish? They were questions she'd never even thought to ask herself before; she was only twenty, after all, and she and Sam had been on a little more than a handful of dates.

But was there any real reason to refuse him, especially when she didn't even want to?

"Yes, Sam," she told him. "If you want me to, I'll be your girl."

Because, Sophie acknowledged, she certainly wasn't anyone else's.

Sam smiled and kissed her, and she smiled and kissed him back, putting her arms around him, drawing him close. Yet even as he held her to him, she fought a sweeping sense of sorrow, that yet another person in her life would be leaving her. She was the one who had done the leaving before, of course, she reminded herself; she'd fled in the night with no more than a hurried goodbye.

Sitting there with Sam as the sun's dying rays sank behind the barge, Sophie acknowledged that being the one who was left didn't feel any better. If anything, it felt worse.

CHAPTER 20

JULY 1941

"There's someone here to see you, Sophie!"

Sophie turned from the reports she'd been filing, surprise as well as a wary apprehension rippling through her at Sadie's words. Someone to see her? She didn't get many visitors at the Center, if any at all. Since Sam had left for Puget Sound back in September, her days—and evenings—had been quiet indeed. She lived for his letters, as well as the precious few that had come from Europe, and the news on the radio. Quiet nights in with a book and a cup of coffee were some of the few pleasures she allowed herself. Nearly a whole year had passed in this way, while the news from Europe had become darker and darker.

Great Britain had been bombed relentlessly, and Hitler had invaded Yugoslavia and Greece. British forces had had some victories in North Africa, but dozens of convoys had been lost in the Atlantic. And, even more worryingly, the *New York Times* had reported on the "destitution, destruction, and every infamy" regarding the treatment of Jews in Poland; according to "unsubstantiated reports," they had been herded into ghettoes in cities such as Lublin and Lodz, the doors sealed against the rest of the world, the Jews treated worse than prisoners or even beasts;

they had no good food or clean water, and dysentery and typhoid were rampant, as was suicide.

The day after the *New York Times* had reported the alarming news, it had retracted it in an editorial, saying that they "chose to disbelieve unofficial reports of such horrors as exaggerated." Reading that, Sophie had had no idea what to think. She knew well enough that reports *could* be exaggerated, and often were for effect, but she could not get the image of the sealed doors, hundreds of thousands of Jews forced into a few city blocks square with nothing but the clothes on their backs, out of her mind. Surely such a thing would not happen in Belgium? In the last letter she'd received from Margarete a month ago, her family was still safe in Antwerp, which had both bolstered her spirits and filled her with relief.

Smoothing her hands down the sides of her plain, dark skirt, Sophie left the filing room for the foyer, stopping in surprise when she saw who was waiting by the door, his hat in his hand.

"Mr. Howard!"

She hadn't seen John Howard since he had approached her over a year ago, while she'd been eating her lunch with Mattie at Logan Circle. Sophie recalled wondering then why he had talked to her at all, and especially asked her about her ability with languages, but with so much else to worry about, she'd forgotten about the odd conversation almost completely... until now.

He smiled at her, faint lines fanning out from his hazel eyes. "You remembered me."

"As you, me."

"I did." He rocked back on his heels, that assessing gaze of his sweeping over her thoughtfully. "I wondered if I might take you out to lunch?"

"Lunch?" Sophie could feel Sadie's avid curiosity like a palpable thing behind her.

Sadie knew that Sophie had agreed to be Sam's girl, and

that they'd been writing each other nearly every week for the last ten months. She'd loved hearing the details of their romance, and thought Sam was a "stand-up sort of fellow", to which Sophie of course agreed.

On his leave before Christmas, Sam had come back and taken her out to see the lighting of the National Christmas Tree on the White House's Ellipse, a magical occasion as the tree had blazed with lights under a wintry, starry sky. They'd gone to Roma for dinner afterward, something of a tradition now, and, all in all, it had been a lovely evening, made all the sweeter by its unfortunate brevity.

On Miss Bryson's porch, he'd kissed her with more passion and feeling than he ever had before, and in response Sophie had wound her arms around his neck, leaned into him, their bodies pressed against each other from shoulder to hip, Sophie's heart beating hard. She could feel Sam's thundering in his chest, and she'd pressed even closer. They'd clung together for a few minutes, needing no words, until someone had come down the sidewalk and they'd been forced to spring apart, Sam smiling ruefully at her, while Sophie's heart had continued to race and her lips had tingled.

He'd returned to duty soon after, continuing to help with the maintenance of one of the country's biggest battleships. In January, it had finished its refit and Sam had gone with it, posted in Hawaii. Sophie had found the scattered green dots of the islands in Miss Bryson's atlas, amazed at how far away he was—more than halfway around the world, even farther away from Washington than anyone in Europe.

Now, Sophie focused on John Howard, and the question he was asking her. No matter how scandalized or censorious Sadie might seem, Sophie knew the man wasn't asking her out on a date, not out of the blue and after all this time. So why *was* he asking her? A thrill of something like excitement ran through her like a streak of lightning, radiating out from her fingertips and right down to her toes. She didn't know why, of course, she couldn't possibly, but she thought—*hoped*—that it might be something interesting. Something important even, perhaps... Or was she being ridiculous, to think such a thing, even for a second?

"That would be very nice," she told him at last. "Let me just get my purse."

Sophie hurried back to her desk to get her purse and light cardigan, while Sadie frowned daggers at her.

"What are you doing—" she hissed under her breath. "Sam Jackson is a very nice man—"

"Oh Sadie," Sophie protested on a half-laugh, "it's not like that. I would never two-time Sam, you know that."

"Yes, I know," Sadie replied after a moment. "And you know he's crazy about you." She'd taken quite a liking to Sam, on the few times that she'd met him. In December, they'd gone out again to the Mayfair, and he'd come to one of the dances on the Center's roof terrace. Sadie clearly thought Sophie was a very lucky woman... and she was, when it came to Sam. "It's just, that man clearly has his eye on you."

"It's probably just business," Sophie dismissed, and Sadie's eyebrows rose.

"What kind of business?"

"I... I'll tell you when I get back," Sophie promised, and then she rejoined John Howard in the foyer, before they headed out into the warm, sticky afternoon.

"I've got my car," he said, gesturing to a Buick Century parked in front of the Center. "I thought we could go to Sholl's. Nothing fancy, I'm afraid, but they do a good lunch."

Sophie nodded her assent. Sholl's cafeterias were popular in the city, especially among those who worked in the government. They offered simple fare in a bright and clean environment, with a few German offerings on the menu as well, such as schnitzel and strudel.

They drove in silence to the cafeteria, just over a mile away on 14th Street. John had rolled the windows halfway down, and Sophie was glad of the cooling breeze that blew over her. She was desperately curious as to why he'd sought her out, but she wasn't bold enough to ask, and in any case, she suspected he'd tell her in his own good time.

A few minutes later, they were seated at one of the tables in the back of the mostly empty restaurant; it was a bit early for lunch. The waitress had poured them both cups of coffee and left them alone, studying the menus.

"What do you feel like?" John asked. "The sirloin steak is always dependable."

It was also the most expensive thing on the menu. "I'll have the roast chicken, I think," Sophie said.

They served themselves at the buffet and returned to the table; by this time, Sophie's stomach felt like a ball of nerves. What could he possibly want? After all this time?

"Your English is very good now," John remarked as he spread a napkin in his lap and they both tucked into their lunches. "I know I've said it before, but you almost sound like an American."

"Well, I try to," Sophie replied wryly, and he raised his eyebrows.

"Is that because you've encountered anti-German sentiment?"

She shrugged, thinking of Jack Wells storming out of Miss Bryson's. Since then, she'd noticed little things—sideways glances on the bus or trolley; a discarded copy of the viciously antisemitic paper, *Social Justice*, edited by the notorious Father Coughlin; the casual cartoons even in the *Washington Post* and other newspapers that depicted Jews as wealthy, avaricious, big-nosed. She had once hoped she'd left behind such things in Germany, but it seemed they were, to some extent or another, everywhere.

"Anti-Jewish, perhaps," she replied quietly, and John nodded thoughtfully, not debating the point.

"That must be a disappointment to you," he remarked.

"I've learned to accept it. Or at least," she corrected herself, "if not accept it, then expect it."

"Unfortunately, that is probably wise." He paused, a forkful of mashed potatoes halfway to his mouth. "Have you heard from your family?"

The way he asked the question made Sophie think he knew they were still in Belgium. He hadn't asked if they'd been able to emigrate, certainly. "There have been a few letters, through the Red Cross," she replied. Each one had been unbearably precious. "They are still in Antwerp, waiting to emigrate."

In the last year, all Jews in Belgium had had to register with the German government; Jewish business owners had had their premises and assets seized. Recently, the government had required a *Judenrat* to be formed—an administrative body purported to "help" the Jews but which really just ended up being a way to control them. It was life in Berlin all over again, Sophie had thought as she'd read Margarete's news with a plunging sensation in her stomach, a racing of her heart. There had been no mention of her father or Heinrich, besides them both sending their love. At least, she told herself, they were safe. For now.

"I'm sorry," John said, and Sophie could only nod.

She'd also heard from Rosa, Rachel, and Hannah, although infrequently; Rachel and Hannah's situations seemed similar to that of her parents, and Rosa had not said anything of her own circumstances at all, which made Sophie wonder what on earth she could be doing. Was she still at the internment camp? Why hadn't she said so? There was, she'd reflected more than once, so much she didn't know. So much her friends and family seemed to not want to tell her...

"You must be wondering why I've asked you to lunch," John

said after they'd finished most of their meal, and Sophie kept her expression carefully neutral.

"It did cross my mind," she replied, and he let out a soft laugh.

"I'm sure you follow the news."

"Every day." She folded her hands in front of her, her appetite vanished. What was he going to tell her?

John lowered his voice, although there was no one around to hear. "I think I told you before, way back in '39, that America would get involved in the war. It was just a matter of when."

"Yes." Sophie's mouth was dry. "I remember." In the last few months, the United States had relinquished its alleged neutrality, by providing aid to Great Britain through its Lend Lease program. It was a start, but Sophie knew it wouldn't be enough to stop Hitler.

"It's still a matter of *when*," John continued. "But that when is moving closer, as I'm sure you can imagine. In the meantime, the United States needs to be ready—not just militarily speaking, but in terms of intelligence." He reached for a cigarette from the packet inside his jacket, proffering it to Sophie first.

She shook her head; she'd never got the hang of smoking, and didn't particularly care to.

"We're hiring for a new governmental agency," John explained as he lit his own cigarette. "I'm afraid I can't tell you much more than that. We're looking for all sorts—analysts, economists, historians, linguists." He paused, and Sophie nodded slowly.

"You want to hire me as a linguist?" Even as she said the words, she could hardly believe them. She might speak German and French, but she was little more than a schoolgirl. She had no university education, no formal training. She wasn't even an American citizen. The US government surely couldn't be so desperate as to hire someone like her.

"I can see what you're thinking," John remarked, smiling as he blew out a ring of smoke. "Why you?"

"Yes," Sophie admitted, "that is exactly what I'm thinking." It certainly seemed a sensible thing to think.

"There are quite a few reasons, as it happens. We're looking at recently arrived foreign nationals for a reason—they have recent experience of the country they came from, its mores and values, its slang and jargon. Far more so than a fusty academic who has been reading Goethe somewhere in Illinois." He smiled again, inviting her to share the joke.

"Still," Sophie replied slowly, "I'm hardly qualified."

"Besides," John continued, as if she hadn't spoken, "we've got to have the right sort of person, if you get my meaning. No pinkos or socialists, or anyone like that. Not at this level, anyway. Some of these academics... well, we can't be as choosy as we'd like. But if we find someone with the right sort of beliefs, well, that can only be a good thing."

Pinkos—anyone with communist leanings. Sophie was familiar with the term; many Americans seemed to regard communism with the same disdain and dread that they viewed fascism, although some, especially in education, were, like Samantha, quietly pro-communist.

"How do you know I'm not a communist?" she asked, daring to be so bold, and John laughed softly.

"My dear Miss Weiss, do you imagine we'd be having this conversation if you were?"

A chill stole over her, replacing the excitement she'd felt, which now seemed almost childish. Of course, he must have researched her—her background, her beliefs, her *family*. That was why he hadn't asked if her parents had emigrated yet.

Sophie lurched forward, driven by a need so deep it felt as if it was taking her over. "Do you know something about my family?" she demanded hoarsely. "Do you know more than I do?"

John's face softened in something like sympathy. "I know they're in Antwerp," he said. "As you do."

Sophie had the sense that even if he knew more, he wouldn't have told her. Whatever this new government agency was, she thought, it dealt in secrets.

"What is it you wish me to do?" she asked after a moment.

"Nothing terribly exciting, I should say that straight off. We have the more experienced people dealing with anything remotely sensitive, you understand. You'd have some security clearance, but you wouldn't be given any information that is truly classified." Sophie nodded her understanding and he continued, "What we do need are good linguists and translators. You've been doing a fair amount of translation at the Jewish Community Center, I understand?"

She gazed across the table at him, her lips pursed. She wasn't fooled by his deceptively casual tone. "You *know* I have."

He laughed again, an admiring sound, his head cocked to one side. "You're right, I do. We'd like you to translate some German for us. Like I said, nothing top secret. Most of it will be German newspapers we've managed to get hold of—not the propaganda ones, you understand, such as the *Völkischer Beobachter* or *Der Stürmer*. We're not interested in reading more of Hitler's lies."

Sophie couldn't hide her moue of distaste—both newspapers were violently, virulently antisemitic. She'd dreaded seeing the lurid headlines of *Der Stürmer* in its red display boxes on the street back in Berlin, often filled with stories of ritual murders and sadistic practices supposedly carried out by Jews.

"Yes, exactly," John remarked, agreeing with her as if she'd spoken out loud. "We're not much concerned with what Goebbels wants everyone to believe. We're more interested in what little titbits might be slipped into a regional newspaper— the *Frankfurter Zeitung*, for example, or the *Hamburger Abendblatt*."

Sophie supposed she could understand the reasoning behind that, although she couldn't really imagine what the so-called *titbits* they'd be looking for could possibly be. She presumed it wouldn't be her job to guess. "So I would translate such newspapers?" she surmised.

"Yes. You wouldn't have to analyze anything—in fact, you wouldn't be allowed to. Your job is strictly translation and leave the analysis to those trained to do it. We have very clear responsibilities in the government—you do your own job, and no one else's."

Just as she'd thought, then. His words were patronizing, but the tone was not.

"I'm afraid it won't be very glamorous," he warned her wryly. "You'll be stuck in a little broom cupboard somewhere, with a stack of newspapers and a typewriter. That's all."

It didn't sound glamorous at *all*, Sophie thought ruefully. She'd miss working at the Jewish Community Center—the companionship, the friendliness, the shared sense of purpose. And yet she suspected that, for the last year, she'd been employed out of pity as much as usefulness; she wasn't needed nearly as much as she'd been back in '39, when the refugees had been flooding into the country.

And if she could do anything, anything at all, to help win this war... this war that America hadn't yet entered into, yet perhaps one day would. One day soon, if John Howard was to be believed...

"Well?" John Howard asked, and Sophie gave a decisive nod. She knew she didn't even need to think about it. She would do whatever she could, no matter how insignificant or dull, to help with this war effort. To bring her family to America, and to rid the world of Hitler and his evil forever. Working in a broom cupboard by herself was a very small sacrifice indeed compared to what her friends and family had to endure. Sophie knew that in her own head and heart it didn't balance the scales;

she still felt wretched for being safe in America when everyone she loved was elsewhere, but it did go some way to assuaging her guilt. At least now she would actually be *doing* something to bring them closer to her.

"Yes," she told him, her voice ringing out firmly. "I accept."

John's eyes crinkled. "I haven't told you your pay or anything like that yet."

Sophie shrugged. "I don't really care, but it's got to be at least as much as I'm making at the Jewish Community Center."

"Twenty dollars a week? It will be a good deal more, in fact."

So he knew how much she made, as well. Sophie wasn't surprised, but she was a little shaken. What else did John Howard know about her? Was there a file on her somewhere deep in the bowels of some government office? She imagined there must have been; she was a German national, after all. And what might he know of her family? Or of Rosa, Rachel, Hannah? She suspected someone had been monitoring her mail.

Well, she had nothing to hide, and everything to gain. Her family's freedom. The world's freedom. Of course she would do her part, no matter how small.

She gave John a direct, bold look. "So, when do I start?"

CHAPTER 21

AUGUST 1941

John Howard hadn't been exaggerating when he'd told Sophie she'd be working in a broom cupboard. In fact, he'd been generous in describing her office in such terms. When she'd reported to work at an anonymous address on E Street a week after John had approached her, Sophie had had no idea what to expect. She'd been terrified and excited in equal measure, having only been able to tell Sadie and the others at the Center that she was going to work as a typist for the government.

"I'm sorry," she'd told Sadie. "But the pay is a bit better, and I need to save all I can, in case my family..." She'd let her words trail away, knowing Sadie would be sympathetic, which, of course, she was.

"So, you'll be a government girl, eh?" Sadie had shaken her head slowly. "I suppose it will come to that for a lot of us, if we get ourselves into this war. It will be all hands on deck, and more besides." She had let out a sigh as she gave Sophie a wry smile. "Well, I don't begrudge you leaving. Of course I don't."

The address on E Street was a squat yet substantial brick building, in what used to be part of the US Navy Bureau of

Medicine and Surgery, on Navy Hill. As Sophie had walked up to the front door, she'd wondered if she was even in the right place. There was no placard saying it was a government building, no sign telling her to keep away, no one about at all.

As soon as she had knocked on the front door, however, she had been whisked away by a blank-faced man in a dark suit. In a small office crammed with files, she was given a whirlwind explanation of where she was—the anonymous-sounding Office of the Coordinator of Information—and asked to sign a document ensuring her secrecy about just about everything. After scanning its many paragraphs, Sophie had thought she'd be reluctant to admit to anyone so much as what she ate for breakfast, but she signed willingly enough, eager to begin this adventure and start being useful to the war effort.

Although outside of the building on E Street, it had been quiet and almost abandoned, inside it was a chaotic scramble of people rushing everywhere—secretaries with tottering piles of files, doors opening and then slamming shut, and hammering and sawing coming from other places, where the building was still being renovated for its new purpose—whatever that actually was. Sophie might have signed her soul away, but she knew little more than what John Howard had told her at Sholl's.

She did learn, over the course of the next few days, that she worked in the department of Research and Analysis—or R&A—with a few other linguists and academics. Anything she translated and typed up was put on a metal cart that was trundled to R&A's main library, where six women worked around the clock filing all the pieces of paper they were given. Sophie wondered if anyone ever even looked at the articles she translated so laboriously. As far as she could see, they seemed to go right into a dusty metal filing cabinet.

No one was encouraged to chitchat, although the girls in the catalog library did, at least a little. Sophie listened sometimes, but she didn't say much, since she knew so little and everything was meant to be secret, anyway. It could feel rather lonely, beavering away by herself in a broom cupboard, but at least, she told herself, she was doing something useful... even if it didn't always *feel* useful.

Translating the *Frankfurter Zeitung* was a job anyone with a passing knowledge of German could do, and most of the articles seemed as if they wouldn't be very helpful at all—never mind the vicious lies found in *Der Stürmer*, every German newspaper seemed to be a vehicle for frothing-at-the-mouth propaganda. It had given Sophie an unpleasant jolt, the first time she'd turned to the paper and scanned the melodramatic German headlines in the old-fashioned Gothic font the Nazis preferred. *The Fatherland Defeats Red Spirit. In the Poison of the Three Mouths of our Enemies. Triumph in Finland.*

If she was to believe what she read in the German papers, the Nazis were absolutely trouncing the Allies, with victory parades in the streets of Berlin every day of the week. Even though Sophie knew it *had* to be an exaggeration—something propaganda minister Goebbels was well known for, acknowledged even by his most ardent disciples—it made her stomach curdle with nerves.

It also made her realize how much the Allies needed America to join the war, and yet it was already nearly September of 1941. Great Britain had been going at it more or less alone for two years already, and the United States was continuing to stay stubbornly out of the conflict. When would it finally join, as John Howard had promised?

Two weeks after Sophie had started at the Office of the Coordinator of Information—otherwise known as COI—she made her first friend. She'd gone to the small kitchenette on the ground floor, little more than a gas ring and a sink, where there was usually a pot of coffee on the boil, and found a pretty, dark-haired woman perched on the windowsill, smoking.

The woman turned guiltily as Sophie came in, stubbing her cigarette out and waving the smoke-filled air. "Sorry, I know I shouldn't," she said, "but I can't be bothered to go all the way outside, just for a smoke. Why do they keep us in these cupboards, do you think? Sometimes I think I'm going to go blind in here, groping around in the dark, squinting like some underground mole."

"I know what you mean," Sophie replied with a little laugh as she poured herself a cup of coffee; it had been stewing in the pot for a while and looked as thick and black as treacle.

"Oh, are you German?" the woman asked, and Sophie stiffened slightly in surprise. Over the last two years, she'd tried to eliminate her accent as much as possible, and it was galling that a stranger could tell her nationality from just the few words she'd spoken.

"Yes, I am," she replied after a pause, trying to sound matter-of-fact, even though she felt guarded.

"And Jewish, I suppose?" the woman continued in her candid way, seeming bright-eyed and unfazed.

Sophie couldn't keep from feeling—and, she suspected, looking—even warier. "*Ye-es*," she said slowly, taking a sip of coffee, mainly to hide the expression on her face, which she wasn't sure she could trust. The coffee felt like sludge in her mouth, and she had to force herself to swallow it.

"There are quite a number of Jewish refugees here, you know," the woman remarked. She had perfectly waved dark hair and very red lips, and she wore a sweater and skirt set that made the most of her curvy figure. Sophie thought she looked like a movie star. "On the Europe desk, naturally. Donovan recruits them in particular, because he says they've got a fire in their bellies. Did he recruit you? Can you say?"

"I've never met him," Sophie replied. Surely she was allowed to admit that?

She'd heard of the director of the COI; the actual coordinator of all the information they were gathering was "Wild Bill" Donovan, a Major General and the most decorated American soldier at the end of the Great War. He was a lawyer and a Republican, but with the President's ear, and his methods of operating were considered unorthodox, potentially unethical. No one had said so outright, but there had been veiled hints, and Sophie thought she understood what they'd meant. Who knew what the men and women working here got up to; Sophie suspected it was a lot more than translating three-month-old newspapers, as she was doing.

"Do *you* know him?" she asked the woman, who had unabashedly lit another cigarette.

"Oh, yes," she replied, taking a deep drag. "That's how I was recruited. I'm from Buffalo, like him. Old family friends and all that. He played golf with my father, and I rode ponies with his daughter—she died in a car accident last year, poor thing. Anyway, a lot of us here are from that circle—people he knew from his club, or university, or what have you. He went to Columbia Law, and there's a lot of them from there, as well, although I heard the Comms unit hired almost exclusively from Dartmouth, because that's where they went." She rolled her eyes as she took another drag of her cigarette.

"Did they?" Sophie remarked. She had no idea about any of it. She'd more or less been sitting in her office for the last two weeks, poring over German headlines, squinting to decipher the Gothic script, and speaking to hardly anyone at all. She could have been working in an empty building, for all the people she'd seen or spoken to.

"Of course, it's different for women, isn't it?" the woman continued with a grimacing twist of her lips. "No Columbia or

Dartmouth for *us*. Someone told me that Donovan has said the perfect COI girl is a cross between a Smith graduate, a Powers model, and a Katie Gibbs secretary. All in one package, eh?" She raised her eyebrows sardonically. "I doubt they're rating the men for looks, that's for darn sure." She blew smoke out the window, her eyes narrowed, before turning to Sophie with a suddenness that startled her. "I'm Maude Welton, by the way." She stuck out a hand, her perfectly shaped nails lacquered a deep crimson. "Pleased to meet you."

"Sophie Weiss." She took Maude's hand, and the other woman shook it heartily.

"I don't suppose I can ask what you do, although I can probably guess. Something with German language? Do they have you poring over German cookbooks or something, to decipher if Germany has any food shortages? 'How to make a loaf of bread with some engine grease and a handful of grit—for the Fatherland, *Hausfrau!*'"

Sophie let out a small, startled laugh. "Not quite."

"I'm on the Far East desk," Maude told her. "I think I'm allowed to say that much since we both work here, although who knows. They really read you the riot act, don't they, when you first start? Talking of *treason*, for heaven's sake." She shook her head before resuming, "I spent some of my childhood in Japan, you see. My father worked for the embassy, way back when. I can speak the language a *little*, but I guess they're pretty desperate." She shrugged. "They hire all sorts here, don't they? Have you *seen* some of the mad professors, mumbling to themselves? I've seen two girls I knew from Vassar, as well, in the catalog library. Thank God I'm not stuck filing, although typing is almost as bad."

"So what do you do?" Sophie asked. "If I'm allowed to know?"

Maude rolled her eyes. "Type up intelligence reports, that

sort of thing. Nothing earth-shattering so far, a lot of naval coordinates and not much else. But mum's the word, obviously, on anything they contain." She stubbed out her second cigarette. "It's all a bit when-and-if, isn't it? I mean, we're not in the war yet, of *course*, but we're acting as if we are."

"I hope the United States enters the war soon," Sophie replied quietly. "I have family in Belgium."

"Do you?" Maude smiled in sympathy. "That's rough. They're hoping to emigrate, I suppose?"

"When their quota number comes up. It's been two years."

"Goodness." Maude eyed her speculatively. "And you've been here all on your own?"

"Yes." Sophie gazed down at her cup, the coffee undrinkable. "It had to be that way."

"Well, it sounds pretty lonely to me. Have you met people?" Sophie shrugged. "A few."

"Well, you've met one more today," Maude told her cheerfully. "Why don't we go out one evening? I'm so tired of the Vassar girls and their silly little social club. All they want to do is catch husbands, and I'm not interested. Have you got a boyfriend?"

Sophie smiled, admiring Maude's forthrightness even as it took her aback, at least a little. "Yes. He's an engineer in the Navy."

"The Navy? Where?"

"Hawaii, at the moment, but he'll be heading up to Bremerton Yard for a rehaul shortly, and I think he'll stay there for the winter." Or so Sam had said in his last letter.

"Hmm." Maude frowned briefly. "I suppose most of the Navy is stationed in Hawaii at the moment, what with Japan circling the Pacific like a school of sharks." She pursed her lips. "Is it a *school* of sharks, or something else? Oh never mind, you know what I mean."

Yes, she certainly did. Sophie tried to suppress the vivid and violent image that came to her mind at Maude's words. She realized she'd been so focused on what was happening in Germany, she hadn't truly considered that Sam could be in actual danger, yet she knew, of course, that tensions between the United States and Japan had been steadily increasing over the last year.

Japan had signed the Tripartite Pact with Germany and Italy and had also made treaties with the Soviet Union and Vichy France, which had allowed it to invade the former French territory of Indochina, in an attempt "to protect its interests." The US had demanded Japan withdraw; the ultimatum had not yet been met.

Maude was quiet for a moment, seeming reflective, and then she suddenly snapped to attention, her eyes bright and fixed on Sophie. "Well, even if your fella is all the way in Hawaii, you can still have fun right here in Washington! I adore jazz. Do you like it? We could go to one of the clubs on U Street. None of the Vassar girls would be caught dead there, you know."

"They wouldn't?" Sophie had lived in Washington for over two years now, but she hadn't heard about the U Street jazz clubs.

"Well, coloreds go there, don't they?" Maude said practically. "Not that I mind. But you know how uppity some of those girls can be, and U Street is a little racy."

Sophie didn't know, but she supposed she could guess. "My friend Mattie is black," she remarked, a bit recklessly. "Could she come with us?"

Maude looked delighted by the prospect. "You have a colored friend?" she exclaimed. "How *wonderful*. Of course she can come."

It wasn't quite the response Sophie had been expecting, and it left her feeling a little uncertain. Maude's tone had made it sound as if Mattie was some specimen in the zoo, to be trotted out simply for the thrill and shock of it.

"All right," she said after a moment. Mattie was well used to people's attitudes, and Sophie thought her friend could handle any of Maude's potentially unguarded remarks. And it would be fun to experience something different. She smiled at Maude. "When would you like to go?"

CHAPTER 22

NOVEMBER 1941

Sophie had been working at the COI for nearly three months when she came across the first news article that truly gave her pause. By that time, she thought she'd become at least somewhat inured to the broad and bombastic statements found in the Nazi press, and the headlines declaring triumphant victories against the Soviets and British rolled right off her, or almost. She'd learned to ignore the sweeping declarations of the Reich's total victory or mass annihilation of the enemy, knowing it was simply how the Nazis operated. They would, she suspected, be marching in victory parades even when, God willing, Allied tanks swept down the Unter den Linden, in the very heart of Berlin.

But this article wasn't like one of those trumpeting headlines; it was barely two inches square, on a back page, of seeming little notice, in the *Breslau Zeitung*, a small, regional newspaper in the city of Breslau in Silesia, near Germany's border with Poland.

The headline declared "The German New Order in Poland" and the short article decried the "terrible atrocities" that Jews had committed in that country, and their "reign of terror" that had been unchecked for far too long. Sophie had read such sentiments before, and did her best to take them in her stride, but it was the next sentence that truly chilled her: *"This reign of terror will soon come to an end as the government has had no choice but to implement policies that will resolve the Jewish question forever, and rid the Reich of this parasite. Already the Jews of Breslau have been moved into* Judenhauser *and will shortly be deported by rail."*

She looked up from the newspaper, gazing unseeingly in front of her as she pictured the possible scene—trains like the one Margarete had described traveling on in Belgium, little more than boxcars, doors locked, or even nailed shut, stretching down a railroad track, under a bleak, gray sky... and filled with frightened Jews. In the silence of her cramped room, she could almost hear Rosa's matter-of-fact voice. *They want to destroy us...*

Was this the beginning of such senseless yet systematic destruction? Would her parents, would Rosa, Rachel, and Hannah, be squeezed into similar *Judenhauser*, shabby tenement apartments without clean water or good food, teeming with disease... or, even worse, into sealed ghettos like the ones in Lublin or Lodz? Would they be deported by train, to who only knew where, as some kind of way to resolve "the Jewish question" *forever*? What did that even *mean*?

News had been trickling through to America from Europe about the increasingly harsh treatment of the Jews for over a year now—ghettos in Poland, pogroms in Ukraine, stories of expulsions, persecutions, even executions. Some of the Jewish newspapers in America had railed at American Jews for seeming so indifferent, demanding why they had not kept a "death watch" by the German embassy in Washington, or worn black armbands in solidarity, until the defeat of the Nazis? Why, some had demanded, were American Jews so unconcerned, so *smug*, about their fellow Jews in Europe, losing their lives?

Sophie suspected she knew the answer. Because Jews all the way over in Europe didn't concern them, not really. Even the Jews like Sadie who worked at the Jewish Community Center had regarded the events in Europe with sorrow and concern, but not, Sophie thought, much more than that. They were almost all American born and bred, often to the third or fourth generation, as Sadie had admitted when Sophie had first met her. They didn't have any family in Europe, or at least none they remembered or cared about. They weren't fearing and praying for their loved ones the way she was, the threat of danger to them a panicked constant in her mind.

Again, Sophie pictured that train, under a darkening sky. She could almost hear its shrill whistle, piercing the chilly air. She could see Heinrich clinging to Margarete, confused and afraid as her stepmother bundled him on board, her father weeping behind, the whole world lamenting... except, of course, they weren't. They *weren't*.

A sound escaped Sophie, close to a sob, and she pressed a shaking fist to her lips. *No.* Her imagination was galloping away with her, surely, because she was so afraid. It simply couldn't be true. It couldn't be so awful, so hellish, as that. Like the *New York Times*, she "*chose to disbelieve unofficial reports of such horrors as exaggerated.*"

Except what if she couldn't?

Sophie lurched upright, her chair scraping across the floor in a squeal. She needed to escape the suffocating confines of her room, of her mind, for just a little while.

The little kitchenette where she got coffee was empty, the view of Navy Hill outside bleak in the throes of fall—gray sky, leafless trees, the grass dead and brown. Sophie took a shuddering breath, forced her shoulders back, and then poured herself some coffee. She wished she had someone to talk to, although she had no idea what she'd even say. Still, she would have appreciated Maude's irreverent cheerfulness just about now, her easy ability to distract.

Over the last two months, she'd become good friends with the smart-mouthed socialite, although Sophie still remained a little in awe of her. Maude clearly rubbed elbows with the highest echelons of society; she'd even met Roosevelt once, and she hadn't seemed to think all that much of it. She lived in an elegant studio apartment in the Mayflower Hotel, paid for by her parents, and often went to the U Street jazz clubs and other seemingly less salubrious places, not caring a whit for her reputation, perhaps because, with her family connections, it was so very secure.

Sophie's one foray to a jazz club on U Street had admittedly been fun, especially since she'd been able to go with Mattie, who had absolutely adored the wild thrill of it, but the extortionate five-dollar cover charge meant she was not in much of a hurry to repeat the experience.

Still, Sophie had gone to Maude's apartment on several occasions and felt quite sophisticated as they'd sipped gin and tonics and ordered steak and potatoes dauphinoise from the restaurant downstairs, Maude blithely charging it all to her father's account. Maude had regaled her with gossip about various COI staff, as well as other Washingtonian theatrics, none of which affected Sophie, but which were amusing to hear about.

Maude seemed to think working for the COI was something of a lark; Sophie supposed she didn't take anything with much seriousness. She'd lived too charmed a life for that. Yet Sophie could hardly begrudge Maude her lightness of spirit, and she could certainly use some of her friend's levity right now, when the memory of that article—and the awful images it had conjured—was so fresh in her mind.

Bolting down the rest of her coffee, Sophie forced those images away as she headed back to work.

Several hours later, in a deepening dusk, she was heading toward the bus stop on E Street to go back to Miss Bryson's, when she saw Maude walking quickly down the sidewalk, her head tucked low, a scarf wrapped around her throat and covering her mouth.

"Maude!" she called. Her friend did not turn.

Sophie had never seen her look so determined and yet dejected, something purposeful but also resigned in the way she walked. Following an instinct she couldn't name, Sophie abandoned her trek to the bus stop and hurried after her.

"Maude!" she called again, breathlessly this time. "*Maude!*"

Finally, after what seemed like a second's hesitation, her friend turned to face her. Sophie could only see Maude's eyes above her wool scarf, narrowed against the cutting wind.

"Oh, it's you," she said, rather flatly, as she looked away. "Sorry. I was miles away."

Somehow, Sophie didn't quite believe it. She had a suspicion Maude had heard her—and had deliberately kept walking. She just had no idea why. "How are you?" she asked. "Are you all right?"

Maude shrugged, still not meeting Sophie's gaze. "Why wouldn't I be all right?"

Sophie stared at her helplessly. "I don't know..."

"Do you fancy a drink?" Maude asked abruptly. "You could come back to mine. I'm meant to be at some cocktail party tonight, but I don't think I can face it alone. Let's have a drink together, and order some supper in."

"All right," Sophie replied after a moment. She would have to call Miss Bryson to let her know she wouldn't be home for supper; her landlady had at long last installed a telephone in the hall of the boarding house.

"Wonderful," Maude replied, her tone managing to sound bright and grim, and then she kept walking.

They took a streetcar on the Metropolitan line to Connecticut Avenue, and then breezed through the elegant lobby of the Mayflower, up to Maude's studio on the second floor. As soon as she'd unlocked her door, Maude shed her coat and scarf and went to the drinks table by the fireplace to pour herself a drink.

"I'm parched," she announced as she sloshed gin into a glass. "G&T all right?"

"Yes, fine," Sophie replied after a moment. Carefully, she unbuttoned her own coat as Maude mixed their drinks with a sudden, determined, and absolute focus. She should call Miss Bryson, she knew, but she was too concerned about Maude to worry about that now. "Maude—"

"Bottoms up," Maude cut across her as she handed Sophie her glass and tossed back most of hers in one swallow.

Sophie didn't take a sip. "Maude," she asked slowly, "is everything all right?"

Maude raised her eyebrows as she drained her glass. "Why shouldn't everything be all right?"

"I don't know..." Sophie paused, hesitant. "You seem... funny," she said at last.

"Funny?" Maude let out a hard laugh. "Darling, I'm *always* funny."

A frisson of unease rippled down Sophie's spine. This wasn't at all like the Maude she knew. "You know what I mean," she said quietly.

"No, I don't, actually." Now Maude's tone sounded almost cold.

Sophie couldn't keep up with her lightning changes of mood. She watched uneasily, her untouched glass still in her hand, as Maude whirled away from her. She lit a cigarette and smoked it silently for a few moments, her back to Sophie. *What on earth was going on?* Sophie knew she'd come here to Maude's apartment in large part because she'd wanted a distraction from her own worries; now she felt as if she had even more to fret about.

"I don't think I want to stay in, after all," Maude announced suddenly, stubbing her cigarette out in one rather vicious movement. "Let's go out instead."

"Out...?"

"I told you there was a cocktail party I'm meant to go to. You can come as my date."

"Your *date*—?" Sophie couldn't keep from sounding a little bit scandalized.

"Not really," Maude said in exasperation as she whirled around. "Honestly, Sophie! No one will care, anyway. It's one of those massive shindigs where everyone is trying to impress everyone else. It's right here, downstairs in one of their ballrooms, so it's no trouble."

Sophie glanced down at her wool skirt and plain blouse. "I'm not exactly dressed for a party," she pointed out, trying for a wry tone.

"You can borrow something of mine," Maude replied dismissively. "We're about the same size. Come on." She lurched forward and grabbed Sophie by the arm, almost causing her to spill her drink. "We'll have something of a fashion show." She pulled her into her bedroom, Sophie half-stumbling, half-laughing, and yet also feeling even more alarmed by her friend's behavior.

Maude dropped her arm to move to her wardrobe, which she threw open with abandon, tossing dress after dress onto the bed, in a froth of silk, satin, taffeta. Sophie had never seen so many dresses.

"Maude, I..." she began, stopping when she realized she

didn't know how to finish the sentence. Something about this whole evening felt off, and yet she didn't know what it was. And really, Sophie thought with a sudden surge of rebelliousness, why should she even care?

She took a sip of her drink, let the alcohol fire her blood. Maude seemed as if she wanted to forget something, and, as it happened, so did she. Why shouldn't they enjoy a night out together?

"All right," she declared, taking another sip of her gin and tonic, the alcohol firing through her. "Which one do you think I should wear?"

"That's the spirit," Maude replied in approval. "Why not go in black? You're twenty-one, now, aren't you, a woman grown? Show your sophisticated side." She reached for a black cocktail dress with spaghetti straps and jet beading along the bodice and tossed it toward Sophie, so she had no choice but to catch it with one hand, the other still holding her drink. "Try that on."

Sophie took another sip of her drink. With no dinner, the alcohol was already starting to go to her head and it made her feel wonderfully reckless. "All right," she said again, and she turned away to try on the dress. She felt giddy with both nerves and excitement as she peeled off her blouse and skirt, and then slid the dress on over her underwear and slip.

It was gorgeous, far more expensive than anything she could ever own, and fit her even better than Maude had said, like a second skin. Sophie worried it was almost indecent.

"Don't you look *stunning*!" Maude exclaimed. "Like Veronica Lake."

"Hardly," Sophie protested, but she couldn't deny she felt beautiful in the slinky dress. She glanced at her reflection in the window, the night dark enough outside that she could see her own silhouette. Was it a bit shocking? she wondered as she ran her hand from her shoulder to her hip.

A movement outside caught her eye. Sophie moved slowly

toward the window, standing right by the glass as she gazed out at the darkened street. It was mostly empty, save for a dark-colored coupe parked directly across from Maude's window. A man in a plain suit and overcoat stood by the car, silently smoking, the brim of his hat pulled down low as he gazed up at the Mayflower. He almost seemed as if he were looking right at Sophie.

Instinctively, she took a step back, away from the window. Her heart skipped a strange beat. From where she stood, she could still see the top of the man's head, the brim of his hat, and a shiver of apprehension rippled through her.

"Maude..." she began, but then didn't know what to say. *There's a man outside your window?* Maude would think she was ridiculous. She lived in a hotel, after all, one of the most renowned hotels in all of Washington. Of course there were people outside her window. There were even people staring up at the hotel, because plenty of famous people lived or visited there. It didn't *mean* anything.

"How about this dress?" Maude asked, holding a rather skimpy froth of pale pink satin to her. "Too shocking?"

Sophie turned from the window. She let her mind clear, and then empty out, as she reached for her drink. "I think you'll look absolutely lovely," she declared firmly.

CHAPTER 23

The Mayflower's ballroom was ablaze with lights, filled with music and laughter and the tinkle of expensive crystal. Sophie had had two glasses of champagne as soon as she'd arrived, and her head was swimming. She didn't care; she craved even more.

Every time she let herself stop and think, she pictured that news article: *The government has had no choice but to implement policies that will resolve the Jewish question forever and rid the Reich of this parasite. Already the Jews of Breslau have been moved into* Judenhauser *and will shortly be deported by rail...*

No. She wouldn't think of it. She couldn't. She reached for more champagne—anything to forget, even if just for an evening —as conversation and music swirled around her.

As Sophie moved through the crowd, she cast her glance around for Maude, who seemed to have disappeared into the throng. Snatches of conversation drifted on the air—most of the talk seemed to be about politics. Everyone was well-heeled and in the know, or at least seeming to be. Sophie hadn't rubbed shoulders with such people since that long-ago evening at Friendship House, when she'd felt so alone.

As if conjured by the memory, a man caught Sophie's

glance, standing about a dozen yards away. His florid, jowly face, the checked suit, the air of importance... it was Stanley Tyler. Sophie hadn't seen him since he'd assaulted her in her bedroom. Now the memory of that awful evening came rushing back, and she tasted the acid tang of bile in the back of her throat.

Tyler's assessing gaze moved slowly around the ballroom while Sophie stood there, transfixed, horrified. She wanted to dart out of the way so he wouldn't see her, and yet she couldn't seem to move. Inevitably, as she'd known it would, his gaze came to rest on her. His lips twisted. She drew a hitched breath as he started walking toward her.

When he was halfway across the space between them, Sophie straightened her shoulders and lifted her chin. She wouldn't run; she wasn't a frightened, vulnerable girl anymore. She could face down Stanley Tyler now.

His slow stride turned to more of a saunter as he came to stand in front of her, eyeing her up and down in a way that was bold enough to seem lewd.

"Well, look at you," he slurred. "Haven't you changed."

Sophie knew he was already drunk. With a gin and tonic and several glasses of champagne to her credit, her head was spinning, too, but when she spoke, her voice was cool. "You clearly haven't," she remarked.

His eyes narrowed. "Smug little miss. We took you in, you know. You'd be *nothing* without our charity."

"I'm grateful for the kindness you showed me," Sophie replied with dignity, although such *kindness* had been grudging indeed. "But I have managed on my own for two and a half years now."

As she said the words, she felt a quiet thrum of pride reverberate through her. She *had* managed on her own. Yes, people had helped—lovely Esther, and Sadie at the Jewish Community Center, and even John Howard—but she'd still done the work and made her own way. She owed nothing to the Tylers now. Maybe she never had.

She gave the man she'd once been so afraid of one long, level look, and then, very deliberately, turned away. She heard him mutter under his breath as she walked away from him, her shoulders back, her head held high.

As soon as she rounded the corner, however, her shoulders sagged as a shaky breath rushed out of her. That had been harder than she thought and had brought up too many painful memories. She decided to find Maude and tell her that she was leaving. It had been foolish to think that a party and a few drinks would distract her from what she'd read that morning. *Will be deported by rail...*

After searching for nearly a quarter of an hour, Sophie finally found Maude in the ladies' powder room, blearily looking into the mirror as she tried to reapply her lipstick.

"Maude." Sophie gazed at her friend in concern; her hand was shaking too much to apply her signature crimson lipstick. "Maude, please, tell me what's wrong."

Maude lowered her head as the lipstick fell from her fingers, clattering onto the sink. "I can't."

"What do you mean?"

Maude looked up again, gazing at her pale reflection—the only color in her face was two bright spots of rouge and her mostly bitten-off lipstick. "It's top secret, doncha know." She said the words in a singsong voice before turning around to face Sophie, stumbling slightly. She was even drunker than Sophie had realized. "*I'm* not even supposed to know. Nobody is."

Sophie stared at her uncertainly. She knew better than to ask questions; they'd both signed the same paper, swearing them to secrecy, threatening them with treason. And yet Maude seemed so *tormented*. "How do you know, then?" she finally asked.

"I don't really know," Maude replied in something almost

like a moan. "But I can guess, that's the damnedest part. I've been typing up naval intercepts from Japan—I don't suppose they even *think* about the secretaries who do that, do they? Secretaries who happen to know a little Japanese?"

"Maude..."

"But that wasn't it, of course. Everyone knows Japan is getting ready for an attack—"

"*Are they?*" Sophie felt a frisson of fear pass through her in an icy shiver. She'd been so focused on what was happening with Germany... yes, she read the headlines about Japan's foray into Indochina, the Japanese envoys who had just this week failed to meet with Secretary of State Cordell Hull—the same man who had made the decision to turn away the SS *St Louis* from American waters two and a half years ago. But none of it had seemed very close, somehow, and the newspapers hadn't said anything of an actual *attack*. Besides, Germany was a thousand miles closer.

"Of course they are, Sophie," Maude retorted, and now she sounded irritable. "The question is where and when, and, more importantly, what the United States is going to do about it." Before Sophie could reply, Maude continued in a flat voice, "And do you know what they're going to do about it? *Nothing*."

Sophie stared at her. "What do you mean, nothing?"

Maude shook her head. "I've said too much." Her voice rose shrilly. "It's not my fault he let something slip, is it, when he'd had a few too many whiskey sours? I wasn't asking for answers—"

"*Who* let slip—"

"Never mind. You don't need to know. You *shouldn't* know." She ran a shaky hand over her hair. "Do you know, I think the FBI might be watching my apartment. I saw a man in an overcoat across the street this morning, when I went to work. He *looked* like FBI, with his stupid brown hat. His coat was dreadful."

Sophie was jolted, remembering seeing the same kind of man that evening. "Why would the FBI be watching your apartment, Maude?" she asked unsteadily. She already knew the FBI kept a close eye on the activities of the COI, as the "eyes and ears" of the nation; all the intelligence services were in direct competition with each other.

"Because they know I know something!" Maude exclaimed in a near-shriek. "And the truth is, I don't even know what I know. But the United States is expecting an attack from Japan, and I'm afraid they are going to let it happen. They *want* it to happen. They've been poking and prodding at Japan like a kid with a stick at a hornet's nest!" Her voice dropped to a whisper. "And I'm afraid they might even know where—and they still won't do anything."

Sophie stared at her, stricken. "But if they know where... they'll evacuate, surely..."

"And give the whole game away? No." Maude shook her head decisively. "It's a good thing your fella is up in Bremerton Yard, because I have a feeling it might be Hawaii that they attack. Not that I know," she clarified quickly. "Not entirely. It's just a guess..."

But if Maude had been translating naval intercepts... she must know more than a guess. Sophie felt as if her stomach were coated in ice. "Why Hawaii..."

"Because people have heard of it, haven't they?" Maude replied, still sounding shrill, as well as exasperated. "Roosevelt needs the American people to *care*, and I'm not sure they'll be all that bothered by an attack on a few ships in the middle of the Pacific somewhere—Wake Island or the Midway. But Hawaii? An American territory that so many have heard of? Yes. They'll care about that."

"But it could still be an island somewhere," Sophie protested numbly. "Or the west coast. San Francisco or—"

"No." Maude sounded sure. "An attack on the mainland

would be too damaging for public morale. The government wouldn't allow it."

Surely the government wouldn't *allow* any attack, Sophie thought in a blaze of incredulous panic. She found she had to stretch her hand out to the basin to steady herself. "You sound like you know what you're talking about."

"Maybe I do, maybe I don't," Maude replied. "I'm not paid to think, am I? Just to type and translate, the same way you are. And most of the Japanese naval intercepts are as dull as ditch water—it's a needle in a haystack, to find something—*anything* —of note. Nobody would think I'd find it. And I *wouldn't* have, I didn't!" A strangled gasp escaped her. "I wouldn't have put any of the pieces together, if a boring old coot in Naval Intelligence hadn't talked my ear off when he was sauced at a party." She let out a long, shuddering sigh. "He didn't know what I did for work, of course, or that I knew anything about what he was talking about. Anyway. It doesn't matter." She straightened, her face still deathly pale, her lipstick all but bitten off her chewed-looking lips. "I can't breathe a word of it to anyone." Maude looked at her fiercely, in something close to a glare. "And you can't either."

"I won't," Sophie replied, but she was wishing, rather desperately, that Maude hadn't said anything to her at all. She didn't want this information; it was too heavy a burden to bear. It clearly had been too heavy for Maude, which was why she'd shared it. But Sophie had no intention of telling anyone else ever, not even a whisper. "I think we should go," she said at last. "You need to sleep, and I need to get back to my boarding house before the buses stop running. We won't talk about this ever again. In fact, we'll forget we even had this conversation."

Maude nodded, almost frantically. "Yes. Yes, let's forget." She reached her hands out to grab Sophie's own. "Oh Sophie, I want to *forget*."

"I know you do." Briefly, Sophie embraced her friend, while

Maude pressed her face against her shoulder, a shudder wracking through her. "And you will," she added, with more conviction than she actually felt. "But first, sleep."

They left the party with little notice, and once upstairs, Sophie boiled the kettle to make a hot-water bottle for Maude as she changed into her nightgown. She was as docile as a child as she let Sophie help her into bed, tucking the cover up nearly to her chin.

"Now get a good night's sleep," Sophie instructed her as she handed her the hot-water bottle. "And I'll see you tomorrow."

Back down in the lobby of the hotel, Sophie pulled her coat more tightly around her. The party was still going strong, and outside it looked chilly, and windier than before. She was not looking forward to the journey back to I Street.

She'd almost reached the hotel's entrance when, to her surprise, she felt a hand clamp firmly down on her elbow. A startled gasp escaped her.

"Miss Weiss," a voice said, familiar and urbane. "Let me give you a ride home."

Sophie turned to see John Howard smiling at her, although his eyes were narrowed, and his tone had been implacable. He was still gripping her elbow.

With a plunging sensation, Sophie feared she knew what this was about. Somehow, she managed to summon a smile. "That's very kind of you, Mr. Howard. Thank you."

Outside, still holding her elbow, he led her to his car, a dark, anonymous-looking coupe, similar to the one that had been outside Maude's window. But John Howard wasn't FBI, Sophie knew. He was Naval Intelligence. This had to be about what Maude had told her—yet how had John Howard known Maude had spoken to her? She must be being watched even more closely than she'd thought.

"Thank you," Sophie murmured as he opened the door and she slid into the passenger's seat.

He didn't speak as he came round the other side, climbed in, and then started the car.

"I Street, yes?" he asked after a few taut moments.

"Yes."

Neither of them spoke for several minutes, and Sophie started to wonder if she'd been imagining things. Maybe Mr. Howard was simply being kind, giving her a ride home on a cold autumn night.

Such frail hopes vanished when, halfway through their journey, he remarked in a casual way, "Your friend Miss Welton seemed a little restless tonight. Do you know what's gotten her into such a state?"

Sophie's body went tense before she forced herself to deliberately relax. "I didn't know you knew Miss Welton," she replied, amazed at how casual she sounded, as if they were having a normal conversation, which she knew they weren't.

"Her father is in the foreign service, her brothers in the Navy. I think most people in government know Miss Welton, one way or another."

Sophie turned to look out the window, the blur of lights streaming by. "She's overtired, I think," she said after a moment. "And a bit nervy, perhaps. I imagine you know the nature of her work." She turned back to face him, managing a small smile, even though her own nerves were twanging like the strings of a violin.

"Do *you* know the nature of her work, Miss Weiss?" John Howard asked after a pause.

Sophie gave a little shrug. "None of us talk about what we do."

"I imagine you talk a little, over coffee and a cigarette. Or gin and tonics?" He turned to her, one eyebrow arched, and Sophie went cold. Did he know about their drink earlier, in Maude's apartment? *How?*

"A little," she agreed after a moment. "But not much. I

know she works on the Far East desk, but not much more than that." She hoped she hadn't said too much; she didn't want to get either Maude or herself in trouble.

John Howard's fingers flexed on the steering wheel. "I believe Miss Welton has got some rather ridiculous notions into her head," he stated. "Like you said, she's nervy. I wouldn't want a sensible girl like you to think she's talking sense when she very much *isn't*."

From somewhere, Sophie dredged up a light laugh as she made herself turn to look at him. "Mr. Howard, if you know Miss Welton, then you know she very rarely talks any sense at all."

To her surprise, Sophie thought she saw a gleam in Howard's eyes, almost like approval. Did he believe her? Or had she just done the right thing, claiming ignorance? She felt as if she were flailing in deep water, acting out of instinct as much as fear. Deny everything. Admit nothing.

Yet what exactly was she scared of? Could she be arrested, simply for knowing what she did? Although, like Maude, she wasn't even sure about what she knew. The United States was attempting to provoke Japan into an attack, and they might do nothing to prevent it when it happened. And the attack might be on Hawaii. It was all hearsay, rumors, warmongering, whispers... wasn't it? Roosevelt had been conciliatory toward the Japanese, according to some newspapers. *They* were the aggressors, not America. Of course the government would not allow an attack on its own shores, its own *citizens*, without defending and responding appropriately. It was absurd, offensive, to think otherwise. Maude must have got it wrong. Sophie could almost believe it.

"Ah, here we are." Howard smoothly pulled the car up to the curb. He turned off the ignition but didn't move from his seat, and neither did Sophie.

"Thank you for taking me home," she said after a moment, her tone carefully polite.

"You're a sensible girl, Miss Weiss," John Howard remarked. "I've known that from when I first met you. And you want the United States to get involved in this war, don't you? For the sake of mankind, not to mention your own family?"

She paused before stating quietly, "It is the only way Hitler's evil will be destroyed."

Howard nodded slowly. "Indeed."

Another pause while Sophie waited, sensing something more.

"You've been stepping out with a naval engineer, haven't you? Lieutenant Jackson?"

Of course he knew absolutely everything about her, even her relationship with Sam. "Yes."

"Where is he serving?"

Sophie suspected he knew this, as well, but she answered anyway. "On the *USS Arizona*. It's being taken up to Bremerton Yard in Washington State for an overhaul."

"Ah, yes. Of course." John Howard nodded again, and then he gave her a sudden, wide smile. "Well, then. Goodnight, Miss Weiss."

Sophie stared at him uneasily, feeling as if she'd missed something just then, but she had no idea what it was.

"Goodnight," she replied after a moment, and then she slipped out of the car.

The unsettling conversation lingered in her mind as Sophie headed for work the next morning, after a restless night's sleep. Reading and translating the headlines of German newspapers provided a distraction from her worries about Maude, although they made her remember what she'd been worried about in the first place... that tiny bit of print about the scheduled deportations.

She tried to find more articles about the Nazis' resolution to the so-called "Jewish problem," but she saw only headlines about the "new generation" of Nazi youth in Heidelberg; Roosevelt's visit to Newfoundland with Churchill where they announced the Atlantic Charter; more cheerful propaganda about the Nazis' "Strength through Joy" program of holidays, offering hiking trips and swimming excursions. Sophie stared at the black and white illustration of a young woman smiling widely as she rode a bicycle, blond hair blowing in the wind; most of Germany's regional newspapers had few photographs. Her head pounded and she decided she needed a coffee. She also wanted to check in on Maude.

But when Sophie went to the kitchenette, there was no one there, and when she dared to ask one of the girls in the catalog room if they'd seen Miss Welton, she was told that Maude had called in sick.

Well, Sophie thought, that was probably all for the better. But she still felt uneasy as she finished her work and headed home in the deepening dusk. It was nearly Thanksgiving, and Miss Bryson—or really Lorna—always provided a wonderful home-cooked meal—roast turkey, mashed potatoes, pumpkin pie, everything. Sophie was looking forward to it, even as she couldn't quite shake the anxious feeling that had dogged her since she'd first seen Maude walking home from work yesterday.

As she turned onto I Street, her steps faltered. There was a familiar-looking dark coupe parked across from Miss Bryson's. A man sat in the driver's seat, smoking, the brim of his hat pulled low over his face. It had to be the FBI, Sophie thought. For intelligence agents, they didn't much try to disguise themselves.

She forced herself to walk slowly past, as if she didn't have a care in the world, before heading up to the front door of Miss Bryson's. The man didn't get out of the car. Sophie's hand trembled as she turned the knob.

"Sophie, thank goodness you've arrived," Miss Bryson's exclaimed, her hands pressed to her cheeks. "You've got a telephone call! It's your young man, Mr. Jackson. I would have hated for you to miss it." With a kindly smile, she pressed the receiver into Sophie's hand.

"Sam?" Sophie spoke into the receiver with surprise; he'd never telephoned her before. She'd only used the device a handful of times herself.

"Sophie, are you there?" The line was crackly, Sam's voice sounding tinny and far away. "I can't believe this actually works! I wanted to call you for Thanksgiving... I know it's not a big holiday for you, but I miss you all the same. No roast turkey for me out here, though! Can't talk long—it costs a fortune, let me tell you, not that I mind. I don't mind at all."

"Where are you?" Sophie asked with a laugh. It was so good to hear his voice, the easy and cheerful affection that she so loved, his simple and warm enthusiasm. It made her breathe easier, just listening to him. It reassured her that the world was not the dark and dangerous place it so often felt like. "Are you in Washington State, at Bremerton Yard?"

"Meant to be," Sam told her. "But a couple of weeks ago we had a run-in with the *Oklahoma* in deep fog. We're going to be dry-docked for the foreseeable, unfortunately."

"Dry-docked? At Bremerton?"

"Nope," Sam told her cheerfully. "Lucky me, I get to spend the winter in the sun! We're in Hawaii, at Pearl Harbor."

CHAPTER 24

The FBI agent was still parked outside the boarding house the next morning, when Sophie peeked out of her bedroom window, dry-mouthed, her stomach feeling as if it were lined with lead.

She'd barely slept last night, after her telephone call with Sam. He was in Hawaii! She'd believed him to be tucked safely away, up in Washington State, but now she knew he was near the possible threat of attack... as John Howard must have known, when he'd asked about Sam. He'd been happy to let her go on believing Sam was at Bremerton Yard, Sophie thought bitterly—not that she entirely blamed him. Of course there were bigger interests at stake than the whereabouts of a single naval lieutenant.

Even so, it had been unbearably painful, to speak with Sam, to hear him talk about the palm trees waving in the tropical breeze, the white sand beaches stretching to an endlessly blue horizon, and not say a word about what she feared she knew. Her mouth had felt like sandpaper as she'd forced herself to ask, "Will you be stationed there long, do you think?"

"Through the winter, and then who knows what's coming."

His tone had grown serious, although not without a certain enthusiasm, or at least an acceptance. Like many in the military, Sophie suspected, Sam was tired of waiting. He wanted action, and she had a terrible feeling he was going to get it, and soon. "You know there will be a war," he said quietly, a statement rather than a question.

"Yes." That was painfully clear to her right then. "Will you get leave?" she had asked after a moment. "At Christmas?"

"I don't think so, not with the way things are. And not enough to get all the way back east." His voice had lowered, softened. "I miss you, Sophie..."

Sophie's knuckles had ached from clenching the telephone receiver so tightly. "I miss you, too," she'd whispered.

"Sophie..." He'd lingered on her name, turned it into an endearment, a caress.

Sophie had closed her eyes. "Sam."

"I love you, Sophie." He spoke quickly now, with determination.

Sophie's lips had parted soundlessly. He'd never said those three wonderful words to her before.

"I wanted to say it in person," he'd continued in a rush, "but who knows when I'll get the chance, but I do love you, and I want you to know it. Will you still wait for me? I don't know how long it will be—"

"Yes." The word came out on almost a gasp. "Yes, I'll wait."

"That's all right, then." She had heard the smile in his voice, but also the expectancy. He wanted her to say those words back, and she should—she *wanted* to, desperately—yet somehow, with the knowledge of what Maude had told her like a stone in her stomach, she couldn't. She was too scared, too tangled up, too emotional. The words simply wouldn't come to her lips.

"Take care, Sam," she had finally managed, her voice breaking on the words. "Stay safe."

· · ·

Now, as Sophie got ready for work, she felt exhausted yet also nervy—just as she'd said Maude was—with the FBI agent standing across the street, the knowledge of an imminent attack pulsing through her in a hectic, staccato beat. Would it be today? Tomorrow? Next week? Never?

Maybe Maude had been exaggerating, she told herself—far from the first time. She'd simply got the wrong end of the stick. Talking nonsense, just as Sophie had said she always did.

But if she had been... would John Howard have sought Sophie out and warned her the way he had? Or was he covering his bases, being thorough, just in case? It was so hard to know.

Sophie knew what she wanted, *needed* to believe—that Sam would be safe, and that she had no dangerous, insider knowledge with its accompanying responsibility either to speak or to stay silent. She didn't want to have to choose to act—or *not* act—on something she had absolutely no control over, and yet she feared she was already in that position, and not by her own doing.

The FBI agent was still sitting in his parked car when Sophie left Miss Bryson's, walking down the sidewalk toward the bus stop with an uneasy prickling between her shoulder blades that didn't let up even after she'd boarded the bus and the bus had driven away, leaving the agent far behind.

At COI headquarters, Sophie tried to focus on translating the ever-present stack of newspapers on her desk, but the Gothic script blurred before her tired eyes. *Tax Relief for Wives. Penitentiary as Warning Drove Bicycle Thieves.* Did any of it even *matter*? Did any analyst even look at her translations, did they have any relevant information at all, or were they just filed away in some dusty folder, never to be seen again, never needing to be seen?

She pushed away the newspaper she'd been working on and then pressed the heels of her hands into her eye sockets, hard enough to hurt. Thoughts thudded through her mind—*deported by rail. Imminent attack. I love you, Sophie.*

A groan escaped her, and she rose from her desk, deciding she needed a respite, if not from her own racing thoughts, then at least from the grim headlines of the newspapers. She headed to the kitchenette for a cup of coffee; it was empty as usual, and Sophie wondered if Maude was back at work. She hoped so, for her friend's sake. Perhaps she'd seek her out at lunch.

But at lunch, Maude was nowhere to be found, and when Sophie asked the catalog girls if they'd seen her, one of them raised her eyebrows, dropping her voice as she stepped closer to Sophie.

"You haven't heard? She's not coming back."

Sophie's stomach dropped. "What...? Why?"

"Who knows? You don't ask, do you? Not in this place." She turned back to her filing cart, clearly not wanting to talk about it anymore, and Sophie could hardly blame her. Any more chat and the filing clerk could have an FBI agent outside her boarding house, too.

Had Maude quit—or had something worse happened?

Several days passed in a similar manner, with Sophie feeling as if she couldn't concentrate on anything. She felt as if she were viewing life through a cloudy haze, as if everything was happening at a distance. At least, after two days, the FBI agent must have decided she wasn't worth following anymore, for his car was gone from the street. That had provided a small amount of relief.

After work one day, she'd gone to the Mayflower, hoping to see Maude, only to be told Miss Welton had left to visit her family in Buffalo. The doorman did not know when she would be back.

Perhaps it was just as well, she thought uneasily as she'd

headed back to I Street. Maude clearly wanted to lie low, and Sophie should, too. In any case, the next day was Thanksgiving, and Sophie, along with Samantha, was busy helping Lorna and Mattie in the kitchen, as they prepared a feast to celebrate the fact that, as Roosevelt had proclaimed, "Our beloved country is free and strong. Our moral and physical defenses against the forces of threatened aggression are mounting daily in magnitude and effectiveness." Sophie had been heartened by his further words, "In the interest of our own future, we are sending succor at increasing pace to those peoples abroad who are bravely defending their homes and their precious liberties against annihilation."

War was coming, she thought, but with it, she hoped, was salvation.

In any case, it was lovely to enjoy such a huge meal—turkey and stuffing and giblet gravy, cranberry sauce and sweet potatoes with orange, green beans and mashed potatoes, and a gelatin salad with cabbage and pineapple, followed by coffee and pumpkin pie.

By the time Sophie had helped Lorna clear it all away, she felt as if she were waddling from all the food she'd eaten, and the anxiety she'd been feeling had thankfully eased a little. It was hard to fret when her stomach was full, and everything felt lazy and relaxed and warm.

As they sat in the living room that evening, listening to Glenn Miller and his Orchestra, her thoughts unspooled like a golden thread—of *course* Maude had been talking nonsense, Sophie told herself. Her friend was dramatic at the best of times, and she liked to act as if she were in the know. She'd probably taken some old naval coot's mutterings as the last word, and then added a few of her own, for good measure. Yes, everyone was gearing up for war—Roosevelt had said as much in his Thanksgiving proclamation. But that hardly meant the government knew an attack was imminent and intended to do nothing to stop it. Maude had jumped to conclusions, and her overreaction had cost her her job. Sam was as safe in Pearl Harbor as he would have been at Bremerton Yard.

As for John Howard, he'd simply spoken to her to reassure her, and also, understandably, to make sure she didn't go around spreading untoward rumors and causing panic. If Maude had been forced to leave the COI, well, that might have been for the best, too. Considering how she had gossiped, perhaps she wasn't particularly well-suited for the role.

As the days slipped by into December, Sophie's sense of not quite ease—no, but almost—grew. She missed Maude at work, but she kept busy herself, and even went out with Sadie and a few others from the JCC. She wrote to Sam, and impulsively she added the three words she hadn't been able to say on the telephone.

I wish I'd told you when you told me, but I suppose you took me by surprise—in a good way, though, the most wonderful way! But the truth is, I love you too, Sam, and I will wait for you as long as I have to. I hope you are able to get some leave soon so we can celebrate together. Love always, Sophie

She posted it on the second of December, and that evening, when she returned from work, she was delighted to see two letters on the hall table for her—one from Hannah, and one from Rachel.

Hannah's was brief but heartfelt:

Dear Sophie,

I do not know when I will be able to write you again. As you can imagine, things have become worse for us Jews here in France. I knew it would happen, but it's hard to see it—and live it—all the same.

There is talk that they are going to send us somewhere, heaven only knows where. Far away, no doubt! They arrested thousands of Jews over the summer, but they were all men and foreigners. I'm sure it won't be long, though, before they turn to women and children. I'm not going to stand for it this time, though, which is why I won't be able to write. I can't say anything more, but please know I am thinking of you and imagining the day we all meet at Henri's—the second of June, the date we were all last together, the year after the war is over.

I've written Rosa and Rachel to tell them the same. Let's make it a promise, Sophie—sometimes imagining us all toasting each other with champagne is what keeps me determined to stay alive. That and Lotte, keeping her safe.

Yours, Hannah

Tears pricked Sophie's eyes and she blinked them away as she reread her friend's letter. Dear Hannah—and Lotte, too, for whom she must be so worried. What on earth could Hannah be doing, that would keep her from writing again? Was it dangerous? Sophie supposed everything was dangerous in France these days, with Hitler in charge.

With a shuddery sigh, she opened Rachel's letter, bracing herself for whatever news her friend might have. She knew it couldn't be good; it was simply a question of how bad it was.

Dear Sophie,

Well, well, life in Amsterdam is never dull! Today I spent four hours—yes, four—trying to buy a loaf of bread. And not a nice, fresh, white loaf, as you might imagine, but just a stale heel of black bread. I walked around half the city, queued in line at a dozen different bakeries, and in the rain, as well. At the last bakery, there it was—my poor little loaf. Nothing ever tasted so good! I could have been eating Sachertorte in the dining room of the St Louis, *that's how good it was. I know it all sounds dreadful, but sometimes you simply have to laugh, because what else can you do?*

Franz had a job working as a clerk in a law office, but he was fired months ago, when the Judenrat *was forced to enact laws that kept Jews from working in the legal profession. Then he got a job sweeping floors—and him, with a law degree!—but that came to an end when yet more policies were put in place.*

A neighbor was allowing me to tutor her girls in history for a few guilders, but eventually that had to stop as well, and so we struggle for money for food. A kindly woman here in Haarlem helps—she's the daughter of a watchmaker, and she and her sister bring us parcels of food, sometimes. And your parcel of potted meat and jam was wonderful, just wonderful! Somehow, we manage, and I know—I know*—one day this will all be over.*

In the meantime, I try to find what small joys and pleasures I can—"if things are not as you wish, then wish them as you are"! There is a little robin outside the window of our apartment that greets me every morning. Her bright eyes and morning song are a delight.

As ever, Rachel.

"Oh, Rachel," Sophie whispered. Were all her friends struggling this way, with not even enough to eat? And what about her own family? She hated to imagine Heinrich hungry, his plump cheeks sallow and thin.

It tore at her heart, and once again that ever-present guilt came rushing up, back in full force, sweeping over and consuming her. How could she be sitting here, in comfort, in *luxury*, having enjoyed a huge Thanksgiving meal only last week, while her friends suffered so? It was unendurable, and yet she could do nothing about it but send a bit of meat and jam. She'd been sending her family as well as Hannah and Rachel parcels of food as often as she could; she no longer knew Rosa's address, and her friend had assured her things were much better in England. Yet as much as Sophie knew Rachel and Hannah both appreciated her parcels, it felt almost like an insult, a patronizing sop when her friends were struggling so much, and she was not.

With a sigh, Sophie folded up the letters. She would send another parcel that week, she decided. It was so little, but it was something.

That weekend, the temperature dropped suddenly, the weather turning frigid and gray as winter sunk its claws into the frozen earth. Sophie spent most of the weekend tucked up in her room with a book, trying to keep warm, until, on Sunday afternoon, Samantha coaxed her downstairs to listen to a Philharmonic concert on the radio.

"You don't need to be a hermit," she told her with a laugh. "And Lorna has laid a fire. Come join us."

Sophie had to admit that it was cozy in the living room, with the fire blazing away and the curtains drawn against the bleak, gray afternoon. It was just the ladies present, as William had gone out; Samantha was writing letters, Miss Bryson knitting, and Sophie rested her book in her lap, her eyes closed as the strains of Shostakovich's Symphony no. 1 in F Minor drifted over her, a sense of peace hovering near her, a wispy, elusive thing, yet closer than it had been in some time.

Lorna had just brought in a tray with a pot of coffee and cups when the music was suddenly interrupted by a newscaster's voice.

"We interrupt this program to bring you a special news

bulletin. The Japanese have attacked Pearl Harbor by air, President Roosevelt has just announced. The attack also was made on all naval and military activity on the principal island of Oahu."

Sophie jerked upright and Samantha dropped her pen. Miss Bryson let out a little gasp and Lorna pressed her hand to her chest as, inconceivably, the music resumed, as if nothing had happened.

"What on *earth*...?" Miss Bryson whispered, the color draining from her face.

Pearl Harbor. *Pearl Harbor*. The words thudded through Sophie as her insides turned to ice. Sam. *Oh, Sam...*

"Are they not going to tell us anymore?" Samantha exclaimed, the symphony drawing to its mournful close, followed by a beat of awful, electric silence.

Then the tense voice of the announcer returned. Everyone leaned forward, straining to listen, breaths held, utterly alert.

"Japan has attacked Pearl Harbor, in Hawaii, and Manila, in the Philippine Islands, from the air. The attack is developing. Today, Deems Taylor's usual commentary will be replaced by a further report on the Far Eastern situation. We pause now for fifteen seconds. This is the Columbia Broadcasting System."

In the silence that followed, all the women exchanged glances, both somber and frightened. Pearl Harbor had been attacked, was maybe being attacked even at this very moment, fighter planes swooping, bombs exploding, Sam fighting for his life, or, God forbid, already dead...

A wave of dizziness swept over Sophie, and the room seemed to whirl around her in a blur of color. The last thing she heard was Samantha's shocked cry before she slumped forward on the sofa, and then slid, crumpled, to the ground.

CHAPTER 25

DECEMBER 1941

In the immediate aftermath of the attack on Pearl Harbor, the whole nation seemed to be in shock, reeling and dazed; it was as if a hushed silence had suddenly fallen upon the country, an overwhelming incredulity that the United States of America, that venerable, invincible behemoth of a nation, could actually be *attacked*. And yet it had been, and terribly so.

After she'd fainted, Sophie had been revived by Samantha gently slapping her cheeks. She'd blinked up at her friend, her mind still a dazed fog.

"*What...*" she'd mumbled.

"You fainted, dear," Samantha had said. "It must have been from the shock. Let me help you up."

Samantha had hoisted her back onto the sofa as Sophie had done her best to adjust her skirt, which had rucked up over her legs. She still felt too disoriented to be embarrassed.

"I'm so sorry..." she'd murmured as she struggled to regain her bearings. She'd never fainted before in her life, and her head had felt as if it were filled with cotton wool, the room still spinning around her. Miss Bryson had turned off the radio, but the newscaster's voice still throbbed through Sophie's temples. *The*

Japanese have attacked Pearl Harbor by air. "I didn't mean to cause a scene..."

"It's the shock," Miss Bryson had offered, patting her hand, and then she'd thrust a small glass of brandy into Sophie's hand. "Take this, dear, it will help. It's such a shock to us all..."

Except it wasn't, Sophie had thought numbly, for her. She'd *known* this was coming, hadn't she? She just hadn't wanted to believe it. She'd let Sam go into danger, maybe even his death, without a single word of warning. How could she have been so cruel?

She'd taken her sips of brandy like spoonfuls of medicine, grateful for the fiery warmth of the alcohol, even as a deep and pervading misery invaded her soul. *Sam, Sam...*

"Are you worried for Mr. Jackson?" Samantha had asked in concern. "Wasn't he up in Washington State?"

"He was meant to be," Sophie had whispered, the taste of brandy still on her tongue. "But the *Arizona* was damaged and so it was put into dry dock at Pearl Harbor at the end of October."

Samantha's eyes had widened, her face paling. "Oh, no, my dear..."

"He might be all right," Miss Bryson had insisted, clearly trying to sound bracing. She looked tiny and wizened, and suddenly very old. "He might have been onshore..."

"Yes," Sophie had replied, more for Miss Bryson's sake than her own. Her landlady looked visibly distressed, her face crumpled as she wrung her hands. "Yes, he might have."

The next day, the newspapers had blared the awful headlines —*Fifteen Hundred Dead, Japan at War*. In his speech to Congress, President Roosevelt had declared it a date that would "live in infamy" when the United States was "suddenly and deliberately" attacked by Japan. He asked Congress to declare war on the Axis Powers—Japan, Italy, and Germany—which they promptly and unanimously—save one—did. Sophie had finally gotten her wish—America had entered the war not just to fight Japan but to liberate Europe, and yet at what price?

She had discovered the personal cost a few days later, after news had come trickling in—not fifteen hundred dead at Pearl Harbor, but two and a half thousand. All eight battleships at the base had been damaged, and four had been sunk, including the *USS Arizona*, which had been bombed by Japanese gunners, causing its stores of gunpowder to explode and turn the ship into a deathly fireball. It sank in just fourteen minutes, with over a thousand crew members on board, who had all died in the explosion... including Sam.

His name had been published in the newspaper, along with all the others. She'd traced the typed list with her finger, knowing even before she got to the Js that she'd see his name there. She'd felt it in her bones, in her very soul, as soon as she'd heard about the attack. In some ways, Sophie felt as if she'd known even before; she'd hoped and wished and just about convinced herself that Maude had made it all up, that Sam wasn't in danger, but in her deepest heart of hearts, she'd always known. She'd known... and she'd said nothing.

When the letter that she'd posted just the week before was returned to her, "addressee unknown", it made her loss only harder to bear. He'd never read her reply, never known that she'd loved him. He'd died without hearing her say the sweet words he'd told her so touchingly, just a few short weeks ago.

It felt like too much to bear, too much guilt to accept, and so for the next few weeks and months, Sophie moved through her days as if she were a ghost herself, showing up at work, at home, and yet not truly present. Her mind felt both empty and buzzing; sometimes she felt as if she were existing outside herself, viewing this slip of a woman with such a pale face and wide eyes as if she were a sad stranger. There she was, reading newspapers and translating; now she was walking to the bus; and here she was, sitting in the front room, listening to the radio, looking so weary and forlorn. Soon, she would go to bed, try to sleep, and then, poor woman, she would have to do it all over again. How could she keep bearing it? Every time she closed her eyes, she saw Sam's smiling, open face, the tenderness and warmth in his hazel eyes. *I love you, Sophie...*

Meanwhile, after its years of isolationist fervor, the United States had suddenly sprung into action—and found a fierce and exuberant patriotism. It was almost as if the country had never been determined to avoid the "conflict in Europe" for so long; suddenly, it had become *America's* war—sending boys overseas to save the world, everyone doing their part.

Seemingly overnight, Washington was draped in red, white, and blue, and men who had had to register for the draft the year before were now actually marching to war, or at least to training camps that had appeared all over the country. Women were volunteering, as well, for all sorts of government positions, taking the jobs that men would have had, before they were conscripted. The once sleepy city was suddenly overwhelmed with people who had come to help with the war effort, and boarding houses were soon packed, with the government setting up a new housing authority to deal with the situation.

By the end of January, Miss Bryson had not only found a replacement for Jack Wells, but managed to squeeze in another boarder besides, turning the attic room into one for a paying tenant; Mattie now had to share the basement with Lorna. Maude wrote Sophie a letter apologizing for leaving the city so abruptly, and saying she was happier in Buffalo, at least for now. Sophie sensed that some of the fizz had gone out of her friend, and she felt sad for her, as well as for herself. War changed everyone, it seemed.

In February, the government announced that anyone of Japanese heritage would be interned in camps, whether or not they were US citizens. Over one hundred thousand Japanese were sent by bus to camps in newly militarized zones in the northwest of the country, just another casualty of war. Sophie felt as if it were Germany all over again; if both sides of this terrible conflict were sending people away and locking them up, what on earth were they fighting for? What did liberty even look like? She wondered if anyone actually knew.

It wasn't a sentiment, however, that she voiced aloud; the national mood had swung sharply against anyone who even looked Japanese, and there sometimes was, she felt, a hostility behind the country's patriotism that she didn't fully understand, even as she recognized it. Fervor of any kind, she supposed, was a double-edged sword.

The office of the COI was expanding to several buildings on its now fenced-in campus on Naval Hill, and with its expansion came change—it was rebranded the rather innocuous-sounding Office of Strategic Services. More and more staff were recruited for its secretive operations, although Sophie's job did not change, save for her articles seemed to be more in demand, now that the Europe desk was staffed by at least a dozen people. It was some small comfort that she didn't feel as if everything she wrote was being filed away on a dusty shelf somewhere, without even being perused.

As the months passed, the days marched by in a dreary line, while Sophie went to work, came home, listened to news, and went to bed, often unable to sleep as she thought of all the people she'd abandoned and disappointed. Her father, Heinrich, Margarete. Rosa, Hannah, Rachel. *Sam.*

Lying in bed, staring up at the ceiling, an overwhelming guilt would sweep right through her like an empty, icy wind, as she thought how she'd never felt so alone, so *anguished*. America had entered the war, yes, but she now felt guiltier than ever. She didn't deserve this safety; she didn't even want it. If she could be back on the *St Louis*, facing whatever fate awaited her, she would have chosen it in a heartbeat, even if it would have meant she'd never met and fallen for Sam. No matter what the poets and songwriters said, she would have rather never loved than to have loved and lost so disastrously. She could hardly bear to think of him, picture his dear face, remember his easy laugh. *Oh, Sam...*

Sometimes, she took out her sliver of emerald and studied it, noting the way the light caught the jagged edged of the precious shard, its dark green depths glinting as if possessed by their own fire. She thought of the promises she, Rosa, Hannah, and Rachel had all made back on the *St Louis*, and wondered if any one of them would actually be able to keep them. Then she wondered if she even deserved to keep such promises, to waltz into that little café without a care in the world, when she already knew that if her friends made it at all, it would be at great cost and sacrifice, a painful and hard-won victory.

Here she was, tucked up safe in America's capital while everyone else she knew—everyone she felt she'd betrayed—suffered and struggled on. And survived, she hoped, even if it was too late for Sam. She couldn't think of him without feeling a rush of grief and guilt, the two emotions so tangled together that she could not separate one from the other.

There were no letters from her family and friends, and as the months passed, the silence ate at her, a torment of ignorance as the news from Europe grew darker and darker. The US was fighting in North Africa and the Pacific; the Germans were occupied with the Eastern Front, and their assuredly doomed invasion of the Soviet Union. The Japanese took control of Singapore, Java, Burma, and New Guinea; the RAF bombed Germany, including Hamburg, and the port where Sophie had once, what felt a lifetime ago, boarded the *St Louis*.

In April, as the city exploded with cherry blossoms and spring sunshine, Sophie discovered another scant two inches of column space on one of the back pages of a regional newspaper, with the simple, stark headline—*Jews Deported*. She read that "tens of thousands of Jews" had been deported from Lodz to a place called Chelmno. Sophie had never heard of it, and she went to the R&A's library to look it up in one of the many maps they kept there.

As she traced her finger from Lodz north to the tiny black dot of Chelmno, she saw it was nothing more than a village, a mere fifty kilometers or so north of the city. Why on earth would the Nazis send tens of thousands of Jews to such a small place, and so nearby, as well? What could it possibly mean?

She was afraid to think too deeply about it, and yet it was *all* she could think about, especially when the news on the radio mentioned other deportations were starting—from the Netherlands, from Belgium, from France. Were her family and friends about to be taken? Why—and where? Would they be resettled, would they be able to live normal and busy lives elsewhere? She wanted to hope so, but it felt naïve. No one seemed to know what it all meant, or even to be much interested. Far more concerning were the victories and defeats of various battles, all of which were described in detail on the radio every night; the movement of Jews east through Europe attracted very little notice indeed.

In June, as the United States announced its first round of food rationing, with sugar, Sophie was summoned from her cupboard to the office of her superior in Research & Analysis, only to find a man she didn't recognize waiting within—and sitting next to him was John Howard.

Sophie stopped abruptly in the doorway as John Howard favored her with a kindly enough smile, his eyes crinkling at the corners as they had before. He looked older, and a little more careworn; the years had taken their toll on him as they had on so many others, Sophie supposed.

"Miss Weiss. Do come in and take a seat."

Slowly, her hands shaking a little, she closed the door behind her and then sat down opposite Howard.

The man she didn't recognize was looking at her in an assessing way, his blue eyes narrowed. He looked to be about thirty, with brown hair and a large, muscular build.

Sophie folded her hands into her lap to keep them from trembling. Why on earth had she been summoned here?

"I was sorry to hear about your loss," Howard said quietly, and Sophie could only nod in reply. She was afraid that John Howard had known about her loss well before it had happened, before the USS *Arizona* had been hit, or Pearl Harbor had even been bombed. She wasn't about to say any of that, however. She didn't think she could say anything at all.

"We've asked you here, Miss Weiss," he stated without preamble, "because there is a sensitive and top-secret operation that is being considered, and I recommended you for its initial stages." He nodded toward his companion. "This is Lieutenant Casey. He works in Special Operations."

Sophie managed a jerky nod. Since its expansion, the newly formed OSS had far more departments than it had before, with oblique names that hinted at secrecy and covertness—Morale Operations, Field Experimental Unit, Foreign Nationalities. She had no idea what Special Operations entailed.

"What kind of operation?" she asked after a pause, and the two men exchanged glances.

"I'm afraid it's not possible to describe it at present," Howard told her, completely unsurprisingly. "But, suffice it to say, it is likely to be incredibly important, as well as very danger-ous. And, naturally, you must speak about it to no one. To do so would be considered an act of treason." He spoke in a calm, almost friendly voice, as if he hadn't practically just threatened her with potential execution...! If Sophie hadn't felt so flat inside, she might have laughed, or at least smiled. Instead, she simply stared back at John Howard.

Lieutenant Casey lit a cigarette.

"And on that basis, I am meant to agree?" she asked, more curious than condemning. Everything in the OSS was on a need-to-know basis, and very little, she'd discovered, needed to be known, at least by the likes of her.

"To serve your country," Howard replied with a brisk nod. "Yes."

Her country. Was the United States really her country? She'd lived there for three years, but she still sometimes felt like a stranger, and now more than ever. And although she had a visa, she wasn't yet an American citizen. The United States was not really her country, and yet...

"Not to serve my country," she told Howard quietly, compelled to be honest, even though she knew in these patriotic days saying such a thing could practically be considered an act of treason, like John Howard had just said. "But to serve the war effort, yes." She kept his gaze as she gave a swift, firm nod. "*Yes.*"

Lieutenant Casey blew out a plume of smoke through his nose. "Are you sure she can be trusted?" he asked, as if she was not there in the room with them.

Howard gave Sophie a look that felt weighted, full of meaning. "Yes," he replied quietly, his gaze still resting on her. "She can."

Sophie knew he was thinking about that strained chat they'd had in his car, when he'd warned her off Maude and she'd shown him she could keep her mouth shut. Oh, how she could...! To the *death*, she could.

Bitterness welled up inside her, along with a sudden, towering rage, directed as much at herself as the man seated before her. She could have warned Sam. She *should* have. She could have stayed on the *St Louis*. She could have cast her lot with those she loved, rather than taking the easy way out, running away, saving herself...

Sophie's hands clenched into fists in her lap, and she struggled to take several even breaths. She wasn't angry at John Howard at all, she realized, but only at herself. For having made it this far. For having left so many behind. For being willing to, not once, but again and again and again... What kind of person did that make her? How could she possibly face the future, knowing who she was? Who she'd let herself become?

The only way, Sophie thought, was to choose differently this time.

When she trusted herself to speak, she asked the most pressing question. "Why would this operation be dangerous?"

"Because," Howard replied, "you'd be in direct contact with the enemy." His gaze was level, steady, with only a hint of challenge. "You'd be involved in covert operations in Europe."

Covert operations in Europe. The words reverberated through her, sinking in slowly. Could he possibly mean as an actual *spy*? A thrill went through her, more of terror than excitement. To go back to Europe, to Germany even, as a spy... and still as a Jew. To face all the fears she'd fled, once upon a time, come up against them even harder than before...

To find her family and friends.

Sophie's hands were clenched so tightly together that her knuckles ached and her nails bit white crescents into their backs. "What does that mean, exactly?" she finally asked, not fully expecting an honest answer.

John Howard leaned forward. "You'll be trained in England," he said. "In all manners of self-defense as well as operating under... difficult conditions." He paused before stating deliberately, "Make no mistake, Miss Weiss, we are asking you to do something very dangerous. You will be fraternizing very closely with the enemy. You will have to operate under an assumed identity, one that you will have to learn very well, indeed. And if you are captured, you are likely to be tortured and killed. You will have a cyanide capsule in your possession, for that very reason."

She eyed him coolly. "To kill myself, you mean, before I spill any secrets?"

John Howard leaned back with a nod, a gleam of approval in his eyes. "Exactly."

A silence descended upon the room; it seemed as if they were waiting for her answer.

And she knew already—oh, how she knew!—that she would give it. Easily, gladly. This, Sophie thought, was what she'd been waiting for. A chance to both absolve and prove herself. To fight this war properly, to find the victory. And maybe, just maybe, to save her family. To see them again, somehow, some way...

"All right," she answered evenly, looking first at Howard, and then at Casey. "I'll do it. When do I leave?"

CHAPTER 26

JUNE 1942

It did not take long, Sophie discovered, to dismantle her little life in Washington. Three years she'd been there, and yet they blew away like a puff of smoke, or the downy head of a dandelion clock, gone in the summery breeze, dissipating into the air.

She had only forty-eight hours before she had to report to duty at Brooklyn Army Terminal, in New York. A convoy of troopships would be carrying over four thousand soldiers to Belfast, in Northern Ireland, and then Sophie would travel on to England, where she would receive her initial training, learning how to "operate under difficult conditions." Sophie could only speculate as to what those would be—would she be smuggled into France, even into Germany? Would she be asked to spy on Nazi officers, cozy up to the SS to discover the secrets? The prospect filled her with terror, but also purpose.

The thought of being in danger, of being in the presence of Nazis who would likely kill her if they knew who she was, both a spy and a Jew, did not even faze her now. Safety and security, those soft-spoken impostors, she found, to her own surprise, held no power over her anymore, no allure. She welcomed the prospect of danger, the very thing she'd once been so afraid of.

Now she wanted to do something that required risk, for at last—
at *last*—she would be contributing in a way that was not just
useful, but important. No longer would she be hiding away,
staying safe and secure while everyone she loved risked and
lost.

It was surprisingly easy, Sophie found, to lie. She told Miss
Bryson she was being sent on a secretarial course for the government, and that she shouldn't keep her room for her. Miss Bryson
kissed her on both cheeks and told her she was a good girl; it
would not be hard, Sophie knew, for her to let the room out
again, now that Washington was bustling with conscripts of all
stripes and sizes. Everyone worked for the government these
days, it seemed.

The day after her meeting, she took the bus to the Jewish
Community Center to say goodbye to Sadie and the others who
worked there. Once again, the lie tripped off her tongue—she
was going on a secretarial course, she didn't know when she'd be
back, maybe a month or two.

"You really are a government girl now," Sadie exclaimed,
hugging her.

Sophie hugged her back, thankful for the friendship Sadie
had offered her over the last three years. The older woman had
given her so much—opportunity, work, camaraderie. She hoped
her friend knew how grateful she was.

"Everything so *hush-hush*," Sadie continued as she let her
go, eyeing her speculatively.

"There's nothing very secretive about it," Sophie replied
with a smile. She sounded breezy, light, and the truth was, she
finally felt it. The guilt was gone, or at least not nearly as
present, as oppressive, as it once had been, dragging her down
time and time again. "I suspect I'll be in some tempo somewhere, boiling to death and bored out of my mind." Tempos, or
temporary buildings, had sprung up all over Washington,
including on the Mall.

"You'll be in touch, won't you," Sadie asked, "when you get back?"

For the barest second, Sophie hesitated. She did not know when, or even if, she would be back, and the slight wistfulness in her friend's tone made her wonder if Sadie suspected there was more to her story than she was admitting. Would she ever see Sadie again? She had no idea.

"Of course," she finally replied, and she hugged her friend again, glad not to have to meet her eye.

As Sophie headed back down the steps of the center, she paused to look up at the stone building with its impressive pillars. The Jewish Community Center had given her so much hope, when she'd first arrived. She'd come here feeling lost and destitute, reeling from so many painful events, and she'd found a purpose, as well as friendship, within these walls. She would be forever grateful for that, Sophie knew, but it was time to move on... even if she didn't yet know to where or what—not exactly, or not even at all. Yet she felt ready for this next step, whatever it was.

The morning of her departure, Sophie took the bus to Dupont Circle, and then walked past the impressive plaza with its marble fountain, to the grand house on Massachusetts Avenue where she'd stayed when she'd first arrived. The day was already hot, even though it was only a little past eight o'clock in the morning, heat radiating from the sidewalk in humid coils, the sky the pale, hazy blue of summer. After walking just a block, Sophie's dress was sticking to her back and her hair had curled into damp tendrils from the humidity.

She stood before the large brick house with its three floors of windows glinting emptily in the sunlight. It felt like an absolute age since she'd first come here, so confused and frightened and alone, barely able to stammer out any English, everything seeming so unfamiliar, her family and friends still on board that ship of the damned.

Now she walked past the front door, round to the back. She had no need or desire to see Barbara or Stanley Tyler again, but she did want to say goodbye to Esther, who had helped her so much.

She rapped once on the kitchen door, and then poked her head around to see Esther stirring something on the stove, her face glistening from the heat. When Sophie came into the room, the housekeeper turned, one hand pressed to her heart in surprise, her face wreathed in smiles.

"Miss Sophie, Lord, child! It's so good to see you."

"It's good to see you, too, Esther," Sophie replied. "I've come to say goodbye. I'm leaving Washington."

"Is it your family?" the housekeeper asked, her tone turning eager, hopeful. "Have they come at last? Oh, Miss Sophie—"

"No." Sophie gave a small, sad smile. "They won't come, not till the war is over, at least." And maybe not even then. She had no idea what the future held. "But I have to go away for work. Government business, nothing very interesting."

"Government business! Aren't you fancy." Esther grinned as she said it, and Sophie smiled back.

"Not too fancy," she replied. "I'm just a secretary, really." Then she stepped forward and put her arms around the older woman, clearly to Esther's shock, for the woman stiffened in Sophie's embrace. "Thank you, Esther," she said quietly, "for being so kind to me, especially at the beginning. I don't know what I would have done without you. I would have been utterly lost."

"Oh, child." Esther's arms closed around Sophie, hesitantly at first, for it was unheard of for a black woman to hug a white one, but then she let out a shaky laugh and embraced her tightly. "You take care of yourself, you hear? It's a dangerous world out there."

Did even Esther suspect something of what she would be doing, Sophie wondered, or was it simply the kind of warning anyone gave, in times of war?

She hugged the housekeeper for one more moment before she stepped away. "I will," she promised. She might relish the prospect of danger, but she wouldn't court it unnecessarily. At least, she didn't think she would, but who could tell? She knew she still had something to prove.

As Sophie left the house and walked back around to the front, she paused in front of the imposing edifice with its many windows glittering in the sun. It had all the trappings of beauty and wealth, yet they had offered so little joy for either of the Tylers in the end.

Taking a deep breath, she headed for the station.

A single suitcase was all she had to take with her to England; besides a few clothes, Sophie hadn't bought much in the three years she'd been in this country. She'd made so little mark upon it, she reflected, and she wondered if that had been, on some level, deliberate. She'd found refuge in Washington, yes, but it never truly felt like her home. It had never been where her heart was, even after she'd fallen in love with Sam.

Several months on, Sophie viewed their relationship now with more bittersweet nostalgia than painful grief; they'd had so little time together, and sometimes she wondered if their love, such as it had been, had been a product of the uncertain times they lived in rather than a sure and true emotion. If Sam had returned from Pearl Harbor, after the war, whenever it ended, would they have married? Would she have lived in some house somewhere with him, with a picket fence and a dog, a child or two, and been happy?

She found she could not imagine any of it anymore. It was like a fairy tale, a story that had almost happened to someone else. And, she knew, it was a chapter of her life that was forever closed, the page truly turned.

She took a bus from Dupont Circle to Union Station, watching the city, now a hive of important industry, blur by under the bright summer sun. Soldiers stepped smartly along the sidewalks, and women in the new workwear suits of khaki or navy blue looked just as briskly purposeful. Washington was a city on the move, fighting for a cause. Patriotism was like a metallic tang in the air.

At the station, Sophie boarded a train to New York; the troopship the *Cristobal* would be leaving for Belfast on the evening tide, with eleven hundred soldiers and civilians on board—almost the same number as had been on the *St Louis*.

The trip to New York was slow and cumbersome, the train near to bursting with conscripts as well as civilian passengers. Everyone had somewhere to go, it seemed. Sophie sat scrunched up on the edge of a bench seat, her suitcase hitting her knees, the window cranked open to let in a breath of hot air for the train carriage was stifling. When a soldier tried to flirt with her, she just smiled and looked away. She felt, oddly, as if she'd gone from this place, as if she was halfway across the ocean already, on to this new, unknown life of hers, whatever it might hold.

When she arrived at the Brooklyn Army Terminal, it was heaving with military—thousands of soldiers milled around or sat on their kit bags, playing cards and smoking, waiting to board the ships moored in the harbor, their gray sides stretching upwards, blocking out the light. Stevedores and sailors hurried here and there with an air of bustling importance, and cranes teetered high in the sky, hauling crates of goods that swung dangerously to and fro while men below shouted instructions. High above, seagulls screeched and cawed, wheeling through the summer sky. The air smelled of salt and seaweed and tar.

Sophie breathed it all in, her senses reeling. She could not believe she had come this far, and yet she knew she had so much farther to go... first to England, and then to Europe. The future loomed in front of her, unknown yet also certain.

The *Cristobal* didn't look anything like the *St Louis*, save that it was a big ship with dark sides and white smokestacks. Unlike the *St Louis*, it positively bristled with anti-aircraft, or ack-ack, guns and artillery, and its sides were painted in various stripes of gray, a form of camouflage for when they were out in the ocean, at danger of being sighted by German U-boats or cruisers. The two troopships would be escorted by a convoy of four destroyers until they were off the coast of Iceland.

And yet despite all that... standing there on the dock, the tang of salt on the air, the breeze blowing her hair into wisps about her face, Sophie was catapulted three years back in time, to that May morning in Hamburg when she'd been about to board the *St Louis*.

She'd been so hopeful then and yet still so afraid, Heinrich clinging to her hand, her father huddled next to her, Margarete so fiercely determined and Sophie believing her whole life finally was about to begin. She'd had such fairy tale notions back then, such silly schoolgirl hopes. Looking back on her old self, Sophie felt a flicker of pity, as well as of compassion, for that girl, so young, so naïve, so afraid, so hopeful, was long gone.

And yet that young girl had made such wonderful friends, lifelong friends, or so Sophie hoped. She knew she would do everything in her power to make sure she, Rosa, Hannah and Rachel all met again, toasted each other in a little café under the shadow of the Eiffel Tower as they'd promised each other, the four glittering shards of emerald made whole and perfect once more.

For a moment, standing on the quayside, staring up at that ship, Sophie let herself imagine Rosa, Hannah, and Rachel... she pictured the four of them together, standing on the deck of the *St Louis*, staring out at the horizon, dreaming about their futures...

Where were her friends now, and more importantly, *how* were they? Rachel, in Haarlem, struggling to find food, Franz with no work... how were they managing to survive? What would the future hold for them, now that the Netherlands was under the Nazis' control? And what about Hannah, living in Paris, seeming so secretive, telling Sophie she didn't know when she'd be able to write next? Was her friend in danger? What about Lotte?

And then Rosa... Rosa, in England! She might even be able to see her, Sophie realized with a thrill of wonder. She was amazed she had not thought of it before; her friends had seemed so far away for so long that she simply hadn't considered it. But if Rosa were in England, even if she'd been taciturn about where she was or what she was doing... well, surely Sophie would be able to find her, or at least find a way to contact her. The thought filled her with hope, with tremulous joy. She'd make sure she found a way.

And here *she* was, Sophie reflected, about to start on this new adventure. So much had happened... and so much had *not* happened that she'd longed to. She had danced and laughed and tasted champagne; she'd loved and feared and hoped and grieved. She'd lost her family, her friends, and yet she'd made others, as well as fallen sweetly in love and then lost it. She'd strived and worked and overcome; she'd struggled and wondered and failed and tried again. Now she was about to cross that vast ocean, once more into the utterly unknown... and yet this time she felt ready. She felt fierce.

"Miss!" A soldier called to her, a look of wry humor on his face, for she had been, Sophie realized, simply standing there, staring, a woman alone, a single suitcase clasped loosely in her hand. "Do you know where you're going?"

Sophie glanced back up at the ship, the harbor stretching out into the ocean and beyond, glinting blue under the summer sky—so much unknown, and yet for the first time in her life, she felt utterly certain. She slipped her free hand into her pocket, her fingers curling around that sliver of emerald, hard enough to hurt, the pain giving her an even deeper strength of conviction —to serve the war effort, to find her family and friends.

"Yes," Sophie told the soldier. "I know where I'm going."

With her head held high, she started toward the ship—and her future.

A LETTER FROM KATE

Dear reader,

I want to say a huge thank you for choosing to read *The Girl on the Boat*. If you enjoyed it, and would like to keep up to date with all my latest releases, just sign up at the following link. Your email address will never be shared and you can unsubscribe at any time.

www.bookouture.com/kate-hewitt

This novel was inspired by a friend's ancestors who had traveled on the *St Louis*. The plight of the doomed ship caught my imagination, and when I learned that the refugees had been dispersed between different countries, I immediately imagined four young friends, each assigned to a different place, and the adventures and trials they would all have. Many of the characters in the story are based on real people, and the events on the ship are all taken from firsthand accounts. Of the 937 passengers on the doomed *St Louis*, 267 tragically ended up dying in concentration camps.

I hope you loved *The Girl on the Boat* and if you did, I would be very grateful if you could write a review. I'd love to hear what you think, and it makes such a difference helping new readers to discover one of my books for the first time.

I love hearing from my readers—you can get in touch on my

Facebook group for readers (facebook.com/groups/ KatesReads), through X, Goodreads or my website.

Thanks again for reading!

Kate

www.kate-hewitt.com

X x.com/author_kate

ACKNOWLEDGEMENTS

I am always so grateful to the many people who work with me on my story, and help to bring it to light. I am grateful to the whole amazing team at Bookouture who have helped with this process, from editing, copyediting, and proofreading, to designing and marketing. In particular, I'd like to thank my editor, Jess Whitlum-Cooper, as well as Sarah Hardy and Kim Nash in publicity, Melanie Price in marketing, Laura Deacon, Richard King in foreign rights, and Sinead O'Connor in audio. Most of all, I'd like to thank my readers, who buy and read my books. Without you, there would be no stories to share. I hope you enjoyed this one as much as I did. Thank you!

PUBLISHING TEAM

Turning a manuscript into a book requires the efforts of many people. The publishing team at Bookouture would like to acknowledge everyone who contributed to this publication.

Audio
Alba Proko
Sinead O'Connor
Melissa Tran

Commercial
Lauren Morrissette
Jil Thielen
Imogen Allport

Data and analysis
Mark Alder
Mohamed Bussuri

Cover design
Debbie Clement

Editorial
Jess Whitlum-Cooper
Imogen Allport

Copyeditor
Jade Craddock

Proofreader
Tom Feltham

Marketing
Alex Crow
Melanie Price
Occy Carr
Ciara Rosney

Operations and distribution
Marina Valles
Stephanie Straub

Production
Hannah Snetsinger
Mandy Kullar
Jen Shannon

Publicity
Kim Nash
Noelle Holten
Myrto Kalavrezou
Jess Readett
Sarah Hardy

Rights and contracts
Peta Nightingale
Richard King
Saidah Graham